Willie, My Love

JUDY ANN DAVIS

WILLIE, MY LOVE
Copyright © 2019 by Judy Ann Davis

Print: 978-0-9990896-2-0
eBook: 978-0-9990896-3-7

All rights reserved. Except for any review, the reproduction or utilization of this work in whole or in part in any form by any electronic, mechanical or other means, now known or hereinafter invented, including xerography, photocopy-ing and recording, or in any information storage or retrieval system is forbidden without the written permission of the author.

This is a work of fiction. Names, characters, places and incidents are either the product of the author's imagination or are used fictitiously, and any resemblance to actual persons, living or dead, business establishments, events or locales is entirely coincidental.

First Printing
Printed in U.S.A.

Cover Design and Interior Format

*A woman is like a tea bag—
you can't tell how strong she is until
you put her in hot water.*

~ Eleanor Roosevelt

CHAPTER ONE

Central Pennsylvania, September, 1856

AT THE FIRST CRACK OF gunfire, Jonathan Wain dove face down onto the rocky cliff and peered into the valley below. Relentless autumn rains, dogging him all the way northward from Maryland, threw a thick blanket of morning fog over the land and obscured his view.

Somewhere beyond the haze lay the West Branch of the Susquehanna River and the small logging settlement of Clearfield, Pennsylvania. Slowly he inched his way backward and stood, swatting at an irksome mosquito droning near his ear. He hated mosquitoes worse than the tiny black flies that plagued the oceanfront on a warm spring night.

For the past two weeks, he had ridden over two hundred and fifty miles of wilderness trails just to arrive in these God-forsaken mountains. He had roasted under the rays of the hot sun and shivered in the cold downpours at night. He had picked his way around rattlers and through swarms of insects. And he had tangled with Indians, bears, and possums, each wanting a share of his belongings, a piece of his hide, or a portion of his food.

Removing his hat, he jammed a hand through his hair and tried to think things through.

Beyond the volley of gunfire lay a hot meal and a soft bed. This was no time to let a little fog get in his way—and certainly not some ruckus that didn't concern him. What if the gunfire was little more than someone with a hunger for a wild turkey or some rabbit stew?

And yet, from the sound of the ammunition being exchanged, he knew it wasn't that simple. There was a fight going on.

Swearing under his breath, he scanned the forest behind him to locate his horse. The Indian pony, well-trained and accustomed to the wilderness, had taken cover near a copse of leafy maples as soon as the first shot exploded in the air. The horse and hand-tooled saddle had been a gift, or maybe a bribe, from his father shortly after he wheedled him into making the trip northward to meet their logging partner, Dalton Wydcliffe. The man had run his three mills almost single-handedly over the years. More recently, his youngest daughter had become involved in the business as well.

It was said the girl was as wild and tough as the river during flood season and still unmarried—though Jonathan never believed a twenty-three-year-old woman was headed toward spinsterhood as others did. He snorted out a low chuckle. At thirty-one, folks considered him an old bachelor.

Together, Wain and Sons Shipping and Wydcliffe Lumbering had been in business for over four decades. Each spring, rafts of white pine surged down the muddy Susquehanna River to the Chesapeake Bay, where they were loaded into the holds of Wain-owned ships bound for the Eastern Seaboard or as far away as Europe. Nothing surpassed the durability of Pennsylvania white pine for ship masts and building. Orders for spring timber had already started to pile up on his desk back home.

With a fleet of new clipper ships in the Chesapeake awaiting his attention, the last thing he wanted was to embroil himself in another man's troubles. But he had promised his father he would take a look into the operations. Wydcliffe was an old man now, and he had acquired an unknown enemy and a sack of troubles weighing heavily on his shoulders. Someone wanted him out of the timber business. Tallies for spar timber had come up short when rafts had been mysteriously lost or destroyed on their long journey down to the shipyards.

Even if Dalton Wydcliffe could afford the sizeable loss, he and his two brothers could ill afford to have their vessels lying idle, rotting at the docks and collecting barnacles, as they waited for cargo that would never arrive. It was the swift clippers with brimming holds of white pine, baled cotton, and imported goods that made the silver in their pockets jingle.

Tightening the girth more securely around the stallion's damp sides, Jonathan gathered the reins and spoke softly, "Well, Trade Wind, your backside must be twice as weary as mine. Let's pick our way around the commotion, find old man Wydcliffe, and scare up a decent meal for both of us."

The horse, impatient with the lengthy pause, snorted an irritable response.

"My sentiments exactly."

He'd barely swung his leg over the horse's broad back when the stallion reared without warning and tossed his head in frenzied motions. A stinging shower of tawny mane lashed out into the air. Struggling to keep astride, Jonathan bit off a curse, jammed his boots into the stirrups, and drove his knees deeper into the horse's ribs.

"What the hell?" he snapped and yanked solidly on the reins. Only when he brought the horse's flying feet back to earth did he realize the reason for the stallion's odd behavior.

High on the top of the southern ridge, a silver-colored horse with a small slim rider raced toward a stand of trees and headed for cover. Crouched low in the saddle and clinging to the mount with expert skill, the boy looked like he was born in the saddle. Together they flew over the ground as if the devil himself was nipping at their heels.

Some distance back and gaining steadily, three riders—one with a rifle drawn and aimed directly at the youngster's back—pursued them.

A shrill shot rang out, echoing in the air, followed by another.

A muscle tightened in Jonathan's stomach as he mentally calculated the odds of three armed men against one small boy.

He didn't have to think it out.

He kneed his horse and headed toward the ridge.

CHAPTER TWO

THE SLIGHT-FRAMED RIDER RACED ACROSS the meadow and reined the silver horse sharply into a clump of maples and oak.

This is no game, Wilhelmina Wydcliffe decided as a bullet whistled through the air and ripped a hole in her felt hat. For one horrible moment she thought she might be sick, but she steadied her trembling hands, pulled the hat farther down over her forehead, and slipped off her mount. With a pistol in one hand and a saddle bag in the other, she ducked behind a large tree. Her horse galloped onward.

"Good-for-nothing buggers blew a hole in my new hat," she sputtered. "Now Papa will have my hide if these thugs don't get it first. Second one ruined in two weeks." Dropping the saddlebag at her feet, she reached up to finger the damage to the crown and tuck a loose strand of whiskey-colored hair under the brim where the rest of her locks were hidden.

Unaware her pursuers had separated, she waited in a catlike crouch and watched the trail she had just covered. Not even a hint of a breeze rattled the brilliant red and gold leaves clinging to the maples around her. The forest, dim and eerie in the fading afternoon light, was so still that the only disturbing sound was her own erratic breathing.

For over a month, the weekly payroll, sent by horseback to her downriver logging crews, had been stolen along one of the most desolate trails leading to the mill. This time, with a handpicked group of men who could handle a horse as well as a gun, she decided to personally escort the money to its destination. She never imagined her plans would go amiss.

They had rehearsed every detail.

Except one.

No one ever expected the robbers to jump them in the valley outside town. Pinned down on three sides with only brush for cover, her men were easier targets than a flock of crows in a barren tree. If she hadn't high-tailed it out in hopes of drawing the gunmen away, someone might have been killed.

Without warning, a squirrel sent up a vicious chatter high in the top of a nearby pine.

A warning bell clanged in the far corner of her mind. Chills prickled up her small unprotected back.

The leaves rustled

A twig snapped.

Her stomach lurched.

"Ok, boy, drop the gun," a rough male voice growled a foot from her shoulder blades.

Eyes wide, Wilhelmina stood and turned, swallowing back a lump in her throat as she stared at a filthy-dressed man. A dirty red bandana covered his lower face and a grubby hat shaded his forehead and eyes. He pointed his pistol so close she could see the layers of grime on his knuckles.

He backed away carefully and waved his pistol at the saddlebag lying at her feet. "Do as I say. Drop the gun and throw that saddlebag over here. Ain't nobody but you and me, kid. And it looks like I got the upper hand."

Wilhelmina didn't need him to tell her she was alone and in a pickle. After all, it had been her idea to have her crew flee in the opposite direction. The thought settled in her stomach like a stone.

Her gaze swept the forest carefully, looking for a way to escape. There was no place to run without taking a bullet in the back. Even her horse had taken cover.

"I ain't got all day," the man said. Muffled by the bandana, his voice was gruff and irate. "Do it now, boy, unless you want to pick your scrambled brains off the trunk of that yonder tree."

Wilhelmina took a fortifying breath. The pulse in her neck pounded in unison with her heart, but anger seeped into her sense of fear. She was not going to make things easy for this thieving lout. Leaving the saddlebag lying at her feet, she pitched her gun instead. It flew through the air to land in a pile of leaves a few feet between them. Hands unburdened now, she steeled them into half-clenched fists.

"What are you going to do?" It took all her courage to keep her voice calm.

"Nothing, sonny, unless you don't cooperate. Move an inch and I'll blow your ears off. All I want is that nice plump saddlebag." He waved his pistol at the bag again. Kicking her gun farther away, he stepped closer and bent to retrieve it.

A series of penetrating shots rang out from the bottom of the ridge. Shifting his position to level his gaze toward the ruckus, he snarled, "Damn! Looks like trouble."

It was the chance she had been waiting for. With lightning speed, she reached down and deftly pulled a pearl-handled stiletto from the side of her knee-high boot. In one fluid motion, she swept it upward, plunging the blade into the right shoulder of her assailant so solidly only the handle was visible.

The gunman's eyes widened in pain and disbelief. He pitched forward, dropping his gun and howling like a wounded animal. With blood seeping through his sweaty brown shirt, he rolled and stumbled up, dragging the saddlebags with him as he made his way to his horse.

Her lead feet unable to move, she watched the repulsive man fling the bag over the rump of a dappled mare, then pull his injured body into the saddle. With a vicious kick to his mount, he disappeared into the tangled undergrowth of the forest.

Seconds later, the sound of another rider crashing into the shaded clearing forced her to wheel around. A giant of a man now emerged through a narrow opening between the dense laurels and skidded his horse to a halt, sending up a swirl of leaves. He wore no face covering. His drawn rifle was pointed toward the path where the gunman had disappeared. He hesitated, as if he might follow, but decided against it. Slipping his rifle back into his scabbard, he swung around to face her instead.

Wilhelmina blew out a breath of pent-up air and reset her floppy hat farther down to shade her eyes. All at once, she felt dizzy and disoriented. Rivulets of sweat raced down the sides of her cheeks. She wiped them away with her shirt sleeve.

"Are you all right?" The stranger nudged his horse closer.

Now overwhelmed by the size of this opponent, she could only nod. The man was tall and lean with dark gray eyes the color of cold steel. His face was well suntanned as if he'd spent his life working outdoors. And he sat atop the most magnificent chestnut stallion she'd ever seen.

"I...I...I..." The words stuck in her throat. "I..I thank you for your help," she choked out.

"Here, kid. Have some water." He sent the canteen flying from his saddle.

She deftly caught it, still cautiously staring at him.

"Go ahead," his deep voice coaxed. "It's fresh this morning."

She uncorked the flask and lifted it to her lips. The cool water barreled out and spilled down her chin, but she managed to take a gulp, wiping away the droplets with the back of her hand.

"You aren't a runaway, are you?"

She stared at him, baffled for a mo me nt, and shook her head. She had purposely decked herself out in clothes to look like a poor logger's son. Her faded plaid shirt, elbow-worn and in need of some soap, swamped her small frame. Its long sleeves, which would have buried her hands, were rolled up to her wrists. Luckily, she had found a piece of twine to keep her too-large trousers, now bunched about her waist, from falling off. She hoped the stranger, like the thieves, would be fooled by her disguise.

A low chuckle erupted from the stranger's throat. "Didn't think so," he admitted. "Sometimes it takes a minute to catch your breath."

He fell silent and threaded his fingers though his hair to rake out any bits of debris which had hitched a ride though the dense forest paths. He scanned the ridge and checked the clearing again before he spoke. "Are you sure you're not injured?"

"Only my pride."

A ripple of laughter bubbled up from his broad chest. "Lucky for you, kid, your horse can run like the wind or your pride would be buried with that scrawny body of yours." He studied her intently.

Behind them, a snort and rustling of leaves made them pivot with a start.

Wilhelmina watched the stranger's hand flash to his rifle. Simultaneously, his gaze darted to the edge of the clearing where her horse emerged among the tangled laurel.

Her mind whirled. Who was this man? He obviously was no stranger to trouble. Astride his horse he looked like the evil Roman god, Pluto. She tried to remember her grueling Latin lessons. Yes, he was sinister Pluto, all right, galloping out of a chasm in the gloomy earth to snatch a helpless young maiden and carry her back to his dark, shadowy underworld.

She prided herself in knowing most of the area's residents. But this man's face sparked no recognition. None. Certainly, she would have never forgotten the horse. Even burr-covered and trail-worn, the stallion was so well bred it would compel any horse lover's head to turn and take a second look.

Her gaze traveled to the stranger's saddlebags. They were too light to be a peddler's and too heavy for a drifter. His hand-tooled saddle was intricately etched with scrollwork and was much too expensive for a farmer or poor logger. Even the clothing he wore was not that of a common man. His homespun shirt and copper-colored riding breeches had been specially tailored to fit his large, well-muscled frame, and his boots were not the kind stocked in a general store. In fact, a man with feet that big would never find any kind of boots in a store within a hundred-mile radius of Clearfield.

All of a sudden a horrible thought gnawed at her. Was he an outlaw, too? Had he just moved into the territory? Had he been waiting in the forest, hoping to drive the others off and steal the payroll himself?

Criminy! She almost groaned the word out loud at the plausible idea. Now here she stood, weaponless, with only a vented hat to throw at him.

Frantically, she searched the area for the pistol she had dropped. It was no more than six feet away, tucked beneath a few shriveled leaves. Several feet away, the pistol from the thief she had knifed lay on a bed of pine needles.

"Are there any homes this far from town?" he asked.

"At least three families within earshot. I'm sure they heard the gunfire." It was a bloody lie, but it might persuade him to light out.

"What's your name?"

Without answering, she inched toward the pistol. "I wouldn't touch the gun, boy. He gestured toward the spot where it lay. "I'm not overly fond of having my last clean shirt ruined with a bullet hole."

He swung down from his mount and stalked toward her.

Her mouth dropped open.

He stood at least three inches over six feet. Midnight black hair fell in careless waves over his forehead and the back of his collar. His chis-eled aristocratic nose flared above an angular chin, sporting a day's growth of beard. Why, he's almost as good-looking as his horse, she thought, and edged towards the pistol again.

"I said I wouldn't do that." He stopped several yards away and planted his hands on his hips. "Does your father know you're out here?"

"Yes," she lied again.

"Yeah, and I'm President Pierce." He snorted and rubbed the back of his neck. "Now before my patience completely runs out. What's your name?"

"Willie." At least that wasn't a lie. She had been named after her mother, Elizabeth Wilhelmina, but to avoid confusion, they had called her by her middle name. But Wilhelmina was a name she'd vehemently disliked, so along the way, close friends had resorted to calling her Willie. Now even her family and the logging crews used her nickname. If she kept her wits, the overgrown fool would never know she was a girl.

"Listen, Willie, let's hurry this conversation along. Tell me, why **were** those men trying to run their horses up your backside?"

What was with this stranger's endless questions? Would he *not* give up? Despite his good looks, he was beginning to wear on her already jangled nerves. She needed to get back to the mill in town, check on her crew, and get to dinner on time.

"I don't know." Perspiration beaded on her nose, and it started to itch, but she resisted the urge to scratch it.

"You don't know?" His gray-eyed stare drilled into her. "You don't know why someone was chasing *and* shooting at you?"

Twenty-three years of backwoods life had taught her some simple lessons. Caution determined the length of an earthly life, and strangers were to be handled with prudence until they proved themselves otherwise. It was best never to offer too much information. The Wydcliffe name was not the most popular one at the moment. Someone was out to destroy their lumber business. She nodded. "Yes, that's right."

The big man moved closer, obviously following an instinctive urge to get a closer look. "Listen, son, my backside is raw from the saddle. I'm tired. I'm hungry. And my patience is about worn thin." He paused. "Let's start with the truth. I'd hate to have to dust your britches."

Willie gasped and pulled herself up to her whole five-feet four-inches. "Listen up yourself. I appreciate your help, but I don't make it a habit of answering questions from strangers, despite the condition of their backsides." Lips thinned in irritation, she waved a hand toward the clearing. "And you'd best hightail it out of here. You're trespassing. This is private land."

The big man kicked the ground with the toe of his boot. There was a cold edge of irony in his voice when he looked up. "Trespassing? If I hadn't intervened, you wouldn't be sucking in this bug-infested air. I want an explanation."

"And you'll not get one!" The minute the words flew out of her mouth, she realized she'd made a disastrous mistake.

Eyes ablaze, the giant stormed toward her.

"Touch me, mister, and I'll bite your arm, rip your eyeballs out, and destroy any hope you have for an heir." She skidded backwards.

"If you bite me, kid, or touch my eyes, you won't sit down for a week. If you kick me where I think you're planning to, you'll never sit down again." He closed the gap separating them with long, sure strides.

Alarmed, she flung the canteen aside. Her mammoth savior now seemed even more evil at closer range. Whirling sideways, she lunged for the pistol, but Jonathan was quicker. With one pounce, he sent her flying onto the ground. Her hat flew off and her hair tumbled out from beneath it. She landed squarely beneath his broad chest and shoulders.

For one split second, his gray eyes locked with her angry brown ones as he rolled off her, over her hat, and away. But not before she boxed him beside his ear.

"Ouch! Holy hell," he yelped.

"Consider yourself lucky I didn't get a swipe at your eyeballs." Her voice echoed through the forest. She grabbed at her hat while still prone and secured it. Peering at it, she flung it aside with disgust. "Now look what you've done. Bad enough those thugs shot a hole through it, but now you've completely smashed it to bits. Looks like a flapjack now."

Sitting up, she dusted debris from her clothes and stole a quick glance at the big man, recalling the surprised, yet angry, look on his face as he rolled over and snatched up her pistol along the way. With catlike grace, he had maneuvered himself to his feet.

Her heart fluttered wildly in her chest. This is no clumsy logging hand. He was too quick and way too light-footed.

He grabbed the other gun her earlier assailant had dropped and snarled a few curses. "You've got a lot of explaining." He jammed the pistols behind his belt and strode to the spot where she was still seated.

Willie scrambled up. The front of her shirt had come undone in the fall and now exposed a full view of her creamy breasts beneath her transparent chemise. Glaring at him with rage-filled eyes, more chilling than the gun barrel he had just touched, she yanked her shirt closed.

"Most gentlemen I know would turn their backs and allow a lady to properly dress herself."

"And let you club me to death? Don't press your luck, little lady."

Fumbling with the buttons, she finished as fast as her trembling hands would allow. She hitched up her coarse male trousers to settle more comfortably around her waist. "I should be the one who's angry, you big oaf," she said. "You almost knocked the pants right off me."

It took every ounce of patience for Johnathan to remain calm. He eyed the petite figure with wary interest. The girl stood at least a good foot shorter than he. Her black silk bandana around her throat only heightened the color of the gold flecks in her brown eyes and made them glow like miniature stars. A mass of honey-colored hair, now dislodged from her hat, fell in haphazard curls down her back and around her face. Even in her ragged clothes, she was the most beautiful woman he had ever seen.

"I asked for an explanation," he reminded her.

Willie snickered, ignoring his remark. "You're just sore because I walloped you." She plucked off a twig clinging to the sleeve of her shirt and unfastened the scarf from her neck. She lowered her head, gathered up the annoying locks of hair fanning her face, and secured them at the nape of her neck with a hastily tied knot. "In fact, you're sore because you're too stupid to tell the difference between a girl and a boy." She stooped to gather up the fallen canteen.

"And do you always make it a habit of trying to kill people who lend a hand?"

"I thought you were one of them."

"One of whom?"

"One of them!" She flapped her hand toward the southern ridge. "Payroll robbers."

"I suppose you're going to tell me you planned to single-handedly capture them from the front while ducking their bullets?"

"No. I was acting as a decoy to get the payroll

downriver."

"You can't be serious." The words flew through his lips in a mixture of awe and disbelief. His gaze swept over her body, now posed stubbornly, feet apart, one thumb hooked behind her waistband. He tried to calculate her age. She appeared to be little more than twenty years old.

"We've been having trouble in these parts with outlaws stealing downriver payrolls," she confessed irritably. "This time they jumped us earlier than planned, so I lit out to divert them a bit. I sent the payroll crew in the opposite direction with the money."

She laughed a low throaty chuckle. Her coffee-colored eyes glowed like polished agates. "Wait 'til those scoundrels find out they have a saddlebag full of old newspapers."

"Holy Hell." His tone was laced with fright and disbelief.

The hair rose on the back of his neck as a cold chill slipped down his back. "We both could have been riddled with bullets for a bag of useless newspapers?" he asked.

She nodded. "Now don't fly off the handle, mister. It didn't happen." Still annoyed, she scooped up her battered hat and stalked past him, slamming the canteen against his chest as she passed and headed for her horse.

Had he not been expecting her move, the force of the canteen would have knocked the air from his lungs. He took the solid blow, unblinking, grabbed the canteen and pitched it aside. He followed her retreating back. Anger surged in his chest.

"Hold on, now. We're not finished."

Unfazed, she marched onward. "Oh yes, we are. I don't have time for a pointless conversation."

"Hellfire. That's all you have to say for such a ridiculous charade?" All at once, he felt a throbbing in his temple like his blood was boiling inside his brain.

Willie stopped short and whirled around. "Lord in heaven, you could test the patience of a preacher." Throwing her hat-free hand up into the air, she slammed it down on the front of her dusty trousers with a sharp crack, sending up a powdery cloud. With the other hand, she clutched the deformed hat and slapped it smartly against the side of her thigh to dislodge the wrinkles. When her vigorous efforts netted little results, she balled her fist and thrust it inside the hat's mangled crown, punching and poking at the felt to try to reshape it. A look of frustration wrinkled her dainty forehead.

She waved the mangled hat at him. "I've been chased, shot at, knocked down on my backside, and some good-for-nothing thief has my knife. And you...you...have only added to my misery by con-fiscating my pistol and ruining my best hat."

Pausing, she gulped a mouthful of air, scratched her itchy nose, and lowered her voice. "And let me tell you something else, you big buzzard, I've seen mules with sweeter dispositions than you have."

Stunned, Jonathan could only gawk at her. He felt his face flush hot from beet red to purple. "Are you finished?" He barely choked out the words.

"No, but I'm trying not to be late for supper." Without waiting for a reply, she plopped the mutilated hat on her head and covered the final distance to her horse.

"Hold on. Is there anything you just might like about me?"

Maybe she truly *was* demented, he thought. He had heard his father tell of people who had lost their minds from living in the wilderness. He, himself, had seen young sailors who had become unbalanced from just a few weeks at sea. He watched as she deftly untangled the horse's reins and slipped easily up into the saddle.

With a safe distance separating them, she reined her gray horse southward and turned in her saddle. Suddenly, she rose to his bait like a catfish hitting on a night crawler. "Yes, there's *one* thing I like."

"What? What in heaven's name could it be?" He swore softly under his breath and glared at her.

She grinned. "Your horse."

CHAPTER THREE

LIKE A SWARM OF BEES were chasing her, Willie raced her horse into the wide circular drive of the manor, past the imposing front entrance steps of gray flagstone, and off to the stables in the rear. She was late for dinner again, having stopped at the mill in town to check on the safety of her crew.

Halting her lathered mount before the stable doors, she slapped him lovingly on the neck, bent down, and whispered, "I owe you an extra bucket of oats for this one, Silver Cloud."

A young stable hand darted out before her boots hit the ground. "You're late, Miss Willie. Your pa is already here with that Eastern guest you were expecting."

"I know, I know." She rushed toward the manor, skidded to stop, and spun around. "What did you say?"

"Your pa is already here."

"No, the second part."

"Your Eastern guest is here, too."

"Jonathan Caleb Wain? What's the Limey doing here two days early?"

"Dunno." The stable boy shrugged.

"He wasn't expected until Friday." She squinted down at her mud-encrusted trousers and, in one horrible moment, wished she could crawl under a rock and hide. "Drat! I'm going to have to shed these britches faster than a trollop late for work."

She dashed toward the manor again and barreled through a thicket of rhododendron, a shortcut she often used to reach a footpath leading to the backdoor of the kitchen. With Jonathan Wain about, this was certainly no time to make a grand entrance through the front. Ripping the door open, she plummeted through and fell flat against the lanky caretaker on his way out to the pump. The empty water bucket he gripped tumbled from his hand.

"Forgive me, Conrad," she blurted out and realigned her slight frame to dash around him.

"You're late, Miss Willie." The reprimand directed at her back was in unison with the clanging of the bucket hopscotching down the outside steps. "Your father has warned you repeatedly to be on time for dinner. Promptly at seven, Missy. And your sister is anything but cheerful."

"I know. Oh, how I know." Willie felt the pressure of time bearing down on her like an anchor around her neck. She darted across the kitchen, under the disapproving eye of Hannah, the manor's somber cook, who backed her robust body against the pantry door and frowned at the muddy boot tracks trailing the girl over the wooden floor and up the back stairway.

Seconds later, a sharp rap sounded on her bedroom door, and her half-sister bolted in. Unlike Willie, Raven was a tall, dark-haired beauty with ebony eyes.

Her annoyed voice stabbed the air. "You can't come to the dinner table in those clothes. Papa will have a stroke. Do you realize how late you are?"

Willie flung her crumpled hat into a corner and tore at the buttons of her mud-stained shirt. "Eeeegads. I've never met so many clever people at *one* time."

Raven cocked a brow at the distorted piece of felt. "Please don't tell me that's your *new* hat. It's barely a week old. What happened now, Elizabeth Wilhelmina?"

Willie shed her shirt and flung it beside the hat. Leaves from the thicket fluttered to the floor. "I wore the bloody thing while lying down."

She flopped to the floor and tugged unsuccessfully at her boots. She paused and glared at her sister still puzzling over the hat.

"Never mind the blessed hat. It's a long story. We don't have time. Get the housekeeper. Get me a bath. Get these stupid boots off. Please do something besides gawk like a lovesick owl during a full moon." She waved a foot at her sister.

Raven bent and grabbed a boot and yanked it off. The second was removed with just as much effort. She hurriedly stepped aside as Willie peeled off her socks and scrambled up.

"I have a bath drawn for you and your clothes laid out." Raven slapped her hands together briskly to remove any traces of dirt. "You'd better hurry before Papa gets wind of this. Jonathan Wain has arrived, and he is no ordinary guest. He's Papa's business partner—and yours, I should add."

Willie shoved an arm into the sleeve of her robe.

"You have to stall them before Papa works up a temper hot enough to melt lead. Go down to the study and strike up a conversation with the little Limey."

Raven frowned. "The man is far from little, and he's already made quite an impression. Conrad tells me the household staff—after meeting Mr. Wain—has been parading around the manor with smiles on their faces like they've discovered an oil well under the back steps and are planning to tap the wealth, divide the profits, and retire."

Willie splayed her arms, palms up. A wave of panic washed over her. "We've no time to quibble over the man's size and his ability to astound people. Please don't dilly-dally. Go, go!"

Raven sighed before she nodded and hurried toward the study.

Willie's tardiness was an all too familiar habit.

Downstairs, Jonathan barely accepted the glass of rum Dalton Wydcliffe held out to him, when the study door flew open. An attractive young woman hurried toward him, lifting her red taffeta skirt to prevent a fall. Despite her height, she had grace and a proud air about her. Her dark hair, tied away from her face, framed eyes as dark as inky pools. There was little doubt this was the daughter of Wydcliffe's first wife, an Indian maiden, who had died before the lumber mills were built. Wydcliffe's second wife had succumbed to pneumonia when his second daughter was only three years old.

She gave her father a cautious glance, but her

welcoming smile was genuine. "Welcome to Clearfield, Mr. Wain," she said. "I'm Vivian LeConte, but most folks call me Raven. It's a childhood nickname."

Jonathan took the hand she extended. "Thomas LeConte is a lucky man to have such an attractive and lovely wife."

"He certainly is," Wydcliffe interjected. "And I'm a lucky man to have at least one sensible and punctual daughter." He glanced toward the study door.

Raven gave an anxious little cough and said in a low voice, "She'll be down shortly, Papa. I just checked on her."

She turned to Jonathan. "I understand you're the oldest of three brothers and everyone is involved with the shipping industry."

Jonathan took a sip of the rum and smiled. "Yes, but it's Jacob who handles most of the timber sales and the dock operations—and who's content to have his feet on solid ground. I'm certain his marriage is responsible for his contentment."

"So your youngest brother and you are not married?" She studied him thoughtfully.

"No, just Jacob. Although Jeremy has a delightful, red-haired, Irish lass who has been trying to drag him off the ship and to the altar. As for me..." His voice trailed off as he silently grasped for a polite way to explain. "Well, all the charming women such as yourself seem to be already taken by more fortunate men."

He neglected to tell her that he was tired of dull city women who wanted only his money, fine clothes, a big home, and a secure life. He wanted a girl with fiber, with sparkle, and someone who would give him a challenge each day instead of drooling over him like an old hound dog. His mind rushed back to the girl in the forest. There was a female with sparkle. Despite her shabby outfit, it radiated from her like light from the sun.

"So you must enjoy the sea."

"I still have an itch for the sea, a wanderlust longing every so often. Since Father retired, I'm moored close to the coast. I hire our crews, adjust the shipments, open new trade routes, and often obtain new cargo like cotton, Eastern silks, and spices. Oh, and California gold." He took a sip of rum. "You have a sister, I understand."

"Yes, she's unmarried as well."

"And all of us, including the Almighty, knows why," Wydcliffe muttered.

Blushing, Raven gestured toward the study doors. "Let's move to the dining room. She's probably waiting for us there."

Minutes later, they entered through a set of double French doors and arrived at a spacious room far more elegant than Jonathan thought possible in such a small, backwoods settlement. In the center of the dining room, a huge double pedestal cherry table, surrounded by Chippendale pierced back chairs, had been set with four place settings of fine bone china and crystal French goblets. A rustic centerpiece of fall flowers spilled out over the rim of a basket to accent the colors of the oriental carpet covering the gleaming hardwood floor.

But the dining area was no less commanding than a cozy breakfast salon beyond. Jonathan walked onward to admire the nook enveloped by rows upon rows of glass windows.

"My young daughter loves this alcove because of the view." Raven trailed behind him. "Our caretaker leaves food outside the center window so she can watch the squirrels and birds while she eats."

"Is your sister always in the habit of being late?" Jonathan glanced at her anxious face.

Embarrassed, she confessed in a whisper, "I was hoping you hadn't noticed."

"With your father's incessant pacing? The poor man's sweating like a rock on a humid day." He gestured toward the elderly man. "You'd better go and reassure him before he passes out on the carpet."

A noise from the hall startled the group.

Dashing through the doors, Wilhelmina Wydcliffe glided up to her father.

Jonathan's jaw dropped unable to hide his astonishment. All day the picture of the hoyden had plagued his thoughts. He finally vowed to himself he would make it a point to discover who she was before he left the area, hoping for a chance to see her, hoping that she wasn't spoken for. And now, like a careless breeze, she had swept in. Elizabeth Wilhelmina Wydcliffe was Willie from their encounter in the forest.

"I'm sorry, Papa. It won't happen again, I promise." She turned from her father toward Raven and Jonathan. When she spied him, her mouth flew open, and then clamped shut like a trap door. Suppressed anger flitted across her face. She glared at him.

He returned her stare and felt a ripple of excitement in his chest. So the spunky little enchantress, the golden spitfire, now standing just yards from him was Wydcliffe's youngest daughter. Stunningly beautiful in a powder blue dress, she appeared almost angelic. An errant thought hit him like a ton of bricks. This sharp-tongued, little hoyden was by far no angel, but rather *his* business partner instead.

Big buzzard. Oaf. He recalled her string of warm compliments. His brow arched in ironic amusement as he offered her the first move in an obviously tricky situation. To her credit, she recovered with grace and charm. Squaring her shoulders, she crossed the distance, placed her hand in his, and shook it.

"Why, Mr. Wain, how delightful, at long last, to be able to meet you."

"Big buzzard, at your service," he whispered, still holding her hand. Aloud, he said, "Yes, what a delight. This may sound outlandish, but you remind me of someone I've recently met."

She yanked her hand away. "Highly doubtful." Lowering her voice, she whispered, "Let's not overdo the theatrics. You realize you weren't expected for two days?"

"I have an excellent horse."

"Yes, you do. You must be sure to give him an extra ration of oats as a reward for your swift arrival. We are *so* blessed."

She led the way to the table where courses of succulent stuffed pheasant, oven-baked trout, and roast lamb in mint sauce were piled high. Nearby, a sideboard of hot apple pie, peach tarts, and hot blueberry cobbler sent up a tantalizing fragrance in the room.

Once seated, Raven leaned forward. "I can't

believe you've already charmed Hannah, our cook, and you've barely met her. She has outdone herself with this meal."

He laughed. "It seems your gracious cook is weary of small appetites, and I'm tired of beef jerky. She's promised to keep me stuffed from head to toe."

Willie raised her wine glass in a mock toast. "Well, that ought to take some doing especially if she starts with your feet. Best of luck to our diligent cook and all her efforts in the future."

Across the table, Raven shot her a quelling look. "You've chosen the most beautiful time of the year to travel," she said. "The Indians call autumn in these mountains the season of rainbow leaves. Our settlement was named after the Indian village of Chinklacamoose. When the first settlers arrived along the banks of Clearfield Creek, they found acres of land resembling a clearing. Supposedly, buffalo destroyed all the undergrowth and left the face of the country as bare as though it had been cleared by the pioneer's grub-axe."

"And the Indians?" Jonathan recalled his father telling him that the Delaware Indians were a fierce tribe. "What happened to them?"

Raven shrugged. "Shawnee are a migratory people, not too fond of intruders, but not content to remain in any area for a considerable time. They scattered, moved westward, made friends with those they respected, and raided livestock and horses from those they didn't. Many still wander the mountains, often coming into the area in search of good horseflesh. Only a sharp eye will catch them permanently borrowing the goods."

"Speaking of horseflesh." Dalton Wydcliffe paused between a bite of food. "When you get a moment, Willie, check out the beast Jonathan rides. You would appreciate its bloodlines."

Grinning, Jonathan couldn't resist tormenting her. "Oh, do you ride, Miss Wydcliffe?"

"Willie. I prefer Willie." Her face turned the color of ripe strawberries. She stirred uneasily in her chair and hurriedly swallowed a mouthful of food. She coughed fitfully into her napkin, starting to choke.

"My daughter," Dalton Wydcliffe said and followed it with a weary sigh, "rides anything with four legs, bareback or saddled, whichever pleases her at the moment. Sometimes I think she's permanently attached to the back of her gray mount."

Jonathan nudged a goblet of water toward her.

She took a sip and dabbed at her watery eyes with her napkin. "Now, Papa, remember it was you and Raven who taught me to ride."

"I imagine there's a great deal of importance placed on being able to handle a horse in a rural area." Jonathan set his fork aside.

"A good horse can save your life," Wydcliffe agreed. "My mare has outrun packs of wolves many a time, and sometimes they were human." He rose from the table. "You'll have to excuse me, but I promised our neighbor, Nate Sheldon, I'd stop over to see his mare. She should be dropping a foal anytime now, and he may need some help."

Raven stood. "I have to fetch Nicole at the neighbor's, so I'll ride part way with Papa. Willie, please take Jonathan to the study for an after-dinner drink."

Finally, when the room cleared and they were alone, Jonathan leaned back in his chair and grinned, not trying to hide his delight.

"Nicole?" he asked.

"That's Raven's six-year-old daughter, Nicole Marie." Willie's stare stabbed holes in him like icepicks. She dropped her napkin and stood. "She and Raven stay with us quite often when Thomas is overseeing his trapping operations in Canada. Papa enjoys Nicole's flamboyant French personality. She has a way of putting energy and joy into this dreary house. Shall we adjourn to the study, Mr. Wain, where you can have a brandy at your leisure?"

"It's Jonathan."

"Ah, yes, it would have been nice if you'd had told me that earlier today."

Of all the rooms in the manor, Jonathan had earlier decided the study would be his favorite place. A cathedral ceiling held up by huge hand-hewn pine beams sheltered the entire room. A ceiling to floor fireplace built of rough country stone covered most of the west wall except for stout oak bookcases on each side which held works of Rousseau, Shakespeare, and Byron. Opposite it, a row of triple windows splashed morning light into the room. White French doors on the southern side led to a rear terrace of inlaid stone lined with what looked like well-tended roses and masses of marigolds. Brocade draperies on all the openings could be pulled shut to invite privacy. It was a place of warmth for working or relaxing.

"Do you think, Miss Wydcliffe, we could call a truce for the time being?"

Ignoring his question, Willie strolled to her father's well-stocked liquor cabinet. "A brandy?"

"Rum, please." He followed her to the cabinet. With deliberate insolence, he inspected her from head to toe. She was flawless and lovely, and she smelled deliciously like rose water and a summer breeze. "Please answer my question."

She removed a squat crystal tumbler. "I'm not in the habit of making peace with the devil, but you have me at your mercy. What do you intend to tell my father?"

She poured the amber liquid from a decanter and handed him the glass. The high-pitched clinking of glass against glass was the only sound in the room as she replaced it among the other bottles. Her task finished, she moved to the open French doors and stared out into the starry night.

Jonathan had enough irritation still seething under his skin to make her pay for her afternoon antics. He walked to where she stood and looked out into the inky night. Warm, moisture-laden air was alive with the sound of crickets grating their wings. Far off, a disgruntled dog howled. "I haven't decided what I should tell your father...if anything. It's not often I risk getting myself shredded with bullets for a bundle of old newspapers."

She turned to face him. Lightning flashed in her eyes. "You risked your own neck. Did I ask for your help? I should point out you knocked me flat on my back, crushed my brand new hat, and stole my gun."

For a moment they silently assessed each other.

He broke the stillness first. "Did you recognize him?"

"Who?"

"The thief you knifed in the woods, Miss Decoy."

"How would you know I knifed him?"

"I heard no gunfire from the clearing, but from the amount of blood scattered all over the place, you more than just playfully tickled his ribs. Actually, it looked like you went for the poor fellow's jugular vein."

"I wish I had. I only stabbed him in his shoulder. I wasn't aiming to kill, just slow him down a bit."

"With men that ruthless, Willie, it's best not to extend too much compassion. Those three riders on the ridge weren't exactly trying to miss your backside in the true spirit of Christian charity."

"Next time, I won't let them get that close."

"There won't be a next time," he snapped. "You pull a fool stunt like that again while I'm here, and I *will* tell your father. The closest you'll ever get to a logging operation will be sewing buttons on your crews' shirts. So tell me, did you recognize him or the horse he rode?"

"No. If I had recognized him, or his blasted horse, I would have spoken to the proper authorities." She paused and wagged a slim finger at his face. "You realize, mister, you're a pain in the—"

"Don't even say it!"

"Neck. But your first conclusion might be a more appropriate location."

Their dueling gazes met and he reached out and captured her against his chest.

Suddenly conscious of the fact that he either wanted to shake her mercilessly or kiss her senseless, he released her gently, disturbed by the discovery she had aroused far more than anger. He stalked to the fireplace and gripped the mantel, his head bent in thought. He had always been good at logical reasoning, but this wisp of a backwoods girl defied every civilized rule he ever learned. Her nearness stoked a gently growing fire that he'd never felt before with any other woman. And she was oblivious to it all. How would he ever be able to work beside her?

A lengthy silence elapsed before he spoke in a calm voice. "Is there a possible way we can come to terms since we have to share the same roof over our heads?"

Shifting like the wind, she concurred. "Unfortunately, I agree with you."

Turning, he pinned an astonished gaze on her. "You mean there's actually an ounce of compassion in that tiny body of yours?"

Willie grinned. "Don't compare my size with my compassion, or any other of my abilities, for that matter. The venom of a rattlesnake is deadly regardless of its size."

She thrust her hand toward him in an honest gesture of friendship. "If you promise not to tell Papa about the payroll, I promise to forget the apology, hat, and gun. A deal?" Her mischievous brown eyes twinkled. She shrugged. "After all, a stalemate is always better than a loss."

He relaxed. "Deal."

Smiling, he took her proffered hand and shook it, without releasing it. "To show you I bargain in good faith, I offer your pistol as well." With his free hand, he pulled her small, single shot, dueling pistol from his waistcoat and placed it in her open palm.

"But I have absolutely nothing to trade," she said

with a haughty theatrical voice.

"Ah, ha," he whispered, pulling her close to him. "A kiss, perhaps?"

Her voice exploded as she tried to push him away. "Why you arrogant scoundrel, I ought to shoot you with this gun."

His face moved closer. She gasped in surprise before his mouth swooped down on her lips. The kiss was brief, but soft and bewitching, and when he released her, she skidded safely backward.

"Now tell me," he crooned in a velvet voice. "Why do you carry a loaded pistol?"

"For rattlesnakes." Her hand fell to her side, the pistol enclosed in the folds of her dress.

"And the knife?"

"To cut off their rattles."

He laughed, his hearty chuckles filling up the room and silence around them. "I'd rather sit naked with the rattlesnake than with you so heavily armed."

CHAPTER FOUR

A SLIVER OF MORNING SUN SNEAKED in through the rose damask drapes in Willie's bedroom and landed directly on her face. The rays danced about, retreated behind a cloud, and reappeared to plague her again.

She slipped out from beneath the quilts on her four-poster bed, padded on bare feet across the floor to the window, and flung it open. The fresh, sharp breeze of autumn wafted in bringing the clean, pungent smell of drying leaves, wet earth, and frosted grass. Stretching, she yawned, wishing she had been able to secure more sleep. But her father had not returned until after midnight, and she was forced to spend most of the evening with her head bent over a chess board, avoiding Jonathan's nimble queen. Later, they both conned her into a few hands of poker, a game she could never resist.

She turned from the window and smiled at the coins resting in towering stacks on her nightstand. The card game had been more successful than she'd imagined. And she hadn't cheated. Well, almost hadn't. Except for the few hands she had stealthily dealt Jonathan from the bottom of the deck. It served him right. It had been the first time in years she had lost a chess match to anyone. Having him around might prove to be entertaining. He certainly was pleasant to look at. Classically handsome, he projected a polished veneer like it was second skin. The smell of his after-shave, bay rum with a hint of pine, would make most women swoon.

With elevated spirits, she moved to her washstand and splashed water into the porcelain basin. She had just finished washing when a shrill childish yell echoed from the hallway, followed by the pounding of little feet. Nicole Marie burst through the doorway without knocking, darted up on the bed amid the wrinkled bed linens, and started bouncing up and down on the mattress.

"Good morning." The young girl shrieked out her greeting as the old bed springs sagged and creaked out their displeasure. Her dark, loosened hair flew out around her face in undulating waves with each rhythmic movement. "Why aren't you dressed yet? You promised to go shopping with Mama this morning."

Willie groaned. "Oh, Nicole, I forgot." She knotted the thin sash to her robe about her waist and searched for her rosewood hairbrush on her nightstand. It was missing. She dropped to her knees to look under the moving bed. "Where's your mother?" she asked in a muffled voice.

"Here."

Startled, Willie jerked her head upward and slammed it against the low bedframe. She howled, staggering to her feet

"I didn't mean to frighten you." Raven's apology

had less of an effect on her than the hair brush she thrust at her. It was one of the few possessions Willie had from her mother. "I found this with a bundle of soiled laundry on your floor."

Willie tenderly traced the carved rosebuds etched on the handle with her fingertips. "I was afraid I'd lost it."

Raven looked disapprovingly at her daughter doing a quick somersault over the edge of the bed, only to land nimbly on her feet in an upright position. "If we're going to have time to look at those dolls at Irwin's Store, we'd better let Aunt Willie get dressed, Nicole Marie. Please go to your room and find your socks and shoes, and I'll be over in a minute to braid your hair."

Obediently, the little girl skipped merrily through the doorway.

For a few moments, Raven studied her sister's still form, her hand still wrapped around the handle of the hairbrush. "I know how it feels, Willie. I have nothing of my mother's either, except a quilled shirt she once sewed for Papa and a silver bracelet he gave her long ago."

Willie nodded glumly. "This is a shabby clue to understanding a parent I can't remember."

"I know, but you were only three years old when she died." Raven touched her arm gently. "Your mother was a kind and loving person. She liked to read, and she was beautiful, organized, and tidy as a pin."

Willie watched her dark-haired sister scrutinize her room, her gaze darting to the ribbons tangled on the floor, circling the room from corner to corner. Her dress she wore last night was tossed over the back of a chair, followed by petticoats and a camisole. Books haphazardly piled on the night table shared space with stacks of coins and a half-filled glass of water. On the bookshelves on the far wall, treasures lined the shelves. Eagle and hawk feathers, an Indian necklace made from bright stones, a huge shiny black rock the size of a man's fist, a dog-eared Latin book, a small replica of a clipper ship, rattles from a timber rattler, and a delicate porcelain statue of a dun-colored stallion were scattered about with no semblance of order. Willie cringed when her sister's gaze alighted on a shelf and she frowned. Rusty rings from an old bridle were pitched together with an expensive mother-of-pearl necklace and matching earrings.

"Don't say a word," Willie ordered. "Papa said our rooms are our domains. Sua cuique voluptas."

"*Every man has his own pleasures*, but Papa obviously hasn't seen clutter as charming as this." Raven's glanced at the rock again, and she shook her head at the black dust it made on the lower shelf. "Magna est via consuetudinis."

Willie laughed. "*The force of habit is great.*" Those moth-eaten tutors had drilled a few boring Latin phrases into her head.

"Papa would be proud. He only hired six of them in four years to tutor you because you were so obstinate and rambunctious." Raven crossed the room to the closet and pulled out a pale violet dress.

Willie's lips bowed into a grim line. "Oh no, I'm not wearing a dress *again*. I wore one yesterday. We're verging on being pretentious here."

"Be reasonable, Willie. Jonathan Wain is having

breakfast with us in the salon. The least you can do is look presentable. Papa seems so pleased he's here."

With a huff, Willie snatched the dress, poked her head into it, and jammed her arms into the sleeves. "I don't know how one obnoxious, East Coast pirate has been able to throw this entire manor into such a tizzy. Father is pleased. You are charmed. Conrad is in heaven. And Hannah is cooking like there will be no tomorrow. I'll bet the man is so cold-hearted he eats nails for breakfast."

"He's really quite handsome." Raven waited until her sister's head popped through the opening in the dress. Spinning her around, she started buttoning her dress up the back.

Willie had noticed, but it was the last thing she'd ever admit. She slipped her feet into her shoes.

Together, they descended to the first floor. Raven searched the kitchen and study for her daughter, but returned empty-handed to the breakfast nook. "I do wish Thomas would find a proper home for us in Canada." She pursed her lips and looked out the window. She seemed to be choosing her words carefully. "Nicole needs to be with her father and away from these mills. The other day she told old spinster Larson her mouth flaps more than a lumberman's underwear. Where does she hear such crude expressions?"

A wave of heat crawled steadily up Willie's neck. "I'm afraid to venture a guess."

On the third floor of the manor, Jonathan Wain

was awake at dawn. After an early morning ride, he had returned to his room to bathe and shave before breakfast. A huge white marble fireplace sputtered and crackled, driving away the early morning chill from every corner of his room. Across from the two dormer windows at the far end of the room, Dalton Wydcliffe had thoughtfully placed a large secretary to allow him a private work area of his own. Richly done in emerald green, the room had a masculine aura and comfortable charm, right down to the Oriental rug beneath his feet.

Whistling, he concentrated on his shaving in front of a mirror above the washstand in a bathing alcove. A large canning jar, filled with water and a fat bullfrog, sat on a ladder-back chair beside him. In the corner of the room, an old scuffed pair of boots, dripping water, was propped upside down against the wall. Sneaking a glance at the frog, he smiled and reminded himself to thank the caretaker for securing the old worn-out boots and warning him about the pranks played on new guests at the manor.

As he shaved, he caught a ripple of movement near his open door. Two small eyes peered at him from around the jamb.

Laying his razor aside, he wiped the foamy lather from his face and turned, speaking to the plump frog. "I have peppermint candy, but I've yet to find someone who likes it besides me."

"I do," a tiny voice said from the shadows.

He laughed. "A talking frog?"

"Non. It's me."

Giggling, the little girl revealed herself. Two glossy black braids with matching pink ribbons framed her delicate face and chocolate eyes. There was no doubt she was Raven's LeConte's daughter. The child was the mirror image of her mother, right down to the distinct cheekbones and burnished gold skin.

"You must be Nicole Marie." Jonathan pulled out his watch. "Am I late for breakfast?"

"Oh, non, monsieur." She spoke with a French accent. "Mama must not know I'm here, or she'll scold me soundly. She told me not to disturb you, but I had to see what you looked like."

"What am I supposed to look like?" Jonathan knelt before the child.

"Aunt Willie said you're an obnoxious pirate. What does obnoxious mean? I've come to see your eye patch and sword."

He bit the corner of his lip, choking back a chuckle. "Obnoxious means unpleasant. But I assure you, I'm a very likable pirate. And I'm sorry to disappoint you. I don't have an eye patch or sword." He watched the child's lively face fade into a disappointing frown.

"Why, you even have all of your fingers," she lamented, inspecting his large calloused hands. "Do you have any teeth marks from fighting with sharks and alligators, or maybe scars from a sea battle?"

He rose and rolled up his sleeve. High on his upper arm, a large ugly white scar zigzagged halfway down from his shoulder. "Only this one," he said dramatically, pointing to it. "It's from my last battle with a group of pirates who I chased over-board into the sea."

He watched the girl's eyes brighten as she studied the ugly scar now faded with time. It was the memory now that still hurt, much more than the flesh had, when he had to withstand the gruesome stitching to lace the skin together. His best friend had lost his life, and the scar was a nagging reminder of the ache he sometimes felt for him.

"Oh, monsieur, you are so brave," the little girl whispered. She glanced at the chair beside the washstand. "And you've found Toby."

"Toby?"

"Oui, monsieur, my pet bullfrog. I caught him at the mill dam two days ago, but he disappeared from my bureau last night. I was afraid he was lost forever." She skipped to the jar, scooped it up, and looked adoringly at the slippery green frog with balloon-like eyes staring back at her through the side of the glass jar.

"Did you let Toby try to wear my boots? I found him in one this morning."

"Oh, non, monsieur, don't be silly." She giggled. "Frogs don't wear boots."

"Of course," he agreed with a sheepish grin. He took the glass jar from her hands and set it back on the chair. "You'll have to get Toby later. He probably wouldn't be welcome at the breakfast table."

"Oui, monsieur," she agreed. "It is a good thing you have captured him. You really area kind pirate." She wound her arms around his legs and hugged him tightly.

It was a noisy pair that scuttled down the stairs and entered the breakfast salon minutes later.

"Ahoy, mates," Jonathan greeted Raven and Willie. He swung Nicole up and around and into the high-back chair beside him. She held a peppermint stick in her hand.

He glanced around the table. "Did Dalton leave already?"

"Papa is meeting John Pierce at the mill," Willie told him. "He's a rogue merchant who's able to locate anything from ammunition to the finest furniture made in New England."

Jonathan took a sip of steaming coffee the cook graciously slid before him along with a plate filled with eggs, sausage, and bacon. "Do you know what the meeting is about?"

"I suppose it's the same weary conversation. Pierce is eager to buy a thousand acres we own on the western part of town." She picked up a slice of bread and began to butter it. "Half of it was once deeded to your father, but my father bought it after the lumber was removed. It's totally useless. No gold, silver, iron, or clay to be found. It might be decent for farming with a lot of work."

"Is your father selling?"

"No, but he's tossed the idea about several times. Papa's sentimental about that particular piece of property. It was one of the first parcels he acquired for the company."

He drummed his fingers on the table. "So tell me, would you sell?"

She pondered over her answer. Would she? Sometimes she thought there was something binding her father closely to it, something mysterious, something he refused to disclose.

"Only if I needed some ready cash." *But not to John Pierce.* She neglected to add there was a rumor he once supplied renegade Indians with guns and ammunition, and some of his goods, if not stolen, were secured by less than honest means.

"Do you think this Pierce fellow has anything to do with the timber being ruined or the lost rafts sent downriver this spring?"

Willie shook her head. "He's not the type to get his hands dirty. I can't imagine him getting knee-deep in river mud to drive some spikes and nails into our logs. He'd never climb aboard a crib of rafts and cut the lashings."

Nicole patted Jonathan gently on the arm. "Are you going shopping with us, monsieur?"

Willie resisted a groan. The last thing she wanted was to squire Jonathan Wain about town. It was going to be tiring enough later in the afternoon when she had to escort him to see the various logging operations.

He came to her rescue unknowingly. "No, I'm afraid not. I'm counting on you three to plunder and loot the stores without me."

Disappointed, Nicole hung her head.

Jonathan fished in his pocket, pulled out a shiny half-dollar, and handed it to her. "A coin for more sweets. Select something for me, too, that I might like."

Brightening, Nicole smiled. "Merci, monsieur. Now when are you going to eat the nails? Before or after we leave? I don't want to miss it."

He stared curiously at her.

The little girl barreled on, her words pouring out like water from a flood gate. "Aunt Willie said your heart is so cold you eat nails for breakfast. Are they little tacks like the shoemaker uses or those big ones like Grandfather uses at the mills?"

Raven flew out of her chair as if she was shot from a cannon. "That's quite enough Nicole Marie LeConte."

Grinning, Jonathan motioned to her to take a seat before he yanked one of Nicole's braids good-naturedly. "Pirates don't eat nails anymore, little one. But I've heard they use them to pin mutinous scallywags to the mast by the seat of their pants."

His dangerous gaze found Willie's. "And who should I credit for the frog and wet boots?"

The room grew deadly silent.

Stains of scarlet appeared on Willie's cheeks. She stood, scraping her chair against the floor, and bolted from the room.

CHAPTER FIVE

THE BUGGY UNDER CONRAD'S SKILLED hands rocked gently along the picturesque countryside, aglow with colors splashed from autumn's frosty paint box. Red apples dipped the branches of orchard trees to the ground in prayer, and a profusion of green and purple grapevines clung proudly to weather-worn fences along the way.

Oblivious to it all, Willie rode in silence beside her sister and Nicole. Many thoughts warred in her mind, and now Jonathan Wain had arrived to further confuse an already unsettling situation. She needed to formulate a plan to deal with the mills. The spiked timber that ruined the mill's saws and stolen payrolls were not chance calamities resulting from meandering gangs of thieves or rival logging crews. There was no jealousy among the lumbering operators. The year had been a profitable one for all and the demand for timber was growing voraciously. Many men had grumbled they now had the cash to erect a large home near town and live like a king, but not the energy or time to do it.

Willie scowled, wishing she could have injured

her attacker sufficiently to have him identified or apprehended. It might have meant an end to their problems. Soon, with fall logging upon them, the weekly transfer of payrolls to the mills would cease, and all men would draw their paychecks in town at the Hornet's Nest mill. The violator might never be discovered.

The arrival of Jonathan Wain also troubled her. His visit had to be more than a social call. She should have realized it as soon as his trunks, sent earlier by flatboat and wagon, arrived. The man was now armed with enough clothes and belongings to spend the entire fall and winter. She'd have to find a way to send him packing. He was an outsider. He didn't belong. And, good heavens, she didn't need a Limey from Baltimore to involve himself in a fight that didn't concern him. As long as she could draw a breath of air, she'd do what was necessary to protect the Wydcliffe logging operations and her crews.

Without conscious thought, she clenched her fist, trying to recall the feel of her old stiletto with its smooth handle, razor sharp edges, and a blade bright like ice. It had been a gift from Thomas LeConte before he became Raven's husband. She and Raven had wiled away many an afternoon at the Indian village situated north of town. Even though it was seven years ago, she still missed the outings and the village with its smoky fires and aroma of fresh roasted meat.

She knew Raven used to go there to see her people and to see Thomas, who frequently stopped when he was overseeing his trapping lines or trading with the tribes. But she went there to watch the young braves practice their horsemanship and knife skills.

It seemed like only yesterday when she was caught hiding in the ferns, watching the warriors lob their knives into the bark of the pines with a force and speed that made her dizzy. She had begged Lone Wolf, a friend of Thomas, to teach her. Each week, thereafter, she secretly stole away to practice with the eighteen-year-old brave who wore a gray wolf's fur draped over his broad shoulders. He had taught her well, the ways of the singing blade and the ways of the forest.

He was born into a family with a long line of shamans. He once told her of an unsettling vision. He dreamed she was walking along an icy riverbank, swollen by winter rains, and in her hands she held a fiery ball so hot, it slipped from her grip to fall hissing into the cold snow before its scarlet tongues rose up to engulf her. He couldn't explain its meaning. It had been the last time she had seen him. Her heart ached when they parted for she could never tell anyone, including Lone Wolf himself, a naive sixteen-year-old white girl admired him. Yet, she suspected he knew.

It took a moment for Willie to realize the carriage was no longer swaying along the rocky road, and they had arrived at Irwin's General Store.

The shop assistant, Harold Young, his Adams apple bobbing, greeted them instantly, wiping his hands on a dusty cotton apron and skirting crates and barrels of goods stacked on the walk in a fetching display.

Nicole flew down an aisle toward the doll corner. Raven headed for the yard goods. And Willie sauntered to the back of the store where long glass-covered cases held guns, knives, and costly items like delicate china, porcelain, and glass jewelry.

Seconds later she heard a familiar voice behind her. "Why Wilhelmina, surely you're not in the market for a knife?"

She didn't have to turn to know who was behind her. Matthew Reed was the only one who called her by her given name. One of the youngest operators in the area at only twenty-five years old, he owned a small saw mill operation along Montgomery Creek, west of town. He was a slight built man with sandy hair. Despite his sometimes cocky attitude, Willie genuinely liked him. He was a pleasant sort around her, always willing to talk with her after the monthly lumber meetings and escort her to her father's buggy. She knew her father had no charitable words for Matthew Reed. They had come head to head many times at the loggers' meetings, and more recently over script money and owning company stores. Her father believed it was cruel and unjust to pay a man for his hard work, and later collect it back by charging ridiculously high prices for the same goods he could buy for less in town at the General Store. Wydcliffe Lumbering never owned a company store. And never would.

Slowly, she eased away from the gun case. "Why, this is a surprise, Matthew."

"I missed you at the meeting last week."

"Yes, Raven cajoled me into shopping for yard goods for a dress she's making for one of the singers performing for Clara Ferguson's party."

He chuckled gently. "So you're planning to

attend? I hear Clara's father has returned from London and brought her a new game called croquet. It's a lawn game where a hard ball is struck with a mallet through a high arch of iron. The person with the least strokes wins the match."

If the truth be told, last thing she wanted to do bat some ball over the grass with Clara Ferguson. They had never been friends. But she knew of no way to decline the invitation. The whole town had been invited.

"I heard they're clearing out the sitting room just to accommodate the dancing." He nudged her to one side of the counter where the shadows were deep and smell of wool and leather clung in the air. "You'll save at least one dance for me?" His eyes roamed appreciatively over her body.

She drew her shawl tighter around her shoulders. "I will."

"Splendid." Matthew Reed shoved his hand in his pocket, fingering some loose coins. "Rumor about town is you're having trouble with your mills."

Willie forced a smile. "It's nothing we can't handle." Heat rose in her cheeks as she thought about the episode in the woods. She had no desire to tell him about her confrontation with one of the bandits. Her father's fury was less threatening than that of the townspeople if they got their hands on that choice bit of gossip. A wounded thief would get more sympathy than a knife-wielding female masquerading in logger's clothes.

"Be careful." He frowned. "I hear there are thieves plying the area, and they're a fearless lot." He leaned an elbow on the counter. "How's that silly old codger? What's his name?"

"Sam Bradley?" The last word she'd ever use to describe Sam Bradley was silly. "Oh my stars, we can't keep Sam off his stubborn old mule. He plans to go out cruising this fall to select timber stands for our winter logging operations."

A perplexed look flitted across Matthew's face before he disguised it. "The whole town is a buzz, eager to meet your Eastern guest."

Jonathan Wain, in Willie's estimation, was far from a guest—a thorn in her side perhaps, but not a guest. She surmised some sort of correspondence between her father and old Isaac Wain was responsible for his sudden appearance. "Johnathan's father is a close friend of Papa's," she explained. "I'm showing him our mill in town this afternoon and the downriver one, near your operations."

"How long is he planning to stay?"

"I don't know. He just arrived."

Offering her a quick nod, he turned toward the back door of the store. "Well, time is money. I'm off to buy feed for my stock. Don't forget to save a dance for me."

Willie watched his retreating back for a few moments before she stepped around a keg of nails to reach the aisle. She found her sister selecting yards of bright calico. After agreeing to meet at the buggy in an hour, she hurried to the front of the store. Outside, she quickened her pace, weaving her way among boisterous children rolling hoops and skipping ropes on the boardwalk. The air hummed with the clop of hooves striking the dusty road and the chatter of people. Shopkeepers stood in their doorways, greeting customers, gossiping, or wielding brooms to keep the dirt out.

She was so caught up in her thoughts, Willie barely noticed a slim girl with hair the same shade as her own come barreling around the corner. Packages went flying in all directions as they collided and tried to recover their poise. The girl wore a simple red gingham dress with a white cotton collar that had undergone many starchings. Her eyes were sparkling blue.

"Willie Wydcliffe. I should have known." She giggled, the corners of her pert mouth turning upward.

"Drat, I'm so sorry." Willie scrambled to collect the scattered packages. "It's a good thing you weren't old biddy Minnie Larson. Almost knocked her over when I was taking my saddle to the harness shop. I had to listen to her chew me out for half an hour. Her mouth flaps more than a lumberman's underwear."

Together the girls stacked the packages on a wooden plank bench nearby.

When the last one was recovered, Willie dusted her hands. "I finally received my invitation to Clara Ferguson's party, and I'll wager mine was the last one delivered. The twit never throws a party unless she plans to flaunt something."

"It's her twenty-first birthday, and she can flaunt whatever she wants," Rachael pointed out. She's one of the richest females in town."

"You mean her father is."

"And the lucky man who marries her will never starve." Rachael swallowed nervously. "I'm not going. I always feel out of place at Clara's parties.

To be honest, I don't own anything suitable to wear." She lowered her head, a blush like a shadow crept over her cheeks.

Willie studied her a moment. They were the same size and height. She had a closet full of dresses more than suitable for the party, dresses she'd never wear. "I have an ice blue silk to make your mouth water, Rachael. It would match your eyes perfectly."

"Oh, I don't know…" Rachael hesitated.

"I even have the perfect jewelry for you to wear, a mother-of-pearl necklace and earrings." Willie patted her on the arm. "Stop at the manor on Thursday afternoon. We'll have some tea and rummage through my closet. No excuses, hear?"

A gust of autumn wind swirled about and billowed her skirt as she left Rachael and headed to the buggy where she dropped off her packages before crossing the street to the jeweler's. A tiny bell above the door merrily tinkled as Jonathan Wain stepped outside and blocked her entrance.

"I've been chasing your shadow all over town," he admitted.

"Looks like my luck just ran out."

"I hope you're not going in there to purchase a knife." His voice had a terse tone to it.

"It's really none of your business what I buy."

Anger flashed briefly across his face before he turned her, grabbed her by the hand, and pulled her down the walk to a spot in front of the assayer's office devoid of people. "Think! What would happen if word was spread around town you were buying a poker for yourself? The man in the forest, the one you made mincemeat of, thinks you're a boy."

The incident with her assailant flashed through her mind. Her stomach did a nose dive.

A disgruntled sigh escaped his lips. "You can't afford to get careless with a thief still on the loose. And for future reference, your town jeweler is less than honest. He tried to overcharge me on a purchase I made."

He fell silent and pulled her up the street toward the buggy, pausing to nod and smile at an elderly woman who curiously watched them. Too late, Willie realized it was Isabelle Payne, the wife of her father's lawyer.

She tried to jerk away from his viselike grip. "Jonathan, let go of me. What will people think?"

He held on despite her efforts to dislodge him. "I could give a tinker's damn what the whole town thinks." He tugged her onward.

Before they reached the buggy, a tall woman with flaming red hair flowing from beneath a white satin sun hat passed them and he greeted her warmly as well. When Willie recognized her, she had the urge to sink into the walk. Did he not know he had just publicly greeted the proprietor of the town's saloon and local brothel?

When they finally reached the buggy, he left her.

Nodding in farewell, he sauntered away in a carefree gait, whistling a repetitious little tune which Willie later recognized as the very same one she had often heard drifting out of the doors of the Sawdust Bin Saloon.

CHAPTER SIX

THE BURNT ORANGE SUN RADIATED an umbrella of warmth over their heads when the trio arrived back at the manor and alighted from the buggy.

Nicole, still simmering with glee, raced up the walk, her little legs churning madly. The hatbox she clutched under her arm jiggled wildly and threatened to escape before it reached its destination. Her mother, fearful of the new bonnet's fate, hurried after her.

Lingering behind, Willie watched Conrad unpack the many boxes and packages from where he had carefully stored them in the back of the buggy. His thinning, straw-like hair fluttered in the breeze, and he looked like a scarecrow come to life. Despite all the loyal years he had spent working as their caretaker, Willie realized she knew little about him. His stern, aloof demeanor kept everyone at a distance.

He had been hired before she was born, just after the manor was completed, and Raven had once confided in her that she heard he had come from the British Isles seeking work after the well-to-do family he worked for went belly up in debt. He had been in his mid-thirties, and another twenty years of backwoods life had only softened his English twang. Well-read, he often borrowed books from her father's library. A man of impeccable manners, he held fast to propriety, often voicing distaste over her tomboyish appearance and her involvement with the lumber mills. Lately, they seemed to have come to an agreeable stalemate and were learning to tolerate each other's differences.

He unhitched the horses from their traces and led them to the stable doors where he turned. "I'm supposed to remind you that Mr. Wain is waiting for you. You're responsible for giving him a tour of your Papa's mills. And you haven't eaten, so you better hurry."

Willie lowered her head, brooding. She didn't need to be reminded about her obligations or Jonathan Wain. Why would a man leave the luxury of a grand house in the Chesapeake Bay area and come to a settlement in the wilderness? And why would he choose to visit with winter almost upon them? What did she know about him? Nothing really, except for the fact that every spring timbers were sent to Wain and Sons Shipping, and later, tally and profit sheets came back with his neatly penned, bold signature on them.

"Please have Roy saddle Silver Cloud for me and Blackjack for Mr. Wain."

Conrad eyed her suspiciously. "Blackjack hasn't been exercised recently and he'll be difficult to handle. He might try to kick up his heels like an ornery mule."

"They ought to make a perfect pair. Mr. Wain's

horse has been ridden hard the last few days and needs to rest." Hiding a snicker, she headed for the manor.

Later, after a hurried meal, she returned to her room to don a riding habit from her clothespress. She was surprised to discover a thin, rectangular package, tied with string, sitting on her dressing table. Unwrapping it, she found a stiletto with a black onyx handle similar to the one she had lost. It had to be from Jonathan Wain, she concluded, recalling his visit to the jeweler's. Smiling, she dropped her pistol into her coat pocket and yanked on her worn riding boots. She slipped the shiny the blade inside her right boot and climbed the stairs to the third floor.

She was hardly prepared for the sight greeting her outside the opened guest room door. Chest bared and clad only in a pair of buckskin breeches, Jonathan leaned over his desk and poured over mountains of papers and maps. He was a well-muscled man with gigantic shoulders. A white scar, thick and ragged, zigzagged down one arm like a lightning bolt. Black hair fell carelessly over his forehead and framed his angular face, deep in concentration. Her father had indicated he was in his early thirties, given his place in the birth order of his brothers.

She called into his room. "If you need more time, I can return."

Maps and papers, rolled and unrolled, covered every available flat surface. Occasionally, a breeze from the opened window fluttered a pile of pages and sent them scuttling across the floor.

Jonathan reached for his shirt and shrugged into

it, jamming his shirttails down behind his belt, never lifting his eyes from the desktop. "No. Come in."

"Thank you for the knife." She moved beside him and peered at a pile of maps, some recently new, others yellowed and time-worn. None were foreign to her. She recognized the latest geological survey of their lands at the western end of town. Clay deposits had been neatly penned in.

"If you're looking for gold on these thousand acres, forget it," she said wryly.

His gray eyes traveled over her small frame. "I think I've found gold right here in this room." His voice was low and silky.

"And our Pennsylvania sun has already fried your brain."

Chuckling, he turned back to the map and pointed to the uneven boundaries of the one-thousand acres of land John Pierce wanted to purchase. "Why don't the other areas outside this tract of land show changes in the rock formations?"

"The entire area is limestone." She squinted at it again.

"All of it?" He peered at the map with a dubious look.

She shrugged and stepped backward. "After the land was timbered, lime and blue stone quarries were opened, but they weren't very productive. The stone of the manor is from a nearby quarry Papa owns." She leaned over the map again, her head almost touching his. "William Kramer is the best geologist in the area as well as a respected friend of the family. His daughter, Rachael, is my best friend."

And Kramer had no reason to tamper with the surveys, Willie thought, as she re-examined the area closely one more time. He had nothing to gain by misrepresenting them. She knew Rachael's father was not wealthy enough to even purchase fifty acres of land, let alone a hundred or more, even if there was anything worthwhile on them.

She straightened and gripped the back of the desk chair. "It doesn't make sense these wouldn't be accurate."

"The idea of anyone destroying timber doesn't either." He removed a book from his nightstand and laid it on top of the papers to secure them should an errant breeze slip in from the open window. It was in French, and she picked it up, leafing through it. "You can read this?"

"Are you surprised a pirate can read…or he can read French?"

Willie cringed. She prayed Nicole hadn't repeated every glum detail with her usual unbridled enthusiasm after she had eavesdropped on the conversation she and Raven had exchanged the other morning.

"It's a translated collection of folktales by the Grimm brothers. I'm trying to stay one step ahead of Nicole. We're going to trade stories in the evenings," Jonathan explained.

"How did you learn French?"

"My father is fluent in many languages, and he thought it would be helpful if each of his sons learned one, what with the shipping business. I learned French from a Paris governess. Jacob knows Spanish, and Jeremy is studying German." He sauntered to the washstand in his dressing alcove. "I have another surprise for you. Actually, it's a gift." From a shelf, he removed a hatbox laced shut with a red velvet ribbon and handed it to her.

Willie's mouth dropped open in surprise.

"Well, open it," he urged. "I assure you nothing will leap out."

She tugged the ribbon and lifted the lid. A fawn-colored suede hat was nestled inside, protected by the four cardboard walls. Its wide brim, turned up around a semi-high crown, was accented by a thin gold braid. The color matched her riding boots to perfection.

She removed it from the box, flew to his mirror, and perched it on her head. She cocked her head at all angles and reverently touched the suede as soft as moss on river rocks. Turning from the mirror, she grinned. "It's exquisite. How do I look?"

"Beautiful," he said, his voice a whispering caress.

She giggled, turned back to the mirror, and rattled on. "Oh, it's just what I wanted. How can I ever thank you?"

"I'll think of a way," he said in a low allusive voice fading into silence.

Jonathan had to force himself to pull his gaze away from Willie's enraptured face in the mirror's reflection. The woman was incredibly fetching, like a mountain spring, pure, sweet, with inexhaustible flowing energy. Without a doubt, he knew if he spent the rest of his life, he could never satisfy his thirst for any other woman but her. The thought was so jolting, he found himself saying in an awkward tone, "Ah, we'd better hurry. Your father is waiting for us."

Unaware of his warring thoughts, Willie stole another glance in the mirror and followed him outside to the stables, where a red rooster, atop a white-washed fence, cocked his head fitfully and started to crow. His squawk was near deafening.

Amused, Jonathan stopped to watch his antics.

"The crazy rooster goes into a frenzy every so often." Willie threw it an evil look, flailing her arms. "Shoo, shoo. Get out of here."

Ignoring her, the rooster stretched his slender neck, ruffled his scarlet feathers, and strutted back and forth along the rail. Another deafening series of squawks sliced the air.

"Does he have a name?"

"Crazy Red." She chuckled. "He belongs to Roy, the lad who works in our stables. We think the poor thing is confused. He crows at every time of the day except daylight. Hannah, our cook, wants to put him in the soup pot, but Roy's taken a shine to him."

"What about his other natural abilities?"

"What other abilities?" Willie's forehead wrinkled. "Ahhh," she finally said, blushing. "Well, the chickens don't seem to be complaining, do they?"

He laughed and followed her to the stable doors where the Roy appeared with her mount. She snatched the reins and stepped into her saddle before addressing him. "I decided you'd probably want to give your horse a rest, so I had Roy saddle Blackjack."

The stable boy slipped inside the stable and appeared with the second mount, a prancing black stallion. He was sleek, massive, and looked like he was capable of riding to hell and back. Snorting, he pawed the ground and rolled his eyes.

Jonathan heard Willie offer a partial warning in her sweet, but oh so cynical voice. "Blackjack's rather lively at first. If you need a more docile beast, I can have Roy saddle another."

The gauntlet had been thrown. The little spitfire was testing his riding ability and trying to set him up to fail.

"No, the stallion will do. I've no doubt you have a perfect nag already picked out for me should this one prove unsuitable." He stepped closer and moved to the stallion to recheck the saddle and girth. "Hold his head steady," he commanded the stable boy.

Without warning, the horse laid its ears back and reared.

With a tug on the reins, Jonathan pulled the stallion back to the ground. With a gentleness belying his huge stature, he ran his hand down the snorting stallion's smooth neck and patted him affectionately before he eased himself up into the saddle.

Blackjack, aware of the weight on his back, sidestepped, jerked his head, and threatened to rear up again.

"Eeeasy now, boy," Jonathan soothed.

The stallion danced sideways, then as if calmed by the rider's voice and his light, but firm hands on the reins, settled down like a meek stable cat.

The stable boy hooted. "Holy cow! Nice work, Mr. Wain. Never saw a stranger calm Blackjack so dang quick. First time out a rider usually gets himself knocked flat on his britches."

"You don't say." He threw a scathing look at Willie who had wheeled Silver Cloud toward the Hornet's Nest and raced off.

Blackjack's hooves rang out a sharp staccato on the brick drive as he followed and gave the stallion his full head. They raced onto the dirt road, kicking up a cloud of dust and eating up the distance to surpass Willie and Silver Cloud. The stallion was born to run. He could feel it in the animal's powerful muscles straining beneath him. The wind whistled in his ears. For a second, it reminded him of the carefree feeling he always felt when one of the ships was flying hell bent over the ocean.

Moments later, she raced in, and he moved to the hitching rail to help her from the saddle. He searched her face for a split second, his heart pounding in his chest as a spattering of sparks leaped between them. He was certain there was an invisible thread of some undefinable emotion pulling on them.

She jerked away as soon as her feet hit the ground and started to speak, but quickly cocked her head to listen. From the mill floor, the thunderous hum and whine of the saws and the clang of iron striking iron split the air.

An alarmed look crossed her face. She rushed toward the mill, yanking its thick-slabbed door open, barreling up the steps and down a narrow hallway, and sending the door to her father's office crashing against the opposite wall.

Startled, Dalton Wydcliffe sprung up from his chair behind his desk. The pipe he was filling clattered onto the desk top and spilled tobacco over his papers. When the old man recognized his intruder, he gave her a cross look. "Wilhelmina Wydcliffe, must you always tear every door from its hinges?"

Jonathan skidded to a halt behind her.

"It sounds like we have another saw down." She ignored her father's reprimand.

"Yes, someone tampered with the saw blades last night." Wydcliffe sank down in his seat. "Fortunately, one of the men noticed the loosened bolts before we started them up this morning, but more spiked logs got past the men loading our saw carriages. A blade was ruined."

Jonathan buckled into a chair near the door and frowned at the bits of sawdust accumulated on his boots and covering the old threadbare carpet.

Wydcliffe motioned towards the sawdust trail. "We've hired a woman to clean the offices starting next week. We had one of our workers' wives helping. Lydia Henderson. McGee caught her nipping the spirits from the liquor cabinet and fired her."

"The same McGee who started as a paymaster for my father?" Jonathan recalled his brother, Jacob, had only the best words to say about the man and his accounting skills. He'd never been a penny off when spring rafts arrived at the Chesapeake docks along with the tallies.

Wydcliffe nodded.

Willie blew out a weary sigh. "Let's hope we can make the fall quota."

"We'll certainly try," Wydcliffe said soothingly. "We sharpened one blade this morning. I sent the last one we had downriver to the Black Widow mill last week, so we're short one." He rubbed the back of his neck. He was a tall, gray-haired man who had once been lean and tough, but the years had chiseled much of the sharpness from his features. Now his face was drawn and pinched. The last few months had taken its toll on his health.

"Maybe we need to assign a night watch," she suggested.

"This isn't the work of an outsider," Wydcliffe said, "and it's impossible to guard every pile of timber we own."

"This crew in town is our most loyal bunch, Papa."

"Except for one. All you need is one greedy man who likes to line his pockets with our pay and a bonus from someone else. One man who easily can be bribed."

"Maybe a smaller mill will loan us one." Willie went to her father and placed a hand reassuringly on his thin shoulder.

The elderly man slumped farther back into his chair, his body sagging with fatigue. "Why would our competitors want to lend us a hand? Winter is far too near for anyone to be generous."

"We've always helped them." She bent and placed a quick kiss on his forehead. "I'll take Jonathan to the upriver mill and stop at Matthew Reed's mill on Montgomery Creek. If he has an extra blade, he'll loan it to us."

Wydcliffe scowled. "Yes, when pigs fly."

She gave him a hostile stare.

"You probably should know Sam Bradley was injured this morning."

Her face paled.

"A chunk of wood flew off when a file hit the blade. Lucky old coot came out with just a nasty bruise above the eye. I told him to take the rest of the week off. I assigned another foreman. We need Sam to recover so he can scour the woods and mark our timber for winter lumbering. When you head out to show Jonathan the other mills, take Sam his usual supplies and some medicine." He let out a long audible breath. "And take Jonathan out back and show him the operations here."

Willie nodded. She searched her father's face. "Slow down, Papa, will you?"

Outside, she led Jonathan on a well-worn path to the back of the mill where a burly young man wrestled a huge log onto a ramp with a peavey hook. As soon as Daniel Barrett recognized her, he turned, waved, and shouted at her, "Rachael said you're going to the party at Clara's."

"I am," she called out and hurried onward.

Sweeping her hand across the water of the millpond, she explained, "This is the largest operation in the county, producing over forty thousand feet of lumber a day. With the splash dam above, we can hold a log boom; and below, in the millpond, we can have timber ready to feed the saws."

"How do townsfolk get finished lumber?"

"We send to the coast. Our mills only produce rough cut lumber for framing houses, and for building bridges or barges."

As they walked along, she stopped occasionally to chat with a mill hand. Jonathan was astonished to discover she knew them all by first name, and even more surprised when she recalled the names of their wives and children.

Farther on, they rounded a corner following a small footpath winding up a knoll to a splash dam above.

"I'll race you to the top," he challenged and tore off.

She reached the top, just inches behind him, and flung herself, exhausted, in the soft mossy grass. Hugging her knees in her arms, she looked out over the water. A small rowboat bobbed in shimmering waves, anchored on the opposite shore.

"That's Nicole's clipper ship, the Godspeed," she explained. "Other times it's a steamboat, sometimes a raft, depending upon her imagination on any particular day."

Jonathan listened as she spoke. He liked the sound of her voice. It was deeper than most women. Soothing. She radiated a vitality that drew him like a magnet. He was powerless to resist. The thought was so jolting he forced himself to tamp it down into the far reaches of his mind.

"What do you want in life?" he asked abruptly, watching her with a critical squint.

She swept her hands over the landscape and water. "I have everything I want right here."

"If you could have one wish, anything at all, what would it be?"

"There's only one thing I've wanted all my life." She stood, smoothing her hands down the front of her britches. "Promise not to laugh?"

"Promise."

She pushed some wispy tendrils of hair from her face. When she spoke, her clear voice was cool and calculated. "I want to be the owner of the largest lumbering operation east of the Mississippi River."

Stunned, he stared at her. Despite her fragile outward appearance, there was something more to her than he had first thought. Plucky boldness.

Strength. Ambition. Even reckless determination.

He shook his head and whistled long and low under his breath. "Whew, you really want to corner the market, don't you?"

She looked out over the gleaming waters shining like silver in the sunlight. "I don't want to," she said. "I intend to."

CHAPTER SEVEN

THE RIDE UPSTREAM TO SAM Bradley's cabin was peaceful and unhurried. Squirrels chattered in the trees and the soft rustle of dried leaves was the only sound the forest gave up. The trails were so narrow Jonathan was unable to ride beside Willie as they crisscrossed along paths winding up the mountainside covered with laurel, ferns, and stands of sharp-smelling pine. Two miles onward, they veered off onto another badly rutted path and worked their way along it until they reached a clearing and stopped. With two fingers between her teeth, she whistled shrilly. Shortly thereafter, a soft whistle returned her call.

"All clear," she said. "Let's go."

A few yards onward, they entered more dense growth which broke into a large, cleared hollow, secluded by massive oaks and bordered by thick brush on all sides. Below a cluster of tall white birch, a weathered log cabin with an attached stable and corral sprawled out. A rickety porch, encircled by a rough plank railing, jutted out from the front of the cabin. On a well-worn cane rocker, Sam Bradley sat whittling and chewing, his feet propped on the splintered rail. A rifle was leaned against the windowsill behind him and faded blue gingham curtains fluttered in the breeze.

"Well, Elizabeth Wilhelmina, if you aren't a sight for sore eyes," he called out. He was a small, bow-legged man with a mop of salt-and-pepper hair, and when he laughed, the whiskers on his face twitched with each ripple.

Willie reined her horse in at the stable, slipped off, and tore up the stairs. She squinted at the huge blue-purple knot above the old man's left eyebrow. "Did you see the doctor?"

"Naw. It'll take a lot more than a piece of flying timber to kill old Sam." He chuckled gleefully, delighted the girl had stopped by.

"Howdy, son. My, oh my. You are surely the spittin' image of your father, Isaac." He nodded to Jonathan before his little round eyes searched out Willie again. "Did your pa happen to send any medicine?"

"Gracious, I almost forgot." Like a sprite, she scampered down the steps past Jonathan and returned with a small flask of whiskey and two pouches of tobacco, laying them carefully beside his creaking rocker.

"Papa said to remind you to take the rest of the week off. He hopes you're a better fisherman than a sawyer." She grinned an impish grin, and he winked at her, his blue eyes twinkling.

"You know, Willie, your father has enough troubles without me taking the rest of the week off. Those bullheads can wait a few more days to get a belly full of grub worms. What with Henderson off until the end of the week, we'll be short-handed if anything comes up. I'm dragging these old wretched bones in at sunrise, like always."

"Why is Henderson not working?" She raised a quizzical eyebrow.

"Dunno, except his wife stopped yesterday morning and said he wasn't feeling so good."

"Henderson's one of our boom rats," Sam Bradley explained to Jonathan. "Sure are a tall one, ain't ya'?"

It was Willie's turn to explain. "We hired Henderson a while back when one of our regular boom rats quit. He's mighty quick at sorting brands on the logs and separating the types of timber held in the mill pond for the saw carriages. He only has one fault." She grimaced. "He has a surly attitude and doesn't get along with the crew. But he works alone most of the time so it's not a problem. I guess I'd be cranky if I fell off a few logs in the pond and got dunked every so often."

From the corral, Tess, Sam's old mule, brayed a stream of hideous bellows of disapproval at the intrusion of visitors.

"The old gal never likes to be left out of the excitement." Sam chortled and spit a wad of tobacco juice over the rail.

"I know, and I forgot her carrot."

"The old gal will survive, but she may hold it against you. You headed back downriver?"

"No, to the upriver mill, and onto Matthew Reed's place to see if he has an extra blade to lend us."

The old man's face turned dour. "Well, my pa once told me never to trust anyone who appears dumber than your mule."

"Sam!"

"God almighty, girl, he can squeeze a copper penny so tight Lady Liberty jumps off." He squinted at the sun. "You better get movin', you got a long ride ahead. Those woods get dark right quick once the sun sinks."

She nodded and clambered back down the rickety steps. "Take care of yourself, will you, please?" Tenderness was evident in her plea.

"You do the same." He uncorked the flask and took several long healthy swigs. He peered over at Jonathan who had halted at the top of the steps. "Tell me, lad, how are you and Elizabeth Wilhelmina getting along?"

"I wouldn't know, old-timer. With Willie, you never know whether you're afloat or drowning."

The old man grinned from ear to ear. "Ah-ha. So you've taken a shine to her?"

Jonathan's mouth twitched with amusement. "What does a crazy old logging hick like you know?"

"Crazy, maybe," Sam agreed slapping his hand on his thigh, "but not blind, son. I see the way you look at her. Even I was a young once."

"And which century was that?"

The old man belted out another peal of laughter. "Lad, you've been bitten so bad, the itch is going to drive you crazy. It's writ all over your ugly face." He leaned forward in his rocker. "Now don't take it to heart. It really ain't so dreadful looking, but if I were comparin' you to the fine horse you rode into town on, he might win hands down."

Jonathan shook his head. The old coot was as downright exasperating as the girl. He remembered his father saying Sam Bradley had crossed more mountains and streams, fought more Indians, and tamed more bears than any man he knew.

Rubbing his whiskers, Sam Bradley spoke in low raspy voice, "I'll give you a little advice, son. Give the little lady enough rein or you'll spook her. Wil-*hell*-mina is like a well-bred horse with a mule's disposition. Riled, she's got a temper as hot as a smithy's poker."

Jonathan turned and watched her fix her saddle girth. Her hands were no stranger to the labor as she tugged it tight and refastened it. His gaze still glued to her, he heard the old man add, "Watch the blade she keeps in her right boot. She'll shred a man like cabbage if she's threatened."

He bit off a plug of tobacco. "One more thing, big fella. Keep your head up and a sharp eye open. Someone's not too fond of the Wydcliffes right now, and a bullet hole below the belt could take some spark right out of you."

Jonathan resisted the urge to roll his eyes skyward. "Before you start giving out advice, I suggest you spend more time learning how to duck."

Sam's hearty snickers followed him all the way to his horse where he lifted his lithe body into the creaking saddle, turned his mount, and followed Willie out into the shaded forest.

The ride to the upriver mill was not long, but it afforded Jonathan some undisturbed minutes for reflection. Who would want to put an old man out of business after forty-some years? There were a lot of reasons why men took the time to ruin others, and most of the time it was for wealth or power. Yet, whoever was harassing the mills was wasting good lumber and snarling everything just enough to hamper the operations, but not shut them down. If anyone really hoped to gain control of the land, was it because of the timber or something else? Something more valuable? And did they know time Wydcliffe's time on earth was running short? Was it possible they wanted Willie in control?

He was so pinned down by his thoughts he barely noticed her pointing out the mill in the distance. Much smaller than the one in town, the upriver one was crudely constructed, but strategically located among a vast area of endless, wilderness timber. Mountains of scented white pines rose up around it on all sides and, from the face of each slope, long log slides snaked down to feed the river, just above the timeworn structure.

They crossed the stream in a shallow current well below the dam and allowed their mounts to climb the rocky bank at their ease. Eager to be given rein, the horses cantered along the muddy path leading to the front of the mill and would have continued their reckless pace had their riders not slowed them to a safer speed.

Beside the milldam, a huge stocky Swede stood, his red woolen cap pulled down over his white-blonde hair. With hearty wave, he motioned them over to the edge of the glassy pond.

Willie barely alighted from her horse, when he grabbed her like a feather pillow, hoisted her into his brawny arms, and swung her up into the air, enveloping her in a bear hug. "*God dag*, little one. Still as light as a leaf." He set her on her feet, cupped her face with his huge hands, and planted a quick kiss on her flushed cheek.

He turned to face Jonathan. "And you must be Jonathan Wain, the big fella from Baltimore who everyone is yammering about, no?" He thrust out his thick hand. "Olaf Svenson, foreman for the upriver operations. Good to finally meet you."

Jonathan studied Olaf. The giant of a man appeared to be just over forty, but his youthful ruddy face, massive shoulders and broad chest made him appear much younger. When he moved, it was almost catlike for a man so large.

"I've missed you, flicka," Olaf said, pulling Willie close again and rattling her shoulders until Jonathan was sure her brains would fly out. But she took his frolicking antics all in stride.

"I've missed you, too," she said, "but the Hornet's Nest has us dancing like a grasshopper at the end of a fishing line."

"Well, vhat can I do to help?"

She smiled. "Papa thought Jonathan should see all our operations up close."

The big man surveyed Jonathan from head to toe. He waved a hand at the mill. "This old shack we call the Wasp. Sam Bradley, Dalton Wydcliffe, and your father, Isaac, helped to build it many years ago before your father got an itch for the sea. Sam cut a deal shortly after, sold out, and went to work for Dalton at his mill in town." It was obvious the Swede prided himself in his history and work. He spoke in a voice which begged anyone to differ.

Jonathan's gaze roamed over the steep slopes rising up on each side of the mill. A splash dam farther up the river was surrounded by rocky cliffs. They had chosen the spot as protection from the Indians when the only thing they were trading was scalps.

He could understand why this mill hadn't been tampered with. One would have to be as nimble as a goat. The only way to it was through the front door, and anyone looking for trouble would have to get past the big Swede as well.

"Sam was hurt today when more spiked timber went through the saw." Willie's voice faltered, and she blinked several times to hold back the tears puddling in her eyes. "He has an ugly old bump above his eye from a piece of white ash."

Olaf spoke gently, "Stop your worrying, flicka. You can't be responsible for everyone or everything that happens with these dang mills. I vill stop by on my way home and check on the old man." He pushed his cap out of his eyes." I vill take him a bundle of good dried wood to whittle, though I doubt he will stay put very long, ja? Where you headed?"

When she told him, a cold silence fell between them. "Vasting your time, flicka, and you've got little time left." He looked across the waters of the pond. Long shadows fell in inky patterns over its shiny surface.

"No lectures, please, Olaf," she said sullenly. "Matthew Reed has been a good friend."

He shook his head "Nej. If you're big enough to run the mills, you're big enough to decide vhere your heart is...and who you choose as friends." He laughed nervously, dissipating the strained tension between them. "Maybe Olaf is a little jealous, no? . . . to give you to another?" He thumped her lightly on the back. "Hurry now, before the sun sleeps, before Hannah is angry because you are late for dinner."

"I'll tell her you send your love." Willie's eyes lit up with a mischievous glint. "I'll tell her you miss her cooking."

"Oh, ja, for sure. Especially meatballs and kringles." He patted his stomach. "And tell your Papa everything is on schedule here. If he has a few slack hands, he can send them to me. Olaf vill keep them busy."

Willie nodded and walked to her horse with the big Swede following silently behind. He secured the reins while she mounted, then handed them to her. "You be careful, little one, you hear me?" he asked tonelessly. His eyes were so light blue they seemed white as he looked at her. His hand snaked out and he grabbed the horse's bridle, speaking even more sharply, "I *am* serious. You get yourself killed and ve might as vell dig the old man's grave with yours."

She nodded and veered her horse toward a path leading around the pond, pausing only long enough for Jonathan to fall in line behind her.

The dark, dank swamp she led him through was alive with the croaking of mud frogs and the humming of angry swarms of mosquitoes. Thorny thickets huddled around the swamp's edge and cattails grew in profusion, jutting toward the sky.

Familiar with the area, she guided them to the far rim where an opening brought them onto another path which weaved its way up a small ridge. Wild grapevines crawled up to entwine themselves in the tree tops. On the crest of the next ridge, she halted amid a cover of laurel and slid soundlessly down from her mount, her booted feet sinking into the thick pine needles. She stared silently into the dim woods behind them.

Jonathan pulled up beside her and dismounted. Faint sounds, similar to the call of a wild turkey, echoed faintly in the air.

"I heard it a mile or so back. Maybe turkey?" he asked." An uneasy feeling settled over him.

She shook her head.

For a long moment, neither spoke. Finally, he whispered, "Maybe it's your friend returning the newspapers."

Despite the tension, she chuckled. He reached over and touched a gold curl which had escaped from her tightly coiled chignon, rubbing the silky strand between his fingers. They stared at each other for several seconds, drowning in each other's eyes. He reached out and stroked her cheek gently and moved closer. So close he could smell the rose water in her hair and he lowered his face toward hers.

Slowly, oh so slowly.

Without warning, a pair of ruffed grouse flew from the bushes beside them, their thunderous wings beating the air and sending them flying apart like they had been touched by a shower of hot coals.

He cursed under his breath.

Color rose in her cheeks. She stepped backward, turned, and climbed into the saddle. "If we value our hides, we need to get out of these woods before dark." She urged her horse quickly under the lush green canopy of the forest and up another meandering path leading to a slope above a muddy creek. On the top of the knoll, she halted and pointed. "There's Matthew Reed's mill."

Recently built, the mill stood like a little card-board box beside a pond, no larger than a lazy puddle compared to the one at the Wasp. As they neared the structure, a figure, leaning in the door-way, stepped across the soggy marsh grass to meet them.

"Why, this is a pleasure, Elizabeth Wilhelmina. Twice in one day." Matthew Reed smiled and helped her down. He led her horse to the hitching rail outside the mill and secured the reins.

"Do you have mill hands working the woods?" she asked. Behind her, Jonathan dismounted.

Matthew stared at her with a puzzled look. "No, not yet."

She turned to Jonathan. "This is. . ."

"Jonathan Wain," Jonathan said curtly and shoved his hand toward the younger man whose gaze had dropped lower to Willie's open jacket and her silk blouse where the soft outline of her breasts were visible. He felt his irritation spike. With a voice defying calmness, he asked, "Didn't you want to check with Reed about something, Willie?"

Teeth clenched, she flashed him a disapproving look. "Give me a moment, will you? Criminy, we just arrived. You'll have to excuse my partner. His brain grows feeble on thin mountain air." She threw Jonathan another warning glance before proceeding to tell Matthew Reed about the recent happenings."

When she finished, he offered her a nervous smile "Golly, I'm sorry, Wilhelmina, but I can't help. I don't have a spare blade. I just sent an order to the coast three weeks ago and still haven't received word about its arrival. I would. . ." he paused, stammering, "do anything to help you."

Jonathan snorted. The man's excuse was as transparent as onion skin.

She nodded. "Well, it was worth a try. Thank you, Matthew."

He fell in step with her as she walked to Silver Cloud. "I heard Wain is planning to spend some time here. Do you know how long?"

She shrugged and shook her head.

"How long you fixing to stay, Wain?" Reed asked brazenly, gazing at him over the top of her head.

Jonathan winked at her. "As long as it takes my partner here to teach me all I need to know about the lumbering business."

The men scowled at each other, trading steely looks.

"Menfolk here don't take too kindly to outsiders, especially if they move in on our territory." Reed turned and nodded at Willie, who had mounted and was waiting to nudge Silver Cloud into the dim forest.

"Well, let's hope I'm not a slow learner." Jonathan's nostrils flared and the muscles in his jaw tightened.

Matthew moved to Willie and placed a hand on her saddle horn. "If you still come up short finding a blade, I can lend you one we're using and we can come to terms on a percentage of the lumber you put through. I know how crucial your operation is near town."

Jonathan's voice rose sharply into the autumn air. "We're not making any deals, Reed." He mounted and prodded Blackjack closer to her mount. "Let's ride, Willie. We're wasting daylight."

Within minutes, they were cantering off deeper into the forest. Leading the way, she turned only once and long enough to look over her shoulder to catch Jonathan's eyes boring holes in her back.

Her thoughts went sour. For the life of her, she couldn't figure out what had blackened his mood. Since the moment she had laid eyes on him, since the moment he had arrived, he had only caused her grief. And, if he continued in his usual reckless fashion, she wouldn't find a person left in the county to call a friend. She should be the one who was furious.

Minutes onward, they reached a clearing. Jonathan halted his mount and swung his lean body down. "Let's take a rest," he said.

When she dismounted, he led the horses to a grassy spot and returned. Propping his booted foot up on the trunk of a fallen oak, he removed his hat, wiping the bead of sweat above his brow with the back of his hand.

He gestured gallantly to a seat on the log and tossed his hat there. Cautiously, she walked over and dropped down, just a few inches from the toe of his boot. She slipped her hat off and propped it on her bent knee. The day had been long, and she was weary.

"Do you always carry on like you have a thistle up your britches?" She flung her arms disgustedly into the air.

"I'll ask the questions," he snapped. "How *well* do you know your mill hands?"

"All of them quite well except for anyone recently hired."

"And just what does *quite* mean?"

"They're my workers, my friends. I grew up with everyone around the mills."

"Tell me about Sam Bradley."

"Sam is Papa's right hand man. Your father knew him well. He's pushing past seventy, but he's our landing man, cruiser, Hornet's Nest foreman, and the closest thing to a grandfather I've ever had. He taught me how to shoot a gun, run a mill, balance on the logs in the millpond, and yes, curse. He used to tell me if Papa couldn't have a son, he'd have a hell of a daughter." She pushed on, a tightening lump forming in her throat. "For your information, it was Sam and Olaf who taught me how to swim and run a millpond during the most backbreaking part of the lumbering season."

The taut set of his jaw told her he had not been appeased. Where was he going with this inquisition? And why? Her feeling of irritation intensified.

"All right. Let's move on to Svenson now."

She squinted up at him. "Olaf is the best upriver foreman we're ever had. He's taken more meals at our table than at his own."

Jonathan's voice cut her off. "The man is almost twice your age and old enough to be your father. And he's married, isn't he?"

"Yes," she agreed. "What difference does it make?"

"Do you always flirt with married men?"

"Oh, I see where you're going with this. You *are* demented," she mocked. "Olaf Svenson is our cook's younger brother. Raven, he, and I grew up together under the same roof." She watched Jonathan's demeanor soften.

"I didn't understand the relationship."

"Then ask." She spit the words at him, furious he would make a bald assumption they were anything but close childhood friends.

"I will," Jonathan assured her. "What about Matthew Reed?" His gray eyes bore into her.

"He's not one of our mill hands," she pointed out and glared back at him. "Matthew Reed and I are…" She paused. "…good friends. For quite some time we both shared the same thing, an insatiable interest in our mills, which you couldn't possibly understand."

"Are you a couple?"

"That's none of your business." She slapped her palm furiously on the bark of the log.

He reached out to grab her arm, but she was quicker and came to her feet. Her hat flew off her knee. Stepping backward, she swiftly drew the stiletto from her boot. The knife flashed in the fading sunlight, but Jonathan saw it and stepped back in time to put enough distance between them.

She knew she couldn't get away from him and onto her horse, but she was weary of his verbal assaults. If he wanted to vent his anger further, it wasn't going to be on her. She had enough of his insinuations, and she was not about to answer any more questions.

"I suggest you get on your horse and ride." She gripped the knife more firmly as anger rippled along her spine.

"Put the knife down before someone gets hurt." His voice was dangerously low.

She shot him a cold look. "You've been like a burr under my saddle since you rode in here forty-eight hours ago. You have turned my life inside out and upside down. Some dang partner you are. You hardly know me, and yet, you have the audacity to accuse me of sordid romantic involvements."

He held his palms out. "I made a mistake. I'm sorry. I didn't like the idea that the little weasel back there, you call a friend, was all too eager to take advantage of your misfortune."

"For heaven's sake, do I look demented, too? I had no intention of making any deals. If we don't find the saw blade, we close down the Wasp, set up an early lumbering crew, and use the Wasp's blade at the Hornet's Nest in town. Now tell me why you're here. Who sent you?"

Jonathan expelled a long breath of air. "Actually, it was my father who decided I should come."

She scoffed. "Try again."

His mouth twitched with amusement. The tension around them eased. "It's been ten years since my father was in Pennsylvania. My brothers and I are now involved in the shipping, and he thought it was high time one of us saw the operations from all angles. I drew the short straw. If you don't believe me, write him a letter and ask. But put that poker away before I get hurt with a knife I paid for."

Reluctantly, she slid the knife into her boot.

He walked up to her and offered her his hand. "Truce?"

Even more reluctantly, she placed her hand in his. She felt a hot spark shoot through her entire body.

He must have felt it too, because he lowered his head towards her and with something between a groan and a slow curse, pulled her close and placed a kiss on her mouth.

Somehow, she met him half way, and the kiss

deepened until it became a tender, sensual caress. Her heart hammered in her chest as he molded his mouth to hers and tangled his fingers in her hair. Slowly, he released the pins holding her hair, cupped her face in his hand, and stared into her flickering eyes. "My God, you are so beautiful," he whispered, crushing his mouth down on hers again. He parted her lips with his tongue and teased the inside of her mouth, inviting her to caress him back with hers.

When the kiss ended, his mouth traveled to the sweet hollow of her neck and up over her cheek to claim her mouth again. His hand trailed a path, burning and warm, from her throat to the top of her shoulder. She shuddered and started to pull away.

"You're so perfect," he murmured softly against her lips.

"Stop. Please stop," she half-whispered, half-choked and wedged her hands against his chest. She pushed him away. "No, I can't do this."

He pulled back, emotions in check, and wrapped his arms around her shoulders and buried his face in her sweet-smelling hair. He held her against his chest until her trembling ended, and they both gained control.

"We'd better get back," she said and shrugged out from under his nearness. "It's getting dark." She moved to her horse and fumbled with the reins.

He walked up behind her, pulled her loosened hair from around her shoulders to tumble down her back, and placed her forgotten hat on her head.

"If I scared you, I apologize. I never meant to hurt you," he whispered. "I want you, Willie Wydcliffe. More than I've wanted any woman in my life. And it scares me, too."

He turned quickly and mounted his horse.

The ride to town was still and silent with both caught up in their own churning thoughts.

CHAPTER EIGHT

JONATHAN AND WILLIE ARRIVED AT the manor just as the feeble sun hid behind the hills and chased the heat from the day. Roy was waiting for them, seated atop a rail of the white-washed fence outside the stables. At his feet, the bantam rooster fluttered about and searched for bits of grain or insects not yet taken shelter from the cold moisture settling in.

Immediately, Willie grew alarmed. The stable boy never waited outside, unless he had something important to tell her. She had formed an easy alliance with the orphan two years ago when she had begged her father to take him on. Initially, everyone had protested that a twelve-year-old was too young to manage a stable. But they had been wrong. The kid was a natural around animals.

Willie vaulted off Silver Cloud, sending the squawking rooster into a frenzy as it scurried for cover. Roy jumped from the rail and met her half way. "You're late."

"Drat, Roy, you know how I detest being reminded about that."

The boy grabbed Silver Cloud's reins and started

to unfasten the saddle. "Explain it to Conrad, because he's working himself up to a quick death. You're having company, and you're supposed to go straight to the house and get ready." He looked up to find Jonathan tending to Blackjack. "I'll take care of him, sir."

Jonathan shook his head and dismounted. "No, I'll lend a hand. I'd hate to ruin the good relationship I've worked up with this rascal." He glanced at Willie. "Better see what Conrad needs."

Minutes later, she faced the caretaker pacing inside the steamy kitchen.

"You look like you've seen the devil." Her mouth twitched with amusement.

"No, he's dining with us." Conrad's lips thinned in displeasure.

"Who is?"

"Charles Ferguson. Your father sent word from the mill."

A sense of relief washed over Willie. "Well, Hannah will see to the table setting and seating arrangement. I don't see a problem."

"This is business and social, Miss Willie. He's bringing the Mrs. and Clara."

At the sound of Clara's name, Willie's shoulders slumped and she stared speechless at the caretaker. The last thing she wanted to do was deal with Clara Ferguson after a long day. She headed toward the back steps leading to the upper floor. "Let Raven handle this one. Tell Papa I have a dreadful headache and extend my apologies. I'll take supper in my room."

Conrad stood his ground. "You'll have to, Missy," he insisted. "Raven is having supper in town with a family whose daughter is friends with Nicole."

She regarded him with a frosty air. "Let Papa handle it. I'm not in any mood to entertain the wicked little troll and her acid tongue."

"But Miss Willie. . ." Conrad's voice trailed behind her as she vanished up the stairs.

Leaning on the back doorjamb, Jonathan watched the display in silent amazement. The two had squared off like roosters in a cockfight, and it appeared the light-weight, feisty one had won.

"Wicked little *troll*?" Jonathan raised an eyebrow at the caretaker.

Frowning, Conrad gave Jonathan a withering glance and shook his head. "Now we have problems, sir. Mr. Wydcliffe won't be pleased. Wilhelmina knows Ferguson is an important business associate. I don't know what gets into the young lady."

Jonathan shrugged. "Does she always act like she should be institutionalized when she hears the name Clara Ferguson?"

Conrad sighed. "Mr. Wain, that display was one of the calmest reactions to date."

Willie slammed her bedroom door and leaned against it, her legs trembling and her head hammering. Taking a gulp of air, she flung herself across the bed. What had she done? She had kissed Jonathan Wain like a wanton trollop. That's what. Of all the mule-brained things to do. If his intent was to come barging into Pennsylvania to take over the operations, she just flung out the front doormat in welcome. She had to admit, he was a powerful individual with an appeal capable of drawing unsuspecting women in with his cultured charms.

And now, Clara Ferguson. Could the day get any worse? She pushed her palms against her throbbing temples and tried to determine how she could have fallen into such a sorry state of affairs.

She looked around the room. Behind her dressing screen, a bath had been thoughtfully drawn and steam curled up vanishing into the air. Floundering to the edge of the bed, she tugged off her boots and tossed them in a corner. Next, she peeled off her jacket, trousers, and undergarments and sent them sailing across the room to rest with the boots. Slipping into her robe, she slumped glumly onto the bed.

It was then a realization struck her as if she had been hit alongside the head with a fence post. She stared at her crumpled riding jacket. There was no sound when the jacket hit the floor. No thump. No thud. Nothing.

"My pistol," she whispered hysterically. Crossing the room, she snatched the jacket up and rummaged through the inside pocket and came up empty-handed. Disheartened, she sank back down on the bed again. She'd lost it.

Seconds later, a light rapping on the door startled her. A deep voice said, "I need to talk to you."

"If you're Jonathan Wain, go away or please shoot me."

"I only need a minute," he pleaded.

"Either let me wallow in my misery or help me end it. Your choice."

"Doggone it, Willie, open the door."

Sighing, she opened it and found him leaning against the doorjamb. "I'm in no mood to listen to anything you have to say."

He stepped in and quietly shut the door.

"Does the word, *no*, mean *anything* to you?" she persisted.

"Shhh. Keep it down," he whispered, "or the entire household will know I'm here." He drew in an exhausted breath. "You are the most difficult woman I've ever met. I thought perhaps you'd want your hardware." He pulled her gun from his coat and handed it to her.

Her eyes narrowed, her dismay evident. "You found my pistol?"

"If I tell you where, do you solemnly promise not use it on me?"

She nodded.

"I confiscated it when I kissed you."

"You're a pickpocket to boot? Why am I not surprised?"

"You already had threatened me with a knife, Willie. I had no intentions of getting my brains blown out."

"I thought it was lost for sure." She took the pistol. "It was a gift from Sam. Let me guess—you unloaded it?" She gave him a sour look as he dropped the bullet into her palm.

Before she had time to realize what was happening, he moved to her rose wingback chair and, with one swipe, dumped a heap of clothes onto the floor. He eased his huge frame down and put one booted ankle on top of the opposite knee. In a chair as small as hers, he looked like a bear in a teacup.

"You said a minute," she reminded him. She flapped her hand at the door. "Time's up. Get out."

"Not until you tell me about Charles Ferguson." They stared at each other for a moment before she moved to the stool by her dressing table and sat down. Frowning, she picked up her comb and turned it over and over in her hand.

"He owns the largest construction company in town and is our biggest customer for rough-cut lumber," she said. She set the comb aside and fiddled with the loose end of the sash on her robe as she continued to collect her thoughts. "He builds stores, feed mills, and bigger buildings around our area. Any timber we don't send to the coast to ship north or to England, we sell to him because he buys in quantity and always has ready cash."

"Sounds like a powerful man."

"Well, he's regarded as one of the town's prominent leaders," she agreed. "His wealth, and the fact he spreads it around backing others, affords him immense pleasure and exposure. He bankrolled a woolen factory in Curwensville, a flour mill in Bridgeport, and has dabbled in processing brick. Supposedly, this area is one of the richest for clay deposits. He also has the land adjoining the thousand acres we own."

"Besides throwing his money around, does he have any other interests?"

Her laugh was scornful. "Fergie, as some of his close friends call him, loves to be recognized and have his name in our local newspaper, *The Raftsman's Journal*. He sits on the town council and acts like he's a philanthropist, pushing for public schools and donating money for a town marker along the river. Lord knows we need a fire department first. We can't protect the buildings we have standing now."

Jonathan stood, walked to the window, and parted the curtains. A harvest moon hung in the pitch black sky. "Tell me about Clara."

"Clara? Oh, such a joy. I don't want to spoil your encounter with her."

"Do I detect a note of sarcasm? A droll look flashed briefly across his face.

She returned it with a withered one of her own. Should she tell him Clara was a rich and spoiled young woman with a haughty air and sharp tongue? Or that she was a sorry and pathetic individual whose only interest was deciding what dress to wear or discovering the next man she could woo with her father's money? Willie knew she was only included in her soirees because her father did business with Charles Ferguson. Her birthday party in three weeks would speak for itself. Nothing would be too good for dear Clara.

"At twelve, at twenty-one, Clara has been obsessed with only one thing. She wants a way out of here," Willie said. "She equates her rural life to the existence of a heathen. When she was not spending her father's cash, she spends her time entertaining."

"If she hates it here, why does her family stay?"

Willie straightened and shrugged. "Her father, like everyone else, came here with a few thin coins in his pocket and as much chance as the next person to succeed. With a little ingenuity and a lot of sweat, he made a good life. But for everything you get, you give up something else. It's a risk, but it's also a challenge. Ironically, like most, he fell in love with the rugged territory and small town. But Clara didn't. She yearns for a fast and easy way out of here."

Jonathan chuckled. "I can't wait to meet her."

"Your funeral."

A comfortable silence passed between them, and they sat assimilating their conversation.

Willie suspected Clara couldn't wait to meet Jonathan once she got wind he was from Baltimore. She probably wheedled her father into setting up this dinner meeting. She should probably warn him that Clara was also looking for a husband, and her mother helps to facilitate the search.

"Well, if I'm going to be tossed to the wiles of a crafty woman," Jonathan said at last, "I can't believe you wouldn't want to see it."

"Under normal circumstances, I would. But Clara is exhausting. At the end of a tiresome day, she can stagger the imagination. We have nothing in common. My life doesn't revolve around attracting a husband."

"I'd be the last one to disagree with that statement." Jonathan rose and crossed the room, towering over her and grinning as if Lucifer himself had crawled inside him. "Be it as it may, you're going to this dinner even if I'm forced to dress you myself. You owe your father the courtesy of entertaining guests properly."

"And if I refuse?"

His voice was low with no vestige of sympathy. "Hmmm…let's see. I can divulge to all your fascinating guests you cheat at cards and deal from the bottom of the deck. You play decoy for your father's payroll. I could add you are a knife-wielding, blood-drawing she-cat. Take your pick."

"Why, that's blackmail!"

"No. I'd call it friendly persuasion." He gave her a long steady look. He turned to look at the drab gray dress with a white collar someone had laid out for her at the foot of her bed. "Wait, what in blazes is that? You can't go down there looking like you just jumped off the boat with the Pilgrims."

Horrified Willie watched him move to her closet and rummage through her wardrobe. Even more horrified, she saw him pull out a peach confection, studying it thoughtfully. It was an exquisite creation with a daring neckline and short billowing sleeves which fell immodestly off the shoulders. A ruffled hem, encircling the bottom, was caught up with tiny ribbons to reveal a lacy underskirt.

"Oh, no. That's one of Raven's, and it's close to indecent," she choked out. "She had it altered for me, but knew I'd never wear anything…anything…so revealing."

He shoved the gown toward her, ignoring her appalled look "It's perfect. Put it on," he ordered, "and I'll be back to get you. We'll face the enemy together. He slipped out, just in time to hear what sounded like a hairbrush bouncing off the opposite side of door and landing with a solid thud on the hardwood floor.

A half hour later, when Jonathan returned, he found Willie standing in front of her dressing mirror struggling to fasten a string of pearls around her neck. Her chestnut hair tumbled in wild disorder down her back, and her exquisite face glowed alluringly above the lusty peach color. Like a starved man whose eyes have located food, he scrutinized from her creamy throat to her soft rounded breasts barely concealed under the provocative neckline of the dress. She was totally unaware of her ravishing beauty.

He crossed the room in long strides to where she stood, exasperated. The string of pearls was tangled in her hair.

"Here," he said, "let me help you."

Fearing she would lose her temper and courage, he took the pearl necklace and loosened it from the troubling curls. His fingers, unfamiliar with work so delicate, fumbled trying to fasten the clasp. Her nearness was overwhelming, and he had to fight to keep his hands from caressing her.

He barely finished before she swallowed nervously and spoke. "You better go down. I'll join you later after I've done my hair."

He swept up the hairbrush from the floor and handed it to her. "Oh, no. I'll wait." He crossed his hands at his chest and watched as she pulled the brush through her tangled locks, wincing as she tugged the snarls free, and pinned the sides up with two pearl combs.

When she finally finished, she took a deep breath and turned to him. "Time to be a hunk of bear bait."

Grinning, he pushed her out the door and down the staircase into the spacious sitting room where the Fergusons were enjoying a glass of wine.

The group paused in their conversation and

turned to watch as they entered.

A look of astonishment fell across Dalton Wydcliffe's face when he saw her enter. He took a step, closing the gap between them, and proudly allowed her to plant her usual light kiss on his cheek. "You look beautiful," he whispered.

Jonathan crossed the room and clasped Ferguson's hand in a friendly fashion. "I've heard so many things about you and your family, Mr. Ferguson."

The pot-bellied man puffed out his chest and pulled on his red-whiskered face. "Call me Charles. A ship's captain, I'm told. You must tell me about the sea." His eyes wandered to Willie, standing quietly beside Jonathan. "But first, allow me to escort this lovely young lady to the dinner table."

"And I shall escort the delightful Miss Ferguson," Jonathan offered. He shot a devious glance at Willie, who beamed mischievously.

Dalton Wydcliffe offered his arm and saved a gaping Mrs. Ferguson.

Once seated, Clara leaned close to Jonathan. Enveloped in a frothy pink dress, she giggled, her brown, frizzy curls bobbing. "Wilhelmina never told me she had such a handsome man hiding under her roof. How long will you be staying?"

"A few weeks, perhaps."

"A pity. You may reconsider once you've seen our little town."

His gaze drifted over to Willie, who was deep in conversation with Charles Ferguson. There was only one reason why he would consider extending his stay, and to date, she wasn't encouraging his presence in the least.

They ate in comfortable silence until minutes

later, when Clara looked intently at Willie. She took a sip of wine and lifted her haughty chin. "Oh dear, Wilhelmina, haven't I seen that gown before? It looks sooo familiar. Isn't it one of Raven's old castoffs, perhaps?"

Before she could reply, Jonathan leaned forward. "I'm sure Raven would have looked elegant in it, but Elizabeth Wilhelmina looks dazzling beyond words, don't you agree?" His voice was deep and filled with an easy grace. "You strike me as one who recognizes excellent taste."

Clara squirmed. "Well, I. . . I suppose so," she stammered.

Jonathan turned to Charles Ferguson. "I hear you've been instrumental with the new building for the town's common school."

Mrs. Ferguson interrupted, dabbing her lips with her napkin. "Yes, poor dears must hold classes in the town hall. You understand our children are educated under only the best tutors and schooled in all the proper etiquette befitting a young lady. We wouldn't feel comfortable letting them just mingle with the town riffraff." She scowled at Willie for a moment. "Why, they could compete with your most cultured young women in Baltimore. Some of them, that is."

Dalton Wydcliffe, obviously tired of Martha Ferguson's prattling, spoke. "Tell Charles about your plans for enlarging our mills, Jonathan. I don't believe Willie has heard the details, yet."

"It's rather simple. What we need here is a good finishing mill. The shipping costs to bring machinery from the coast wouldn't be cheap, but if you weigh them against the costs to bring in finished goods, I'm willing to bet the local cabinet makers, craftsmen, and builders like yourself will pay for the convenience. Dealing with a local supplier has its advantages as well."

Jonathan stole a peek at Willie. He could see the gears inside her head spinning at the thought of a new adventure. And one involving profits.

"Where would you locate it?" Ferguson asked.

"I haven't thought it through yet."

"Next to the Hornet's Nest," Willie said. There was joyful intensity in her face and voice. "A perfect match."

"Now, now, Elizabeth Wilhelmina," Mrs. Ferguson patted the back of her wiry bun, "this doesn't concern womenfolk."

"Quite the contrary." Dalton Wydcliffe frowned. "There are many men who value their wives' opinions. Since Willie will inherit the entire operation someday, I see nothing wrong in her taking an active role now."

Rushing to her mother's defense, Clara rejoined, "I find women in business quite repulsive. You've only to look at the town's painted floozy who runs the Sawdust Bin."

"*Wealthy*, painted floozy," Willie corrected her. She smiled an impish smile Jonathan had come to know. "And alas, whose money has been earned from our gallant menfolk."

Charles Ferguson's lifeless face came alive. A flush slipped up his thick neck to his jowly face. He cleared his throat uncomfortably.

"Saloons, sawmills," Clara babbled on, "are all quite boring, besides being dirty, crude, and filled with ill-mannered men."

Willie lifted a brow. "That's strange, Clara. I'm certain I've seen your buggy take a detour and drive past the Hornet's Nest on its way home."

Beside her, Mrs. Ferguson's fork clattered to her plate.

Jonathan kicked Willie under the table and threw her a black look.

She winked at him and lifted her wine glass in mock salute as if to say, *tit for tat, Clara.*

Charles Ferguson leaned back in his chair and turned to Dalton Wydcliffe. "I hear you haven't closed the land deal with Pierce yet. He made me an offer as well. To be honest, with the timber removed, my land is useless. If I don't sell, I'll hold it for Clara Jeanette. She'll need a home someday and the area is good cleared land. Pierce must know the particulars, too, because he's toying with the idea of raising horses."

"A gentleman farmer?" Wydcliffe shrugged dismissively. "He seems to being doing quite well as a supplier for the inland communities. Everything from guns to furniture is sent from the river here to remote settlements—and at an inflated price."

The men fell silent, returning to their meal.

Across the table, Clara leaned seductively toward Jonathan and purred. "What do you do for excitement in this shabby little town?"

"Right now, I'm learning about the settlement and the logging activities." He reached for his glass of rum which Hannah had shrewdly substituted for his glass of wine. If he had to continue a conversation with this twit for another hour, he'd have to brace himself with a dozen more glasses. "Do you ride, Clara?"

"Horses?"

"Of course, *horses*, my dear," Mrs. Ferguson said, interrupting. "I understand Mr. Wain is quite an equestrian."

Clara squirmed uncomfortably. "Occasionally, I ride. Father bought me the best English saddle in Pennsylvania."

"Perhaps both of you can get together for an afternoon to ride," Mrs. Ferguson coaxed. "And you must come to Clara's birthday party at the end of this month. It would be the perfect opportunity to meet some of the prominent people in our town and show you off to our gentle, single womenfolk. You'll not be disappointed, I assure you."

Across the table, Jonathan's gaze landed on Willie's impish grin as a silent discourse unfurled silently between them. *I told you so,* her crafty expression seemed to say. She was finding a perverse pleasure in the exchange, he realized.

He heaved a sigh and leaned back in his seat as Clara chattered inanely on about some diamond earrings and some place in England where they grew acres of bluebells. Tired and bored, he wondered how long the blasted dinner would last.

It was well past midnight before the Fergusons' carriage pulled away from the front drive and the lamps from the manor were finally extinguished.

CHAPTER NINE

"IF A LOGGER TAKES THREE bottles of whiskey into the woods at daybreak, how many will he drink before nightfall?" Willie asked.

She and Jonathan were standing on a cliff above the same haze-filled valley where he viewed Clearfield for the first time. She loved to be high above the town. Down below, the tall white pines loomed like massive sentries in the feeble morning, their treetops shrouded in autumn fog. Some of the gigantic trunks climbed over one hundred-twenty feet into the sky and were at least four feet in diameter at their bases.

Just below the forest line, nestled between two mountain ridges, the settlement seemed little more than a meager anthill on a cleverly-sewn quilt. The wide Susquehanna River, running through the center of the settlement, was jammed in sections with logs in splash dams above a chain of sawmills. Its stormy grayish blue waters snaked its way onward, around a bend, and out of sight toward the Chesapeake Bay.

Jonathan eyed her with amusement, attentive to the gabble from a flock of geese overhead, winging their way south to avoid the forthcoming harsh winter. "Two. One's for pain, one's for pleasure, and the last is full of oil to lubricate his saw. Can we move away from this cliff? I don't know why you like heights. This makes me uneasy." He took a step back.

"Nicole told you."

He smiled indulgently, his face attesting to the fact that Raven's daughter had subjected him to a long list of logger's riddles. "I'll wager she knows more than this stand of trees," he said.

Willie took a deep breath of crisp mountain air. She watched him shrug into his leather coat. He was so strikingly handsome, her breath caught in her throat. She was playing with fire. She should never have agreed to accompany him to the downriver mill. Yet, before she had the chance to voice any reservations about the trip, he had commissioned the cook to pack a picnic lunch. It was divided between their already heavily loaded saddlebags.

They set off and rode in silence, conversation impossible above the rustle of the dried vegetation beneath the horses' hooves. Several minutes later, he asked, "Did you ever discover why the downriver payroll has been the favorite target for thieves?"

"The land has cover. Deep forests, thick brush and laurel, and desolate swamps," she explained. "It also has a hefty payroll compared to the smaller mills." She had a hunch the thieves had set up a camp in the area. They knew every move, even when she randomly altered the days to try to sneak the payroll through.

"Did you think it was odd when Charles Ferguson inquired about the land your father was thinking of selling?" He urged his horse closer to her so they could ride side by side when they entered yet another clearing.

She shook her head. "Ferguson is an excellent businessman and builder. I hear he's bought up several prime lots on the west side of town on speculation the town will someday outgrow its present limits." She veered off the trail into laurel so thick it reached the flanks of their mounts and led Jonathan to the top of a low ridge. Below them, leaves still clinging to the oak rattled in the breeze.

"See the oak! 'She flung her arm out excitedly. There was a heightened color in her cheeks. "It's like hair on a hound's back. If we get a finishing mill erected, we could supply all a cabinetmaker's needs. There's good maple, cherry, and even ash for boats, buildings, and furniture. Yonder is walnut—the gunsmith's favorite."

He chuckled. "You're expanding before we have a building in place."

"But look at the possibilities." Reaching behind, she fidgeted with the fastening on her saddlebags until she was able to wedge open a flap and pull out a small brown sack.

"This is a present from Nicole." There was a playful glint in her eye. "Something for your foul disposition and black moods,"

"Mine? Surely you're jesting."

She withdrew two pieces of hard rock candy and handed one to him. "You ride well," he admitted as he accepted a piece,

"For a woman, right?"

"No, in truth, you ride better than most men."

"My father would be pleased to hear it." She felt her face blush. "He and my sister were excellent teachers, but Silver Cloud deserves most of the credit. Papa picked him out for me on my tenth birthday when he was down in Kentucky. He has some Arabian blood to get the light gray color." She patted his neck affectionately. "He's getting up there in years. I need to find a younger mount."

Her eyes slid over Jonathan's stallion. "The animal under you was sired by some prime stock."

He laughed and ran his hand over the horse's mane. "Trade Wind and I got tangled up recently when I needed a good horse for the trip north. My father said he wrangled with a toothless Delaware Indian to buy him and set the man up with enough whiskey to quench his thirst for the next three years. This old boy can pick his way along trails, alert me of trouble, and run like the wind when danger is near."

A bluejay screeched its harsh cry above their heads and both horses picked up their ears and rocked their riders, sending a tightening surge in Willie's chest. The hairs at the back of her neck felt like a column of ants began to march up into her hair. She slid her boots deeper into her stirrups. She didn't need to be told there was someone or something was out there just beyond their vision.

"Are you expecting company?" Jonathan scanned the area, checking the perimeter of the forest for a path to escape.

She knew the forest trails by heart. She pointed to a small opening through the trees to her right. She leaned forward to resettle the knife in her boot before she casually placed her hand on the pommel of her saddle.

"Should we meet with more than one unfriendly soul," he said with grave seriousness, moving his horse next to her, "how many can you handle by yourself?"

"Two. I rarely miss with my gun," she admitted with a nervous chuckle, "but I never miss with my knife."

"You know, you can almost be amusing when you put your mind to it." A glint of cynical humor flashed across his face. He rested his hand on his upper thigh where a pistol was hidden beneath his coat. "We'll wait and let whoever is out there come to us."

She nodded, her pulse beating erratically. He moved his horse several feet away. The sound of a horse's hooves resounded farther down the bush-lined trail.

They waited without speaking.

A few minutes later, a dark horse with white stockings emerged from an opening in the woods, and Willie easily recognized the heavyset rider. She blew out a breath of pent up air and felt the knots shake loose in her stomach.

John Pierce approached.

"Beautiful day, Miss Wydcliffe." Solicitously tipping his hat, he drew near and stopped beside the couple. "Howdy, Wain," he added.

A stocky, corpulent man, Pierce wore elegant clothing which belied his true brute strength. Muscles on his brawny shoulders bulged beneath his snug black jacket with satin lapels. He wore matching dark trousers and a splashy gold brocade vest over a starched white shirt. He reminded Willie of a vulture. She stared at him as a flicker of revulsion coursed through her.

"I'm giving Mr. Wain a scenic tour of our properties," she said. "We even planned a picnic." She patted her saddlebags.

Pierce's mouth curved upward. His thick hand, curled around his saddle horn, was bedecked with a solid gold ring with three large diamond chips. The gems flashed brilliantly in the sunlight. He glanced indifferently at their saddlebags. "Once the fog burns off, it will be a warm one. Perfect day for a picnic."

He resettled his hefty body in his saddle to the sound of creaking leather. "Rumors about town says your father is still having trouble with the Black Widow mill."

A suspicious little voice whispered in her head. *Was this idle saloon talk or did people really know about the episode with the payroll?*

"They're wrong," she lied. "The weekly payrolls have been delivered without a hitch."

Pierce grunted as if in approval and flipped out a silver pocket watch dangling from his vest. "Glad to hear it. A hard-working man deserves to get paid on time."

Says an opportunist who takes advantage of others, she thought, and one who sells ammunition and guns to thieves or marauding Indians, just as easily as he does to the common man.

He snapped the watch shut and tipped his hat. "Give my regards to your father."

Willie watched him head in the direction of town before she turned to Jonathan. "How do you know John Pierce?"

"I met him in town the other day."

"You sure get around for someone who just arrived."

"Willie, Willie," he said and followed it with an exhausted sigh, "pull in your claws. I'm not your enemy. If we don't strike up a cordial relationship with the man, we'll never find out why he's so eager to buy your father's property."

"Maybe I don't want a cordial relationship with him."

"Enemies have many faces. A word of advice, my dear, keep them close so you have a chance to discover what they might be scheming."

"I'm not your dear." *Maybe I should take his advice to heart myself?* She threw him a penetrating look and tugged her hat down on her head before nudging her horse forward.

Later, as the sun crawled high in the sky, they stopped and dismounted atop a rolling green valley cut in two by the river curling around a medium-sized mill, not as elaborate as the Hornet's Nest in town, but not as crude as the Wasp.

With wind-blown curls swiping at her face, Willie explained how the mill was important to the outlying regions. Settlements in the southern region depend upon it with its well-located position on the river near the mouth of Clearfield Creek. In years to come, as settlers move in, it would become even more strategic. Although Wydcliffe mills owned several thousand acres, they also leased, traded, share-profited, and arranged for mutual lumbering agreements with other surrounding landowners.

Together, they gathered the horses' reins and picked their way down the grassy slope carefully avoiding the rocks piles where rattlesnakes might linger to catch the last warmth of the season.

"This mill was the second one built a year after I was born," she said. "I'd sell it at the drop of a hat if the price was right, and I'd put the money toward the finishing mill."

"Too far out?" He matched his stride to hers as they walked along, spellbound by her knowledge and uncanny business sense.

"Yes. It needs a lot of attention. But I don't want to spoil the fun. You'll see why when we get there."

Approaching from the front, they tied their horses to the rail, amid the groan and whine of the carriage saws.

Jonathan leered at the front above the double doors and below the peak of the roof. A monstrous spider had been fashioned on the rough planks. Huge hemp ropes dipped in tar were shaped into what appeared to be the eight legs of the insect.

"The black widow spider is just a symbol for the widow who was involved in a murder at the mill just after it was opened," she explained. "According to the story, a young man named Matthew Rowles and a man called Sidney Pierce, both loggers at the mill, were playing cards and drinking. Some say Rowles was a poor card player, others say Pierce, some twenty years older, was known to be a cheat. Rowles lost not only the card game, but also the deed to five hundred acres of land. Angry by the loss of his deed, Rowles called Sid Pierce an outright cheat and challenged him to a midnight duel. Unfortunately, poor Rowles lost both his life and the deed that evening. The next morning, when Sid Pierce was entering the mill, Matthew Rowles's young pregnant widow, in mourning clothes, arrived and shot Pierce straight through the heart. She disappeared before the law had time to arrive.

"This Sidney Pierce, is he any relation to John Pierce," Jonathan asked.

"No, I don't believe so. John Pierce came to this area a few years back from New England. Massachusetts, I hear. The land, though, was part of the thousand acres my father and yours later purchased.

"What happened to the widow?"

"Some say she took refuge in New York State, others say she had Rowles's baby and died shortly thereafter, by childbirth or suicide. Nobody knows for sure."

They both stood, side by side, staring at the mill's spider, each lost in thought.

Without any warning, a gruff voice rasped behind them, "Welcome to the Black Widow."

Willie jumped and swung around, almost falling into the gritty-looking man before her. Ezra Hawkins, the mill foreman, grinned at her with brown, tobacco-stained teeth.

"Edgy, Miss Wydcliffe?" he taunted, scowling at her.

Irritated, she glared back at the scrawny foreman of the mill. "I don't take a shine to people who sneak up on me without warning, Ezra. However, since you're here, we can take care of business. We've got next week's payroll divided between the bags on the back of our mounts."

"Well, I'll be go to hell. Ya' mean ya' brought it in

alone? No guards, no nothin'?" Ezra's beady eyes pinned themselves on the bags.

Willie studied him disapprovingly. It took every ounce of her stamina not to let her temper spin out of control. Hawkins's appearance alone was enough to rankle her. His hair was long and unkempt, and his beard was stained with tobacco juice. Layers of caked dirt made his face and hands several shades darker than the best suntan.

"We decided we had a pretty good cover," Jonathan said. "Who would stop a romantic pair taking a scenic ride through the woods in hopes of discovering the perfect spot for a picnic?"

Willie threw him a murderous look. "I'm assuming you've already met our self-appointed jester, Jonathan Wain from Maryland?" Before either man could respond, she turned and looked about the mill yard. "How are things running?"

She was sorry she asked when Ezra's faced darkened.

He snorted and stroked his grubby beard. "Nothin's ever runnin' on time down here. It's a damn fact. Ya' can't get these fool men to do anything right. They drag their backsides and foul up the whole blasted operation." He cursed out a string of expletives. "I got me a candy-ass yardman who can't sort or stack and careless pike men who have their brains up their—"

"Thank you, Ezra," she interrupted, "that's quite enough." She walked away toward the lumber yards.

Jonathan followed on her heels. "Pleasant fellow," he said, falling in step with her.

"It gets worse," she stated flatly. "Any time you

feel like it, don't hesitate to jump in and offer advice. Everyone knows we could use help, even if it's not divine-inspired."

She circled around to the far side of the mill, and they looked down into the soft hollow. Piles of wood, unsorted, lay in tangled heaps. To their left, a group of mill hands lounged under the shade of an oak and played cards. Those who were working moved about in a sluggish gait of indifference, except for one ambitious, but hideous-looking man. When he noticed them, he stopped to wave. She returned it.

Everything seemed in order on the man's face, but on closer inspection, Jonathan could see he was missing a nose. Two irregular holes, where the nostrils should have been, protruded from among surrounding layers of scar tissue.

"What happened to him?"

"Old Joe?" she asked. "He doesn't talk much. Word has it, his nose was ripped off in a river fight some years back. Others claim his opponent was so ferocious, he literally bit it off. He's the best worker we have." Brows furrowed, she paused, deep in thought. Finally, she spoke. "I'm going to talk to the paymaster. You poke around by yourself. I'll meet you back here."

When he returned a short time later, she was leaving the paymaster's office and was as mad as a wet hen. Shipping tickets for two barges of lumber, already three days overdue, lay collecting dust on the desk of the paymaster.

"We have to find the yardman." She headed in the direction of the river with Jonathan following. "His name is Leb Luther."

Without warning, a rough, cantankerous voice from behind them called out, "Lookin' for me, Missy?"

Together, they turned to find a lanky man with dark mole-like eyes limp up. Soap and water were obviously his vilest enemies, and lice, his life-long friends. The man slouched before them. His filthy clothes emitted an odor that would have knocked a horse to its knees. The yard worker hitched up his pants and ran his grimy hands through hair hanging in greasy strings.

Did every member of this crew have an aversion to water, Jonathan wondered, and moved upwind from him.

Willie's lips thinned with anger. "I understand our last shipment was delayed and the shipment down there on the bank is already a day late. Why aren't we loading barges?"

Leb Luther's face contorted into a freakish sneer. "What do ya' think? We all have six friggin' hands, Missy? I'm moving their damned lead arses as fast as I can."

"Move them faster," she snapped. "You have ten hands down there stacking, but none are loading. Break up that card game under the tree and round up the men to load those barges. Confound it, man, settlers are counting on us for their lumber before winter sets in. If the snows fly early, they won't have a makeshift shack to keep the cold off their heads."

"Just because your pa owns the mills doesn't mean you can come skimble-scambling in here and order me around." He glowered at her with outright contempt.

"Yes, I *am* telling you what to do," she insisted. Her voice cracked, and her brown-eyed gaze burned holes through the sweaty flannel shirt beneath his dirty coat. "We have more orders to fill. They're lying on the paymaster's desk as we speak. Your job is to see our shipments get out of these yards *on time*."

"Why, you good-for-nothing, little snot. No one tells me what to do, or how to do it. I'll throttle you." He reached out a grubby hand to yank her by her jacket, but she skidded backward and squared off.

"I wouldn't touch the lady, if I knew what was good for me," Jonathan ground out and took a step forward.

Leb pulled his hand back, stepping sideways and glaring. "Who are you, mister?"

The muscles in Jonathan's jaw tensed. "The other half of Wain and Wydcliffe."

Luther's glare lifted to the huge man towering menacingly over him. "The Eastern dandy, eh?" He scoffed and spit a stream of tobacco juice onto the toe of Jonathan's polished boot. "You ain't tellin' ol' Leb what to do. No one tells me how to run these yards—especially some cocky sea captain who doesn't know a thing about lumbering."

"Even a sea captain, who know nothing about the lumber business, can see this place is full of lazy no-accounts."

"Then ride out of here," the filthy man sputtered, "and take this little she-booger with you. No one tells me how to do my job." He lunged forward and grabbed the lapels on Willie's jacket, shoving her towards Jonathan. She stumbled and would have fallen if he hadn't reached out and righted her.

Leb Luther turned and walked away.

Jonathan stormed after him. His temper, now unshackled, blew sky high. He reached out, grabbed the man by the collar of his shabby coat, and spun him around, grasping him by his front lapels and lifting him off his feet. "Let's get a few things straight." His face was hard and cold as steel. "Where I come from, we treat our bosses with respect. Secondly, we treat our ladies with even more respect—and if our boss just happens to be a lady, then she gets a double portion." His temper gained renewed momentum. "More important, if you should ever, *ever* lay a hand on Miss Wydcliffe again, I'll kill you."

He shoved the filthy yardman away from him with revulsion. "I hope I've made myself clear. Pick up your pay at the paymaster's office. You're fired! You hear me? Sacked." He cursed a string of expletives and briskly began to brush himself off.

"You can't sack me!" Luther backed away from the huge man.

"I just did."

"I'll remember this," Leb shouted. "I won't forget. Not ol' Leb."

"Out. Now!" Jonathan barked.

The filthy man turned and trudged toward the mill.

"And do your next boss a favor," Jonathan called after him in a flat bottomless voice, "get yourself a bath."

The mill hands who had stopped their work to witness the scene stared at the powerful man who had just ripped up one side of their yardman, down the other, and fired him. Jonathan looked up to catch them cautiously watching him. "Anyone else have problems that need to be resolved?" he bellowed in a tart tone. The mill hands turned and scrambled to resume their tasks.

Moving to a grassy spot, he dragged the toe of his boot over the ground, pawing it like an angry bull. His face was knotted in disgust and muscles bunched along his jaw. He let loose another string of expletives that could have peeled the bark from the nearest tree. Finally, he swallowed a few deep breaths and rejoined Willie who was staring apprehensively at the riverbank and empty barges.

"Are you all right?" he asked.

"Yes." She could not bring herself to look him in the face. She had just as much anger simmering below the surface as well.

"Now we need a yard foreman," he said, lowering his voice. He jabbed his fingers through his unruly hair.

"Let's put Old Joe on," she suggested. "He's dependable, and no one could be worse than what we already had. He's not a big talker, but I'm betting he can get the work done. I'll call him up."

Seconds later, hideous Old Joe approached her. Jonathan watched her twist the brim of her hat 'round and 'round for a few minutes and stare at the ground, deep in thought. When she finally looked up, her voice was fearless and as commanding as Dalton Wydcliffe himself.

"We have a yardman's job open immediately, Joe." Unflinching, she peered up at him, despite his deformed face. "I need a man who can move our lumber down there on time, someone who can work with these evil-tempered mill hands, and someone who's not afraid of hard work. Think you can fill the position?"

Joe nodded.

She smiled. "Looks like you have yourself a new job. I'll tell Ezra and let the paymaster know he needs to double your wages."

She cupped her hand around her mouth and yelled down to the crew now scurrying about. "Listen up! Old Joe is the new yardman. Anyone who doesn't like working for him, gather your wages at the paymasters office now and hightail it out. Otherwise, get those barges loaded before nightfall. He also has my permission to fire any slacker."

Jonathan watched as a hint of a smile twitched on the new yardman's lips.

"And Joe," she said, turning and halting him before he could leave, "do you see those piles of green lumber by the side of the mill?"

He bobbed his head in assent again, still not uttering a word.

"Well, shake a leg, man. If we don't get them stacked properly, they'll be warped and ruined." She stormed away toward the paymaster's office.

Jonathan and Old Joe watched her retreating back against a cobalt blue sky.

"Whew," Jonathan said. "I'm glad I'm not Hawkins or the paymaster. I hope they're smart enough not to rile an already annoyed woman."

Joe nodded for the third time and grinned outright before he turned to lumber down the slope to his now bustling crew.

CHAPTER TEN

THE LAST DAYS OF SEPTEMBER offered skies the color of ashes and pelting rain, but Jonathan plowed through the three weeks heedless of the damp chill with his attention riveted on learning the logging business. Not afraid of hard work, he was learning the operations with alacrity and was more than willing to help with the most loathsome tasks. Even the mill hands accepted and respected him, eagerly following his slightest requests.

He also spent tedious hours collecting drawings, sketching designs, and exploring possible building sites for the finishing mill. It was finally decided to locate the building below the Hornet's Nest, where strategically it could be supplied with vast quantities of lumber.

Determined not to frighten nor upset Willie, he pursued their fragile alliance through the facade of their partnership and forced himself to remain detached in her presence. But the weeks were long, and at times Jonathan felt he would go mad when he dined with her or they worked shoulder to shoulder at the mills. His patience was stretched to the limit. Yet, he was determined to wear down the wall keeping them emotionally at odds. And he vowed his actions would not betray his true desires.

The deception worked, even though the thought of it gnawed at him incessantly. Their relationship materialized into a warm camaraderie, and much to his amazement, he found her witty and knowledgeable and kind. She opened up like a flower unfurling its petals and began to accept him as a companion and friend.

Now, as she sat across the breakfast table one morning, he watched her excitement build when he handed her a stack of papers with the supply list for the new mill. Oblivious to her food, she shuffled through the stack.

"Surely you can eat first," he said. "The papers can wait."

A sly smile appeared. "I'm too excited to eat. I've waited for weeks for these."

He chuckled. "Did you just tell me I did something right?" He watched her carefully. She was beautiful even when deep in thought.

"So what will it be like tonight?" he asked and leaned back in his seat. He toyed with his fork. "It's not customary where I come from to attend birthday parties of your enemies and wish them many more."

Startled, she jerked upright, eyes wide. "Oh tarnation, I forgot." She grimaced. "It's going to be ghastly. Shoot me now and end the misery."

"How ghastly can it possibly be?" The corners of his mouth turned up.

"The evening will be a feeding frenzy with Clara Jeanette ready to chew her competitors up and spit them out."

"But I'm told it's the social event of the year." He took a final sip of coffee and set the cup aside. "I wouldn't miss this for the world. Clara's mother has promised she'd introduce me to all the eligible women in the area."

Willie threw him a withering glance. "Good luck. I'd be skeptical about Martha Ferguson's kindness extending to *all* eligible females."

He stood. "Come, I've something to show you."

Within minutes, they paused outside his third-floor room. "I should warn you," he said and flung the door open, "your housekeeper is having apoplexy about the order of my room."

Willie gasped.

"What the devil?" she choked in a half-whisper. It was an explosion of paper. Books, piled in heaps, littered the chairs and window seats, and unfolded maps covered the floor and bed. A small footpath wound through the chaos and led to his desk beneath the window. Jonathan pulled her along through the debris until they reached it. He tapped his knuckles on a set of sketches. A twist of a smile ruffled his mouth. "Here they are. The final sketches for the mill, drawn to scale. There is a place for every machine, every office, and I even included a storage area in the loft."

Willie's gaze fell on the top drawing as her mind tried to absorb all the fine details. "It's perfect. It's everything we discussed—and more. When can we start?"

"If the weather holds, we can break ground in a couple of days."

She squealed, threw her arms around him, and

hugged him with unleashed zeal. His big arms came around to envelope her, and he lifted her off her feet, twirling her around.

When she touched ground again, she tipped her head up and stared into his lean face.

The weeks of being near her, wanting her, needing her, had eaten through his thin exterior of self-control and he was helpless. His eyes smoldered with pent up desire and his breath quickened as a gate opened, sending a flood of emotions loose within him. He bent and cupped her face with his hands while his mouth consumed hers. And when he felt her lips throb back in response, he groaned and responded with an even deeper passionate kiss. Slowly, as the kiss lengthened, his hands skimmed down her throat to her soft shoulders, and downward again to her slim waist as he crushed her against him.

She pulled away and drew in a labored breath, but he cupped her face again and stared into eyes so dark they reminded him of deep rich coffee. He lowered his head and kissed her once more, sending sparks flying and spinning between them. He inhaled the sweet scent of her delicate rose water perfume. When she made no move to stifle his advances, his lips traveled hungrily upward to her ear lobe and back down to the hollow of her neck, raining kisses along the way.

"My fiery angel," he whispered softly in her ear, "when you touch me, I lose complete control." He pulled her more solidly along his hard body again, forcing her so close he knew she could feel his arousal and the heat of his body burning through her clothing. He pinned his lips to hers again, penetrating, probing, and exploring the soft interior of her mouth.

A soft, hesitant cough from behind them brought them both gasping for air. Willie flinched and skidded away.

Jonathan bit off a quick curse and glared at the sound. The caretaker, red-faced and nervous, stood in the open doorway.

"Dammit, Conrad, what now?" he asked peevishly.

Speechless, the nervous man inched a step forward. "A…a… Mr. Cadwell has sent word he can meet you at the Hornet's Nest this afternoon to discuss construction of the foundation for the new finishing mill."

Jonathan nodded, but made no attempt to hide his displeasure. He watched Willie pivot, shove past the caretaker, and barrel from the room.

Obviously out of sorts, the poor man lowered his gaze, still glued to the same spot. "I'm sorry, sir, for the disruption. It won't happen again."

Jonathan snickered, irritation draining away. "To be honest, I'd give anything for it to happen again, but with a little more forethought to privacy."

He watched Conrad beat a hasty retreat.

Clara's birthday party was everything Willie thought it would be. Every resident in a fifty-mile radius had been invited. From every corner of the room, eyes darted out to stare at her, and she felt like she was the side show in a circus.

She took a few steps forward, feeling awkward.

The green organdy dress fell in soft folds from her waist and rustled with each movement. A double flounced neckline, skimming the top of her breasts, revealed her satiny skin from the neck down and bared the top of her shoulders.

Like a nervous child, she toyed with the emerald necklace encircling her throat. It had been a gift from Jonathan just before he announced he would not be able to accompany her as planned. He was meeting the stone mason at the mill to discuss the sketches for the foundation and would arrive later.

Raven prodded her forward with a smug smile. "Smile, Willie. Smile. These gentlemen appreciate true beauty when they see it."

"And I feel like a treed coon with a pack of dogs at my heels. These buffoons can't tell the difference between a good piece of lumber and a toothpick, let alone what constitutes beauty. Tell me again why we decided to come?"

"We can't miss the biggest event of the year." Raven pushed her sister forward with a less than gentle nudge.

Matthew Reed, impeccably dressed, was the first to claim her for a dance. He gathered her into his arms and ushered her gallantly onto the dance floor. "Wilhelmina Wydcliffe, you have turned every male's head in this room."

She scowled. "I feel horribly out of place."

"You're safe with me, I assure you. I'll not let anyone capture you so easily. Everyone tells me you've been a busy lady."

"With the finishing mill? Oh, Matthew, it's going to be truly magnificent."

He twirled her about until she felt like a spinning

top. "How long will it take to build?"

"Jonathan thinks we'll have the groundwork finished within a few weeks, but with winter closing in, we may have to complete it in the spring."

Matthew Reed gripped her hand harder. "You mean Wain is planning to hang around until spring?"

The impact of his words hit her full face. "I'm...I'm not sure."

A million thoughts swirled through her head, each colliding with the others. She recalled Jonathan's hot, burning kisses earlier that morning, and shuddered. Could she work for months beside him?

"Poor dear, you're cold," he said and pulled her closer.

When the music ended, she tried to excuse herself, but was spun away by another and yet another male, all vying for a dance with her. Breathlessly, she declined the fourth request and searched the room for her sister.

John Pierce intercepted her on her escape to the refreshment table. Decked out in a dark gray, pinstriped waistcoat, he looked the part of a wealthy business man, right down to the gold pocket watch on his chest. He offered her an arresting smile. "Can I get you something, my dear?"

It was the chance she had been hoping for. "Some punch. And some fresh air. And freedom from all these raving fools."

Pierce laughed, straining the buttons on his wine-colored vest. "It would be my pleasure to give you all three." He took her by her elbow. "You are a rare breed of woman, Miss Wydcliffe. A *very* rare breed."

They stopped long enough at the refreshment table for Pierce to pour two cups of punch before walking out onto the wide veranda where only one other couple stood deep in the shadows. Night had fallen, and it was cool and misty.

"It looks like you'll have all the male population in town grappling at your feet before the night has ended." He gawked at her scanty neckline.

"And to think, I came to take a break from inhaling sawdust." She leaned against the railing and sipped her punch. "Can we dispense with senseless chatter? I'd rather talk business, if you don't mind."

He arched an eyebrow and pulled out a cigar. "You have a charming way of getting right to the soul of any matter. Do you mind if I smoke?"

When she shook her head, he slipped the cigar between his thick lips. He struck a match and lit it, blowing a puff of the smoke into the night air.

"I know you deal along the entire river," she said. "Word has it, settlers are beginning to pour into the area. Is that true?"

"Are you concerned?"

"As concerned as you are. Maybe more so. If the nation holds together, and we don't go to war over the slavery issue, expansion will happen rapidly. We've already had inquiries about when the finishing mill will be completed."

"But a war might be a bonus for me, my dear. Settlers still need supplies despite the war, and if my competitors shift their efforts to supplying troops, my market would be enlarged considerably." He waved a hand in a grand sweep toward the river. "I'll have a hold on everything—goods going out and provisions coming in."

"Let me guess," she said. "Prices would rise as high as the Susquehanna River in a spring thaw."

"You are a clever one." He looked at her appreciatively. "If I were ten years younger, I'd be among those pups inside sniffing at your feet. A woman with your intuition and brains is hard to come by." He paused. "Tell me, has your father come to any decision about selling the western thousand acres we discussed?"

Aware of his scrutiny, she kept her features deceptively composed. "We haven't made any decisions. It would be a good way to put some ready cash against the expenses of the new mill, but Papa and I haven't discussed it with Jonathan Wain."

Pierce's head shot up. "What's Wain got to do with it?"

She eyed him cautiously. Why did Jonathan Wain's name cause every blockhead around her to panic? "He has nothing to do with it. It's a Wydcliffe decision to determine what happens to our land."

The statement seemed to appease him. He removed a flask from his coat pocket. When he reached to pour some whiskey in his cup, she brazenly held hers out to him and saw a look of surprise fall across his face.

"Not meaning to pry, but do you have plans to dabble in a new business venture once you've secured the land?" She took a small sip, tasting the potency of the rich whiskey and forced herself not to recoil.

"I'd like to raise horses. Race them, perhaps."

"You'll be involved with Standardbreds, I imagine?" she asked as her mind leaped wildly ahead. The man knew nothing about horses other than which way to slap the saddle on.

"Pacers or trotters?"

"Pacers, I imagine."

"Like Jeb Wilson's Red Devil?"

"Exactly," he said.

Willie put the cup to her lips again and stared over the rim into the darkness. Everyone in the surrounding area, including most of the half-wits, knew Jeb Wilson had the finest trotters in the state.

She left him, excusing herself to hurry off to find the nearest bush where she tossed the punch before returning to the dance.

Like a ghoul, Clara Ferguson materialized and sailed up beside her as soon as she entered the room. "Wilhelmina, I'm so pleased you could come."

Bedecked in a mass of turquoise and white lace, Clara looked like she had been yanked from a flowerbed. Daisies, now wilted, were woven into her drooping corkscrew curls. A sickening sweet scent wafted from the air around her. Her gaze fell greedily on Willie's gown and necklace, and her face turned the same shade of green as Willie's dress.

Willie waved a hand before her face, batting at the air. "Whew. What do I smell?"

"My perfume. Father had it sent all the way from France. It's called Phlox in the Night." Clara sneered. "I see all these males are fawning over you like unweaned whelps. What's your secret?"

Willie coughed and sputtered, "Well, rest assured, it's not my perfume." *But yours would make any man or mule run for cover.*

"My mother says men swarm to women who possess heathen natures like yours," Clara said. "Do tell, is your dress another old castoff of Raven's? Green always makes me look antediluvian."

Willie glanced briefly down at her gown and watched the ruffles dance romantically about her hem. "No. The design is from the most recent Godey's Lady's Book, thanks to the ingenuity of my sister."

Clara scowled. "I'm surprised the half-breed knows what's in style."

Stepping closer, Willie went nose to nose. There was enough heathen in her to do some real damage, she decided, although it would hardly be worth the effort. "Careful, Clara. Push me as far as you like, but keep my sister out of this."

She watched Clara's mottled face turn red. A rejoinder was just dying to escape the poor girl's lips.

And here it came.

"Your jewelry is exquisite. Where does one find imitations like those way out here?"

Willie fingered the necklace at her throat. "Imitation? Jonathan Wain would be furious if he thought he paid for anything but the real thing."

Clara Jeanette gasped. "Jonathan Wain?"

Nodding, she grinned. "Yes, it must be my heathen nature."

CHAPTER ELEVEN

MATTHEW REED CAUGHT UP WITH Willie just outside the veranda.

Willie was so distracted disguising her anger from her bout with Clara, she never saw the tall figure in the shadows who had been observing her for the past hour.

"Please," Matthew pleaded, "one more dance." They moved onto the dance floor as the soft swells of violins filled the room. When he pulled her close, she could smell the liquor on his breath. His hand wandered to her waist and slid upward to caress her back. "I hope you're having a good time," he crooned in her ear.

She would have rather knocked herself on her head with her shoe. But she forced herself to nod in agreement.

"You are breathtaking. Simply breathtaking." His fingers moved suggestively down her back again as his eyes silently undressed her.

"Matthew, please…" Her voice trailed off as Jonathan covered the space between them. Ice crystals formed in his steel-colored eyes. He greeted them with unmistakable faked warmth and politeness.

"Good evening," he said dryly. "Excuse me, Reed, but I'd like to dance with Miss Wydcliffe."

She felt him grip her tighter.

"Try the next one, Wain," he said, his voice slurring. "This dance is already taken." He attempted to whirl her away to another area of the dance floor, but Jonathan's hand clamped down on his arm.

Halted, Willie decided the last thing she needed was a conflict in the middle of the dance floor. She pulled away and watched Jonathan scowl. A tic of anger twitched at the corner of his mouth.

"We'll have a cup of punch and another dance later, Matthew," she said in a placating voice. "In all fairness, I owe Papa's guest at least one dance."

Nodding with cool politeness, Matthew strode across the room, his shoulders ramrod straight.

Jonathan captured her immediately and pulled her up against him, moving gracefully in tune to the music. Dressed in a forest green jacket, his broad shoulders and lean tapered waist made him appear even taller. If he was aware the entire population of females was in awe of him, he seemed completely indifferent.

"Your warmth for the man rivals that of a snake locked in an ice house." She glared at him.

Chuckling, he spun her about the dance floor. "And there will be even less warmth when he learns I have announced our engagement tonight."

"Have you been into the spiked punch?"

"No. I've decided we should be engaged."

"And tell me, how did you reach such a conclusion?"

"It seemed like the appropriate thing to do. You

see, everyone was whispering at the punch bowl about my presence here tonight. About living under the same roof as you. So I just casually dropped a few hints an engagement was imminent."

"No, I don't *see*." She ground the words out between her teeth. "Why, you big oaf. How dare you spread such a ridiculous rumor? I already told Clara Ferguson you bought my emerald necklace. And my father...what will my father think when he hears this from anyone but me?"

"I should hope he'll be delighted. And maybe, relieved." He flashed a smug look and snuggled her closer.

"Good heavens, stop it," she snapped. She fumbled a step as her agitation ballooned and she tramped on his toes. "This is not amusing."

"It was not meant to be." He stepped lightly out of her way and squeezed her hand tighter. "Let's not make a spectacle of ourselves, everyone is watching."

It took less than a minute for her to realize he was telling the truth. The rumor must have been quickly passed about the room, and any female who had hoped for a chance to entice the handsome newcomer with her charms watched the virile tall figure and the notorious female tomboy with a disheartened look. Only Bradford Payne's white-haired wife, standing at the refreshment table, nodded her warm approval.

All at once, the thought of what Jonathan had just done made Willie's pulse beat erratically. Her head pounded, and she could feel the blood throbbing in her veins. They had a deal, a partnership. This was a horrid act. Now everything was crumbling right before the entire town. She gripped Jonathan's hand until her fingers were cold and numb. She searched her thoughts for a plausible way to escape while he continued to spin her about the floor.

"Jonathan, please," she finally pleaded, "stop. I'm getting dizzy."

He halted, and she pulled away, storming from the room with a sea of curious faces watching her.

The music ended and the room grew eerily quiet.

She searched the perimeter of the room for a familiar face. Rachael Kramer rushed up to her. "Willie," she yelped and squeezed her in a hug. "Why didn't you tell me you were betrothed? How romantic. And you've only known each other a month. It's like a fairytale."

Bloody nightmare. She felt Jonathan's presence behind her.

"My, my, Rachael, you look lovely this evening," he said.

Rachael blushed and touched the mother-of-pearl necklace at her throat. "Lucky for me Willie is generous, and we wear the same size dresses." She turned toward a young man approaching several feet away. "There's Daniel Barrett. I promised him a dance. You'll have to excuse me." She sighed a wistful sigh. "I can't wait to hear all about the details." She left quickly, dashing away.

Willie looked helplessly about the room. Inside the archway of the hall entrance, she spied Raven. "I need to talk to my sister, Jonathan."

"Don't be too long, sweetheart," he murmured, his breath fanning her ear. "I shall dread every moment we are apart."

Her brown-eyed glare threw imaginary daggers at his gray-eyed gaze. "Oh, stop it, you fool, before I boot you clean to the river and feed you to the fish," she hissed under her breath.

She found Raven buttoning her cloak just inside the door.

Her sister grinned, "I have to go, Nicole is waiting up for me. Papa is already in the carriage, he's not feeling well." She paused and hugged Willie tightly. "I'm so pleased you and Jonathan have considered a betrothal. Papa is bursting with pride. You must tell me all about it tomorrow morning. First thing." Turning, she vanished, leaving her standing bewildered and forlorn.

Jonathan crossed to the archway and stood behind her. "I hope that's not a frown on your beautiful face."

She flinched. The man should have a cowbell around his neck. Over the last few minutes, she had assessed her unfortunate situation. There was only one means of recourse. She needed to get away from the celebration as quickly as possible.

She heaved a sigh. "At the moment, Jonathan, I find everything, including you—tiresome."

A peal of laughter slipped through his lips. "Very well, let's leave."

Without hesitation, she executed a quick pirouette, snatched her cloak from the grip of a surprised doorman, and swept down the steps to an awaiting carriage.

Climbing in, Jonathan gave the driver a signal, and they headed out, the carriage swaying behind the horses' hooves.

For the first few moments, the air around them was thick with pent-up energy. When, at last, he did speak, his voice was like a knife slicing through the dead silence. "It seems we're at a disagreement again."

Eying him with a look of contempt, she remained silent.

"Would you like to discuss it?"

Silence again.

"Fine, would you like to know why I decided we should become betrothed?"

More silence.

"Since I don't hear otherwise, I must assume we are in agreement. Would you like to select the date of the wedding, or do you prefer I do it?"

That blew the cork from the bottle.

Her voice spilled out faster than water over the milldam. "You…you jackass, there will be no wedding. I'd rather be married to Sam's mule."

He leaned back on the seat "Splendid! We're conversing again. I'm sure you're aware Clara Ferguson has been doing everything possible tonight to discredit your virtuous reputation? She has all but publicly announced you're engaged in a business far more lucrative than the mill operations and the oldest since man has walked the face of this earth."

Willie's sniffed. "I don't give a flying fig what lies Clara Jeanette has been spreading."

"Hellfire, I do." Jonathan leaned forward. " And you've only added to the blabbermouth by having every single male vie for your undivided attention."

"I did nothing to bring that pack of dogs down

on me." She pounded a fist on the velvet seat.

"Granted, your beauty alone was sufficient. But think of your father for heaven's sake."

"He knows Clara is a loose screw."

"Agreed. But think about this. Since we're already in business together and share the same wealth, why not love and the same warm bed? Quite frankly, I'm totally enchanted with you."

Crossing his arms at his chest, he challenged, "I dare you, Elizabeth Wilhelmina, to name any one of the slobbering curs at the party who deserve to be called your adoring fiancé."

Willie turned away to look out into the black night.

Jonathan's voice softened. "Let's just sleep on the whole situation tonight and discuss it in the morning."

The minutes dragged on, and her silent cold behavior permeated the inside of the carriage. A rainstorm blew in, drumming on the roof. When the carriage finally halted in front of the manor, he alighted and offered her his hand. Slapping it away, she stepped down unaided into the rain and brushed past him like an ice maiden.

His hand shot out and spun her gently about to face him. The air had turned chilly, but her silent icy look was no match for it.

"We make a perfect couple despite your denial."

A perfect couple? Why the arrogant fool. Willie's voice ripped through the empty air around them. "Be prepared for your life to be a white water hell unless you set me free."

She jerked loose from his hold and marched slowly toward the front door oblivious to the downpour, her head held high like she was walking to the gallows without an ounce of remorse.

CHAPTER TWELVE

IT WAS SENSELESS TO TRY to sleep. Willie had spent most of the night tossing, turning, and tangling herself in her bedclothes. Tearing back the covers, she slipped out of bed and the manor before even faint pink rays of dawn peeked above the mountain ridges.

Irritated with herself and furious with Jonathan, she searched her thoughts for a suitable solution to her dilemma. She could think of none.

Like a nervous logger late for work, she raced Silver Cloud along the hard-packed dirt road toward the river and woods beyond. Worn breeches were molded snugly to the curves of her hips. An old suede coat concealed the patched elbows of her faded red shirt and scuffed brown boots encased her legs. Only her chestnut hair, streaming from beneath her hat, attested to the fact she was a girl.

The bite of the morning breeze stung her face, but she drove her horse relentlessly toward the river before she finally eased him into a walk. They picked their way carefully along a worn uphill trail until they arrived high on a steep overhang. Before them, rock-faced cliffs jutted above the swirling

West Branch of the Susquehanna River stretching itself below like a thread unwrapped from its spool. She loved the fickle river with its many personalities—from its swollen, turbulent waters in springtime to its calm rippling beauty in summer to its murky agitation after a hearty autumn rain to its ice-covered splendor in winter. It was the life blood of the rural lumbering communities.

She stripped the bridle and blanket from her horse and watched him trot to a nearby clearing to graze. A breeze scattered her hair recklessly about her face. In reverent-like silence, she walked out onto the cliffs and faced the eastern horizon as the sun, changing from a drowsy rose to lemon yellow, slid up and cleared the expanse of the mountaintops.

She slumped down on the moss-covered ledge and tried to sort the thoughts swarming in the dark recesses of her mind. She had cried the entire night and was now too weary to weep any longer. She had to find a way to tell her father the truth. But now, since he had formed a close alliance with Jonathan Wain, he would certainly take any decision on her part to end their relationship with bitter disappointment.

She wondered what Jonathan's true motive had been for entrapping her. Surely not love. She was little more than a scrap of paper in Bradford Payne's law office, little more than a business deal, impulsively manipulated to suit the circumstances.

Resting her head on her knees, she dozed, collapsing onto the ledge with the rock a feeble pillow for her head. Silver Cloud's soft snorting roused her some time later, and she immediately sensed she was not alone.

"You have a real fondness for heights," Jonathan said in a low voice. He was sitting just inches from her. "And you certainly have faith in wildlife to sleep so soundly."

Willie groaned and eased her stiff body upright. "It beats what I have in humanity."

He snorted and threw aside the dried straw he had been chewing on. "You always go straight for the throat, don't you?"

"It's a bad habit. What do you want?"

"And you're tactful as well."

"Another bad habit. What *do* you want?"

"I was hoping we could talk. Civilly, that is."

She sighed and looked intently at the waters below. "Unless you can tell me this has all been a mistake, I doubt it."

Jonathan rubbed the back of his neck and drew in a tired breath.

She could tell things were not going as he had planned, but she was not about to let him off the hook. His announcement of their engagement had been an ill-thought-out plan.

"There was no need to return the jewels. They were a present for you to keep," he said.

She chuckled, remembering the look on Clara Ferguson's face when she told her they were from him. "I have no need for something that costly. They should go to someone who could better enjoy them."

"You detest me, don't you?" He paused, measuring her a moment.

"No." She gave him a despondent look before she picked up her hat and swatted at a bee darting about her feet. "There's a tale the Indians repeat to their children about two brothers whose finest string of horses were stolen by their worst enemies. The first brave grew angry. So angry, he ranted and raved and beat his chest, cursing, refusing to drink, eat, or sleep. The second brother set aside his wrath and calmly bedded down for the night, confident he must pursue his enemies when dawn appeared."

She stared at the river. "I don't need to tell you which one retrieved his horses the next day."

She heard him let out another ragged breath of air.

"So now what happens?"

"We calmly tell my father the truth and dissolve the betrothal. Don't worry, Jonathan, I won't soil your fine reputation or mar your ardent friendship with him. I'll tell him it was my mistake. Papa's used to my impulsiveness."

"Why? Why would you take the blame?"

"I gain nothing by continuing my rage," she admitted. "And I do nothing for Papa's well-being either." A tear slipped down her cheek, but she squeezed her eyes tightly together, refusing to cry.

He waited. The ensuing emptiness cut through them like a bone-chilling wind. "How long have you known about his illness?" he asked.

"At least six months, after he came back from a trip to Philadelphia." The words stoically tumbled from her lips. "He never told me, but I surmised it. He was losing strength. Too quickly for even an elderly man. Later, I found the bill for the doctor tucked away in an old ledger in the study. So I did some checking on my own—a blood disease, incurable."

"Is he aware that you know?"

She shrugged.

"He acts like you and Raven don't have the slightest clue."

She rubbed her tired eyes with the palms of her hands. All the fire and spirit in her had vanished. "I've always suspected Papa realizes he can't hide anything from us. It's just a game he plays."

"Willie, I've never asked for anything," he said in a low voice. "Please wait a while before calling off the engagement. Your family seemed so pleased and relieved last night. Now isn't the time to make a spectacle of everyone." He paused, as if waiting for her to say something, but she sat silently.

"What harm can a few weeks make?" he persisted. "Given time, it would be easier for the entire family to handle the disruption."

She considered what he had to say. Unfortunately, what he was proposing made sense, and it would give her time to sort through the calamity and find a reasonable excuse. It would be easier to end it later without stirring up the wretched minds of the entire town. She knew Clara could sink a hook into the mess and dangle it in front of her face for years.

"Yes, let's wait," she agreed.

Silence slid briefly around them for protection.

"Tell me," she finally said. "What possessed you to do such a horrid thing?"

He lifted his chin. "You must admit we make a perfect pair, despite your denial. It's high time we both settle down and find suitable mates. Your father is worried about your welfare, the future, and the business. My father is concerned about my bachelorhood and his lack of grandchildren."

She gave him an annoyed look. "So you'd marry out of sense of duty to our fathers?" And to keep the business intact, she thought wildly. A simple arrangement for business purposes. To please a dying man. To please a fretful father. Only he could be so honest and practical.

"Good gracious, man. You should have been a bloody monk. Oh, but providing the grandchildren would be a problem, right?" Her eyes narrowed. "I'm warning you, I refuse to be a pawn. What about love? Doesn't it account for anything?"

"Who are you waiting for?" His voice was cold and exact. "A romantic logger to come sailing down the river and sweep the rich logger's daughter off her feet? Sometimes good mates come on plain chestnut stallions and as partners."

Willie's eyes glistened with tears. "I could give a tinker's damn about who my future mate might be. One thing is for certain, I'd be the one to make the choice. I would decide. Do you hear me?" she cried out. "I would decide!"

He shook his head. His voice broke miserably. "Why won't you give me a chance? Do you loathe me that much?" A look of tired sadness passed over his face. "You must…because why else would I get the jewels, which I personally took the time to select just for you, flung back in my face? But can't you see we still have to work together?"

"Yes." Tears of frustration splashed down her face and she sobbed uncontrollably into her hands. She cried for the mother she never had and for her sister who would be leaving soon to resettle in Canada. She cried for the fear of loneliness, the fear of abandonment. For herself and for her father who would never see her future children.

Jonathan wrapped his arms around her and pulled her to him. "I'm sorry," he whispered into her hair. "I never meant to hurt you. I did what I thought was right at the time. I hate to see you so miserable."

Willie shoved him away, stood, and tore off the jagged cliffs, her boots silent on the mossy surface. Spying Silver Cloud, she whistled shrilly and the stallion danced toward her.

Jonathan caught up with her and reached for the blanket and bridle to help her, but she jerked them away before he could touch them.

"Leave. Me. Alone." She wiped her tear-stained face on her sleeve, adjusted the blanket, and slipped the bridle over the horse's head. Using only his silky mane for support, she lifted herself gracefully onto his back and kicked her knees gently into his sides, sending him racing in the direction of the manor. She and Silver Cloud fit together like threads of rich oriental silk.

Horse and rider seemed like one.

Trade Wind was already in his stall when Willie rode in to the stable yard an hour later. She had chosen a longer route, needing the time to rethink the conversation she had with Jonathan.

Slipping off, she doled out her usual treat, a sugar cube, and patted the horse affectionately, reluctant to give him up. It had taken her three years, a ton of patience, and hours of hard work to learn to maneuver the gray gelding bareback.

"He seems a little sluggish," she warned the stable boy who took the reins from her.

Roy nodded. "He's getting up there in years. I'll rub him down and give him some extra feed. Maybe we need to turn him into the pasture to roam and rest."

Later in the day, determined to face the rest of the afternoon in a mood that defied the bitter taste of the morning, Willie sought the only person who could make her spirits soar, and the only person who would be ideal to accompany her to the mills where she'd have to face Jonathan again.

Nicole.

The little girl did not disappoint her. With her pigtails bobbing along to the rocking of the buggy, she babbled continually, only stopping long enough to try to mimic a bird she heard in the surrounding trees. Sam Bradley was at the mill entrance when they arrived and his face split into a wide grin.

"Gracious me, Willie. Where'd you find such a beautiful little helper? Under a rock?" He lifted Nicole from the buggy like she was a sack of sugar and turned to Willie. "Jonathan wants to see you."

Willie stiffened. "Do you know why?"

"Dunno. Probably the dad-burned finishin' mill again." He studied her pale face and red-rimmed eyes. "For someone just engaged, you don't look moon-eyed to me."

"Let it go, Sam," she snapped. Seeing the hurt look on his wrinkled face, she relented. "If the truth be known, the engagement was Jonathan's idea, not mine. He was trying to stop Clara Ferguson's wagging tongue and appease Papa. It's probably prudent we don't tell anyone about this sordid mess."

The old man scratched behind his ear, trying to

make some sense of her words. "You mean you're not in love with him?"

"No."

"He'd make a fine mate."

"I'd rather wed a polecat."

"Now don't get sassy, young lady, you know what I mean."

"Why do I need a mate, Sam? Papa doesn't have one. You don't either."

"It's not the same, you're a female. The old man scratched his ear again.

Her arms flew up in the air and came down, slapping her sides. "I give up." She turned to Nicole, who was chinning herself on the hitching post. "You run along with Sam out back. I'll be out shortly. Don't go in the mill unless Sam is with you. Do you understand, Nicole?"

When the little girl nodded, she breathed a sigh of relief. Long ago she had learned to have respect for the saws that devoured log after log, day after day. Flying chips and sawdust could cause eye injuries, and the saw blades themselves were known to cause bodily harm or death.

Outside the storeroom door which Jonathan had converted to a crude makeshift office, she paused apprehensively before entering.

Startled, he glanced up. For what seemed like an eternity, they stared at each other with troubled looks.

"I didn't think you'd come," he admitted and dropped the stack of papers he held on his desk. He stood in the light of the window and looked at her warily.

"No one would ever accuse me of being a coward." She stood with her hands on her hips.

He winced. "I apologize for this morning. I had no right to intrude on your solitude."

"And last night?"

"No," he said flatly. He rubbed the back of his neck. "The engagement seemed like the proper thing to do at the time."

She gave the man credit, he was long on stamina even if he was short on brains. "I never figured you for the type to rob the cradle." She spoke calmly with a look of tired sadness.

He chortled. "A mere eight years between us? Are you concerned about our age difference or my breeding abilities? If it's the latter, I can assure you, we'll be compatible enough. If you'd like, we could start early. I'm not opposed to a little tryst before the wedding."

She shook her head, softening. "There will be no tryst, no children, because there'll be no wedding. As soon as this whole fiasco blows over, we're dissolving this asinine betrothal. I figure a month should be more than a sufficient amount of time to determine we're as incompatible as all—"

"Ah, Ah, Ah." Jonathan raised an eyebrow.

"—heck."

He bit back a smile, backing off, saying **nothing**. He liked her best when she was passionate and feisty.

"The least we should do is pick out a ring," he said. When she started to protest, he held up a hand to silence her. "Just to make the whole relationship seem more believable to everyone. You can have anything you'd like, and you can think of it as a gift from a partner and admirer, rather than a fiancé."

Willie frowned. "I don't want a ring, but as much as I hate to admit this, I'm going to need you. Papa's health is rapidly declining." She blew out a breath of pent-up air. "I can't handle three mills, winter logging, and a finishing mill by myself, even with Sam Bradley's help."

He kept his demeanor neutral. "I understand. Tell me what needs to be done." He watched her relax as if a tremendous weight had lifted from her shoulders.

He pointed to the drawing nailed on the wall behind his cluttered desk. "I have the finishing mill laid out."

She moved to the wall and studied the drawings.

"I don't suppose you'd consider having dinner with me tonight in town?" he asked close to her ear. "To celebrate a truce?" he prodded. "Two crates of rum and top shelf whiskey, packed in straw, will be arriving at the manor by late this morning—delivered by a pie-eyed keelboat operator whom I swear has already sampled the goods. I can't wait for Sam to taste some real Southern whiskey instead of the rot-gut he swigs. I was thinking we could dine with him and go over some of the mill operations."

"Well," she hesitated, "maybe it's not a bad idea. Sam could explain what needs to be done in the woods."

She walked to the window over the millpond and glanced out. Piles of logs bobbed on the black surface, ready to be sent up the carriage and ripped apart by the sharp teeth of the giant saws.

"Oh, good grief," she cried out. "Nicole is down walking on those logs in the mill pond. I told Sam to watch her and keep her out of trouble. I'll bet she conned him into letting her give it a try. We have to get her before she gets her clothes wet, or worse, slips off a log and gets hurt."

Abruptly, she pulled away from the window, grabbed her hat, and sprinted across the storeroom with Jonathan following. When they reached the landing dock, Sam Bradley was gazing affectionately at the little girl as she leaped agilely from one log to another like a real pike person.

"Sam, what the blazes are you thinking?" she shouted in an irritated voice and flapped her hand toward the mill pond. "Get that child in here before she gets injured. You were supposed to be watching her."

"What do you think I'm doing?" He spit out a wad of tobacco juice onto the dusty ground. "Look at her, Willie. She can walk them as good as you could at her age."

"That's not the point," she huffed. "I promised Raven she'd stay safe and *dry*."

"She doesn't look wet to me." Sam laughed and waved to Nicole, who was flapping her arms to get their attention. Willie signaled for her to come toward the shoreline, and the little girl obeyed, hopping from log to log to reach them.

As if sensing something was amiss, Jonathan's gaze shot to the splash dam above.

"Hellfire," he yelled. "Someone opened the chute."

In a split second, all three realized the danger as they looked toward it. Water surged into the pond carrying piles of stored timber. The first string of freed logs fell and crashed against those crowded farther back in the millpond. Soon the entire tangled mass would gain momentum, sweeping the logs under Nicole's feet over the dam below. There was no way to stop the onslaught.

Her heart thumping, Willie stripped off her boots and jacket.

Jonathan leaped toward the shore.

"No," she shrieked. "I'll go out and get her. I know how to do this. Go down near the dam where the current is strong. If I have to do some swimming, I'll need your help to bring her to shore before we both get washed over the dam."

She vaulted onto the first log and felt the sharp bark tear at her stockings and the icy water soak her feet. Wasting no time, she jumped onto another log, and another, and another, inching her way toward the girl. In some places the logs were jammed together so solidly, it was like walking on a wooden floor, and she moved quickly over them. Once, she paused long enough to avoid stepping on a circle of sharp nails which jutted out along the end of a log she recognized as ash.

She closed in carefully a few yards from the little girl. "Nicole," she urged, "come here."

Frozen with fright, the little girl stared at her wide-eyed and gaped toward the dam above.

She followed her gaze where log after log slipped through the chute and tumbled into the water, sending sprays of water billowing into the air. Pushing a wet strand of hair from her eyes, she continued until she was face-to-face with the child.

"Grab my hand, Nicole," she said sternly. "We have to get off these logs." The little girl frantically reached out and clawed at her fingers, and Willie felt a sense of relief momentarily wash over her.

"Move fast," she instructed in a strained voice, dragging the child beside her. "When you feel the log give way underneath you, walk with the slow roll, just like Sam taught you."

"I can't," Nicole wailed, her small body trembling. "I can't do it as fast as you."

"Yes, you can." Willie spoke calmly, vaulting onto another huge muddy log. She stopped it from spinning and pulled Nicole onto it. "I'll help. Balance yourself. We'll work our way toward shore."

They were forty feet away when the last pile of logs slipped though the chute and propelled the mass they were standing on into the rapid current. Willie knew it would only be minutes before they were swept over the dam and buried under the water with the weight of the timber.

Frantically, she grabbed the child and flung her into a wide opening among the tangled logs. "Swim!" she screamed and dove into the icy water behind her.

Taken off-guard, Nicole broke the surface, sputtering and flailing her arms. Willie grabbed her by the collar and pulled her away from a log sailing by. All around her, timbers bobbed in the water like giant tangled toothpicks. She could feel the current sucking at her, and she stroked faster. Somewhere she heard Jonathan's voice as she dodged another flying log. She prayed he was nearby, but she didn't dare look. All her efforts were concentrated on swimming against the rapids and away from the edge of the dam with the child in tow. Her lungs burned, and her arms and legs ached like they were on fire, but the thunderous noise of the water crashing over the spillway urged her onward.

It seemed like an eternity she had been in the water. Each stroke, each movement was a painful reminder she was not safe. Just when she felt she couldn't lift her arm for one more stroke, Jonathan grabbed the floundering child from her. The lessening of the burden provided her with the renewed energy she needed to propel herself forward. She gulped in a fresh breath as she swam wildly toward shore.

It happened in an instant. A giant log rushed up. Driven by the tremendous speed of the current and the other logs propelling it, the log hit her squarely across the back. She went under and struggled up, sputtering, just as another chunk of timber collided with the side of her temple. Her hands and feet went numb. She labored with every effort to swim, but found she couldn't. Far off, someone screamed. Or was it her own voice?

Within seconds blackness enveloped her, and she felt herself being pulled down, down, down into a swirling cold mass.

Then nothing.

CHAPTER THIRTEEN

RAVEN STUDIED THE TINY UNCONSCIOUS form in the big rose-colored bed and glanced surreptitiously at Jonathan slouched in the wingback chair where he had slept, fused to Willie's bedside, for the last two nights. A tray of untouched food, dried and neglected, lay miserably on her dressing stool beside him.

After the accident, he had carried Willie to her room and had even refused to leave when Raven and Helga stripped her of her wet clothes and placed her between clean sheets. Distraught, he had paced the floor long after the doctor had departed and had continued until weariness physically over-took him.

Wondering how she was going to deal with his irrational behavior, Raven turned and regarded him more intensely. Tired, unshaven, his pained eyes were a dull haze. His face was drawn, and he looked sick. Was it love, or guilt keeping him so close? She moved to stand beside his limp form. She knew he was tormenting himself and was verging on insanity, even though he had been the one who had dragged Willie from beneath the dark currents and saved her life.

Nicole tiptoed into the room. "Is Aunt Willie awake yet?" she whispered.

Raven hurried to her side. "No, dear, not yet." She gathered one of her daughter's braids between her fingers to feel the woven corn silk strands. Across the room, Willie's tawny hair lay damp with fever, her eyes sealed. Raven hugged her daughter tightly. "Run along and get something to eat, Nicole. Maybe you can take Jonathan with you."

"No," Jonathan said gruffly and sat up straighter in his seat.

Raven jumped at his sharp tone.

He sighed and said more softly, "I'm sorry. I just want to be here when she wakes up. I'm not hungry." He stood and moved to the window. The rain had begun to drum against the pane and the droplets slid down the slick glass.

"She's going to be fine, Jonathan," she said. "I know it. I'm going to see to my father. I'll be back to check on her." Without another word, she left the room.

"I hope to God you're right, Raven," he muttered glumly to his reflection in the pane before his eyes returned to the motionless form.

Raven found her father alone, hidden away in the study. He had imprisoned himself there since the accident occurred, refusing most of the food offered, refusing to see the many callers who had already inquired about Willie's health.

The tightly drawn curtain cast dark shadows

about the room and seeped around his defeated shoulders. He sat slumped over the desktop, his forehead propped on his forearms.

Raven leaned down and touched his shoulder. Bloodshot eyes greeted her.

They stared at each other mutely for a long time. Finally Wydcliffe spoke, "Why, Raven? Why would God do this to me three times? Isn't it enough he's taken two wives? Now he wants my daughter, too?"

She encircled the old man with comforting arms. "Papa, Willie is not going to die. Trust me. You must not give up hope."

"I've tried," he replied bitterly, "but I've been chasing death away at my doorstep all my life. I've tried to have hope since your mother died when you were only a small babe. I tried when Willie's mother died. But sometimes I get so damn tired of trying. You're looking at an old man now, and I'm tired myself."

"I know, Papa, I know. You'll feel better once you eat. Nicole is waiting for you in the dining room."

Dalton Wydcliffe shook his head in despair. "Food can't help this broken-down body any longer. It's just worn out." He looked up to catch the compassion in her ebony eyes. "Don't feel sorry for me, Raven. You know, don't you?"

She nodded gravely.

"And Willie, too?"

She nodded again, her eyes misting.

"I should have known I couldn't keep a secret from you two rascals. An old man can't even die in peace without causing a commotion. Well, I'm going to fight my way to the devil. At least no one can say

Wydcliffes give up easily. I sure hope the little one upstairs knows it."

"She knows," Raven said, "trust me, she knows."

But it was not only Willie's welfare she worried about. "Papa," she said after a moment, "we have to find a way to get Jonathan out of her bedroom before he becomes petrified rock."

For the first time since the accident, she saw a faint smile form on his lips. "I suppose we're all acting like children, aren't we?" he asked.

Much to his surprise, she nodded in agreement.

A multitude of feelings tumbled through his head as Jonathan slumped down in the chair he had occupied for the last forty-eight hours. He had been crazy to let Willie go out in the water alone. What had he been thinking? What if she had been killed? It was bad enough he had made a shamble of her life in the few weeks since he arrived.

He thought about all the unkind things he had said and done. He had pushed and prodded, taunted and teased her without remorse, without a thought for her feelings. He had even forced a betrothal on her without her consent. Why had he ever been so foolish to think he could tame her? Who had ever captured a wild wind? Now, there were so many things he longed to tell her, and if he got a second chance, he promised silently, he would make it all up to her.

He leaned back in his chair and allowed his burning eyes to fall shut and had almost drifted off when a mumble rose from underneath the bed covers. Brushing aside his grogginess, he bolted upright and rushed to her bedside. He took her cold hand gently into his. "Willie?" he ordered in an insistent whisper. "Wilhelmina? For heaven's sake, speak to me."

She moaned, barely fluttering her eyelids.

"It's Jonathan," he urged gently. "Willie, please say something. Anything, anything at all." Even a curse would sound wonderful to him, he thought, as he gently rubbed her hand.

She blinked and tried to move, but the pain in her head pounded furiously. She heard a voice from afar echo to her like it came from the bottom of a deep canyon. "You're going to be all right." But no matter what the voice was saying, all she wanted was for the grueling pain to end. She felt her whole body begin to throb with her head, and faces flashed before her—a small child, a beautiful woman with hair like her own, an Indian maiden with midnight eyes, and a grotesque face which changed into the likeness of her father and faded into the stone-like countenance of a belligerent Indian. But Lone Wolf was real. Sitting proudly on a paint stallion with a silver wolf skin draped over his broad shoulders, he smiled before he ordered, "Go, little one, and leave this place at once."

Willie opened her mouth to speak, but realized she was fading from the world she had entered. Her eyes fluttered open and she stared up at the ceiling. It was white. It was her bedroom. Her eyes felt heavy like someone had placed stones on them. She slid back into the darkness again, but this time into a peaceful sleep.

"Did she say anything?" a voice asked, startling

Jonathan.

He looked up and carefully rose from the edge of the bed. He watched as Raven moved to the sleeping form with the silence of a ghost and brushed her sister's damp hair away from her forehead.

"How did you know she stirred?" An eerie sensation started in the pit of his stomach.

"A feeling." She shrugged, her eyes avoiding his. "She's my sister. We share Wydcliffe blood. If I tried to explain it, you wouldn't understand." She touched Willie's cheek gently. "The fever had fled and her breathing is normal. She'll sleep now. It's time for you to eat."

He started to protest, but she scolded, "Be reasonable, man, you could use a bath and shave."

Shoulders drooping, he reluctantly left.

Minutes later, in the kitchen, he removed a cup from the cupboard and was pouring his own coffee when the cook lumbered in.

"Good news?" the old woman asked.

"Her fever is gone."

Hannah's concerned look swept over him from his shoeless feet to his wrinkled clothes to his uncombed hair. "You could use a bath and a shave, sir," she blurted out. Her hand flew up to cover to her mouth, and she blushed like she knew she should have bitten her tongue.

"So I've been told," he said dryly, dropping the cup from his lips to look into her embarrassed, round face.

Hannah drew back. "I'm sorry, sir. But you do look…a little tired."

He smiled weakly. "You're a good cook, Hannah Svenson, but you're a horrible liar."

She laughed, the buttons above her apron straining. "Go on, man, Conrad will draw you a bath. Get yourself cleaned up. I'll fix you a tray with your favorites and send it up promptly."

A half hour later and freshly bathed, Jonathan returned to Willie's room to find Dalton Wydcliffe leaving. For a few minutes, he studied the old man standing silently outside the door. Head bent, with the fading light of day playing across his face, the elderly man's eyes appeared more sunken, his skin more gray, and the lines around his mouth more deep. He looked far older than his age.

"How is she?" Jonathan asked quietly.

"The same," Wydcliffe replied. "Though Raven insists she'll be fine."

He nodded. "She said the same to me."

Wydcliffe's voice trembled, but the anger in his eyes was scorching. "Sam found the ropes behind the splash dam cut, and Nicole's boat floating in the pond. Someone deliberately sent those logs through the chute and into our boom below. If I ever find out who, he'll pay dearly. If she dies, I'll spend the rest of my life hunting him down."

"You'll have lots of help." Jonathan wanted the same bitter revenge himself. The thought of injuring a woman and child was totally revulsive. "How's Sam?"

"Near crazy with guilt. Says it's his fault. He even stayed in town last night so he could be close by in case there was a change in her condition."

"What about the mill hands? Have they found anything unusual?"

"No. They were all at their usual locations, except for Daniel Barrett, who is usually on the carriage ramp, trading with Henderson so he could tally stacked lumber. We had no one working up at the chute above the splash dam."

His ancient eyes found Jonathan's anguished ones. "You can't stay locked in that room either, son. We still have mills to run and a finishing mill to complete. Sam is near worthless right now, and I need a good man down there. No matter what happens, we finish what we started."

Jonathan stared at him for a long moment and nodded. He owed him that much. "All right, if there's no improvement by tonight, I'll be back at the mills tomorrow morning. Count on it." The old man turned to go, and Jonathan watched his dejected form trudge down the narrow hall. He wanted to tell him how much he loved his daughter, but the words wouldn't come out, so he walked into Willie's room instead.

Raven was fussing with the covers on Willie's bed when he entered, and she took immediate note of the immaculate man before her. "I see you took my advice."

When he smiled sheepishly, she continued, "Stay for another hour, but no more. You need sleep as well. I suspect she'll be awake soon." She left again, soundlessly, without another word.

He had barely fallen in the chair when Conrad arrived with a tray stacked with food, deposited it, and silently departed. Settling back, he curled his hand around a cup of freshly brewed coffee and waited. He had no idea how many minutes dragged on before she stirred in the bed and moaned softly through lips, dried and cracked. Slowly she raised her hand, but he grabbed it gently and returned it to the bed.

She cried out, tossing about. He rose, sat beside her on the edge of the bed, and grabbed her shoulders, holding her firmly against the mattress.

"Don't touch your head, there's stitches in it," he ordered. "And stop tossing about. You tangled with a gigantic log and lost."

She tried to lift her head from the pillow, but the attempt was futile.

"Nicole!" she cried out in anguish. She struggled to try to sit upright again. Her eyes flew open, large and frightened. "Where's Nicole?"

Jonathan pushed her gently into the softness of the mattress again. "She's fine, Willie. She came out without a scratch. Lie still or you'll start the bleeding again."

Tiny beads of sweat collected above her fine brows, and Jonathan wiped them away with a damp cloth. Her skin was cool, moist, and feverless, but chalky.

Against the white pillow, her eyes were like sunken coals. "How did I lose all my clothes?"

"You were wet and Raven dried and disrobed you. Except for the hat. I must admit, you certainly have an odd way with hats. Last time I saw it was sailing down the Susquehanna and should be at the Chesapeake Bay in a couple of weeks. I'll have one of my brothers fish it out."

Willie squirmed again, and he trapped her again. "You *have* to lie still. Doctor's orders."

She groaned. "Who pulled me out?"

"I did."

"Oh, good grief." She closed her eyes to rest a moment. "Did you have to think twice about it?"

"Stop talking. You need to rest."

"I wish I could, but my stomach aches like I swallowed a patch of briers."

He left her, but returned minutes later with Raven and a bowl of chicken broth.

"Good thing you decided to wake up." Raven spooned the liquid slowly into her sister's mouth. "Any longer and Jonathan, Sam, and Papa would be sitting with Roy's crazy rooster out back."

"Oh, Raven, I had a dream. I saw Lone Wolf. He was on his horse, a monstrous paint. I bent to pick up a crow's feather at my feet, and he became angry and ordered me away."

"You were near the land of the dead spirits, and he was warning you not to enter," Raven suggested. "He was sending you back to the land of the living."

Willie's hand came up in a weak gesture. "He can't be dead, can he?"

Raven shook her head. "No, he just has the power to see the past and future."

His interest piqued, Jonathan stared at Raven. "You believe in these dreams?"

Her dark eyes reflected nervousness. She glanced at her sister for a moment as if they shared some unspoken secret. "My people believe we should welcome our dreams and accept them for what we think they might personally mean." Relief fell across her face when her father chose the next moment to arrive and end their conversation.

The old man lowered himself onto the bed beside Willie. He took her hand in his. "I heard the party was here. You had us worried. Your crews are badgering me for invitations to visit. Sam's first in line." He squinted at the bandage wound tight around her head and scowled.

"Ah, it'll take more than a piece of my own timber to kill me," she muttered hoarsely. "We might want to check all the timber lumbered from upstream before it gets near the carriages again. I think the spiked timber is coming from the area around the Wasp."

"Take it easy, child, you're in no condition to worry about anything." Wydcliffe patted her hand soothingly.

"White ash," she whispered exhaustedly, her eyes falling shut to rest a moment. "Almost every piece I crossed in the millpond has nails in it."

Wydcliffe turned to Jonathan. "The only white ash we get for the Hornet's Nest comes from dense stands along the swamp between the Wasp and Reed's mill. But I can't believe anyone from Olaf's mill is responsible. It must have been spiked after we received it."

It came to Jonathan like he had been battered alongside the head with a log himself. "No, what she's reaffirming is that the spiked timber only comes from one location. It was a piece of ash in the saws when Sam was hurt. Whoever is causing the trouble knows the mill in town periodically puts through special loads of ash for the boatswain and keelboat operators." And the culprit's work is easy, he thought to himself. He only has to tamper with timber stacked in one remote area. Eventually, the operations at the Hornet's Nest would be fouled up when those orders were requested.

Willie's discovery had another implication. Dalton Wydcliffe's earlier assumption had been correct. Only someone from inside, someone who worked at the Hornet's Nest, would know when those orders were requisitioned.

Jonathan glanced at Dalton Wydcliffe. His face was as white as the bed's sheets. Raven must have seen it, too, because she took her father by the arm and steered him toward the door. "You'll have to discuss this later."

After they left, he eased himself down on the side of her bed.

"I owe you my life," she said hoarsely. "I don't know how I can repay you."

His hands warmed her shoulders. He bent down and kissed her forehead, his lips traveling down to touch her lips.

Willie's senses went reeling as their lips met. They clung together for a few seconds before he raised his head. "I'll think of a way for repayment. Does the kiss pain you?"

She barely shook her head when he leaned forward and grazed her lips again.

Exactly, at that moment, the caretaker arrived. Red-faced, he coughed lightly and lamented, "Oh no, sir, I've done it again. I thought you might want more coffee."

He made no move to withdraw from the bed. "Please leave it on the table, Conrad."

"Jonathan, stop," Willie pleaded in hoarse whisper.

"He's gone," he said and chuckled.

"But it's truly coffee, not passion I desire. Just one sip?"

Relenting, he stroked her tangled locks and reached for the cup.

She breathed a sigh of relief and weakly took the proffered cup.

CHAPTER FOURTEEN

Mid November, 1856

THE WINDS OF WINTER BLEW boldly, stripping the trees of their brilliant leaves and turning the land into a blustery white domain as logging camps sprung up in surrounding areas. Farmers, finished with their harvests, enlarged their meager earnings by joining winter lumber crews. Hired on, they drove their oxen, mules, or horses with them into the dense forest to skid logs out to the frozen riverbanks.

Slowly recovering from her accident, Willie was able to handle her occasional bouts of dizziness, but she grappled incessantly with depression. She missed Raven and Nicole who had resettled in their Canadian home, and she hardly had a chance to see her father or Jonathan with winter upon them. Logging camps required constant attention as crews were assigned, temporary buildings constructed, and supplies collected and stored.

Worse yet, she struggled inwardly over her relationship with Jonathan. Although he had made no further mention of their engagement, she felt compelled to stay betrothed. He had saved her life. She dreaded each new day as she warred with her emotions, fighting down the urge to disclose the truth and set them both free. Often she wondered whether he felt obliged to carry on the farce for her father's sake alone.

It was Henry McGee who finally found a cure for Willie's listlessness. With the crews engaged in the woodlands, arrangements had to be made for Irwin's General Store to set up and stock camp supplies. McGee handed the entire intricate operation and details over to her.

But as she regained a sense of renewed spirit, she enveloped herself so deeply in her work and her love for the mills that she began to spin a permanent cocoon around herself, shutting everything and everyone out.

Out in the woods, Jonathan threw himself into the hard work of the logging camp, helping to erect loggers' shanties with huge central chimneys which heated the inside and allowed the cooks to prepare meals on a cambus fire. Logs for cooking were piled on mounds of sand to save the hastily improvised wooden floors from fiery destruction.

Alone in his bunk at night, Jonathan could not shut out the recurring thoughts whirling through his head, and he could not shut out the image of the tawny-haired girl who had carved a place in his heart. Although he had never disclosed his true feelings to her since the accident, he felt if he could work himself hard enough, he could eradicate her from his heart and mind, and set her free. It had worked with other women he knew. He even went so far as to promise himself he would talk to her soon, at the end of his tortuous week, and demand her honesty and search her feelings for some bit of hope she truly cared for him. If he found none he would release her from the engagement, despite the anguish he might have to suffer.

It was a cold day near the end of the week, with sparkling winter snows piled high, when Olaf roused him up before daylight. Together, they trudged northward into the woods where skidders and teamsters were hauling timber out to the river. Sleepy-eyed, Jonathan stomped beside the sturdy foreman who set a driving pace over the icy roadways.

"What's the hurry, man?" he grumbled at the back of the huge Swede who refused to slow down, refused to lose his ever-irritating sense of humor. "Have the beans worked their way to your gut as well?"

Initially, he had dug into the hearty meals of the camp with exuberance, but he quickly discovered he missed the delicate culinary talents of Hannah Svenson. Beans had never been his favorite meal, even aboard his ships, and he daily kept a mental count of the number of slowly dwindling sacks lining the back wall of their shack.

Olaf slackened his pace a bit, pulled his crimson hat farther down over his head of white hair. He wore no coat, despite the bitter cold, only an open vest. His thick red suspenders, holding up his coarse woolen trousers, matched the color of his cap and stood out boldly against the white snow.

"Ve haven't got all day, Jonathan. I need to know how much timber the skidders have hauled out to the roads, so I can forward tallies to McGee. A driver is going into town this afternoon."

"You really are a wood hick," Jonathan mumbled sourly. "How can you be so content away from your family for so long?"

The big Swede laughed. "Because there's a part of every logger's heart in these woods and mountains. It's like the sap running through these trees runs through our veins, too. It's hard to explain—the love, I mean. But even Willie shares it. She has certain Wydcliffe areas protected from logging." He looked at Jonathan with steadfast eyes and smiled. "You get used to the vork, because you come to love these white pines so...and it's such a short time during the vinter months. Except perhaps for you, man. Olaf can tell it's been three long weeks, and you are missing more than yust my sister's cooking."

"Am I that transparent?"

"Oh, ja, for sure," the Swede taunted him.

They walked in silence until they arrived at a man-made clearing. The winter snows had been packed down by workers tramping in and out. Here, skidders chained logs to sleds pulled by teams of oxen and draft horses. The trees, stripped of their bark, slid easily on the snow. The animals heaved their stout shoulders against their sturdy harnesses as they dragged trees to a skidway where teamsters hauled them to the riverbank and piled them in stacks.

"Looks like a good year," Olaf boasted. He stopped to watch a skidder snub a log off the steep side of a hill. One end of the log was chained to the horse, and the other was tied to a tree at the top of the slippery slope. As the animal pulled the log down, a skidder at the top released the rope slowly from around the base of a brace tree.

"Once I saw a log get away and pierce straight through the heart of a huge standing pine in its path," Olaf said. He watched in amusement as Jonathan eased away from the area and moved to a level clearing where choppers were felling trees and hewers were square cutting the logs.

The work was all too familiar to Jonathan, and he could still feel the sting of the blisters under his gloves.

"I could barely keep pace with them," he admitted. The side of the trunk, where the logger who was teaching him to square cut, had been peeled slicker than a smooth cabinet door while his side was like the back of a washboard.

"They keep their axes sharp, so sharp they can cut their hair with them." Olaf chuckled. "I knew an old timer who could also trim his toenails and shave with his axe."

Jonathan rubbed his bearded face. "I think I'll practice a little longer before I give it a try."

Chortling, the big Swede walked down a path, passing a pair of handsomely groomed Clydesdales shouldering a sleigh piled high with logs over twenty-one feet high. Perched like a canary on the top log, the teamster waved and urged his team forward, his long reins flapping in the stiff breeze. Straw had been strewn on the inclines of the icy skid road to slow the descent of cumbersome loads.

"Who marks our timber?" Jonathan asked. He

stopped to listen to the sounds of striking axes and rasping saws spilling out from the mountains. Occasionally, the shouts of *timber* echoed in the air.

"Our landing men at the riverbank." Olaf paused. "Young Dan Barrett does the job best. The lad can swing a wicked brand hammer and never misses a log. He runs the daily tallies to town. It gives the lad some time to court Rachael Kramer."

Olaf pointed to a sleigh which was stopped several feet in front of them with two perfectly matched, dark Percherons. "Look at the old raccoon driving that load."

Jonathan didn't have to ask who. His salt and pepper hair stuck out from all angles underneath his battered felt hat.

The old codger waved. "Hey, big fellow," he shouted. "You are a sight for sore eyes, although you're still uglier than your horse. Thought you had enough blisters on your hands you didn't need them on your backside. Haul it up here, and I'll teach you to drive some real horseflesh."

"I'm not crazy," Jonathan yelled back.

The old man laughed gleefully and slapped his hand on his knee. "You just have to be half-squir..." His voice cracked as he spun around on top of the load and bellowed down, "Look out, son. *Timber... rrr!*"

Together, Jonathan and Olaf dove sideways into the snow at the same split second an enormous white pine crashed down a foot from where they lay sprawled. Jonathan struggled to his feet. His hat was gone, and he was covered in a dusting of snowflakes. He leaped in the direction of the fallen tree.

"Who felled that tree? Find him," he barked savagely. Workers nearby rushed forward under his stinging command.

He cranked his neck around when he heard mumbling from the snowbank beside him. The burly Swede sat up from where he lay like a toppled snowman, rubbed his head, and stood slowly, brushing off snow clinging to his shirt and trousers. "Bumped my head," he mumbled, pulling off his knitted hat and shaking the snow from it. "Must be a rock under there."

Sam scrambled down from the load and rushed over to where the men stood, each one wearing an expression of unbridled anger. "Whew. You got the charm, lads." He whistled. "You both must have lives like a cat."

"I don't give a hoot about cats," Jonathan snarled. "Who in blazes felled the tree?"

"I dunno," Sam replied, rubbing his whiskers and looking up the bank at the fallen tree. "I was too busy watching it tumble your way. I plum forgot to check out who was on the other end."

"Don't tell me this was an accident."

"Nope." The grizzled old man spit a brown stream of tobacco juice in the snow. "I'm crazy and old, but not stupid, son."

They stared at each other in silence, arriving at the same conclusion, each afraid to voice it aloud. Someone wanted him dead.

It had been a long grueling week for Willie, and she welcomed the weekend and a break from her tedious bookkeeping and her monotonous routine. She had poured over stacks of accounts and columns of figures until she thought she'd go blind. Hemmed in by the snowy weather, the days seemed to melt into each other with no beginning, no end.

Looking forward to dinner with both her father and Jonathan, she appeared at the dinner table on time with minutes to spare.

Jonathan's eyebrows shot up the instant he saw her, and he removed his pocket watch to check the time. "You're not feeling well?"

She refused to be needled. "Pray tell, what's growing on your face?"

He rubbed his beard. "You don't like it?"

"It has a certain charm..." She paused and snickered. "...on goats."

He laughed. "I'm glad to see you've recovered, including your sharp tongue."

She slipped into a chair beside him. "Dan Barrett brought the latest tallies from the woods today. It looks like this winter will be one of the best yet. The price and request for lumber is escalating."

"With the market booming, maybe we had better consider lumbering some of the area you set aside," Wydcliffe suggested.

"No, we're not leveling those areas, no matter how profitable the year looks." She reached for her glass of wine and took a sip.

Over the past few years, she had written for reports from logging operations in New England and Canada, all emphasizing the need for forest conservation in order to prolong their productivity. She knew how quickly thoughtless crews could raze a wooded area, destroying even the trees too small to produce lumber in order to satisfy their greed.

She turned her indignation toward Jonathan. "For every tree in the forest which must be hewn in order to be carried in your ships' holds, approximately a quarter of it is wasted by square cutting. The lumber lies on the forest floor and rots. Just rots, mind you."

Jonathan leaned back in his chair. There was a challenge in his voice. "Devise a better plan for stacking a ship's hold to maximum capacity, and I'll consider it."

Willie refused to be baited. She fell silent and watched him stab his fork into a piece of apple pie, and she wondered which of his legs was hollow. The man had not stopped eating since he arrived from the logging camps.

A moment later, the front door blew open, and a brisk wind pushed Roy into the entranceway. Cap in hand, he stood breathless, fat snowflakes falling from his woolen coat buttoned to his neck.

"There's something amiss with Silver Cloud, Miss Willie. You'd better come to the stables and have a look."

Willie bolted from the table, sweeping up her cloak from the hall rack. The blistering cold bit at her face, and snow sifted down in a blinding sheet. Behind her, she heard Roy, her father, and Jonathan treading the slippery path lit only with the eerie light of a lantern Jonathan held high above their heads.

Inside the dimly lit barn, the gray stallion lay sprawled on its side, his withers heaving, laboring to breathe.

"Get another lantern, Roy," she ordered. She knelt in the straw and stroked the horse affectionately on the neck. The stallion's glassy eyes barely moved, but he snorted at the sound of her voice.

Squatting beside her, Jonathan instantly took note of the horse's frothy mouth. "When was the last time you fed him?" he asked the stable boy.

"I gave him his usual feed this morning. Hay and water," Roy said. "Late this afternoon he refused the grain I offered him, but he was still on his feet."

"Notice anyone about the stables?"

The boy shook his head.

He rose and moved to a corner of the stall. A feeding trough held a scant layer of hay covered with molasses. He plunged his hand in and dug through the sticky remainder. Disgustedly, he threw a fistful of hay back into the trough. "He's been poisoned."

Still huddled beside the horse, she looked up horrified. "No," she cried out.

He turned, grabbed her arm, and yanked her up. "Here, have a look. Crowfoot or something like it, I imagine, and deliciously dipped in molasses."

"No, you're lying!" She slapped at his sticky hand and stumbled backwards against the rough planks. Tears welled up and flowed down her cheeks, falling onto the straw beneath her feet.

"Willie," she heard her father say sharply, "the man has no reason to lie."

"Why the horse?" she demanded, splaying her hands. Her pained eyes searched their faces.

Jonathan shook his head and watched a wave of despair wash over her. "I wish I knew," he said softly.

"What should we do?" She choked out the plea. "There's nothing we can do. We can't let the animal suffer. If you like—"

"No, I love him," she cried out again in a ragged voice. Tears continued to course down her face as she dropped to her knees and clutched the horse around his limp neck. "I'm sorry, ol' boy," she said over and over again. "I'm so...so sorry."

Minutes seemed like hours as Jonathan watched the girl, hunched in the cold straw. In the mean-time, Dalton Wydcliffe had ordered a pistol sent down from the manor. In the halo of the lantern, the old man stood, gripping the cold heavy gun. With tired eyes and a heartsick demeanor, he regarded his daughter still kneeling in the wilted straw.

Jonathan rinsed his hands in a bucket, stepped forward, and took the burden from the elderly man's tired hands. "Here, I'll do it," he offered.

"No," Willie said, stumbling up. Her voice was as bitter cold as the snowy weather outside. Tiny pieces of straw clung to the back of her velvet cloak. Her hair, which had come undone, tumbled in confusion over her shoulders and back. For one brief moment, Jonathan was sure he saw hate flicker in her eyes, before she disguised it with her grief. She swiped once at her tears with the back of her hand, and then held it out.

They stared at each other for what seemed like an eternity before he dropped the gun into her cold palm.

CHAPTER FIFTEEN

CHRISTMAS TIPTOED IN WITH A series of snow squalls dumping piles of snow on the landscape, reshaping it into fairyland of white. The snows were so deep Raven and her family were unable to visit during the holiday season. Lost in her own world of grief over her beloved horse, Willie paid no attention to decorating the manor and barely acknowledged the array of clothes Jonathan gave her, including the latest styles sent from Baltimore. She did go so far as to present both her father and him with a new gold pocket watch on Christmas Eve, engraved with the Wain-Wydcliffe intricate insignia.

In reality, she was bitter and angry. She knew nothing could ever bring back her precious horse. When she learned of the attempt on Jonathan's and Olaf's lives, she realized the magnitude of the danger surrounding her. What seemed like a game of sheer harassment had now become a deadly one. The rules had changed. She would have to be careful. She could trust no one.

Her anger turned into fury every time she thought about her father, an ailing old man, who was spending the last precious moments of his life fighting to salvage their business. She knew he would fight to the end, and she vowed silently to fight beside him. No one would ever lay their hands on Wydcliffe mills as long as she was breathing.

Now, as she worked in the study with a blazing fire in the hearth to keep her company, her thoughts circled back to Jonathan. He was leaving for Baltimore soon and would be returning in the spring. She wondered whether he was planning to break their engagement before he left and set her free. Instead of being pleased as she thought she would be, she found herself feeling even more empty and forlorn. He had saved her life. During the time she was recovering, he had shouldered the mills, assuming her tasks along with his. As much as she hated to admit it, she was becoming fond of him. But what did it matter? Now, he was leaving.

She would be alone.

Again.

If Jonathan was unsure of what Willie's reaction would be after the death of her horse, he wasn't quite prepared for her persistent and stoic silence. In rare bouts of conversation, she carried on like nothing had happened. Even though she was painfully hurting, she bottled everything inside, refusing to share her aching loss, spinning herself tighter and tighter into her self-made cocoon. By day, she threw herself intensely into the mills with a hard, cold, and often driving dedication. By night, she locked herself into the study and relentlessly pursued the mounds of paperwork produced from the winter lumbering, often working until weariness physically overtook her.

Only by chance did he invade her privacy one evening when he went to the library to borrow a book. She was hunched over a ledger at her father's desk. They contemplated each other for a moment before she broke the uncomfortable silence.

"I'm afraid I haven't been pleasant company lately," she confessed, closing the ledger and standing to chase the numbness from her body.

"I'd be lying if I said I hadn't noticed." He crossed the study to the liquor cabinet to pour himself a drink. He held up a decanter. "I was hoping we could talk. Can I get you anything?"

She shook her head. "Conrad has been supplying me with coffee and tea." She sauntered to the rosy hearth, sat down on the floor, and tucked her feet under her billowing, black taffeta skirt. She pulled her shawl around her shoulders and watched him pour a liberal draught of rum. His angular profile was highlighted by the crimson glow from the fire. He carefully replaced the top on the crystal decanter and secured a seat next to her on the thick Oriental rug. The heat from the fire was comforting.

"Papa says you're leaving for Baltimore within the week."

"There are a few things I have to finish back home if I plan to come back this spring and supervise the finishing mill." He took a sip of rum. "My brothers will be quite capable of running things on the coast once I get them acquainted with the tasks

I usually perform." He neglected to tell her he was hiring someone to check out the list of names he had collected, including some of her mill workers. He couldn't risk upsetting her more.

He swirled the liquid in his glass. "Most of all, I'm concerned about us. We've never had a chance to talk with the winter logging operations taking up every minute of our waking hours." He promised himself he would discuss the betrothal as soon as she recovered. He remembered the many nights he had heard her crying in her room before retiring late.

"Willie, you can't go on like this," he said, his tone scolding. "Your hurt and anger has locked everyone out. You barely speak to the men at the mill. You refuse to talk to me. No one can even venture a guess about what might make you happy. Even I have run out of ideas, except one."

"And what is it?" he heard her whisper.

"Willie, Willie, Willie," she heard him say, "love is built on trust, not silence and suspicion."

She stared at him for a lengthy moment. "How can I convince myself to trust anyone? Everything and everyone I ever care about seem to slip through my fingers like water. My mother, Silver Cloud...soon Papa...and maybe these mills. My world is crumbling around me, and I can't put it back together, no matter how hard I try." She hung her head and added hoarsely, "You don't know what it's like. You have a family, loved ones who care for you. You've never been alone with nowhere to turn or no one to turn to."

"You're not alone. There's Sam and me, and dozens of other people who care. But you have to reach out."

"It's difficult. Especially after everything that's happened."

"Yes, I know. But it's even more difficult when you deliberately shut people out."

"I don't," she insisted.

"Yes, you do. You've created your own little world. You take breakfast in your room and supper in this study. The rest of the time is spent safely tucked away with work. I feel like a three-eyed toad."

He reached for his drink. Deadly silence, like an invisible wall, isolated them.

"Damn it. Say something...anything."

Hard as she tried, she could not stem the stinging tears starting to spill down her cheeks. "I don't know what to do," she said, her voice faltering. "Don't you understand? Everything happened so fast. Your arrival. The engagement. My horse. Threats against peoples' lives." She buried her face in her hands and choked back a sob. "I need you more than ever, but I need time to sort things through, to discover my true feelings."

He set his glass aside and pulled her gently into his arms while his heart raced with joy at her latest admission. For the first time, he felt whole and complete. He didn't care why she had a sudden change of heart. Be it loneliness, be it security, be it fear. Given time, he would win her with kindness and trust. He held her snugly against him until her sobbing ceased.

"I'll give you all the time you need," he whispered, "but I fear I'll go mad if you take too long."

She smiled and leaned against him. "How long

will you be gone?"

"A month. Maybe two. Please tell me you'll at least miss me a little."

"Yes," she answered, and turning, lifted her hand to touch his face. Unconsciously she was leaning toward him. Her shawl slipped from her shoulders. Unplanned, the proximity was too potent. With their breaths intermingling, their lips sought out each other's and met for an electrifying moment. A surge of energy coursed through his veins as the kiss deepened. He reached up to hold the back of her head in his hand. Her lips were soft and supple beneath the kiss, and he tenderly forced her mouth open to caress her tongue. Gently he drew her down to the rug before the fire and stretched out beside her. He held her with one arm as his other stroked her breasts through the thin layers of fabric. His lips never left her mouth, greedily absorbing the sweetness of her kisses. He could smell the rose scent on her hair, and he was dizzy with desire to love her. She was everything he wanted and more.

He lifted his mouth from hers and trailed a wave of kisses down her throat and back up to her earlobe before he recaptured her mouth again, his lips burning hot against hers. Her hands encircled his neck and she rose up against him and writhed beneath his torso lying half upon her and pinning her beneath.

Abruptly, as if reason overtook desire for both of them, her eyes flew open and she broke the kiss, releasing her hands from around his neck. "Jonathan, please," she whispered.

He felt her pushing against his shoulders, and he raised himself slightly, noting the fear in her eyes and realizing how innocent and vulnerable she was.

"I'm not sorry this happened," he whispered hoarsely, kissing her swollen lips again, wishing his pounding head would grow calm. He rolled away from her, allowing her to quickly straighten her clothes. "Next time, my dear, I might not have any willpower left to restrain myself."

He stood and pulled her to her feet.

Together, silently, they walked upstairs. They stopped outside her door.

"Have a safe journey," she said.

He placed a hand on her shoulder. "There's a favor I must ask." He frowned, a warning cloud settled on his features before he spoke. "Please, whatever you do, don't do anything to draw attention to yourself or the mills. And for heaven's sake, don't provoke anyone unnecessarily, including John Pierce. Understand?"

She nodded, and he blew out a breath of relief. "Can I bring you a surprise from Baltimore?"

But it was he who was startled when she reached up on tiptoe and kissed him quickly on the lips.

"Just yourself," she said.

CHAPTER SIXTEEN

THE NEXT MORNING BEFORE THE winter sun had a chance to take the bite from the air, Willie awoke to see him off. She hated the thought of having to part. She hadn't planned on having feelings for him. She hadn't planned on having feelings for any man. It was a new experience. To her relief, with the caretaker hovering over them and fussing with Jonathan's belongings, the parting was quick, neither tender, nor tearful.

She left afterwards for the Hornet's Nest, impatient to speak with her father alone.

She found him, standing beside his desk, head bent over a letter.

"Just came in this morning." He glanced up and waved it under her nose. "It's postmarked over three weeks ago. Your sister is arriving this afternoon. It seems Thomas has business in the nearby area."

"Today?" Willie clapped her hands and squealed a cry of joy.

"You miss her, don't you?" he asked.

She beamed, and he didn't need an answer.

Moments later, Henry McGee's balding head

appeared around the doorframe. A plain-faced, honest bachelor in his mid-fifties, he had a quick mind and a love for figures. Even though he was well paid, he was a frugal sort and unselfishly spent most of his wages to help support a large family of brothers and sisters. But his best trait was he always had his finger on everything happening at the Hornet's Nest.

"Pierce just rode up to the rail," he warned, ducking back into his office.

Minutes later, John Pierce was seated in a leather chair in front of Dalton Wydcliffe's desk with Willie in a matching chair beside him.

"I have to admit," he said to Wydcliffe, "you have me over a barrel. I'm prepared to pay any price you want for your western piece of land. With spring closing in, I'd like to start construction of some stables."

Willie met his eyes briefly and smiled to disguise her annoyance at his brazen attitude. "There's a lot of other acreage outside town just as suitable," she said.

"But none as accessible to town as yours."

"Ferguson had some acres adjacent to ours."

Pierce frowned, crossing his black cleated boots, impeccably polished, on top of each other. "He's already deeded the land to Clara Jeanette for a homestead."

"Who's the lucky dog she has finally put on a leash?" She didn't try to hide her cynical tone.

Amused, Pierce leaned toward her. "No one yet. But she'll have no problem. Someone will be pleased to marry her, considering—" He stopped short.

"—considering her father is rich. Money makes a poor blanket on a cold night." The words were out before she realized she uttered them. She caught the reprimand in her father's eyes.

"Just how many horses do you plan to acquire?" she asked.

"A dozen, I imagine, to start."

"Hmmm." She drummed her fingers on the chair's arm. "You'll have a hard time getting them around here."

Pierce cleared his throat uncomfortably. "I plan to purchase them in New York, but there are more details to be worked out. The land and building come first." He scowled. "You won't get a better offer. It's been lumbered. Your tract is useless now."

She met his pointed gaze with one just as sharp. "I've never considered land useless, Mr. Pierce. In the next twenty years, this town may grow and push outward beyond our cleared land."

Pierce's face mottled. "That's doubtful."

"Well, I don't want to sell until I have time to think about it." She rose, walked to the window and stared pensively at the sun glinting off the water below in the pond. "Until I talk with our contractor for the finishing mill, the land is not for sale. Eventually, everything we produce with a new mill will have to be stored from the weather. The western land might be an ideal place."

Jonathan's warning came flying back to the recess of her mind. She grew serious. Was it possible Pierce was the cause of their problems? She cast the doubt aside. The man was no fool. He'd never risk getting caught at anything that could bring the law down on his head. He knew the Hornet's Nest crew well. In fact, he knew most of the crews at the Wasp and Black Widow mills. To rile them would be to risk swift vengeance. A thousand useless acres of land would hardly be worth it.

Standing, Pierce stiffened, and tried to mask his indignation with a tight smile. Ignoring her, he extended his chunky hand to Wydcliffe instead. "I'll not waste your time, but if you should reconsider, you know how to reach me." He left, his cleats tapping out a harsh rhythm on the rough wooden floors.

Wydcliffe glanced at his plucky daughter, now studying Pierce's retreating back. "I assume he annoys you so much you had to go to all lengths to annoy him?"

"He's like a mosquito bite. The more you scratch it, the worse it itches."

"You may have made an enemy."

"He was never my friend."

Dalton Wydcliffe chuckled and the strain of the last few minutes eased. "What tact, my dear daughter. What tact."

She shrugged, a puzzled expression clouding her face. "Do you think Pierce wants the land for something besides horses? To pawn illegal goods? To deal in a business where privacy is important and the scrutiny by our townsfolk wouldn't come into play? He's no equestrian, Papa, for sure."

Her father lit his pipe and sent a puff of smoke into the air. "True, but I've checked to see if he's buying illegal merchandise and he's clean as a stripped log. The goods he now peddles come by keelboat from Williamsport, purchased from honest sources."

Willie bit her lip. Nothing made any sense. She felt like she was in a round room looking for a corner. She could think of no one who had not been on cordial terms with them. "I wonder who wants us out of business?" she asked thinking aloud.

"I don't think anyone does." Wydcliffe blew a puff of smoke again and settled the pipe comfortably in the corner of his mouth. "They want me out of business, not you. After your injury, we had no further problems until your complete recovery. The incident at the splash dam was meant for Jonathan, not you. Whoever slashed those ropes never figured you would go into the water after Nicole. Someone wants Jonathan removed permanently judging from the size of the tree they tried to use. Destroying the horse was to scare me off."

"Who would want Jonathan killed?"

"He's been known to be a ruthless opponent if given reason enough. If he married you, he'd be a formidable opponent to deal with. Word has it he tangled with a group of men preying on East coast cargo ships some time ago. They killed his best friend. He pursued them for over a year until bringing two of the four to justice."

"What happened to the other two?"

"He killed them. In a fair fight, I understand."

"He doesn't seem like a killer," she said impulsively, shivering. "Though heaven knows, he can be easily provoked."

He looked at her annoyed. "He's not. He's a good man who believes in justice. When a man acts in self-defense, he doesn't deserve to be branded a cold-hearted killer."

"He has a temper," she rejoined curtly.

"Oh, my dear. A skunk telling the pig he smells."

"Papa, how unkind."

"Yet truthful. You are both so willful and hot-tempered."

"Exactly my point." She stabbed a finger in the air. "We couldn't possibly live a pleasant life if we're constantly warring."

"Maybe not," he agreed with a sigh.

"Tell me, Papa. Honestly, would you be angry if things did not work out, if I didn't marry him?"

Startled, her father looked over at her. "Angry? Of course not. I'm fond of the lad, I admit, but I'd never want either of my daughters to marry someone they didn't love. Are you having second thoughts?" His face was filled with fatherly concern.

She searched for a plausible explanation. There was no use in adding more worry to what he already had. "I think I need more time."

"Give yourself all the time you need, my dear. There's no hurry. I'll make no further mention of your betrothal until you're certain."

Grateful, she smiled, and a comfortable silence fell about them. Her father returned to paperwork on his desk.

Several minutes later, she spoke. "Sam once said he doubts you'll ever sell that piece of land."

Surprised, Wydcliffe lifted his head. "What else did the old coot say?"

"He said Mother wanted it, and you paid Isaac Wain for a clear title."

"Sam talks too much." He grunted.

This time she refused to be rebuffed. "Well, is it true?"

"Yes," he admitted. "But it was a wise investment. We retrieved choice timber stands from it."

"Why did Mother want it?"

"It was pleasant. Peaceful. We often rode out there." The old man fell silent, and a pained look fell over his weary face.

Willie decided not to pressure him further. There was no need to stir up old ghosts. And Sam Bradley probably knew more than he was telling her.

"Let's take the day off," she suggested, "and head back to the manor. It'll give us time to get ready for Nicole and Raven."

The mere mention of his daughter's and granddaughter's names put a sparkle in his sunken, dull eyes.

"I'll drive," she offered and tugged him up by the arm.

"No, it's best if I do," he countered. "You're too impatient with my old nag. She's like an arthritic old man. She needs time to limber up before she can reach a good trot."

Willie grinned.

It was good to see her father back to his old self again.

There was noise, confusion, and gaiety inside Granny Gordon's Tavern as loggers gathered to eat their midday meal, but the conversation at a table in a far corner of the room was anything but pleasant.

"It doesn't look like it will be easy to acquire Wydcliffe's tract of land as we earlier believed," John

Pierce sputtered over a tankard of ale and plate of roasted chicken. "It looks like Wain and his damn finishing mill will keep the thousand acres tied up just in case there's need for expansion. Dammit. We were so close to getting it right from under the old man's nose." He leaned back in his chair, his napkin flapping from underneath his thick chin.

"I can't figure out which one of us is the fool," Matthew Reed replied, his tone coolly disapproving. "I never figured the old man would just up and sell a thousand acres without a good reason. He's got enough money to buy the entire doggone town if he wants." He glanced at Pierce, stuffing food in his mouth like a starved dog.

"We had the squeeze on him until Wain showed up. A few more unfortunate accidents might have convinced him to get out of the business and Clearfield before he lost money and lives." Pierce attacked a dumpling on his plate. "We have to remove Wain when he returns. Then there might be a chance for you to get real serious with Wydcliffe's daughter. In case you haven't noticed, she's a real treasure…but with a iron will." His laughter filled the smoky tavern.

"So I've noticed. But don't get any funny notions about harming her." Matthew Reed leaned close. A shadow of alarm crossed his face. "We'd have every mill hand in the county down our backs if they ever found out we were responsible for the mishap at the dam. Some of those mill hands would tear us to shreds and leave only splinters to pick their teeth with."

Pierce snickered through crooked teeth. "Calm down. The fool woman wasn't supposed to be in the water. I figured Wain would do the heroic honors."

Reed took a sip of ale and wiped his mouth on his sleeve. "Word has it they're still betrothed, but only to keep tongues from wagging. It seems Wilhelmina is having second thoughts." His eyes glittered. The thought of possessing a girl as beautiful as her was sheer joy, and the thought of possessing her father's money was blissful.

"We were so close during winter logging," he continued, "if old man Bradley hadn't gotten in the way. After the horse incident, I know Wydcliffe would have cashed in without Wain around. The old man isn't feeling too chipper. The gal might be independently wealthy soon." He downed the last of his ale and signaled for a serving girl to refill his mug. "What's our next move?"

"What's our next move? You fool! What do you think?" Pierce slammed his chunky hand on the table and released his fork which bounced and clattered to the floor. "We dispose of the Baltimore son-of-a-sea captain permanently. The big lout could mean trouble if he started snooping in the wrong places. He doesn't give up easily. I hear he's pretty decent with quite a few weapons. Killed a few men, too."

Reed's eyes grew round like wooden wash tubs. "According to Dalton Wydcliffe, he's due back in a few weeks."

Pierce grinned maliciously. "Giving us adequate time to come up with a plan for his early retirement from the sawmill business." He licked his thick lips. His ruddy cheeks flushed even brighter from the effects of the ale. His laughter turned into an eerie howl before his fingers tightened on the fork a serving girl had slipped onto the table, and he resumed eating voraciously like a wolf devouring his prey.

CHAPTER SEVENTEEN

THE GRAY SKIES OF MARCH opened up and poured their contents over the land, soaking the emerging grass and swelling the streams. Trees and bushes, just barely budding, drank in the moisture.

A wet spring was usually a welcome one. Winter snows coupled with the rains made for ideal river conditions. Enlarged by the runoff, the streams rose high enough to bring timber down from the mountains into the mills, down the Susquehanna River, and onward to the coast.

But excessive rains created a devil's playground as they flooded the riverbanks and washed rollaways into swollen streams, tangling the lumber with timber from other mills and sweeping the whole lot of them downstream to be lost or discovered at the wrong mills. When it happened, respectable sawmill operators reimbursed the proper mill for the lumber or arranged a trade. It was a headache and bitter loss for many when a mill operator was less than honest and rebranded the lumber as his own.

Throughout the day, Willie could hear the steady

rains drumming against the windowpane, and she hoped the Susquehanna was still at a safe level. It was already the sixth day of nonstop downpours, and the weather was beginning to hamper mill operations. The crews were anything but pleasant as they waded through mud and labored in damp, chilly clothes and water-logged boots.

As she dressed for dinner, she could smell the rich odor of chocolate sneaking up from the kitchen. The only good thing during the soggy week had been the arrival of Raven and Nicole. With the little girl's infectious laughter ringing through the house, everyone's disposition had done an about face. The cook was merrily preparing enough food to keep an army on its feet for a month. Conrad was humming. And her father's face had taken on a renewed shine. Willie's spirits soared as she left her room, and she prayed the gaiety inside the manor would never end.

A knock on the front door sounded the moment her feet touched the bottom step. Startled, she watched the front door open.

Johnathan staggered in. Water splashed off his coarse brown overcoat and his felt hat was pulled down to protect his face. He stamped his boots and shook his head, sending droplets flying over her and the entranceway.

"Heave Ho," he bellowed, peeling his coat off. He tossed the hat on a peg. "Gather the bloody animals. Noah will be here at dawn." His deep voice echoed over the steady beat of the rain hammering on the roof.

"Jonathan," she gasped, "you aren't supposed to be here for another week."

"I finished early in Baltimore and swam straight up the Susquehanna." He crossed the space between them and clucked her under the chin, bent, and brushed his lips over hers for a second. She jumped backwards, her heart thudding from his intimate gesture, and was glad for the icy water falling from his clothes to cool her warm face.

"We're just about to have dinner. Raven and Nicole are here." She shook the droplets from her skirt to distract herself from her reeling emotions. "I'll have Conrad draw you a warm bath."

"Tell Hannah to send a plate of food to my room. I can't wait. I haven't eaten all day." He started up the steps and turned. His look was tender as it touched hers. They stared at each other for a long, lingering moment. "I'll be down for dessert."

"We're having chocolate cake."

"My second favorite," he said, smiling.

"And your first choice is....?"

"Guess." He winked and turned. Whistling, he hurried up the steps.

Willie brushed a curl of hair from her flaming cheeks. She wanted to tell him she had missed him and was glad he had returned, but it seemed like something only a foolish schoolgirl might do. Instead, she rushed toward the dining room with the tune he had begun to merrily whistle following her like a shadow.

A half hour later, Nicole whooped in delight when he strode through the French doors. He held a golden-haired doll in a delicate, aquamarine dress.

"You remembered," she breathed excitedly. "She's just like the one we talked about in the picture book. Oh, Jonathan, thank you." She hugged him vigorously.

He laughed in a deep, rich voice. "It was indeed worth the effort, Nicole. I was afraid I'd have to send this to Canada, but you being here is truly a wonderful surprise for a lonely soul."

"Come, you must sit beside me," she exclaimed and dragged him to a spot near the end of the table and patted the seat beside her chair. "We're having chocolate cake."

Dalton Wydcliffe, waiting until all the excitement subsided, spoke. "Good to have you back, Jonathan. How was your trip?"

"Splendid. Everything is arranged for my brothers to handle the shipping. I secured all the information we need to buy machinery for the finishing mill." He nodded toward Conrad teetering in the doorway with an armload of boxes, "I even had time to do some shopping."

The next hour was spent examining the many gifts he had selected for everyone. For Dalton Wydcliffe, he had purchased imported smoking tobacco and a new rosewood pipe. For Raven, he had selected the latest copies of Godey's Ladies Book and several bolts of expensive East Indian muslin. For Nicole, there was a green velvet riding habit, doll clothes, and a miniature clipper ship in a bottle. And for Willie, an intricate gold inlaid oriental bracelet, an ivory music box, and a fawn-colored hat equally as beautiful as the one she'd lost in the pond.

From across the room, Willie watched him bond with all her family members. Despite the long journey and his weariness, he leaned back in his chair and enjoyed the scene as everyone unwrapped the gifts and squealed or murmured with excitement.

Laughter, warmth, and merriment filled the air.

Jonathan Wain looked contented. Like he had come home. And for a surprising moment, Willie thought to herself...*this is where he belongs.*

A week later, despite everyone's hope for sunshine, the rains continued nonstop, weeping more misery on the settlement, swelling the riverbanks and flooding lowlands. Muscles ached as crews scurried to move timber to higher ground and keep rollaways along the banks of the streams from being washed away under the river's wrath.

Jonathan threw himself gladly into the mill work, overseeing the construction and dividing Wydcliffe's load with Willie. But by the beginning of the second week, she felt an invisible barrier rise up between them.

At first, she mistook his silence toward her as a sign of weariness, but as the week wore on she was certain something was amiss. During the few spare moments they shared, he treated her with an unrestrained aloofness.

Unable to bear it any longer, she confronted him in the library one evening. Slouched in a gold velvet side chair, feet propped on the cluttered desktop nearby, he barely acknowledged her entrance. A brandy snifter dangled carelessly from his hand. **His rumpled shirt, half-open down his chest,** revealed a mat of curly dark hair.

Jonathan Wain was drunk.

In fact, he had hours ago bypassed tipsy and had advanced straight to thoroughly pickled.

It took Willie less than a minute to realize it, and she eyed him with caution. "Change in taste?" She gestured toward the decanter almost deplete of brandy. She knew he preferred rum, especially after dinner.

"I was just about to ask you the same thing, my dear." He looked up with blood-shot eyes.

"I don't know what you mean."

"Let's not be coy," he said dryly. He leveled a deadly look at her. "I had the pleasure of dining at Granny Gordon's Tavern this week. It seems you neglected to tell me John Pierce is still after your land. You also neglected to tell me half the town believes our engagement is dissolved as well."

He laughed a careless laugh. "The entire male population is buzzing with the expectancy of you coming out from under the oppressive chains of our betrothal. Dear old Mrs. Payne even tried to console me in Irwin's General Store. How very clever of you to wait until I was safely out of the picture to start spreading the rumor."

She bristled. "I don't know what you're talking about."

"Come, come, Willie. Even Pierce himself expressed his condolences to me."

"Jonathan, believe me, I haven't said anything to anyone." She fought the heavy feeling beginning to stir in her stomach.

He tried to snarl, but his voice came out as a slurred accusation instead. "You make a good actress, Wilhelmina. You lead me on in the study, send me packing to Baltimore, and spread the rumor our engagement has crumbled. Naturally, everyone will think I'm suffering from a broken heart and turned tail to heal. And you? Well, you're off the hook nicely, aren't you?"

"You're crazy. Besides being three sheets to the wind," she sputtered and marched past him to the fireplace. She bent and threw some logs onto the dying flames. They crackled and hissed and grew bright.

"Maybe both." He unwound his body from the chair to stalk over to where she stood by the hearth. "Tell me, my dear, who's the lucky fop you've set your cap for now?"

"No one, jackass." She threw him a hostile glare. "Since when does the local gossip concern you so much? As I recall, it was you who said you didn't give a tinker's damn what this town thinks. Had I wanted to call off our betrothal, I would have never been lily-livered enough to do it underhandedly. You know I never cared a flying fig what anyone thinks. Give my blackened character at least a little credit."

"Ha! Pity there isn't a darker color than black."

Nose to nose, he was so close she could smell the sweet scent of blackberry brandy on his breath.

"If the truth be known, Jonathan Wain, it's not the town gossip at all that's bothering you," she said. "The idea of being anything but the devoted business partner is as revulsive to you as it is to me. Our engagement has been a bloody farce from the start."

She was on a roll. "You're obnoxious. Overbearing. And I've no need of someone who has such little trust in me. This paltry mess will be fixed tomorrow. I *am* telling my father we ended the engagement. You're free to do whatever you damn well please."

She caught his surprised expression, but spun and headed for the door. When he moved to block her path, she tried to skirt around him, but he caught the soft flesh of her upper arm and stopped her.

"Playing the innocent betrayed role now?" he asked.

"Oh, you overgrown, three-sheets-to-the-wind oaf. This is no flimsy school play." She stamped her foot down hard on his instep and saw pain briefly cross his face before anger returned. "Get out of my way."

"Just tell me, Willie, the name of the man who turned your head and heart so quickly."

She studied him for a prolonged minute. She jerked her arm away. "If there was someone else, do you honestly think I *wouldn't* tell you? When have I ever *lied* to you?"

She wasn't prepared for his next move. He tipped his head and his mouth descended upon hers, stopping any words from tumbling from her lips. He pulled her body against his with a fervor she had never known before. He ravaged her mouth with his lips and tongue, slipping his tongue past her teeth to pillage the deep recess of her mouth.

Crushed tightly against his massive chest, she realized she was experiencing the passion of a man with emotions barely in control. She could taste the brandy on his lips and feel his arousal as he pressed his loins firmly against her body. He continued to kiss her until he was filled, until she thought she couldn't breathe.

Setting her aside, he strode out of the library, slamming the door with a thud.

She shuddered. For a long time she stood, staring into space until the initial shock of their encounter passed before she extinguished the lanterns in the study with shaking hands.

Later, safely cuddled underneath her covers, she watched the flames from the fireplace flicker and make dancing designs on her white ceiling. She rubbed her tired eyes, wondering what had made him act with such boldness. How could he accuse her of being an actress, a liar? She sighed, thinking it was best they were no longer emotionally attached. But if it were so, why did her heart cry out a totally different message? Why did she like the taste of him on her lips? Or his body pressed intimately to hers?

She heard him climb the stairs and stop for a second outside her door, and she lay frozen, motionless, until his footsteps continued onward up to the third floor.

But it was many hours later when she finally figured out what had really happened. The bloody Limey had been pie-eyed, for sure, but he had been spouting the truth. A malicious rumor spread about town was exactly what someone would need to further their unstable relationship and drive a wedge between them. And it was a perfect way to further the rift in their partnership and divide their loyalties.

He had been a fool, a silly fool.

But so had she.

And together, they had fallen into the same trap.

CHAPTER EIGHTEEN

THE DYING FIRE IN WILLIE'S bedroom cast an eerie golden glow over the room, unable to reach the far corners still shadowed and dark, as she rose the next morning and splashed water onto her face from a basin atop her washstand. She moved noiselessly about her room, not wanting to awaken the sleeping household.

Downstairs, she unlatched the door and eased out, the heels of her boots crunching softly on the gravel drive. Outside the air was crisp, needing the warmth of the sun. Long before she reached the stable doors, she could smell the familiar odor of sun-ripened hay and musty grain.

Once inside the semi-darkness of the barn, she made her way to Blackjack's stall and eased in beside him. He snorted in recognition and whinnied in anticipation.

"Mr. Wain said no one is supposed to ride Blackjack," she heard Roy say behind her, just outside the stall. The young boy yawned and rubbed his eyes. "Last time he had him out, he was hard to handle."

"Go back to bed, Roy." She removed her blanket, bridle, and saddle from a row of pegs along the stable wall. It had been months since the death of her horse. She had not ridden since that night, preferring to use the buggy. But now, she had finally worked up enough courage, she was not about to be dissuaded.

"I ain't supposed to let you take him," the boy insisted, yawning again.

"I'm not supposed to," she corrected him.

"That's what I said."

"You forget who owns this horse, Roy."

Her mouth set in a grim line, she hoisted her saddle on the horse's back and tightened the girth snugly.

"I ain't forgot." The boy yawned again.

"Good. You *haven't* forgotten. Go back to sleep." She led the horse into the courtyard with Roy stumbling behind her.

"Say it anyway you like, Miss Willie, but Mr. Wain will be hopping mad. My hide won't be worth two bits, a swig of whiskey, or a trip to hell."

She swung into the saddle and brought the skittish horse under control. "If he gives you any trouble, I'll personally tell him where to go." She turned Blackjack away from the courtyard toward the open road, and she nudged him effortlessly into a trot.

Shivering, Roy watched her ride off. Her hair, sifted by the spring breeze, swirled out in undulating waves. "She can tame any wild creature with four legs faster than I can spit," he muttered aloud, his sleepy voice full of awe.

From the shadows of the paddock, Jonathan nodded. "And she can ride like the devil, too."

The boy flinched in fright.

"I'm sorry, Mr. Wain, I tried to stop her."

He shook his head. "There's no one on God's green earth who can stop Wilhelmina Wydcliffe when she decides to do something. Get some sleep, boy," he said and headed for the manor.

When Willie walked through the kitchen door an hour later, she was unprepared to collide with Jonathan sitting in the breakfast salon nursing a cup of coffee. She halted abruptly and stared at him. His face was drawn and sallow, and he looked like he had been dragged over the stable floor. He returned her stare with a faint smile. His bloodshot eyes studied her flushed cheeks and womanly curves not well concealed beneath her riding breeches.

"The morning ride must have been good for you."

"How would you know?" She turned to retreat to the kitchen.

"Coward," she heard him mumble. "How is it you can manage four-legged beasts so easily, but shy away from those with two?"

She retrieved a mug from the cupboard, poured herself a cup of coffee from the back of the stove, and returned to the salon, leaning against the doorjamb. "The four-legged kind never turn on you like a weasel."

He tried to laugh, but it came out as a pained chuckle. "I'm not good at apologies, nor eating crow, so I'll say this only once. I'm sorry for last night. I had too much to drink. If we have to work together, we can't have this estranged malice between us. I'm calling another truce."

"Ah-ha," she scoffed, her expression one of pained tolerance. "Yes. Let's not disrupt our business partnership any more than necessary. At least we do agree on a few things—keeping money in our pockets and keeping these mills running."

But she wasn't finished. Her voice rose a few decibels as she continued. "Let's get one thing settled. You keep all your advice and orders limited to the mills. Never. Ever. Interfere with the manor, stable, or its operations. And never tell me what horse I can ride."

"Yes, for the love of the Almighty. Yes, just don't shout," he begged, cradling his head between his hands.

She snickered. "You obviously have trouble handling gossip and your liquor." She started to slide into a seat across from him, but a loud rapping on the back door forced her back to her feet.

"Now what?" he groaned, his hands still holding his head.

Willie crossed the distance to the door as Roy burst through, red-faced and panting.

"Someone broke into the Hornet's Nest last night," he said. "McGee's waiting for you there."

"Get the buggy ready," Jonathan instructed, rising. He turned to Willie. Her eyes had widened to the size of wagon wheels. "I'll have Conrad tell your father later. Let's not wake him until we've taken a look." Without further comment, he disappeared from the salon.

The ride to the mill was longer than Willie ever imagined it could be. Yet, she never imagined the shambles that would greet them.

"Holy hell!" The words slipped past Jonathan's

lips when they stepped into McGee's office. The room had been ransacked. Debris was strewn over the entire room. Drawers were torn from the desks, and overturned cabinets spewed papers, receipts, ledgers, and contracts onto the floor. Henry McGee knelt in the center of the disorder and shuffled through a mountain of papers. At the sound of Jonathan's voice, he glanced up.

"I don't suppose we'll ever be able to tell if anything is missing, will we?" His eyes like an eagle scanned the room, and he moved to a spot near a pile of papers. He riffled through them, pausing and squinting at one before he folded it into quarters and tucked it into his chest pocket. "Did they celebrate downstairs as well?" he asked.

"Everything, including the machinery, down on the mill floor is untouched." McGee scrambled to his feet. "Looks like someone spent a lot of time rummaging in the land contract and leasing drawers. The others were pitched out for spite."

Willie blew out a breath of pent-up air. "Or maybe anger? Maybe they didn't find what they wanted?" She picked her way cautiously among the papers and around an overturned chair. She was almost certain she could smell the faint scent of perfume lingering in the air. "Maybe we *were* lucky."

"Lucky?" McGee's eyes flashed with outrage. "You call this lucky? It'll take days, maybe weeks of work to get everything back in order. I was hoping for a few days off to visit my family."

"Would it have been better if they pitched everything into the water?" she asked tersely. "Or lit everything with a match? Or damaged our machinery?"

"For the love of Pete, Willie. Don't shout," Jonathan batted at the air with both hands, palms down. "My head is pounding like someone beat it with an axe. I swear on my mother's grave, I'll never touch brandy again for as long as I live." He rubbed the back of his neck, walked to window, and looked out. "And let's not alert the whole dang town about this either," he added. "We don't want to give anyone more ideas. Among the three of us we should be able to get this sorted into piles so we can operate. When we get it passable, I guarantee you a few days off, McGee."

He glanced at Willie. "Let's go to the tavern for breakfast. It's going to be a long day."

Willie's stomach rumbled, but she ignored it. "I can eat later. I'll stay and help Henry. I'm not in the best of moods for the whole town to see me."

He stood still, studying her with a piercing gray-eyed glare, before he pulled out the paper from his coat pocket and handed it to her. "We'll eat now," he said tonelessly.

She unfolded what looked like a map and studied the soiled mark left on it. It was a boot print, complete with the clear-edged indentation from a cleat.

For a moment, they stared at each other, the air thick with silence. There were a lot of men in town who wore cleats to prolong the life of their boots, but both knew instantly, between them, they could easily name three people—Olaf Svenson, John Pierce, and Charles Ferguson.

CHAPTER NINETEEN

INSIDE GRANNY GORDON'S TAVERN, JONATHAN and Willie found an unoccupied table in the back corner of the room. Jonathan chose a seat where he could see the door and leaned back, propping his heels on the rung of a vacant chair flanking them.

The room was filled with an assortment of tables, covered with scraps of calico and surrounded by mismatched chairs. The dingy gray ceiling was painted only with the accumulation of cooking grease and smoke.

A full-bosomed barmaid hurried over to take their orders.

When she left, Willie asked, "Do you have a hunch who might be trying to ruin us?"

"Somebody who wants something we have. What do we have?"

She gnawed on her lip. "Land, timber, money, machinery, business connections."

"Land," they said simultaneously.

"Well, it's high time we get all the land contracts examined, and the land assessed and surveyed. Jonathan blew out a breath of air. "We'll get new geological studies, too. From an outside source. We need to know everything above and below every piece we lease or own. We'll inventory every stand of timber and determine its size, type, and market value. We'll get to the bottom of this."

The food arrived, and they directed their attention to eating. Afterwards, Willie sipped on her coffee and sighed peacefully.

"I must remember an empty stomach makes you prickly." He winked.

She smiled, knowing he was teasing her and not maliciously. "I was so famished I could have eaten a mule." She looked over at his plate, barely touched, merely rearranged. "Do you know what they call your affliction?"

"Are you going to poke the bear all day?"

"A visit from the spirits of hell." She reached over and stabbed a piece of bacon from his plate.

Minutes later, the door to the tavern opened, and he looked up long enough from her playful face to see who entered. The muscles in his jaw tightened.

Matthew Reed crossed the room.

"Good morning, Wilhelmina." Matthew gestured to the vacant chair. "Can we talk a few minutes?"

When she nodded, he reached for the adjacent chair.

Jonathan hesitated before removing his booted foot from the rung. "I wouldn't get too comfortable, Reed. We're about to leave."

Jaw stiff, Willie gave him a warning look and pushed the chair farther out from under the table. "Please sit down and join us, Matthew."

He made no move to be seated. "I'd like to talk to you, Wilhelmina. Alone." He flashed a frigid look at Jonathan.

Jonathan tipped his chair and leaned forward, his nose nearly touching hers. "I can't imagine what this piece of chum bait would want to discuss with you that I couldn't possibly hear, *partner.*"

If she were a betting person, she decided, her partner's temper was about to hit a rolling boil. She tilted her head toward the door. "Grab a breath of some spring air. Clear that fuzzy head and cool your heels, *partner.*"

Her sarcasm didn't go unnoticed. "Well, the air is certainly much fresher outside." He rose and dropped a wad of bills on the table. "I'll meet you back at the mill, *sweetheart.*"

With a vexed look, Matthew Reed watched him leave. "He has a way of irritating everyone in a ten-mile radius," he muttered and sat down.

"Oh, you're far too generous with the mileage." Her mouth twitched with amusement.

"Rumor has it you're no longer betrothed." Matthew's face reflected a glimmer of hope.

She couldn't honestly decide if the chasm was growing wider or whether she and Jonathan had slowly reaching a stalemate. "Half the relationship says we probably should be, but the other half has yet to formally withdraw," she admitted.

He looked elated by the news. "You know I'm fond of you, Wilhelmina."

"Yes, of course. You've always been a true friend." She rested her hands on the table. Pots and pans clanked, plates rattled, and bottles clinked filling the silence around them. The disgusting smell of hot cooking fat mingled with cigar smoke, and the thoughts of the ransacked office made her stomach feel like it was full of knots.

"What's wrong?" he asked.

Against her better judgment, she briefly related the details of the mill while he solemnly listened.

"The break-in is not for public knowledge," she added.

"I understand. I'm sorry to hear it." His voice sounded genuinely sincere. "I was also sorry to hear about your horse. I know how much Silver Cloud meant to you."

His words only stirred up memories. She felt an odd sense of emptiness. It brought back pain she thought she had recovered from, but it incited anger and bitterness as well.

Frowning, she stood. The last thing she needed was to rehash her losses. "I need to get back to the mill, Matthew. Please do me a favor, will you? " She laid her hands palms down on the table and leaned toward him."Please spread the word around town Wydcliffes are *not* selling land. We're not selling out. And if I personally ever find the culprits behind all this trouble, it will be their backsides this time taking a dip in the mill pond instead of mine."

She saw a startled expression flicker on his face. She patted his arm reassuringly. "I didn't mean to alarm you with such frankness, but everyone's patience is stretched thin. Mine included."

He nodded. "If there's anything I can do, please tell me."

She laid a hand on his shoulder."Thank you, but this is a Wydcliffe fight."

Outside, she crossed the street and headed toward town, past the Sawdust Bin. The local saloon was quiet now with a the loggers at work, but later in the night, its rafters would ring with the sounds of a tinny piano, the shuffling of cards, the tinkling of glassware, and the high-pitched laughter of women of the night. It was a place where cheap whiskey and an iron-clad stomach became friends for twenty cents a shot.

A mangy brown dog, lying in the sun, jumped up to be petted, and Willie bent and scratched the dog behind its ears. She noticed one of the oilskin windows on the saloon was boarded up. Sam had told her once that Red Ruby, the proprietor, refused to spend a dime on glass. It was the scenery inside that counted, and too many rowdy loggers had taken the short route to the street to make the investment worthwhile. Although Willie had only seen the proprietor a few times, she knew she was a tall, attractive red-haired woman who wore paste jewelry and kept to herself most of the time.

Before she reached Irwin's Store, the familiar twang of a banjo caught her ear. There was only one person who could pick a banjo so skillfully, and she hurried down the street to a vacant lot where a crowd was already huddled around a brightly-painted, red peddler's wagon. Perched on the tailgate, a monkeylike figure with eyes as dark as raisins strummed a rendition of *Camptown Races*.

As soon as he spied her, the itinerant peddler laid down his banjo, hopped gingerly down, and invited the crowd to check out his wares hanging from hooks circling the wagon and covering the grassy area beside it.

"It's a joyful day, Elizabeth Wilhelmina Wydcliffe," he roared, looking skyward. "May the sun always shine on peddlers and beautiful women."

"O'Toole, you're always such a hopeful old chap." She grinned and gave him a quick hug.

He let out a rumble of laughter and stroked his scraggly white beard. "Darlin', you sound like Wydcliffe more and more each time I come 'round. How's your pa? Still ailin'?"

"He's doing as well as could be expected. What parts you coming from and where are you headed, O'Toole?"

"The rolling hills of New York and in between. Headed south. Come see the baubles, jewels, and finery I picked up this trip." He gestured to the wagon. A makeshift table was covered with ribbons, combs, thread, buttons, and toilet waters. Cheap glass jewelry shined amid the tins of spices, tea, and hand-made nails. From the wagon's covered roof, pots, pans, and pails clanged in the breeze.

Willie selected two tortoise shell combs and a scrimshaw knife, etched with a clipper ship. "How much?" she asked.

"How much you offering?" he countered.

"You mean I don't get to haggle?"

"Willie, I've known Wydcliffes all my life. I don't have all day or the patience." His weathered eyes sparkled like tiny jewels.

"Five dollars for the knife and fifty cents for the combs."

"Deal." He snatched her money with thin arthritic figures, dropping the coins in a leather bag hanging from his waist. "I was hoping to get to these parts later this summer for the loggers' celebration. Sure enjoy watching the rattler bagging competition. Sam Bradley and Ezra Hawkins still playing with those critters?"

"Sam gave it up a few years back," she said with a twinkle in her eye. "Said the snakes were too sluggish in these parts."

The peddler laughed again. Lowering his voice, he pulled her by the elbow to the side of the wagon. "You know the tale about your pa's second mill, the Black Widow?"

"Only bits and pieces."

"Word had it in New York the Widow Rowles had a son who has now disappeared as well. Folks say he changed his name and probably returned to this area."

The shock of his revelation hit her full force, stunning her into silence. The land, legally theirs, was part of the same piece Pierce wanted. "Why would he want to return?" She stared at him, baffled.

The peddler shrugged. "For what reason do most men return to a familiar area? To find kin, to settle old differences, for vengeance, to make their way in life…and the list goes on."

"Did you catch his given name?"

The peddler shook his head. "Don't think anyone rightly knows. It would've been changed to protect the child. Strange one, isn't it?" He took up his banjo and began to tune the strings.

"Yes," she agreed. "Have a good day, O'Toole."

As she walked toward town, she thought about how everything over the last several months fit the definition of strange.

Later, outside Irwin's General Store, just when the day couldn't get any more wretched, she came face to face with Clara Ferguson. Like a peacock out for a Sunday outing, the girl strolled down the street, twirling a frilly parasol. Layers of pink lace made her figure balloon to barrel size.

"Don't tell me you were shopping at O'Toole's?" Clara asked and gave her parasol a twist until the pink stripes blurred.

"Yes, Clara." Willie stifled a weary groan. The girl's shrill voice alone sent shivers up her back.

"I'm not surprised. Some people think a few shabby ribbons and cheap combs will make them a lady, but I know better."

"Some people think lace clear up to their nostrils will also." Willie cleared her throat and had the pleasure of watching cold fury settle over Clara's face. Many thoughts flew through her head. But one remained. She realized there was a difference between true anger and a vicious hate born out of jealousy and greed. She wondered what had made Clara so spiteful. There was nothing the girl couldn't have, nothing that she couldn't buy. "I hear we might be neighbors."

Puzzled, Clara looked at her.

"The land outside town. I hear your father deeded it to you."

"Oh, that worthless piece of dirt? Yet, no one can ever be too sure when the right man might come around, can they? You should sell your useless land too, now that it's been lumbered." She gripped the parasol tighter. "How's your handsome beau?"

"He's fine."

"Well, I should hope so." Clara emitted a ripple of giggles. "Any man who visits the Sawdust Bin in the morning and later that night isn't there because he needs a drink. He's usually thirsty for something else."

Smirking, she left, brushing past Willie, her skirts dusting the wooden walk as she headed toward town.

Clara's remarks left Willie cold. It would have been better to have been slapped in the face. So Jonathan was at the Sawdust Bin Saloon cavorting with one of the ladies of the night? She watched a couple approach, laughing and walking arm-in-arm. They skirted around her, and she wondered whether she and Jonathan would ever have a relationship with warmth and love and trust. Or would they always be at each other's throats? Distrust made for a poor marriage.

Minutes later, on her way to the mill, she stopped outside the Sawdust Bin and stared at the faded red and white sign above the hand-hewn doors. She had no reason to doubt Jonathan's loyalty. She had no reason to trust him either. With her instincts taking command, she lifted the worn latch. The door drifted open, creaking on its rusty hinges.

It was quiet inside. Light filtered in through the dim oilskin windows and made patterns on the rough floor, sprinkled with sawdust to keep the loggers' feet from slipping when they spun the barmaids about the room. A long bar, worn smooth from bottles and mugs sliding over it, snaked along the entire back of the room. A mirror and gold-framed pictures of scantily-clad women adorned the wall behind.

Red Ruby peered out from behind a curtained doorway in the back. "Sorry, bar's closed 'til seven," she said in a husky voice. Her mouth dropped open when she spied Wilhelmina standing mutely just inside the door. "Well, if this isn't a pleasure.

What brings you into the Bin, honey?"

For one second, Willie had the urge to turn tail and run. She swallowed the lump forming in her throat. "I was looking for some information."

The red-haired woman strolled out and leaned over the bar. She wore a shiny dark taffeta skirt and a blouse as red as Willie's face. "Have a seat." She gestured to a barrel beneath the bar. "Can I get you a drink?"

Willie shook her head and slid onto the barrel. She rubbed her forehead with her hand and felt her head begin to pound like a loose door in a wind storm.

"Tea?" Ruby offered. "It's on the house." The older woman took two squat glasses from the back of the bar and poured some tea from a gallon jug. "My gals drink this on the job," she explained. "Keeps the mind clear and men never know the difference." She splayed her hands on the top of the bar. Slender fingers shone with red nail enamel.

Willie took a sip of tea. For several minutes, neither spoke.

"Listen, honey, if there's something eating at you, spit it out," Ruby finally suggested.

Where to begin? How do you ask if your fiancé is unfaithful? At last, Willie relented and spoke. "Clara Ferguson told me Jonathan Wain came in here this morning and visits at night. I was wondering—"

A low laughter bubbled up and spilled from the older woman's red lips. "I'm sorry, but the mention of that gal's name brings out the worst of my civility. Rabid dogs are more trustworthy friends."

She dropped down on a stool behind the bar.

"Your handsome brute was in here this morning, but he wasn't looking for a woman to relieve his frustrations. He was looking for information to satisfy his curiosity."

Relieved, Willie steadied her hands around her drink. "I guess it's really none of my business to ask."

"It doesn't matter," Ruby answered with a shrug. "He wants me to keep an ear open for information I might hear."

"About John Pierce?"

"Yes, for starters. That smug crow is at the top of the list. I may sell cheap whiskey, Miss Wydcliffe, but I try to send a man on his way before his pockets run dry and his kids are without bread. Pierce is known for fleecing a man's entire paycheck over a game of cards without blinking an eye. Why, sometime back he even took a good chunk of cash from the Kramer fellow. The surveyor."

"Rachael's father?" Willie's words rushed out in disbelief.

"Don't look shocked, honey," Ruby said. "Almost every man from these parts shows up looking to wet his throat, or meet a gal, or wile away a few hours over a smart game of cards. Kramer's no different."

Ruby studied the tea in her glass a moment. "I'm really sorry to hear about your pa. He's a damn solid man."

Willie's head shot up. "You know my *father*?"

"Hell, yes, honey. Your pa and I go a long way back. He's one of the few people in Clearfield who wouldn't cross the street to avoid saying hello. When the Sawdust Bin burned a few years ago, it was your pa who advanced me the cash and lumber to rebuild. Everyone else was ready to run me out, but Dalton said the loggers needed a place to blow off steam, and it was better to have them here than stumbling over the streets and looking for trouble."

Ruby propped an elbow on the bar and held a rouged chin in her hand. "Your father is an honest man, and he treats every woman like a lady. He's not like Charlie Ferguson, who struts around town like he's St. Peter himself, yet slips in here for amusement and slides out the back door."

Willie finished her drink and set her glass aside. "I appreciate your honesty."

"My pleasure. Stop in again for a chat. I like to see a woman in business. Gives the menfolk something to ponder over." She paused and smiled. "If I were you, sugar, I'd snatch up that big fellow you're courtin' before some other gal sets her sights on him."

A ripple of laughter flew though Willie's lips. "Gracious, you sound like Sam Bradley."

"Now there's an old coot with a head full of brains and a good heart." Red Ruby strolled to the door beside Willie. "Tell me, does your fine-looking beau have any brothers?"

Willie looked into eyes of brilliant jeweled green and smiled. "Two, though one's married, and the other's about to be."

"Hmm. A real shame." Ruby shook her head in mock sadness. "A *real* shame."

Willie extended her hand to the older woman. "It was nice meeting you."

Ruby took her hand and squeezed it. "One more thing." Her voice was full of caution. "Hungry wolves run in a pack, kid. Make sure no one gets too close, and don't trust anyone who tries to. Someone is out for Wydcliffe blood."

Willie nodded before she stepped out into the bright sunshine and away from a world far different from the one she knew.

CHAPTER TWENTY

June, 1857

JONATHAN LET THE DRAPES FALL back into place at the window. He had been watching the activity in the stable yard below and hurried down to the breakfast table to intercept Willie before she left for the mills.

He found her at the table hacking a flapjack into a million pieces. It didn't take any more brains than an earthworm to see she was in the vilest of moods for someone about to celebrate her twenty-fourth birthday. Following his explicit orders, no one from the entire household staff had made mention of it, and she was moping.

Whistling merrily, Jonathan dropped into a seat facing her.

"People who are so joyful in the morning should have their hearts ripped out," she muttered and poured more than a generous stream of maple syrup onto the shredded pancake.

A smile ruffled his handsome face. "You're just in a poor mood because you didn't find your birthday presents we stashed in the stables. Everyone knows you've tipped this house upside down in search of them. Think all that sugar might help your disposition?"

"I should have known," she sputtered, coming to her feet, "only buzzard bait like you would stoop to such a childish trick." An unexpected stir of excitement rose inside her. "So what are we waiting for?"

He followed her out into the summer sunshine. The first rays of dawn had already burned off the dew from underfoot. The doors to the stables were flung open, and he had to quicken his pace to keep up with her.

"I guess in all fairness, I should show you where we hid them." Inside the barn, he led her past Silver Cloud's stall to one at the far end of the stables. Her eyes sparkled luminously when she saw a pure white horse, prancing in the stall, still uneasy with its new surroundings. His coat glistened like new snow in the slanted sunlight filtering through the stable windows.

She was so shocked, she could only stare.

"Happy birthday." He leaned a shoulder against the stall. "A new saddle from the staff is arriving from Maryland next week. I ordered it special to fit the mount."

"Oh, Jonathan, he's beautiful. Thank you." She blinked back a tear. No one had ever given her such a splendid gift since the day she received Silver Cloud. The horse must have cost a fortune. And the time and money to have it delivered must have been immense. Another tear slid down her face and she wiped it away with the back of her hand.

"Why the tears?" Gallantly, he handed her his

handkerchief.

"I guess I'm so happy." She sniffed, wiped her eyes again, and shoved the handkerchief into her pocket.

Jonathan stepped toward her, wrapped an arm around her, and squeezed her gently. He gestured toward the stall. "Go. Have a look at him."

Seconds later, she was running her hand over the gelding's silky mane and slender neck. "Where did you locate him?" She giggled when the animal raised its proud head, snorted anxiously, and nudged her on the shoulder like he expected a treat.

"He's all the way from Tennessee. He's still a little spooky since he's not used to your stables." He handed her a sugar cube. "Better make friends with him." He fell silent and watched as she fed it to him.

"Do you think he's ready to ride?" she asked.

"I think he's more than ready to blow off steam."

Willie deftly bustled about the stable collecting her blanket and old tack. She moved like a fairy in the dusty light, her movements flowing and efficient.

"You'll have to name him," he said above the clip-clopping of hooves on the stones as they walked out into the courtyard. "Please be careful."

Nodding, she gingerly hoisted herself up into the saddle and fussed over the horse. Patiently, without flinching, the well-disciplined mount stood quietly, awaiting her instructions. With a dazzling smile and a gentle prod, she urged him forward.

"Come on, boy, let's beat the pants off the wind." Together, they reeled away, flying down the dirt road, gliding over a stone wall, and sailing effortlessly into an open field full of golden buttercups. Horse and rider blended into one total colorful creation of moving art.

Sam Bradley was at the feed store outside town when she rode up. He pushed his battered hat up from his forehead and grinned from ear-to-ear. "I see you got yourself a new mount."

"It's a birthday present from Jonathan." She dismounted and led the horse to Sam. "Isn't he superb?"

The old man ran his hands down the shoulder of the horse and patted its massive white chest affectionately. The gelding refused to shy away, but snorted instead, and rubbed his nose on the upper sleeve of Sam's flannel shirt. "If you mean Jonathan, I suppose he's superb," he said, scratching the horse behind his ears.

"Sam, you know I mean the horse. "

"Yeah, he's superb, too, from the looks of him." He paused. "Comes from gentle Tennessee stock, I'm told."

Wondering how he knew the bloodlines, she looked skeptically at the horse, then back to Sam, then back to the horse again. The animal butted his nose against Sam's chest and snickered. "You knew all along, didn't you? You knew I was getting him for my birthday, and you never said a word."

"Sort of." The old man's face beamed. He pulled out a sugar cube from his chest pocket and fed him. "Jonathan needed a place to keep him for a couple of days, and you know how Tess likes company."

"Sam, you rascal. I should be thanking you for taking care of him. Has Papa seen him?"

"Dunno. You just missed him coming in from the other direction. He was headed for the mill. With this beast, you can probably catch him before he's halfway there." He scratched behind his own ear and regarded the girl with his startling blue eyes.

"Something the matter?" She leaned against the hitching post and waited.

The old man hesitated. "You know, Willie, you pa is not feeling right well, and he has a tendency to worry a lot. It's not like I don't think you can handle this business by yourself, but honestly, honey, you ought to give some serious thought to settlin' down and lettin' a man help you take care of part of these dad-burned mills. Your pa would like to see you in safe hands and the business in strong ones before he leaves this world. Sure would ease his mind."

Willie tenderly patted his arm. She knew he was concerned about protecting Wydcliffe Logging, but she had long ago decided to keep and run the business when her father no longer could—or didn't want to."

"I'll fight to maintain every inch of it."

"You missed my point, young lady. You can't fight alone."

She sighed. "Doesn't love have anything to do with all this?"

He rubbed his chin, pensively. "Sometimes, we don't have to look very far to find someone to love. Sometimes, when someone loves us, we don't always love him in return...that is, not right off. It doesn't mean we couldn't learn to, given some time. He's a good man, you know."

She squinted into the old man's weathered face.

"There are a lot of good men, Sam."

"He loves you, Elizabeth Wilhelmina," he replied matter-of-factly. "You don't give the poor man a chance."

Together, they watched a dilapidated buggy, its springs squeaking, pass by before Willie spoke again. "I don't know whether Jonathan really loves me, or it's just infatuation. As soon as he heard rumors about town, he was right quick to doubt my sincerity." She took the reins of the horse and walked to the edge of the road leading to the mill.

Sam trailed behind her. "Sometimes, when we love a person so much, we're willing to give him his freedom. Some people are like this horse—with a spirit so unique we'd prove nothing by changin' or breakin' it. Think about it, Willie."

She smiled into his wizened eyes which still shone with a youthful gleam. She knew she was one of few who could tug at the strings of his old heart. "I wish you were forty years younger, Sam. I'd marry you."

He stared back at the small girl and returned the smile. "I wish I was too," he said. "I wish I was too."

On her way toward the mill in town, Willie pondered what Sam had told her. Maybe Jonathan really did care for her. All spring he had spent endless hours overseeing the finishing mill. Except for an additional lathe which was on its way by keelboat from Williamsport, the mill was near completion. Even the horse was more than a gift of fondness, too expensive to give to only a friend.

She picked out Jonathan's tall form as soon as she was in visible distance of the mill. She was barely at the rail before he closed the space between them and swung her effortlessly from the saddle.

"You look breathtakingly beautiful," he said.

Willie could feel a blast of heat pass between them, and she stepped away and into the new mill. The sweet scent of fresh cut wood enveloped them. Planers, sanders, and lathes gleamed in sparkling gray and steel, and workbenches, still unmarred, marched around the perimeter of the huge room. The floor seemed to stretch onward forever. Unlike the rough cut plank floors at the saw mills, it was planed to a smooth, shiny finish and varnished.

Jonathan handed her a recently-turned chair spindle. "There are a lot of snarls to be worked out," he admitted, "but Ferguson has already shown a great deal of interest."

Her slender fingers ran over the convex rings on the spindle. She was caught up in the excitement immediately. "We'll have to advertise, and we'll need a name."

"Wain and Wydcliffe Manufacturing?" he asked hopefully.

"Why not Wydcliffe and Wain?"

"It rolls off the tongue better my way."

"I thought this was a fifty-fifty endeavor," she snapped, a hint of a storm brewing in her demeanor. "What makes you think your fifty should come first? It's sitting on Wydcliffe land."

He cursed softly under his breath. "This is silly, Willie, I refuse to fight over a name."

"You know he's right," Sam Bradley said, startling them as he sauntered in. He pulled his battered hat from his head and looked around. "You young folks finally get an entire mill ready for operation, and now fight about what you're going to call the blasted thing? Tell me, does that make sense?" He squinted at the couple with a disgruntled frown.

"Do you have a suggestion?" Willie struggled to be rational.

"White Pine Manufacturing. You can smell the sawed pine a mile away before you see the mill."

Willie thought about it for a moment. "What do you think, Jonathan?"

"I think Sam ought to come around more often." He smiled and winked at the old man.

Throwing them a lopsided grin, Sam walked to the door. "Maybe if you both spent a little more time together and a little less time jawing over these dang operations, you might be able to converse like civilized folk."

He left with both of them staring at each other.

"He's right again," Jonathan said.

He reached up and held her face gently in his hands. "We should be enjoying the moment. It's a true celebration."

She watched his eyes soften from steel gray to fog. Her heart fluttered wildly in her chest. His nearness was overwhelming. He bent his head and brushed a soft kiss across her lips.

The kiss and his nearness had the same effect on her as always. A flood of sensations raced through her, making her tremble uncontrollably. Her head felt dizzy, and she grasped him by the forearms to steady herself. Caught up in the emotional turbulence, she returned his kiss, her eyes closed. Her hands crept up and slid around his neck, pulling him closer.

Their lips caressed each other and their tongues

tangled, sending her senses reeling. When at last they pulled apart, he held her in a warm embrace until both their hearts beat steady again.

And for just a little while, she felt cherished and safe and loved.

CHAPTER TWENTY-ONE

WHERE THE DEVIL IS EVERYONE? Willie walked through the house and slipped outside to sit on the back stoop. The sweet scent of summer roses wafted in the early morning air. It was already tepid, signaling a hot, sultry day ahead.

It was market day in town for Hannah. But where were Conrad and Roy? The clicking of hooves in the courtyard brought her perplexing thoughts to the present. She could tell it was Jonathan by the harried sound of the stallion's shoes on the stones. Trade Wind was always anxious for his feed, and he allowed his mount an easy rein at the end of their ride.

Minutes later, he sauntered up the path. Wiping his brow, he smiled affectionately at her and propped a booted foot on the bottom step. He bent down to kiss her lightly on the side of her brow above her ear.

"I can't find Conrad," she said.

"I sent him into town with Roy to bring the new surveyor I hired."

She yawned. "I supposed it's a sensible idea. It's been a long time since Papa filed those first land deeds." She patted the seat beside her. "Here. Sit down."

"I'd rather stand."

She looked up and realized from his vantage point, he could see the tops of her breasts revealed by her open blouse. She let out a cantankerous huff and patted the seat again.

He laughed and sat down. "Testy this morning, aren't we?"

"Don't you want to know what I named the gelding?"

He reached down and plucked a daisy near the stoop. "Do tell."

"Warrior. Because he's fast, strong, and trustworthy. In many Indian tribes, only the chiefs and warriors are allowed the privilege of riding white mounts. What do you think?"

"I think it's an excellent name." He slid the flower behind her ear. "But let me show you how much I adore Warrior's mistress." He bent and touched his lips to hers before she could protest. The kiss lengthened, and she could feel him demanding her total surrender.

"Jonathan, please." She elbowed him away and removed the flower. "Someone is coming up the drive." She straightened herself as the buggy rolled up to the back entrance.

Conrad alighted and introduced Stuart Cooper, a weathered, lean-looking man with a faint smile who put everyone immediately at ease. Eager to begin his work, he brushed off the suggestion of resting for a day and sent Jonathan to the stables to saddle the horses while he deposited his belongings in the manor.

Willie traipsed behind Jonathan as he went about collecting the proper gear.

"I wish I could come along." She hated the thought of having him leave. She had to admit there was a growing attraction between them. Even though she hadn't planned on having feelings for any man, he was slowly unlocking her heart and soul. It was a new experience. Sadly, she realized the surveying would take weeks of work and many hours apart.

He threw a saddlebag over his shoulder and turned. "Hell fire, Willie, I'd never get any work done out there with you around. My willpower is sorely tried now. I'd have no power of concentration if you were within touching distance." He reached out and caressed the side of her face with his callused hand. "Anyway, someone has to stay here in case there's a problem at the mills."

Before she could reply, Conrad arrived with a saddlebag full of food, a western-looking hat Willie had never seen Jonathan wear, and a Sharps carbine tucked under his arm. Jonathan took the stock and flipped open the brass cover over the spring-loaded priming wheel to check the caps. He opened the patch box to double check the spare priming wheel beneath. Inside his coat, Willie could see the bulge of a pistol.

"Are you hunting or surveying?" she asked anxiously.

He accepted the wooden box Conrad handed him with extra ammunition and caps. "Just watching out for wildlife. Sam says the bear in these parts can get rather friendly."

"I don't know why you're doing this now," she

muttered irritably. Even though they hadn't had any problems in the past few months, she had an uneasy feeling about him riding into the wilderness with so little protection. "Why not take more crew to help?"

He closed his eyes and groaned. "We've been over this a dozen times now. The only way to sort out this wretched mess is to start from the beginning. We don't need extra crew to get in our way."

"Whatever you do," she warned, "don't let down your guard."

The discussion ended abruptly again when Stuart Cooper joined them, leading a roan and a pack horse bearing a transit, tripod, and equipment.

"Don't hold supper for me," Jonathan told her, setting the suede hat atop his rich, dark head.

She reached out to stroke Trade Wind's silky mane. "Please be careful," she whispered, frowning and staring into his gray eyes as another wave of apprehension swept over her.

His mouth twitched with amusement. "I'm beginning to believe you actually care." He stopped to take one last long look at her before he turned his horse down the lane.

Minutes later, after she watched them ride out of sight, she saddled Warrior and headed to the mill where she found McGee sitting at his desk, holding his balding head in his hands, as he poured over a black leather-bound ledger.

"This must be a day for doom and gloom." She paused beside his desk.

"Let's just say the debit side of your new business is using more ink than the credit side."

"We haven't even started up the machines yet,

McGee." She took the pen he had already dipped in ink and signed the orders he pushed under her nose. When she finished, he opened his drawer, pulled out two oranges, and handed one to her.

"Maybe this will lift both our spirits."

"Where on earth did you get oranges?" She brought the fruit to her face, scratched the peel, and inhaled its tangy citrus smell.

"Your seafaring partner had them sent in from somewhere. California or Brazil, I'll wager. Maybe up from Florida. The crates arrived on the same coach with the new surveyor fellow. Mr. Wain told me to be sure all the workers get a few to take to their families."

"Has he lost his mind? These must cost a pretty penny."

"Not when you own your own cargo ships." McGee returned to his ledgers, squinting at the columns and scratching his head.

She left quietly, passing Henderson on the way down the steps. He was dressed in the same ragged clothes he had worn last week. She was puzzled by his appearance. She knew the mills' boon rats, who sorted the many different types of logs in the splash dam, could afford better.

"Your father is above the dam," he mumbled, passing her and continuing upward.

Minutes later, she found him at the end of the twisted path, standing beyond the shade of an elm and gazing at the pond. He was now a thin thread of a man. His face was sunken and tired, his eyes black-ringed. Above them, the sun beat down from its ball of fire hanging in a cloudless sky.

Willie gave him a probing look. "Are you all

right, Papa?" She reached out to steady him, helping him over to a cooler spot on a wooden bench under the elm. "You shouldn't be out in this heat," she scolded. "I'll fetch someone to take you home. Have you seen Sam?"

"He went with Jonathan and Cooper. Come, sit down. We have plenty of time to get these weary bones home."

"For a few minutes only," she agreed and took a seat beside him.

Wydcliffe scowled. "An old man gets no courtesies around this place—even his own daughter orders him about."

"Ah, you must know how I feel when I work with Jonathan." She looked out across the millpond where the hands were working. "How many ships does he own, Papa?"

"I know he and his two brothers own several clippers which carry our lumber to markets up the coast and across the Atlantic." He pulled out a handkerchief and mopped his face. "Sure is a warm one."

"How did he arrange for these oranges?" She turned the one she held round and round in her hands.

"They're a bit of a luxury, but you must remember, Jonathan is an assiduous sea captain who's probably used to having fresh fruit aboard when he sails. He's probably homesick for those things that make him most comfortable. Everyone is allowed a little indulgence, eh?"

"I suppose you're right," she agreed. She scrambled to her feet. "But no more indulgences for you. Straight home to rest."

The old man rose wearily. "Make sure someone takes Henderson's spot in the mill pond. I let him take the rest of the day off. He's been complaining of a toothache. We have a string of orders, and we need those logs untangled and sent up to the carriages as quickly as possible."

"I'll take care of it." Willie signaled for a nearby mill hand to help take her father to the manor.

The ride to the western property was as unpleasant as Jonathan imagined it would be. Sticky heat invaded even the damp undergrowth of the dense forest. He was glad Sam Bradley had persuaded him to wear a hat. Tiny black flies and mosquitoes swarmed around their heads, invading their faces, eyes, and ears, and irritating the horses' dispositions as well. Only Sam seemed to be immune to their persistent attacks. He bantered on, giving Cooper what seemed like a leisurely tour of the countryside.

"How do you stand it, old timer?" Jonathan finally asked, waving his hat to swat at a swarm humming above his head.

"The skeeters?" Sam halted his horse near a stand of trees. "They don't want this tough-skinned old goat. There's not enough blood left inside to feed a half dozen. It's young, tender skin like yours they're fond of." He motioned to a clearing where a small inviting stream bubbled over rocks and meandered onward through the trees. "We'll take a breather here and give our horses a rest."

While Sam watered the horses, Jonathan and

Cooper unpacked the supplies and food, piling them in the shade of a massive oak. The sun, now high in the sky, beat down with unrelenting fury.

"It's so hot you can smell the grass burning," Jonathan muttered as they worked. Sweat poured down the sides of his face, and he felt a river run down his back.

He watched the old man return. Sam tied the horses nearby, seated himself beneath a leafy bough, and pulled his hat over his eyes to grab a few winks of sleep. He wore a light brown woolen shirt buttoned to the neck.

Jonathan found his affable spirit wilting with each passing minute. "So tell me, you old coot, how do you not sweat wrapped up like a mummy in all that wool?"

"When you get to be an old pile of dried-out bones like me, you'll find out." Sam grunted and pulled his hat farther down on his head. "By the way, thanks for the oranges," he murmured. "Willie is starting to question how vast your holdings on the East Coast might be. When are you going to tell her you could buy her out with the coins in your pocket?"

Jonathan mopped his forehead with a handkerchief and tried to collect his thoughts. She would be furious if she found out. Finally, it appeared they had come to amiable terms, and she seemed almost happy. He was certain if he spent the rest of his life, he could never find anyone he could love more. She was spunky, captivating, and beguiling with her own brand of wit and charm. It would serve no purpose to reveal his status or wealth.

"This is not a good time to be spouting off any

truths about me, Sam. We'd be dousing the fire with oil."

Sam snorted. "Well, I'm giving you full credit for that hair-brained decision when she does find out."

Unable to bear the torrid conditions any longer, Jonathan stood, rifle in hand, and shuffled toward the stream.

He'd barely laid his rifle aside, removed his sweat-stained hat, and splashed icy water onto his face when a shot rang out and excruciating pain exploded from behind his left shoulder. The force of the bullet flattened him to the ground. He could feel warm, sticky blood seep down his back. In a daze, he groped for his rifle, recovered it, and painfully rolled underneath a nearby barrier of tangled underbrush. Another series of shots followed him, spraying the leaves overhead.

Cursing silently, he forced his eyes toward the direction of the shots. Sweat mixed with water rolled down his eyelids, his head pounded, and his shoulder burned. To his right, he spied Sam and Cooper pinned down and cut off from the attacker's position by another volley of bullets.

Forcing himself to ward off threatening dizziness, he propelled himself forward on his hands and knees. Shards of pain tore through his shoulder. Briars tore at his clothing. But he crawled his way toward an outcropping of rocks to the right of the line of fire.

Without conscious thought, he rose slowly to his knees and stumbled to his feet, making his way up a steep slope tangled with more brush and rock piles. Now he faced an open slope completely unprotected by even the smallest scrub oak. For a brief moment, he hesitated, contemplating his next move. Another volley of shots flew over his head. A bullet whistled past his ear. From behind him, a horse came crashing through the underbrush without a rider. Sam had cut Trade Wind free.

The Indian pony stopped a foot from him, and he pulled his body up, lying flat against the animal's neck as he urged the mount into a dead run up the slope. Out of the corner of his eye, he caught one of the gunmen just yards ahead of him. He willed his painful arm to grasp the rifle barrel, his right hand on the trigger.

Nostrils flaring, the man swung around to fire.

But it was the explosion of his own rifle that toppled his assailant. He glanced up momentarily toward the wooded forest beyond. A larger man's back disappeared into the thick protection of the trees. Another round of gunfire flew toward him, missing him completely.

Weak and exhausted, he let his body tumble from his horse.

Sam and Cooper found him on the rise, holding his shoulder and hunched over the lifeless body of his assailant.

"Hells Bells, it's Leb Luther," Sam exclaimed.

He stared at the dirt-encrusted body, bloodied on the chest where his bullet had pierced the heart.

Beside him, Sam tore his bandana from around his neck. "Looks like you could use a doctor, son."

He groaned. Pain drew his lips into a tight line. "I could sure use some of your medicine right now, Sam. I think I'm going to pass out."

The old codger snickered and caught his crumpling body before it toppled forward onto the ground. "You're gonna need more than some cheap whiskey, I'm afraid, son."

It was early afternoon and Granny Gordon's Tavern was almost devoid of people who preferred to hide from the brutal summer sun in the shade of their porches.

"Leb Luther is dead?" Matthew Reed's face shone with incredibility. His eyes narrowed as he searched Pierce's face across a table in a far corner of the room. "How did it happen?"

"You know damn well how it happened." Pierce's voice rang with anger as curses fell from his mouth. "The big brute Limey from Baltimore has as many lives as a cat. Unfortunately, Leb Luther didn't."

"Did he talk?" Reed's voice was low.

"From what I understand, Wain never gave him a chance. Shot him straight through the heart." Maniac-like, Pierce threw back his head and laughed uproariously. "At least Luther died with the satisfaction of knowing he tried twice to kill Wain. Too bad all he got for his troubles was the satisfaction of one dead horse." Pierce leaned back in his chair and took a swill of ale. "The way I figure it, it's better with Luther out of the way. One less mouth to spill any details. You know how filthy drunk he used to get. No telling what he might blabber in his stupors."

"What do we do next?" Reed asked. There was an uncomfortable edge to his tone. Nothing was going right. Jonathan Wain was not the easy, vulnerable target he had first thought him to be. "You know Wain will send a crew back there to survey again. This time, he'll be prepared like a garrison. He's no fool."

Pierce glared at Reed with ugly eyes. "Let the fool survey all he wants. He's not going to find anything amiss with those boundaries."

"But what if he starts snooping around?"

"It's taken care of, too. He won't find anything on those acres except mosquitoes and timber rattlers, and there are plenty of both." Pierce glanced at Reed, fidgeting. "Calm yourself, man, I made sure I covered all our tracks."

Matthew Reed sat in silence for a few moments, staring at him with hard eyes. "It still doesn't solve our problem. He's not the kind of man you can toy with and hope he easily forgets. He's a force to be reckoned with. We need him out of the way. For good. And soon."

Pierce's crazy laugh boomed out again. "You just want to edge in on the little Wydcliffe gal, don't you? Wain seems to have her tucked safely under his wing. You'll get your chance, boy. I still have some other little surprises waiting for Wain. I never give up easily."

"I don't want the girl hurt," Reed warned.

"I know. I know."

"I'm holding you to it." he threw Pierce a sharp look. "She's half of the deal, remember? She's no good to me dead."

"Damn, Reed, I told you the incident at the splash dam was a mistake. No one ever figured she'd go out on those logs." Pierce chugged the remainder of his ale and slammed the empty mug down on the table. "Let's get out of here. I don't want to miss Dalton Wydcliffe's little summer gathering and make anyone suspicious."

He pushed his chair back and lifted his stocky frame from the table just as Old Joe entered the tavern. "What the devil? Sometimes this place makes my skin crawl with all the river scum hanging around." He belched and pushed past Old Joe, almost knocking him down, to reach the door.

CHAPTER TWENTY-TWO

WILLIE PICKED UP HER MOSS green skirts with masses of petticoats beneath and raced down the hall, displaying her neatly turned ankles and satin slippers. She was—as always—late and she berated herself for allowing it to happen with so many guests already out on the lawn.

Every summer, they had at least one gathering for the mill workers, their families, and townsfolk. This year, they had chosen the middle of June to celebrate midsummer. The manor was laden with vases of flowers spilling out in colorful displays, their sweet odors permeating the air. Tables with sparkling white covers were strewn around the inlaid stone patio and were heaped with all types of foodstuff from delicate tea cakes to roast chicken and hearty meat sandwiches.

She wound her way through the crowds until she spotted her father where he was seated on a stone bench beneath a rose arbor.

"Everything is so perfect." She took a seat beside him. "Where's Jonathan?"

Wydcliffe gestured to a nearby table, "He's getting me a sip of punch."

She picked him out immediately. Dressed fastidiously in a pair of tan trousers with a dark brown jacket the same shade as the bark of the white pine, he stood tall and proud as the majestic tree itself. His left arm was still in a sling from the ambush with Leb Luther and the other assailants. Despite the doctor's orders, he had been determined to recover as quickly as possible. Despite the pain, he had commissioned a mill hand to drive him into town each morning after just two days of rest.

He smiled and headed toward them with the punch in tow.

"Sir, I'd like to steal your daughter away for a few minutes." He handed Wydcliffe the cup.

"But of course. Young people should take some time for themselves and leave all these older sophisticated women to the wiles of polished old gentlemen like Sam and me."

Willie smiled, wondering how much longer he would be able to keep up his humor. He was pain-fully thin, so emaciated his clothes hung from his body like a scarecrow. His face was pale, drawn, and haggard. It was only a matter of time.

She and Jonathan waited, carrying on a joking disguise of conversation until Sam sauntered up.

Leaving, they meandered down a narrow path strung with lanterns, which would later be lit to expel the darkness of the night. As they walked along the winding path leading to a secluded spot at the end of the grounds, frolicking children and their elders paused to wave or share a tidbit of news.

"I never thought we'd find time to be alone," Jonathan said when they finally arrived. "Everyone in the entire county wants to share a crumb of conversation with you."

She shrugged and tried to boost herself onto the stone wall encircling the property, but her billowing skirts discouraged her efforts. Only on her third feeble attempt was she successful with the help of his good arm.

"You can't imagine how relieved I am about finally having this mill problem solved." She settled herself and straightened her skirts. "It all makes sense now. Leb Luther always had a few teeth missing on his saw blade. He probably was driven to kill you and destroy my horse in hopes of seeking revenge for the day at the Black Widow mill when you fired him. It doesn't seem possible one man could heap so much distress on everyone's head."

He settled himself on the wall beside her. "You're missing one small detail. Leb Luther was stone drunk in Granny Gordon's Tavern the day the ropes to the holding dam were cut."

She blinked uncomprehendingly.

"When we checked the body, there wasn't a trace of a scar on his shoulder from your knife wound. Obviously, more than one person is involved. And there were others in the forest the day I was shot. I'm not counting on them being hired by Leb Luther. The man had no money and no influence to hire anyone. It would be more feasible to think someone hired Luther. Let's not forget the culprit who wrecked McGee's office, either. It couldn't have been Luther. I have serious doubts he could even write his name, let alone read."

"Well, that's discouraging. It's not over as I had hoped." A worried expression marred her face.

"Nothing has changed. Someone will try again." She picked up her reticule where inside she had placed her gun, and she patted it protectively for reassurance.

"Don't worry, we're not easily discouraged." He pulled her next to him with his uninjured arm.

She leaned against the side of his chest and felt the warmth of his body through his snow white shirt. He smelled of the familiar scents of bay rum, pine, and leather. It felt good to be held. Her feelings for him were intensifying each day.

He bent and kissed her, and she responded just as eagerly. They continued to kiss with a tender urgency, their lips hungering for the intoxicating sweetness of each other.

Minutes later, he broke the kiss and released her. "For such a little thing, you sure have a way of melting me to the bone," he said with a rueful smile and jumped down from the wall. He fumbled in his pocket.

"Just to be certain you practice your talents only on me, here's a little token of my love." He dropped a small box into her hands.

Heart thudding, Willie flipped the lid open and stared at a huge diamond twinkling from its bed of red velvet.

Jonathan removed it from the box and slid it on her slender finger. "I've been carrying this around since I returned from Baltimore," he admitted. "It was to be the surprise you asked for the evening before I left. I wanted to give it to you the afternoon at the mill, but somehow my timing was all wrong."

Staring at the ring, Willie's heart began to war

with itself. Her face paled and her hands began to sweat as she realized the finality of it all. This was forever. This was the man she was going to spend her whole life with. "Oh, Jonathan, it's beautiful. Are you sure we should do this?"

"I know you need time to adjust to something this permanent," he said. "I've no intentions of whisking you away to the altar. We have plenty of time to let our relationship grow."

Mollified, she patted his uninjured arm. "I do love you, even when I don't always understand you."

He laughed. "I guess a man can't ask for more." He helped her down from the wall.

They had barely started on their walk back to the celebration when a commotion erupted from the courtyard. Even with the stable doors closed, they could hear the high-pitched snorts and squeals of the horses.

The stables. The horses. Warrior! Willie knew instinctively something was amiss. She hiked up her skirts and tore up the path toward the barn with Jonathan close behind.

Outside, she strained her ears to listen, but the only sound she heard was the splintering of wood as the horses kicked in their stalls, trying to free themselves. She reached for the latch on the stable door when a prickling sensation crawled up her neck.

"A rattler's in the barn," she hissed. "I hear it."

She watched as Jonathan stepped out from the crowd gathered around her. Cautiously, he pulled the heavy door ajar, and the faint buzzing escalated.

On a pile of straw, not more than a few feet from

Trade Wind's stall, a dark timber rattler lay coiled, vibrating its tail in warning.

She slipped her reticule from her wrist and tore at the strings. Jonathan's hand on hers halted her efforts. Pulling out his own pistol from his coat pocket, he shoved the cold barrel into her hands. She noticed he had discarded his sling in the excitement.

"Shoot it," he barked. "One shot, Willie. We want to save our ammunition for whoever put it in there."

She stepped toward the snake, raised the gun, and lined the lean sights on its beady eyes. Taking a deep breath, she steadied her hands, aimed, and fired. The head of the rattler flew off, sending pieces of the skin flying against the wooden planks of the stall. The snake's headless body jerked upward for a split second and landed in the straw, writhing for a second longer before it stilled.

A murmur of amazement spread through the crowd.

"Nice work," Jonathan crooned. Retrieving the pistol, he turned to the crowd, "The party can now resume on the terrace and lawn. Everything is fine here, folks."

He carefully watched the crowd dispersing and noticed the look of awe, followed by rage, pass over John Pierce's face before he blended himself into a group moving toward the food tables.

Sam Bradley, hair slicked down like a flattened hay field, moved inside the barn and nudged the snake with the toe of his boot before he withdrew a knife, bent down, and sliced off the rattles on its tail.

"Little less than six feet," Sam said. "Beats the one we got the summer when you were twelve, Willie. This must be an old fellow, too." He laughed gleefully, holding up the rattles.

Weak-kneed, she slumped against the doorjamb of the stable door and shuddered as a cold chill gripped her. "Oh, Sam," she said with exasperation, "how can you find humor in a situation like this?"

Undaunted, the old man chuckled. "Life is too short, honey, to live without a laugh or two." He grabbed a pitchfork and picked up the snake, its thick body dangling limply on the tines.

Jonathan checked the animals while she waited patiently for him.

"You should've let me use my pistol," she said when he ducked out of the barn moments later.

"No one knows you carry a gun," he said. "I saw no reason to announce it to everyone when they know I have good reason to carry one."

"You should have shot it."

"My shoulder was still bothering me."

Perplexed, she looked intently at him. It dawned on her that he had deliberately wanted everyone to know she could handle a pistol, take care of herself, and keep an enemy at bay if necessary. Before she could speak her thoughts, he gripped her lightly by the elbow and propelled her toward the crowd awaiting them on the lawn.

As they fell into step together, he bent and whispered near her ear, "By the way, my dear, you can run like a gazelle despite those cumbersome skirts, can't you?"

The merriment of the afternoon continued long into the night. Fireworks colored the sky, fiddles hummed and twanged, couples shuffled about the floor, and food and drink quickly disappeared.

But seated off on a bench in the shadows, Jonathan and Willie were oblivious to it all as they wiled the night away locked in each other's embrace.

CHAPTER TWENTY-THREE

WILLIE STOPPED IN FRONT OF Irwin's General Store the next day and watched a dray filled with lumber pass by, kicking up dust from the street. The driver raised a hand in greeting, and she returned the gesture, recognizing the face of a customer.

It didn't matter whether it was one or a thousand wagons, each one filled with lumber from her mills always swelled her heart and bolstered her pride. It was Wydcliffe lumber and that's all that mattered.

She had barely stepped inside the store when Harold Young came rushing over. She sent him collecting supplies of flour, sugar, and chewing tobacco she planned to drop off at Sam's cabin on her way to the Wasp. Sam was busy at the Hornet's Nest working with a crew to repair the mill race and wheel. It was a perfect August day, but a gray tinge on the northern horizon hinted thunderheads would move in before sunset. She wanted to be home before dark.

The orders were collected without delay, and she headed for the cabin, leading the pack horse behind Warrior, displeased with the slow pace they were making.

She hadn't lied, she told herself, the minute she veered onto a path leading into the dense forest at the edge of town. She planned to visit the Wasp. She planned to deliver Sam's supplies. She just neglected to tell anyone she planned to stop at Matthew Reed's sawmill as well. A note had arrived yesterday, asking her to meet him at noon. Even if Jonathan discovered her whereabouts, she was blameless, since she had not initiated the meeting. Despite her betrothal, despite what Jonathan might think of him, Matthew Reed was still her friend.

Her nagging thoughts jabbed her all the way through the forest to Sam's cabin. There, she led the pack horse to the bottom of the old weathered steps and unloaded the supplies inside, safe from the rains. She removed the pack horse's bridle and locked him in the corral. Tess would be pleased to have the company. Sam would bring the horse back his next trip into town.

Minutes later, she hauled herself into Warrior's saddle and followed the creek through the thick undergrowth, making her way toward the Wasp. Delighted with the picture-perfect day, she sang a merry logger's tune as she picked her way around laurel and rhododendron, now pushing their roots deep into the earth with the dry season upon them.

Olaf was at the Wasp when she arrived. His huge frame with a mop of white hair was easy to discern as he stood in the doorway. Around him, the weathered old boards of the mill shimmered in the sunlight like a mirror reflecting light.

"How's the most fetching sharpshooter in the

county?" Laughter rumbled out of his thick chest as she drew near.

She jumped down and rummaged through her saddle bags withdrawing a leather folder of orders and a huge wrapped package. "Hannah packed a midday meal for you and McGee sent orders."

"Oh, good. Let's find a spot on the bank, ja?" Olaf led her to a grassy area beside the millrace and spread the food under the shade of a maple. They ate in comfortable silence. It took only a few minutes for the Swede to polish off a roast beef sandwich and a half loaf of raisin bread. He leaned contentedly back against the trunk and crossed his big hands on his stomach. "Any idea who likes rattlers for pets?"

"No." She tried not to sound alarmed. "Sometimes snakes do wander in looking for mice or insects."

Olaf snorted. "With all those cats around the stables, and those two gray mousers of Hannah's? I'll bet there's not a critter to be found in a two-mile radius. You know as well as I do, there's not been even a blacksnake snooping around those barns for years. Of course, those mousers aren't worth their salt when you feed them."

Willie laughed. "Who told you I feed Hannah's cats?"

"Everyone knows since you were a babe and didn't like the food on your plate, you slipped it to the cats."

"Well, if that don't beat all. Why hasn't anyone told Hannah?"

"And ruin the fun? Even sober-faced Conrad forbid us to tell. He likes a good joke now and then."

She grinned. Having Olaf around was like having an older brother—someone to share your secrets with. He had been only six years old when he, Hannah, and their siblings arrived from Sweden, and after all the years they still had not forgotten their native tongue. She loved the rare times when he stopped by the manor to chat with his sister in their sing-song dialect, which sounded so peaceful, so lulling to her ears.

"Why do you think Sam never purchased this mill when Papa offered it to him?" She remembered her father jokingly tell her Sam, having no faith in safes or banks, probably buried the fortune he had accrued in a tin can on his property. "He could have bought it twelves times over."

"Why would he want to spoil his freedom with the responsibility of owning and running a mill? He's pleased just to be your Papa's right-hand man."

She studied the mill wheel for a few minutes, watching the water rush into the shoot and tumble over the paddles. "I wonder why he never got married."

"He vas married. Supposedly he and his wife and child were attacked by a marauding band of Indians. His wife and child were killed, and they left him for dead. It vas your father, then a young man, who came along and saved his life, taking him into his makeshift shelter and enlisting the aid of an Indian maiden to nurse him back to health. The Indian maiden, your father later married..."

"Was Raven's mother," she finished. "The child who was killed, was it a boy or girl?"

"A girl, naturally," Olaf said as if she should have

known, or at least guessed.

Was that what life was all about, she wondered, as a pain, deep down, jabbed at her heart. A man loses everything in the world meaning the most to him, and he spends the rest of his life never wanting anything again?

"You must bring Bridgette and the boys to dinner some evening," she said, tearing her thoughts away. "Papa always enjoys them, and their tireless energy is priceless."

From the leather folder, she pulled out a stack of papers, neatly bound with string, and handed them to Olaf. "These are the orders with the amount and type of wood we'll need at the finishing mill. Give me a tally of what you can supply."

"Vill do." The big man rose and walked her to her horse. "Now you go straight home, hear me? There are still some wild varmints loose in these parts." He looked at the graying sky, black edged and ominous. "Looks like rain before nightfall, too. We need the rain."

Atop her horse again, Willie paused a moment, crossed her hands on the pommel, and looked down at the big Swede. "Who do you think is behind all this?"

The big man lifted his stocky shoulders into a shrug. "I'm not sure. Sometimes people don't do a thing to receive the wrath of others. Your papa is a wealthy man, ja? But some men, because they lack money, skills, or energy of their own—or the power they think they deserve—spend all their time trying to figure out how to steal it from others. The lazy scoff at the industrious and scorn them for their wealth. Makes little sense, ja?"

He touched her gently on her arm. You be careful, flicka," he warned. "We don't know who they'll go after next. Jonathan was lucky."

With troubled eyes, she watched him amble away as she tried to drive the worry from her mind.

When Willie arrived at Matthew Reed's mill, the first thing she noticed was the mill was quiet with no workers about. She slipped off her mount, tied the reins, and surveyed the area with guarded caution.

The door to the mill opened, and he stepped into the sunshine.

"Getting slow?" She shaded her eyes against the sun. A hot summer often halted activity in the area as farmers returned to their fields to gather their crops and finish their haying.

He faced her, smiling, his hands shoved deep into his back pockets. "Actually, we've near depleted our stockpiles, and we'll have to go back to logging this fall."

She glanced up in amazement. "Skidding so soon? I'd be careful not to overcut your close areas." She knew without winter snows to bring the timber down the mountains to the mills, desperate operators often razed areas close by.

Reed frowned. "Now don't start with those silly lectures about preservation. There's so much timber in Western Pennsylvania, we'll never run out."

Scowling, she countered, "Not if we destroy most of the stands. It'll take a hundred years or more for these forests to replenish themselves. Your grandchildren will be taller than the seedlings."

"I didn't ask you here to discuss lumber," he rejoined sharply. He glowered at her, disgruntled, and fingered a sideburn.

Suddenly, she felt uncomfortable. Alarm bells started ringing inside her head. Something didn't feel right. She wanted to run, climb on her horse, and ride away as fast as possible.

"Come along, I've got a great spot picked out to sit and talk," he said. He led her around the pond's grassy banks until they came upon a small stand of trees. Under their leafy boughs, a tablecloth was spread with food, a bottle of red wine, and two goblets.

"I thought we might as well grab a bite to eat together, unless you're concerned your fiancé might be upset." He gestured for her to be seated.

"You misjudge Jonathan. He knows we're old friends." Willie suspiciously eyed the elaborate spread. She took a place on the ground and wrapped her arms around her knees. "What are we celebrating?"

An unpleasant look played across Reed's face. "You always have to get straight to the point, don't you, Wilhelmina?"

She steeled herself for what seemed like a verbal battle. "I've been told I'm rather blunt."

He dropped down beside her. "You know, most women would enjoy being coddled. They'd enjoy having someone to wine and dine them...and even whisper sweet words in their ears. You're a beautiful woman. Beautiful women should be treated like queens, showered with fine things."

Willie heaved a sigh, weary of his glib platitudes.

Casting tact to the wind, he blurted out, "I don't want you to marry Jonathan Wain."

She searched her scattered thoughts for the right words. "But what if we're in love?"

His lips puckered with annoyance. "He's not the right man for you. He only wants half of the finishing mill business and your money. His kind scours the earth and looks for innocent prey, naïve young women with a fortune."

"That's not true." Oh, dear heavens, now she was defending Jonathan Wain.

"Face it." His voice was laced with malice. "He has nothing in common with our way of life. He'll never be content to spend a lifetime here. He'll tire of dull day-to-day rural activities and long for the roguish, seafaring life again—leaving you without a care or a penny."

She leaped up. "I can't believe you're saying this."

He shot up beside her. "You fool! Don't you get it? You don't belong with him. You belong with me."

Uneasy with his simmering anger, she shook her head and glanced at the sky. Far to the west, dark clouds rolled in. "I don't know what to say."

"Say you'll be rid of him," he snapped. "Say it was wrong from the start."

"I can't, Matthew. I'm sorry."

He snorted derisively at her back as she turned and walked away, toward her mount. "You will be," she heard him mutter just as a big drop of rain plopped down on her head.

Later, as she rode into the forest, the clouds split open. Sheets of driving rain spilled out, flattening the grass, and stinging and blinding the eyes of her horse. Bolts of lightning darted across the colorless sky. Claps of thunder boomed in the distance.

Willie pulled her hat down lower over her eyes to ward off the downpour. Beneath her, she could feel Warrior nervously pushing forward against the wind. Several yards onward, she found an outcropping of limestone with a huge shelf jutting out to form a makeshift shelter. She nudged the horse toward it and dismounted.

A streak of lightening illuminated the horizon, followed by an explosion of thunder. Rearing, Warrior bolted, tearing the reins from her hands.

"Stop!" she screamed above the drumming of the rain. "Warrior, stop."

Stunned, she watched the horse gallop away through the soggy underbrush. Water streamed down her face and rushed over the brim of her hat to land in pools at her feet. Miserably, she glanced down at herself, now soaked to the bone.

"Oh, drat," she shouted and followed it with a stream of blue curses which could barely be heard over the noise of the rain. She took one more miserable look at her drenched clothes and decided there was little advantage in waiting out the storm. Taking the nearest route toward the Wasp, she pushed a handful of wet curls out of her eyes and stepped out into the curtain of water.

Minutes later, as easily as the heavens had opened, they closed, ending the torrential cloudburst. Willie continued along the spongy forest floor, pleased she was wearing her old comfortable boots. She didn't mind the walk. She had no fear of being lost. And she knew her horse would eventually return to the stables for feed. What worried her most was the possibility everyone at the Wasp might be gone before she reached it on foot. It would be even a longer walk to the manor—and in the pitch dark. Already her motions were leaden. She shivered from the dampness.

Several minutes later, accustomed to the area, she squinted through the trees to locate her bearings and recognized a shortcut, up an old animal trail leading to the south side of the mill. She took the path and reached a grassy clearing only to come to an unsettling halt. Her hand flew to her mouth to stifle a cry of surprise and, for a split second, she felt her heart sink to her knees. Ahead, her horse was tied to a sapling and grazed unperturbed.

She dropped to a crouch behind a large tree. Around her, the forest was silent, except for the birds flitting through the leaves overhead. She listened. She waited. She listened and waited for what seemed like hours.

When her nervousness abated, she crept cautiously to the horse. "Now who put you here?" she asked in a whisper as she pulled the reins free.

Pleased to hear his mistress's voice, the gelding snorted. She swung up into the saddle, overjoyed to be reunited with her mount. Yet, a disturbing feeling passed over her. Whoever tied her horse might well be watching her every move. Was his intent to terrify her or hurt her?

Shivering now, more from her thoughts than the cold, she kicked her horse and changed direction, galloping briskly toward the manor with the mystery gnawing at her the entire way.

The same afternoon, Jonathan was not at all pleased with the way the day was progressing. He had missed Willie at breakfast before he could warn her to be careful while in the forest. Even though Sam had tried to put his fears to rest, saying no one knew the woods better than she did, it did little to appease his disagreeable nature.

Things proceeded downhill fast. A planer broke at the finishing mill and a new lathe worker never showed.

Now, drenched from the downpour, Jonathan stood with Sam and prayed their entire morning's work on the millrace would finally pay off.

"Let her rip," he heard Sam bellow to a worker ready to release the water into the chute. "Let's see what we're made of."

Bedraggled and soaked to the skin, the crew watched silently as water tumbled into the millrace and over the paddles on the huge wheel, sending it spinning harmoniously on its axle, gliding like it was greased with butter.

Covered with mud from head to toe, Sam hooted. "Hells Bells, we did it." He slapped his knee and thumped the backs of the workers standing around him. "Now let's get some logs released from the boom and put this ol' gal to work."

Jonathan shook his head. "I don't know how you do it. You find yourself in a dilemma, Sam, and you come out smelling like a rose. And you seem to have a good time despite all the aggravation."

"You worry too much, son. You young folks get so impatient with life. You want everything at once." Together, they watched the logs tumble over the upper spillway into the splash dam feeding the saws. He raised a hand to shade his eyes and squinted across the water. His face paled, and he stood stark still. "Oh, no," he rasped, "there's a body in our millpond."

Jonathan's eyes followed his sight line. Without any words, they both tore off toward the bank above the spillway.

Near the dam abutment, Jonathan felt icy fear twist around his heart and rip at his chest like sharp talons. The body of a woman with honey brown hair floated toward the shore. He instantly recognized the cream and tan checkered riding outfit he had given Willie for Christmas.

"Oh, no," he screamed, grief overtaking him. "Please, noooooo!"

Unable to move, he stood rooted to his spot, his heart pounding so fast, so hard, he could feel it through his shirt.

It was Sam who moved down to the shore and waded knee-deep into the water. Hesitantly, he reached out, grabbed the corpse by the collar, and turned it over, gazing into bright blue eyes which stared lifelessly up at him. He expelled a breath of pent-up air. He searched the bank to locate Jonathan, who had slumped to his knees, his head buried in his hands.

"It's not Willie," Sam called out. "It's Rachael Kramer."

The words shook Jonathan to reality. He rose and rushed down to the shoreline. Together, they pulled the girl from the water and onto the grassy bank.

"Dang gal knew she couldn't swim. I wonder what she was doing near the river to get herself drowned?" Sam asked.

Hands still shaking, Jonathan checked the body carefully, but found no marks on her head or face.

"And what in tarnation was she doing in Willie's clothes?"

Jonathan stood and ran his shaking hand though his thick hair. "Willie always lends clothes to Rachael. Get a blanket from the mill and cover the body. Looks like I'm going to have to tell her father."

He started up the grassy bank, turned, and added, "If Willie stops, Sam, you'd better break this to her gently. This is going to be a dreadful blow."

But it was Jonathan who broke the news to her in the evening, clutching her next to him as she sobbed in his arms before racing up to her room and slamming the door.

Later, as he dined alone with Dalton Wydcliffe, he wondered whether there would ever be an end to the suffering she would have to endure. As if reading his thoughts, Wydcliffe spoke. "She's still got more hurting ahead, Jonathan. You're going to have to help her through it and hope she doesn't have permanent scars from all this."

"I'll try, Dalton," Jonathan replied. He looked into the old man's haggard, watery eyes, "but she keeps putting up walls and they're harder and harder to knock down."

"I know," he answered. "How well I know."

CHAPTER TWENTY-FOUR

Early September, 1857

ASH-COLORED CLOUDS COVERED THE SKY as Willie dressed quickly, brushing her hair and whirling it into a chignon at the back of her neck. Thoughts like a flock of birds flew through her head as she moved about her room and chose a white blouse and navy skirt to wear to go shopping in town.

Despite the fact Rachael's death had been ruled an accident and no witness to the event could be found, she had a pocketful of doubts. At first, the entire town believed Daniel Barrett was involved, though initially, even he was not overlooked when they searched for a reason. But he had been at work at the mill that day, faithfully reporting on time since the day he started.

When she later learned he had quit his job and disappeared, she mulled over various possibilities for days. Why would he leave? Was Rachael with child? Had he refused to wed her? Had shame played a part? Had her parents, upon finding out, humiliated her until she was unable to bear it any longer?

Nothing made sense. Rachael and she had always shared every secret, every problem since childhood. Why hadn't Rachael come to her for help?

In the end, she decided she knew one thing about Rachael Kramer everyone else should have known. She loved life. She loved people. She loved helping people. But she was also a born coward, and it was too far-fetched to believe she'd taken her life and the life of an unborn child, even if she had been highly distraught.

She was also certain she didn't accidently drown like everyone was so quick to believe. At least, not intentionally—or without help. Three summers ago, she had spent weeks at Garret's old abandoned splash dam teaching her to swim. Even though she had developed into an agile swimmer, she was not a strong one. Could she have misjudged her own abilities and swam out too far, tiring before she could reach the shore again? Willie doubted it was a possibility either.

She remembered the day she had lent Rachael the dress for Clara's party. She had been so thrilled with both the dress and the mother-of-pearl jewelry. Why hadn't her parents returned the jewelry? Maybe they never realized who owned the necklace if Rachael hadn't confided in them. Or maybe they were too grief-stricken to remember. To be honest, Willie decided, returning them would only make her pain more intense and the anguish worse.

Still harboring her nagging thoughts, she climbed the stairs to the third floor and knocked lightly on Jonathan's door. He stood buttoning the last button on his shirt. He glanced briefly at his desk before he looked her way. An opened letter from Baltimore lay atop it, where he had carelessly tossed it.

"Sit down," he said, indicating the window seat. He sat on the bed and pulled on one of his black leather boots. "You look beautiful," he added.

"You're not used to seeing me in dresses."

"No, my dear. You look more beautiful each day. Aging is going to be a bonus for you." He pulled on the other boot and retrieved the letter from his desk. "I have a proposition."

She stared at him curiously.

"Let's take a few weeks and go to Maryland together. My family is anxious to meet you, and I have business to attend to."

"Oh no, Jonathan, must you leave *again?*"

"This time, though, we won't be separated." He offered her a hopeful look.

"You know I can't. It's impossible. The finishing mill is busy and needs attention. Papa is feeling poorly. I just don't see how we can both leave."

"Now, now, Willie." He tried to mollify her. "Sam is willing to handle the business for a short time. Even your father thinks it's a good idea. It'll only be for a few weeks."

"Sam can't handle the finishing mill, too."

"I know he can't," he admitted, "but I talked with McGee and he's willing to oversee it. We can set up the schedules and orders in advance. And young Bennie Corbin can run and repair almost all the machinery."

"Why do you have to leave now?" Exasperation crept further into her voice.

"I have business needing my attention. My

brothers have been running my third of the business for over a year. Even if we get married, I can't lock myself away in these woods and ignore other lucrative interests on the coast."

"What did you plan to do with these mills if we were married?" She threw the question at him. A noticeable chill hung on the edge of her words. "We can't abandon them."

"I have no intention of abandoning anything. We'd have to find someone who would be competent to manage these holdings when we are in Baltimore."

"Wait. Surely you're not serious? What makes you so sure I want to live in Maryland? I thought you wanted to live here."

"I do, but not all the time. This was supposed to be only a temporary arrangement. I never had any intentions of giving up all my business interests on the coast. It would be impossible."

Her eyes flashed in indignation. "What would be impossible would be for me to agree to leave these mills...now or ever."

He spoke in a calm voice. "We can discuss this later. I'm asking you to pack and come with me."

"I can't leave the mills."

A muscle clenched along his jaw. "It always comes back to the mills, doesn't it? The mills. Your undying devotion to the mills. Where do I fit into all your plans?"

She faced him, her brown eyes locked with his steel gray ones. "I thought you wanted to share your life with me."

"I do, but I can't compete with the mills, your precious river, and your blasted white pines, Willie.

I'm forever sharing you with them. Two weeks are all I'm asking for."

"What about Papa? I can't leave him."

"You can. You can't tie yourself here waiting for something disastrous to happen. Anyhow, your father wants you to go."

Her accusing voice stabbed the air. "It seems you have this all arranged without even consulting me."

He sighed and rubbed the back of his neck. "And for the very same reason we're discussing this now. I was hoping to get everyone in agreement so you'd leave without any reservation."

She shook her head. "I'm sorry, not now."

He picked up his coat and leveled a wounded look at her. "I'm leaving tomorrow. Conrad will have my belongings packed for the morning. If you are coming with me, make sure you have enough clothes for a two-week trip."

"Have an enjoyable time." She brushed past him and headed to the doorway. "And don't worry about how much time you'll need attending to your other endeavors. We'll manage without you."

She left the room, never once looking back, her dark skirt swishing around her tiny ankles.

CHAPTER TWENTY-FIVE

THE WEEK AFTER JONATHAN RETURNED, bearing a saddlebag of orders from small communities he had visited along his route home, Dalton Wydcliffe collapsed at the mill. The elderly man was taken immediately to the manor with the doctor suggesting complete bedrest.

Willie, knowing his condition was worse than he or the doctor would admit, sent word to her sister and remained close by, spending hours in his room, keeping guard, watching him sleep.

Jonathan readily assumed the work load, never flinching from the long tedious hours. For the brief time he had known Dalton Wydcliffe, he'd been struck with a devotion to him quite unlike that of just a business associate. His heart ached for Willie, and even though he personally understood the pain she was going through, he could think of no way to lessen her burden other than overseeing the mill operations.

Raven's arrival four days later helped to create an air of calmness to the household's pandemonium, but she, too, was unable to alleviate her sister's looming grief.

Even the mill hands showed signs of anguish as they went about their daily tasks. Sam Bradley diligently assumed Jonathan's right-hand position, taking care of problems before he was even aware of them. Still tied to his old friend like an invisible thread, Sam stopped every evening at the manor to check on him before he set off for his cabin in the woods.

A week later, Willie didn't have to be told things were worse. It was written all over Jonathan's face when he came down from the third floor in the morning. She could hear Sam's voice in the hallway, and she raced to the master bedroom door to confront Raven.

"He's been asking for you," Raven said, composed and stoic, "but he didn't want you awakened." Her filmy eyes met her sister's for a brief moment of understanding before she departed.

Willie pushed the old oak door open and watched her father weakly raise his head, recognizing her. His face was drawn and pale in contrast to the cobalt blue quilt covering his four-poster bed. The room was dim, the heavy gold and white drapes drawn shut to blot out the sunlight.

"Come in, Elizabeth Wilhelmina," he said hoarsely. "Open the drapes, I want to see the sun and the pines."

She drew the cords and sunlight poured into the room, falling over the bed and onto the tired old man. Dragging a chair next to the bed, she sat down and swallowed, trying to hold back a flood of tears.

"Don't talk, Papa," she said. "Try to rest."

"No, daughter, it's too late." He breathed shallowly, his listless eyes devouring her as if he needed one last look. He held out an unsteady hand, and she grasped it with her small one.

"I want to tell you how proud I am of you, daughter. No son could have been better. Don't grieve for me, child. Wydcliffes just carry on. Trust Jonathan, he's a good man. You know I love you." His breathing became labored. Tears streamed down her face as she clutched his shriveled fingers, praying she could force life back into them.

"Remember, it's the land, Elizabeth Wilhelmina. The land. It's the only thing permanent and will outlive us all. It brings forth life, it changes, but it will never disappear." His hand became slack in hers. His weary eyes closed briefly and then flashed open. He tried to push himself up from the bed. "It's the key to everything and that's the mystery, don't you see?" he whispered insistently. "The land is cold. Black with cold..." he paused. "Beneath, it's black now and cold as stone." He sunk back on the bed and closed his eyes for the last time as peace enveloped him at last.

Willie never remembered her sister entering. She sat clutching her father's lifeless hand, tears pouring in rivulets down her cheeks. Jonathan removed her from the room, leading her to her bedroom where she sobbed hysterically. He tried to hold her, but she pushed him away. He left, closing the door quietly.

Later, down in the study with Raven, he heard her go out the front door and around the terrace to the stables. He started for the French doors when Raven laid a restraining hand on his arm. "Leave her be," she said softly, "she needs to find her own way to grieve."

It was late afternoon and the mills were vacant, having been shut down immediately upon notice of Dalton Wydcliffe's death. Willie stood high on the ramp where the logs were carried up to the saw carriage. Below her, the cloudy waters swirled and churned in the mill pond. A light drizzle of rain began to fall, but she failed to notice it as she stood motionless and stared, her damp hair hanging limply down her back.

"I thought I'd find you here, young lady," she heard Sam Bradley's raspy voice say from somewhere behind her. She turned to see the bow-legged old man standing on the saw carriage, holding his battered hat in hand. "You always came up here when you were a child and when things weren't going your way. God Almighty, I have no idea why you like heights so dang much."

Her swollen red eyes met Sam's gentle blue ones, and she shook her head sorrowfully. "What's left, Sam?"

"Don't rightly know, honey. Whatever pieces you want to pick up, that's what's left. If you mean what's fair, I can assure you nothin' in life is fair. It's a guarantee the minute we enter this world as squalling babes."

The old man never took his eyes off the slim girl as he continued. "Many years back I felt the same way you do right now—there was nothing left for me. You feel like your world is crumbling around you, and you don't know which way to turn, what to do. And a young man with eager brown eyes like yours told me it took more guts to live in this wild God-forsaken land. Said it was easy to give up and quit. But he wasn't a quitter. He had a dream to become a land baron, a logging king—just for one fleeting moment, he used to say."

"He was different than me, Sam. He was strong, almost invincible." She pushed long wet strands of hair from her face.

"No, you're wrong, Willie," the old man said. "Even the proud and the strong fall to pieces at certain times. When your mother died, he had a lot of mountains to climb to get back on top. Life had dealt him a double blow, losing two women he loved. He had a dream, and he went on despite the anguish, the pain, the problems, and the suffering to carve a place in this valley as he originally planned."

"Don't you see, Sam," she cried out hoarsely. Tears streamed down her face. "I'm weak. I don't have what it takes to become that great."

He walked up to her and pulled her into his grizzled arms as she sobbed. "Oh yes, you do, honey. You have everything and more. You have Wydcliffe blood in you, don't you? And you have a dream."

He took her home, soggy and wet, without an ounce of tears left in her overwrought body. Raven helped put her to bed after administering a sedative to make her sleep.

Jonathan checked on her frequently throughout the night, watching her tiny forlorn form sleeping beneath the rose coverlet.

There was going to be a lot of walls to knock down now, he thought sadly. And he wasn't sure he would be able to do it.

The funeral was held two days later, in the early morning with the heat of the September sun warming the dew-covered earth. Wydcliffe himself had requested a simple burial, but friends, associates, neighbors, and mill hands poured in, many coming from distant outlying areas. All came to honor the man who had helped tame their forest homeland.

Jonathan and Sam had made most of the funeral arrangements. Both stood next to Raven and Willie during the short ceremony at the family burial plot sitting atop a small knoll surrounded by a forest of white pine.

Raven had sent her husband a message relaying the news of her father's death and requesting he remain in Canada with Nicole. She had asked Willie to accompany her back up North for a short stay.

The minister, a serious young man, did not make the ceremony long or tedious. Willie was pleased he was brief. Her father would never have wanted it long-winded or maudlin. Dressed in black, she refused to cover her tear-streaked face with the filmy black mourning net and instead flipped it up over a simple silk hat perched on her head. There was no reason on earth, she decided, not to feel the breeze on her face or to plainly see the cherry coffin as it was lowered into the grave.

At the end of the service, she turned to Sam. His eyes were duller than she had ever seen them in her life. "Think you and McGee could run things here for a while?" she asked. "I need to take some time for myself, Sam."

He placed a reassuring hand on her shoulder and squeezed it. "Sure, take all the time you need. Thinkin' of going up North with Raven?"

She nodded, staring down at the top of the wooden coffin. She glanced up to see the mass of people who were leaving the burial area.

As if reading her thoughts, the old man spoke, "He had a lot of friends, didn't he, for such a wily old cuss?"

A weak smile crossed her ashen face. "I sure hope they have white pines in heaven," she said faintly.

"Hell yes, child. If I know your father, he's already organizing the angels into logging crews. You can stand proud. He was an honest man."

As if drawn by the force of her words, she looked up toward the forest where the tall, white pines stood, reaching skyward. Her eyes caught the glimpse of a figure, dressed in buckskins, standing in the shadows.

"Excuse me, Sam," she said, picking up her skirts and moving toward the stand of trees. "This will take a minute."

The shadow faded back into the recess of the forest as she reached the perimeter. She stood silently a moment before stepping into the dark forest, the soft mossy floor springy beneath her slippers.

"So you've come," she said softly, staring up at the figure who soundlessly appeared like he was a ghost. The Indian stood before her. He was tall with dark eyes and hair, and bronzed skin even darker in the shadows of the dim forest.

"You have grown into a woman, Will..hell..mina," he said.

"And you, Lone Eagle, have become a warrior," she replied. "Many moons have passed since our childhood. Raven's daughter is now seven white man's years. How are your people?"

"They are well, as good as can be expected with all the sickness the white man has brought to our lands. Many tribes are now pushed westward to the borders of the great river." The Indian searched her face. "Have you taken a husband? I see you stand by the tall man at your father's burial."

"Not yet," she replied, "although he and I are supposed to be wed. Have you taken a wife?"

"It is planned this winter. I will take Shining Moon."

The Indian watched her pull out the pins in her hair and remove her hat and veil. "Your father was a great man," he said. "Many of our people will mourn his passing."

She fought back the urge to cry.

"I see much of Wydcliffe in his daughter."

"Maybe not enough," she whispered and turned toward the cemetery. "His footprints are very large."

"But your heart is larger, and your strength will come from it. You must give it time."

"Have you seen Raven?"

"I came today only to look once more upon your father, whose spirit has entered the great hunting grounds above. It is better if Raven and I do not meet in front of the white men's eyes. It would not help her. Her ties to her childhood life are almost forgotten."

"The dream," she said. "The one you once told me of. The one about a fireball. What does it mean?"

He shook his head. "I do not know. It is only for you to discover." Above them, the tall white pines rustled in the wind, and they stood listening for a minute before he spoke again. "You are welcome to come to my village. To mourn. To rest. To recover. To be at peace with yourself."

He held out his hand to her in white man's fashion. She grasped it tightly. They studied each other for a moment, as if sharing thoughts of long ago, before he turned and faded into the forest.

She moved out from the shady glade and back to Sam.

"Lone Eagle," Sam said. "I knew he'd show up."

"Yes, but he doesn't want anyone to know. He felt it was best if no one knew Raven's mother and his mother were sisters.

Sam nodded, removed his coat, and threw it over his shoulder. He pulled at his neck tie, loosening it. Together, they started down the path from the cemetery. The mourning veil from her silk hat dragged carelessly on the grassy ground as they walked along arm in arm.

When they reached the manor, she looked over the crowds of people they had to feed before sending them on their way. Among them, she recognized the bright red hair of Red Ruby, off to one side, chatting with Old Joe. Two outcasts in their own way.

"Thank you, Sam, for being so special," she said, hugging him. As an afterthought, she added, "You know I'm going to need your help with Papa gone."

"I know." He winked and removed his hat, letting the breeze ruffle his mop of salt and pepper hair. "And I'm thinkin' that even if we're in over our blasted heads, between the two of us, we'll keep these dad-burned mills afloat."

CHAPTER TWENTY-SIX

THE DAY AFTER THE FUNERAL, Bradford Payne met with Willie, Raven, Sam, and Jonathan in the library at the manor. He requested the meeting to read Dalton Wydcliffe's will and to process the necessary papers as quickly as possible. A man of often eloquent, but few words, he came straight to the point.

"You might say this is a most unusual will," he began, "but it is the most recent one which I drew up with your father." His gaze circled the group. "Dalton Wydcliffe was more than competent at the time it was made, I assure you. In fact, it's dated two days after the Fourth of July and signed and witnessed as well." He peered at Willie and Raven, and he cleared his throat. "Your father was a wealthy man."

The old lawyer went on to tell them the first part of the will dealt strictly with the household help, who were given generous bonuses and asked to stay on if Willie so desired. The second part gave the Wasp, in its entirety, to Sam Bradley.

"Your father," Bradford Payne said in way of explanation, "had a humorous side to him. He felt

Sam had refused his offer too many times and felt he should have assumed responsibility for the mill long ago. This was his way of getting in the last lick."

Willie listened attentively as he continued, explaining to Raven that she would receive a large sum of money, but would have no interest in the holdings of any Clearfield mills since her father had earlier helped Thomas LeConte set up his fur and tannery business. A trust was set up for Nicole, the only grandchild, until she turned twenty-one. In the event Raven had any more children within ten years, the trust would be split to accommodate the additional grandchildren.

Clearing his throat again, Bradford Payne hesitated. "Elizabeth Wilhelmina, you have been left the manor, the Hornet's Nest, the Black Widow, and all land holdings and business interests of the Wain-Wydcliffe partnership. However, your father has attached certain stipulations to this bequest."

"Go on," she urged quietly.

"Jonathan Caleb Wain has been appointed your legal guardian for all business affairs for the next year if you should not marry, after which, all interests will become solely yours. Should you decide to marry before the year is finished, to anyone besides Jonathan, you must receive his consent to the marriage before he relinquishes the business interests to your complete control."

Bradford Payne looked up.

Willie gasped, her face reflecting a look of shock and horror.

Beside her, Jonathan let out an uncomfortable low groan. His face twisted in agony. He lowered his face to his hands.

"You understand," Payne said, "a husband, by legal marriage, automatically has rights to your holdings and therefore, in reality, he would be releasing them to your husband as well. You have complete charge of all accounts and business dealings of the mills unless the amounts to be spent are so enormous, as deemed by me, at which time Jonathan must also consent to the expenditure. Any interests you share in the finishing mill, White Pines Manufacturing, are yours without reservations or stipulations except you both must mutually agree concerning its operations."

Stopping to scan the pages of the will briefly, Payne added, "Of course, Wilhelmina, should you marry Jonathan at any time, all this is null and void since your husband would legally be responsible for your holdings. In the event of Jonathan's death before you reach the one-year decree, both Samuel Bradley and myself are responsible, upon mutual agreement and under somewhat the same terms, to administer your father's wishes."

"Are you finished?" Willie asked coldly, rising, and throwing a distant, almost haughty look at Payne and Jonathan. The impact of what had just occurred was like a blade cutting through her heart. For the next year, her father had all but cut her off from making any major decisions without Jonathan's consent.

"For now, yes," Payne said wearily.

She stared at him for a disturbingly long time before she spoke. "How strange, even to his death, my father never trusted me enough to give me complete control of what I worked so hard to earn."

"Wilhelmina," Bradford Payne said lowly, "Your father was trying to protect you to the very end. It wasn't you he didn't trust, it was anyone around you who might want to take advantage of you because of your vast wealth. He wanted to be certain you didn't do anything foolish, out of grief or impulsiveness. He felt in a year, you would be in the position to know exactly what you wanted. Until that time, he was safeguarding your holdings in a type of trust."

She tilted her chin up arrogantly. "And I presume making me a ward of Jonathan was the only way he could accomplish this?" She laughed shrilly. "How very demeaning it is to be passed off to a guardian at my age. Thank you, Mr. Payne, I appreciate your time for explaining all this."

Curtly dismissing herself, she walked out of the library, her head held high.

Later in her room, she stood at her window and watched the sun set, a fiery ball glowing on the horizon. With the back of her hand, she wiped the tears from her eyes, red and swollen and ringed with two black smudge marks. What a fool she had been to think her father had actually believed in her abilities to manage the mills. She should have known the minute Jonathan Wain appeared that something was amiss. A guardian. A protector! That's what he had been trying to accomplish. She berated herself for not foreseeing his moves. She had been a puppet in the whole scheme. Now Jonathan Wain would be pulling the strings. Well almost, she decided, but not forever.

Bathing her face in cold water, she sought him

out in the study. He was seated at her father's desk, his head bent over a pile of papers and ledgers. He watched wordlessly as she handed him the black ring box with her hand devoid of the diamond.

"Why?" he whispered. He tossed the box carelessly back on the desktop amid the papers.

"I talked with McGee," she said. "Please don't blame him. If he hadn't told me, I'm sure Bradford Payne would have spilled his guts in due time. It seems you are a very wealthy man—a fact you neglected to tell me. A fact my father neglected to tell me as well. Now I understand the lure of Baltimore and the business affairs requiring your secret devotion. But secrets were one of your better points. I suspect you even knew about the will. Or did you plan it?"

"Honestly, Willie," he said in a husky voice, "I knew nothing about the blasted will. You must believe me. I would never have wanted it to be like this. Your father surprised me as much as he did you." He sighed and leaned back in the chair. "Please believe me. I can explain the other."

She laughed scornfully. "Yes, I'm sure you can explain it all—the hats, oranges, jewelry, clothes, and even the horse. It all makes sense now. Bribes? Or sordid tokens of affection? I admire your charm and your ability to manipulate people, including my father. But it's come to an end."

She walked to the French doors and crossed her arms at her chest. "You were so greedy, you wanted it all. You weren't content with just your half, you wanted to control mine, too. Tell me, was it power? Surely not the money? And was seduction a part of your neat little plot, too?"

"You have it all wrong—"

She cut him off. "All wrong? It doesn't matter now. I'll say this only once." She unwound her arms and a hand sliced the air. "I'm leaving to take some time for myself. Both Sam and McGee have agreed to help with the mills. You can either stay here and run them until I return in a month, and then leave, or you can leave now. Whichever you prefer. But when I return, I do not want to see your face or know your whereabouts. Payne can take care of knowing the latter, just in case your righteous opinion is ever needed."

Her voice grew so caustic it cracked. "Count on one thing, Jonathan, you'll never get Wydcliffe land, not as long as I breathe. It's all mine. And I don't give up easily."

"Willie, please..." he implored.

"No, Jonathan, spare me the damnable lies," she fired back. "Just get out and off my land!"

CHAPTER TWENTY-SEVEN

SAM BRADLEY SHUFFLED HIS FEET, kicking at a pebble in the courtyard and sending it flying into the grass alongside the stables. A wrinkle split his forehead in two. Nearby, Conrad solemnly held Jonathan's hat and waited patiently, not trying to disguise the struggle in his glum face.

Jonathan slipped a rifle into his scabbard and threw his saddle bags over Trade Wind's chestnut rump. The early morning was cool and serene. A hint of a breeze played in the leaves of the trees.

"Looks like this is good-bye," he said in his usual commanding voice. "The lady will be back in a day or two, and we wouldn't want to stir up a Wydcliffe temper needlessly. I sure appreciate everything you both have done."

"It don't seem right. This can't be the only way." Sam shook his head from side to side. He removed a leather pouch, withdrew some tobacco, and filled his pipe. "Surely there's something we can do to convince Willie to agree to havin' you stay on. I'm bettin' she's cooled off, what with a month havin' passed."

"We've been over this a dozen times." Jonathan sighed. "Once she's back and has the familiar things to 'rouse more memories, she'll only get more hostile with me underfoot. She's bitter, and it's going to take some time to heal the wounds." His eyes looked at the stables, courtyard, and up to the manor like he was memorizing it, right down to the last detail.

"Anyhow," he added, "with me gone, this will be the perfect time for whoever's been causing trouble to move in on her. We can't coax the culprits out, so let's try letting them come to her. You both know how to contact me should anything new arise."

"Where are you headed?" Sam lit a match and held it over the pipe under Conrad's disapproving glare.

"Back to Baltimore. There's a lot of loose ends that have needed my attention for the last year. If there are no problems here, I can even take to sea for a while."

"What about Willie?" Sam asked boldly.

A smile played on Jonathan face. The old man was like a burr hooked to your pant leg. A hound with a treed coon. He was never going to give up.

"What about her? There may still be some little girl left in the lady, but she's more than woman enough to handle things here. She'll need your help, Sam."

"Shoot, that's not what I mean. What about you and her?"

"You sure are a persistent old-timer." Jonathan readjusted his hat on his head. "If you want me to admit there's a future, I can't tell you what it might bring. I was once hoping there might be a right time for us—but now, I just don't know."

He flipped open the gold pocket watch Willie had given him and checked the time. Snapping it closed, he turned it slowly in the palm of his hand, rubbing his fingers over the Wain-Wydcliffe insignia before he returned it to his pocket. He swung into the saddle, tipped his hat, and spoke. "I thank you both. Good luck with the hellcat." Seconds later, he was cantering down the road, kicking up a cloud of dust billowing out over the sunlit landscape.

"Things are sure going to be quiet around here," Conrad said. Together they watched the speck of Jonathan disappear into nothingness.

"Take advantage of it, old boy." Sam slapped him heartily on his stiff back. "Will-*hell*-mina is due back any day, and I assure you, all hell *will* break loose."

Willie arrived twenty-four hours after Jonathan had departed, looking more robust than when she had left, but still painfully thin. She rode in quietly to the stables with no one to greet her. She hadn't sent word as to her exact arrival and had taken time instead to visit the Indian village as she journeyed south from Canada. Her skin was now more golden from the outdoors and her hair, streaked with more blonde from the sun. As soon as she reached Wydcliffe land she was so overjoyed at being home, she had taken a day to camp out on the cliffs above the rushing Susquehanna River. There was something peaceful about its steady current, like a heartbeat, drumming over the rocks and flowing forward at its own pace. She was now sure she could deal with her father's death. But she wasn't certain she could deal with the loneliness of the empty manor.

She unsaddled her mount and was leading Warrior into the paddock when she spied Roy sauntering up the dusty drive. Waving wildly, he broke into a churning run to reach the spot where she stood with her shoulder propped against the gate.

"Holy cow! It's sure good to see you," the boy said, gasping, out of breath. He hesitated, not quite sure of what he should do or say next.

Suddenly, she smiled in her old way and, relieved, the boy grinned back.

"It's good to be home, Roy. Is there anyone at the house?" Her eyes shifted from his face to the manor.

"Hannah will be back from town later this afternoon. Conrad is around here somewhere."

"And Sam?"

"He's at the mill. Need a new mount?"

"Maybe later."

She moved toward the familiar path leading to the back door.

The house was quiet and still, almost eerie, when she pushed the door open. In the kitchen, she found a cup in the cupboard and headed for the well-polished cook stove. It had been weeks since she had tasted coffee. Real coffee. Thick as mud and armed with flavor.

"Criminy," she exclaimed, discovering the back of the stove empty. It suddenly dawned on her Jonathan had undoubtedly left, and Conrad had stopped making his daily ration. She headed directly to the pantry and started rummaging through the tins for some fresh beans.

She was so involved in her search, she never heard the kitchen door open, never heard Conrad enter, and never heard him halt before the pantry door until he cleared his throat.

"Good to have you home, Miss Willie. Can I help you get anything?"

She glanced at the lean, serious man. "It's good to be back, Conrad. Do you know where Hannah keeps the coffee?"

"Give me a minute, I'll make it." His voice was soft, unlike the clipped, formal tone he usually used. He brushed past her and removed a round tin from the cupboard shelves overhead.

"Anything amiss while I've been gone?" She leaned against the wooden counter and crossed her arms.

"Here? Or at the mills?"

She shrugged. "Both."

Conrad moved out of the pantry and efficiently about the kitchen. "None I'm aware of, Missy. You'll have to speak with Sam about the mill operations." His sober gaze alighted on her face and flashed down to her dusty riding britches and mud-encrusted boots. "Do you want me to draw you a bath?"

She laughed, pushed the hair out of her eyes, and peered down at her rumpled clothes. "Looks like I need one, doesn't it? Would you bring the coffee to my room?"

"Certainly."

"Conrad." She paused. "Jonathan. I assume he's gone?"

Conrad faced her stiffly, his face expressionless. "Yesterday morning."

She turned to go.

"Miss Willie?"

"Yes?" She turned back to face him.

"I took the liberty of packing some of your father's belongings during the weeks you were gone. There wasn't much to do except ramble around in this old house. I put them in trunks in the attic if you need to find anything."

"How kind of you. Thank you." She wandered into the breakfast salon, where the morning sun had left only shadows, and proceeded through the deserted, hollow-sounding dining room. The house, tomblike and fastidiously in order, smelled like fresh beeswax. The floors and the woodwork had recently been polished to a brilliant shine.

She set her foot on the bottom step of the staircase, prepared to go directly to her room, decided against it, and went to the study instead. She hesitated a brief moment before she pushed the heavy paneled door open.

The sun shining through the French doors threw golden rays of light across the colorful Persian rug. At the eastern windows, she opened the drapes to allow even more light to flood the room. Like a magnet, she was drawn to her father's desk. Her eyes wandered over the chair he always used and the desktop where stacks of papers were divided into neat piles and held down with glass paper weights. The faint scent of tobacco still lingered in the air, despite the fact his pipes, tobacco, and pipe stand had been removed. A parchment letter was propped against a pigeonhole with her name on the envelope, and she easily recognized the bold legible writing. Willie tore it open, extracting the single sheet. It read:

Dearest Willie,
I will make this brief. Should you need any
assistance, please feel free to call upon me. Bradford
Payne knows how to contact me. I know you don't
believe me, but I never played any part in your father's
decision to oversee the mill operations. I know of no
way to convince you otherwise, unless time itself
could speak and disclose the truth. I remain your
zealous admirer and partner...as sure as the
Susquehanna River runs untamed.
Lovingly,
~Jonathan

Willie folded the letter and slipped it in the envelope. Short and sweet. Right to the point. It almost sounded sincere, she thought bitterly. Or was it because he was no longer near? He had a way of crossing space between them even when he was absent.

A peal of laughter at the front door made her forget her thoughts, and she dashed out. Sam Bradley stood in the entrance way. He reached out his wiry arms and grabbed her up as soon as she appeared. "Elizabeth Will-hell-mina, how did you sneak in here without anyone knowing?"

Eyes watering, she pounded him affectionately on his back. "It's good to see you. You must tell me what's happening in town and at the mills."

"No, Willie, it can wait. Tell me about Canada." He hooked his arm into hers and propelled her toward the breakfast salon. "First, let's see if Conrad can scrounge up some grub. This old belly is gnawing at me again."

"I haven't even bathed or changed my clothes," she lamented.

"Hells bells, young lady, you're not eating with a king, just an old logger. You look delightful."

Overjoyed at Sam's arrival, she allowed herself to be swept away to the salon. Some things never change, she decided, and Sam Bradley was one of them. The old man was always in a state of constant motion, oozing a sense of joviality.

"Raven, Nicole, and Thomas send their love," she said.

Conrad entered the salon and poured a cup of coffee for both of them.

She propped her chin on her hands. "Canada is wonderful, Sam. The land is rich, fertile, teaming with beaver, mink, otter, and weasel. There are waterways crisscrossing the entire countryside and miles and miles of forests. Raven's house is outside the city, located on a country estate. Everyone speaks French. Nicole can belt it out so fast you can't keep up. It's so quaint and exquisite, you'd love it."

"I'm sure I would," he answered, laughing gleefully with her, obviously pleased to see her face animated and alive again.

She took a sip of coffee. "What about the finishing mill?"

"You'll have to talk to McGee." He shrugged

dismissively. "Jonathan had everything in order before he left."

Anger mixed with anguish marred her cheery, soft features at the sound of Jonathan Wain's name. "I would assume he would have."

"Now, now, there you go again. You're not being fair to the poor man."

She held up a hand to silence him. "Please. Let's not discuss Jonathan Wain, especially on my first day back."

The conversation would have slid to an abrupt halt had Conrad not materialized with plates piled high with food. They ate in relative silence. Sam watched her nibble at a piece of bread and absently push the rest of her food around her plate.

"What's wrong now?" He eyed her warily. "Spit it out. You always have such a dad-burned pouting look when there's something eatin' at you."

Her lips curved into a smile. "I know you're not going to be hell bent overjoyed with what I'm about to propose, Sam, but think about it before you decide. Why not move into town for the fall and winter? It's a long ride back to the cabin every night, and we have all these empty rooms here at the manor."

The sound of dishes crashing in the kitchen was followed by an anxious cough and a low sputtering behind the adjoining door. Conrad was hanging on to every word being exchanged.

She had a tinge of desperation in her voice. "I have a lot of memories to put behind me, and I know I can't do it alone. I'm going to ramble about in this big old box like a loose marble." She paused and closed her eyes, looking miserable before she spoke again, "It's the silence, Sam. The stillness, the dismal sound of no one, nothing. I hate it. I hate the emptiness. I hate the dang silence. And you'd be close should something unexpected arise."

He stared at her tortured face, and she knew instantly she had him like a bear with its paw caught in a trap. There was no way he would refuse her.

"You know I'm a cranky old fool, and I hanker for the woods and being by myself," he reminded her. "I'm not a real civilized man."

Together they heard Conrad's choking and coughing in the kitchen, and they grinned at each other knowing it would be Conrad who would have to make the most adjustment.

He winked. "What about my mule?"

"Tess loves company, Sam. She'd love the stables. Bring her with you. Oh, please, say yes."

"All right. All right. But just for a couple of months until you get yourself settled in. These old bones do get tired of the long trip back and forth to the cabin, especially when the dad-burned winter sneaks up. Seventy-six years is a long time to be haulin' myself up on an old mule's back. Are you sure you want a finicky old man invadin' your privacy?"

"Oh, yes, I do." She laughed and jumped up, throwing her arms around his weathered neck. "I'll tell Conrad to get a room ready."

The sound of clanking pots and pans echoed from behind the kitchen door.

"I think he already knows," Sam muttered and followed it with a chuckle.

CHAPTER TWENTY-EIGHT

JUST AS SAM PREDICTED, ALL hell broke out less than a week after Willie's arrival. It began with a gentle rumbling from the mill hands who wondered how the operations would be carried on with a female in control. A day later, Ezra Hawkins and four other mill hands at the Black Widow quit outright, leaving the mill without a foreman and short-handed.

Willie knew it was time to clear the air, to set things straight, and to assure them of her leadership abilities. With the help of McGee, she arranged for a meeting of all the hands the following Sunday afternoon at the Hornet's Nest in town.

She now stood in the bed of a wagon and was dressed in shabby clothes similar to those she wore the day she first met Jonathan in the forest. Her plaid shirt was tucked into her logger's trousers and a red banana circled her neck. Her hair was pulled back with a thin black ribbon that fluttered in the breeze.

"Good grief," McGee uttered in disbelief. "She looks like one of them."

"Only a lot prettier," Sam said. "The girl's a sharp

one. She's knows what she's doing. No hand takes orders from anyone in skirts."

She looked out at the wave of faces before her. They were a motley assortment of over one hundred men, some as scruffy-looking as the day they left work, some dressed in Sunday best, having earlier attended church services.

She held up her hand to silence them and waited for the noise to subside. Finally, she spoke, her voice strong and sure. "Dalton Wydcliffe died last month, as you all know. But what you don't know is that Wydcliffe mills didn't die with him. All the mills, with the exception of the Wasp, have been given to me to control and operate, just like we've done the last year when Papa was ailing. Dalton Wydcliffe wasn't just my father, he was your friend, and many of you have worked alongside him and eaten at his table when I was only a baby. Your loyalty had been exceptional. But something is going amiss, and someone has spread rumors our operations won't be handled like they were in the past. I can't promise you everything will be as it always was.

"Times change. We must move forward—be it with new ideas or new equipment. But if you doubt my abilities, I ask you to look back at the past years I've worked beside you. Don't underestimate my desire to see these mills operating on a scale even more grand than they are now. If you want to be part of it, you are welcome to stay on. If you have your doubts, or are dissatisfied, you are welcome to quit and pick up your final pay this week. I'll not accept your sympathies because I'm a woman. I'm a Wydcliffe and will always be a Wydcliffe first. You're either with me, or you have no place at these mills and on my land. Whatever your choice shall be, I hold no grudges, but I want no dissatisfaction once you've made it."

She stopped a moment to give herself time to scan many of the familiar faces, making eye contact with each one.

"I've talked with Sam Bradley. He is willing to consider any man who might not want to work for me, if there's a place available at the Wasp. However, be forewarned. All the mills, including Sam's, will not be run any differently. Olaf Svenson will stay on, but become the foreman of the Black Widow. The shuffle leaves Sam without a foreman. Any man interested should speak to him after this meeting. Anyone who wishes to take the place of someone leaving should talk to me, Sam, or the mill foreman to see if it can be arranged. Anyone leaving, should give McGee notice immediately so he can prepare your pay."

A voice from the back of the crowd shouted, "How can we be sure everything will be the same?" A few low chuckles and snickers followed.

Without blinking, she shouted back, "These mills are your mills and my mills, like always. I guarantee it, and I'll back my word with a challenge to you. Our fall logging operations are already underway. To those who have enough backbone, I dare you to help me have the best year ever. Any additional profit made as a result of your efforts will be dispersed as follows. Fifty percent to Wain and Sons, as owed. A quarter to Wydcliffe mills, with the remaining quarter to be divided equally among yourselves and returned in your paychecks."

She heard a murmur pass through the crowd.

"You can't be serious," she heard a logger shout. "If we increase your profit over last year, you'll divide a quarter of the additional money among us?"

"I guess you're not deaf," she shot back. A wave of laughter ensued.

"Seems a mite too generous," someone yelled out.

"Why?" another man shouted.

"Why not?" she rejoined. "If you helped earn the profit, you can share in the benefits of it. I want Wydcliffe mills on top of the heap when the spring river drive begins. Understand? On top! The question is—can you do it?"

A hoot went up from an old gray-haired chopper in the back. "Sure as hell we can, Miss Willie. I'm game."

She heard the dull roar of the crowd begin to gain momentum. The men began to whistle and clap. She grinned, waved at them, and jumped lithely down from the wagon.

Sam lumbered up, his old tattered gray coat flapping in the breeze. "Nice work, Willie."

"I hope so." She watched the crowd start to disperse, the men murmuring among themselves.

"Got yourself company," he warned.

Daniel Barrett approached her, hat in hand.

"Miss Wydcliffe," He said her name not in greeting as a friend, but in acknowledgement as owner of the mills. "Hear you might be hiring on some extra hands to replace the ones who quit. I'm in need of a job."

"I don't think so," she said.

He looked at her oddly. " You can check at Mc-

Kenney's mill downstream. They'll tell you I was a right good worker and responsible."

His words drew sparks of anger. "Responsible?" she asked. "Tell me, Daniel, is that what you were to Rachael Kramer? Responsible?"

Daniel Barrett frowned, confusion evident. "I'm sorry, Wilhelmina, I don't understand."

"I asked whether you felt any responsibility toward Rachael once you learned she was with child?"

"Child?" He appeared shocked by her words.

"It was all over town. Surely, you heard?"

He back away, bewildered. "No, no. I didn't. It's a lie...a damn lie."

Willie stared at his distressed face. "Are you telling me Rachael wasn't carrying your child?"

"I'm telling you, I'm sure she wasn't. It wasn't possible." His face reddened with anger. "We were in love, but I never touched her, and Rachael would never have been unfaithful before marriage. Yes, we were *planning* to be married. She was supposed to meet me at Garret's old splash dam the day she died so we could go to her parents together and tell them about our plans. I went there after work, but she never showed. Honestly, you must believe me. I loved her. Don't you think she would have told you if she was in a family way? She was your best friend."

"I'm sorry, Daniel," she hung her head, feeling miserable. "After you quit your job, I assumed the rumors were true."

"I left because I couldn't stand being in the area. It hurt too much. I needed time to myself. You have to understand."

Tears stung her eyes. "I do. I'm so sorry," she said. "Who better than me understands what you went through? Find McGee and sign up. Olaf will need some good men at the Black Widow."

"Thank you, I appreciate it." He nodded. "I really appreciate it."

As Daniel walked away, she felt a terrible burden lift from her like a black shadow disappearing. She missed Rachael terribly, but now she could bury the dead properly in her heart, especially knowing her best friend didn't take her life. But someone else did. And now, she would never rest until she got to the bottom of what happened.

"Hiring the lad on?" Sam asked.

"I put him on at the Black Widow, but we still need a foreman for your mill."

"Your mill, not mine." he grumbled.

"No, yours now—*not* mine," she countered. Biting on her lower lip, she threw him a thoughtful look. "I have an idea. Old Joe has more than put the Black Widow back on its feet by running the shipping yard. Let him take over the Wasp."

Sam removed his hat and pushed a shock of hair from his forehead. "Don't rightly matter to me. You know how I feel about the gall darn thing. It's a harness around my old neck. Get him over here. One thing's for certain, the man will scare the devil into working for him."

"Sam," she uttered and shot him a warning look.

She searched the crowd until they alighted on Old Joe, and she waved him over.

"Got another proposition," she said to him once he was standing before her. When he said nothing, but only stared at her and waited, she admonished him in an exasperated tone. "You are one difficult person to talk to."

He smiled, a wide smile that melted her anger instantly. "Sam and I have discussed the possibility of you taking the foreman's job at the Wasp. Are you interested? It's going to mean a lot of work."

He nodded.

She threw her hands toward the sky. "Am I talking to myself, or is it a yes?" She glared at him.

"Yes," he said in a deep voice, alarmingly gentle.

A mill hand sauntered up with her mount. Warrior snorted at the hideous-looking man, and he reached out and patted the gelding gently on its neck. She looked warily at him and saw a faint smile on his lips.

"Animals seem to take a liking to you just like they do to Sam," she remarked.

He took the reins from her and held them while she mounted. He handed them up to her.

"Remember, we're still running the books through the Hornet's Nest," she said and leaned forward in her saddle, enunciating every word on purpose. "If it's not too much trouble, tell McGee you're drawing foreman's wages now with a month's payment as a bonus if there's no interruption in the schedule."

She rode away and missed him grinning at her back, his hands shoved deep into his pockets as he watched the beautiful horse carry its beautiful rider away.

Sparkling chandeliers sent light flickering off the

delicate crystal glasses on the table at the Mansion House where Willie dined later in the evening. Across the table, Matthew Reed smiled at her as she drank in the exquisite surroundings. The gilded wood trim, the ornate wood moldings, and red velvet chairs only added to the beauty of the room.

It was time for a whole new beginning, she decided. And what better way to start up an old friendship than in the luxury of such a grand place.

Still choosing to mourn, she wore a charcoal silk dress which fell off her shoulders, the full sleeves gathered at the elbow and progressed to slim points at her wrists. A simple strand of pearls encircled her throat, and tiny pearls adorned her ears. She tilted her head to see Matthew Reed following her every movement.

"I take it you're pleased with my choice for dining?" His smile was radiant.

"It's perfect. I'm so pleased with Mr. Shaw's redecorating."

"No, you're perfect," he recapitulated and reached out to touch her hand.

She pulled her hand away and folded both in a pose of tranquility. "I suppose you know you'll be sharing the same creek with Sam Bradley."

"Yes," he admitted. "Although I understand the mill will be running the same despite who has control of it." His eyes devoured her. Her features were so perfect, so symmetrical and soft. Any more delicacy would have made her unreal. And now she was exceedingly wealthy. He was pleased Wain was finally out of the picture. Now he was going to woo her properly and win her over. It might take time, but it would certainly be worth the effort.

"I suppose you also know Old Joe is going to be the Wasp's foreman," she said.

"For the life of me, I can't understand what you people see in his grotesque face," he replied, taking a sip of wine. "Rumor has it you're going to share some of your profits with your workers. I never thought I'd see the day when a Wydcliffe threw bones to lazy dogs."

"It's my way of thanking those who have been so loyal," she replied.

"Honestly, my dear, I thought you would have learned by now. Handing those ruffians more money is like pouring more whiskey into a drunk. What they don't give to the Sawdust Bin, they'll waste in a game of cards."

"Maybe," she said, bristling, "or maybe the extra cash will buy them a new plow blade, or an extra bag of flour for the winter, or new shoes for their children."

"You've always been far too generous," he chided.

Fighting the urge to defend herself, she studied him for a moment. "You know, Matthew, I know nothing about you. Where do your parents live?"

He regarded her over the rim of his glass for a moment. He set it quietly on the table. "I don't have any parents living. My mother died shortly after I was born, and my father was a logger who died before I even gulped my first breath of air. I never knew them at all, so to speak."

"I'm sorry," she said softly. "I know how you must feel. My mother died when I was too young to really know her. What about grandparents?"

He puckered his brow and frowned. "None. Just some close friends who helped raise me. I guess we're alike, both orphans."

His words clawed at her heart. It was true, she was an orphan in a sense. Maybe more like a stray. But she still had Sam and Raven. And she had the river and the mills. The mills. Every time she thought of them, her spirits went soaring and the future held promise. She'd never give them up. She would succeed. She'd show everyone what she could do.

Matthew picked up his wine glass and toasted her. "To you, my dear, and everything you wish from life."

"Oh, thank you, Matthew."

They ate in harmony, exchanging laughter and bits of town gossip. The sky was inky black and peppered with a million stars when Matthew finally returned her to the circular drive outside the manor. As soon as the buggy came to a stop, he reached over and captured her hand in his. "This was a pleasure, Wilhelmina. We make a perfect pair."

"Yes, it was enjoyable," she admitted.

Without hesitation, he put his arm around her cloaked shoulders and murmured in her ear, "If you need anything, feel free to call upon me." His hand found her chin and he tilted it upward as his face came slowly down toward her lips.

A hoarse cough from behind the carriage startled Willie to pull away. Without having to look up, she recognized Sam's easy gait on the loose gravel.

"Howdy, Reed," he cackled. "Sure is a nice night. I'm on my way in. How about letting an old gent have the pleasure of escortin' you to the door, my dear? You don't mind, Reed, do you?"

"Of course not," Reed replied. His voice, though unruffled, held an undertone of cold contempt.

Sam helped her alight from the carriage and tucked his hand under her elbow. There was a faint glimmer of humor in his eyes, and his lips hid a smile.

Willie watched the carriage pull away. One thing she knew for certain was that the old buzzard had planned this one.

"Elizabeth Wilhelmina," he warned her, "don't be played for a fool."

"How can I," she asked, "with an old fool watching over me?"

She let out a **ripple** of buoyant laughter and walked toward the light of the manor with Sam glued to her side like a flea on a dog's back.

CHAPTER TWENTY-NINE

Early January, 1858

SNOWFLAKES CAME SWIRLING DOWN LIKE feathers shaken from a down coverlet. Willie pushed her chair away from her father's desk to take time to watch them flutter past the windowpanes of the French doors. A fire dancing in the fireplace made the room toasty warm.

She was pleased she had made it through the holiday season with little mishap besides a few nagging memories. The calendar she kept on a corner of the desk showed she had a little more than half a year until she owned Wydcliffe Lumbering without the entanglement of Jonathan Wain. She knew he was responsible for the crates of oranges delivered to the manor and mills for Christmas, but not even Sam or Conrad had made mention of their arrival.

Try as she might, she could not get his image completely out of her mind. There was an empty feeling each time his name was mentioned at the mill. And it came back to haunt her at the strangest times, especially when she was in the company of

Matthew Reed.

To her delight, the logging operations in the forests were ahead of schedule, exceeding last year's records for December.

If the death of her father had dampened the spirit of Christmas, Sam had lent the warmth which was lacking, plunging forward to bring in a small white pine tree and decorating it with ornaments he had whittled.

On Christmas Eve, she had given him the scrimshaw knife she had purchased from the peddler. For Conrad, she had selected a Greek literary work, and as a part of her Christmas gift to the hired help, she had promised them the entire month of February to visit family and friends.

Gazing out into the wonderland of white, she scratched at the frozen windowpane and fashioned a geometric pattern into the icy surface, similar to the Wain and Wydcliffe insignia.

"Beautiful sight to see the snow fallin' so gently, so silently, with flakes as big as butter pats." Sam's grainy voice interrupted her handiwork.

"Almost too beautiful to be real," she agreed.

The old codger lumbered over to the fireplace and reach inside his pocket for his pipe and old worn tobacco pouch. He filled the wooden bowl, tamped it down with his thumb, and lit a match from the tin box on the mantel to ignite the tobacco. The comfortable sweet smell filled the room.

She chose a seat on one of the sofas near the fire. "Sam, tell me about my mother."

He drew on his pipe slowly and blew out a cloud of smoke. "She was beautiful. But both Wydcliffe wives were beautiful. Look at you youngins." He smiled. "She looked very much like you, Willie. Hair and eyes the same. In fact, every time I hear your laughter, it brings back memories of your mother. She was small, petite like you are, though a tad more reserved. 'Course, she could be, since she wasn't always around an unruly bunch of loggers."

"What was she like? What did she do when faced with a difficult situation?"

The old man chuckled. "Now she was different. She knew how to handle your pa with love and tact, but it wasn't always her way. Raven's mother was the reserved quiet one, always giving beyond what seemed possible. Elizabeth was more flamboyant, more heady, and when Dalton pushed her beyond her limits, he sure heard about it. She had a temper to make most folks shudder. But she was lovely, even when she was angry."

"So she's the one whom I get this ornery nature from?"

"Reckon so." Sam blew a smoke ring and grinned. "But your pa could blow up a storm when riled, too."

"Do you know why mother would have urged Papa to buy the piece of land which was included in the thousand acres Pierce wanted?" She saw a florid color stain the old man's cheeks above his whiskers.

"She and your Pa often rode up there," he said.

"I know, but there had to be more."

The old man hesitated before he spoke. "Your father bought it because the timber was excellent, and it was special to Elizabeth. He killed two birds with one stone."

"Why was it so special?" Earlier Willie had found the deed to the property, not at the Hornet's Nest, but while rifling through the papers on her father's desk.

"Well, if you've ever been in love, the answer is as clear as that pretty nose on your face."

They stared at each other in silence, and Willie watched his cheeks grow brighter. Her mind flew back to the afternoon she and Jonathan spent during the mid-summer festival. Her face flamed remembering the passionate kisses and gentle embraces they shared.

She looked down at her hands in the folds of her skirt and twisted the bracelet Jonathan had given her 'round and 'round on her wrist. "When Papa died, did you get a chance to talk to him earlier in the morning?"

"We talked for a short time. Nothing special and nothin' we hadn't earlier discussed. He was sort of tellin' me it was the end of the line for him." Sam crossed the floor and sat down on the sofa opposite her. "What's bothering you?"

She sighed. "Nothing, I guess. Papa said the land was the key to everything. There's a part of my brain gnawing at me, warning me he was trying to tell me something. A clue. A piece of information. There is also a part of me that believes Papa was so caught up in settling these woods around Clearfield, he was obsessed with land."

Sam shrugged. "People say a lot of things before they die, honey. Sometimes, because it's their last breath, we take their dying words to be more important than they otherwise were meant to be. Know what I mean?"

There was something worthwhile in his answer, and it made her feel better. "You're right. Come, let's enjoy our dinner while we can. In a few weeks, we'll be at the mercy of Conrad when Hannah leaves to see her family."

But they never reached the dining room. A mill hand, tearing through the front door, screamed at the top of his lungs, "Fire! Fire at the Hornet's Nest!"

Snatching a cape from the hall peg, Willie tore through the kitchen to the stables. She was so intent upon reaching her horse, she never felt the cold snow staining the hem of her taffeta skirt or dampening the slippers on her feet. She dismissed the saddle and slipped a bridle onto Warrior instead, and leaped onto his stout back.

Snowflakes bit her face and the bitter wind whipped her cape away from her body, but she pushed the horse to eat up the muddy distance before him. Her heart thudded at the thought of what she might find. Billowing clouds of smoke rose into the cold winter sky even before she reached the river. As she drew near, the stark realization hit her. The acrid scents filling the air were from the finishing mill and not the Hornet's Nest.

Flames licked the sides of its high shaker roof and smoke poured from the second floor windows making the gray sky ever darker. At least a hundred men swarmed the area forming bucket brigades snaking from the river to the blaze.

"Oh, no," she wailed, dismounting and slapping the horse on the rump to chase him away from the hungry flames. **Helplessly rooted to the spot**, she watched the conflagration.

Sam arrived shortly after her and set about shouting orders to the men and organizing another group of idle hands.

At some point in the slow march of time, it was over, and the crowds, which had turned out to witness the town's most feared enemy, began to disperse. Men from the entire town, chilled and sooty-looking, walked away wearily as the last spark died.

Crossing the yard to reach Willie, Sam Bradley noticed the Ferguson's buggy, with Mr. and Mrs. Ferguson inside, plod down the street.

"Could have been worse, Willie," he said with an exhausted sigh. "If the winds hadn't blown from the north, we could have lost the saw mill, too."

His words did little to mollify her. "Don't try to whitewash this, Sam," she said. "Just find out how it happened."

She walked down to the riverbank to find McGee hugging his arms to his chest as he surveyed the damage. His balding head was blotched with soot, and his eyelids, singed. "It doesn't look good, Miss Willie. We've lost a good portion of the roof, part of the second floor, and have at least a half dozen machines covered with debris on the first floor."

"I can see what we have, McGee," she said tightly. "I need to know what we don't have, and how much it's going to cost to replace." She moved closer to the charred building. Only her logging crew remained now, dirty and exhausted, many sprawled on the wet, cold ground. Old Joe, Daniel Barrett, Olaf. All the familiar faces spun around in her mind while she stood and stared at the damages and blackened structure. The sickening scent of wet, charred wood clung to the brittle air.

Sam appeared at her elbow. "Ben Corbin's kerosene lantern was found upstairs tipped over in a corner of the room. Looks like the fire started there. The lad helped to fight the fire."

Willie knew Ben Corbin was the young, seventeen-year-old apprentice they had taken on to learn lathe work. He was a quick and eager learner, often spending more time at the mill than at home.

"Where is he?"

Sam motioned off to his side.

The boy stood alone, his shoulders drooping, his head lowered, staring at the snowy ground. His britches and shirt had been decimated by the fire and smoke.

Willie placed a hand on his weary shoulder and asked, "What happened, Bennie?"

He looked up at her with terrified eyes and hung his head, about to cry. When he finally found his voice, he stuttered, "I-I d-don't know. I-I was h-here early this morning, before daylight, working on some stair railing before leaving before midday. Ma sure was mad I missed church. When I left I made sure everything was in order. I even swept the floor. I was on the second floor earlier to get some wood for my lathe, but honestly, Miss Wydcliffe, I brought the lantern back down. And before I left, I even made sure the flame was out before I hung it on the peg like I always do. You have to believe me," he pleaded. "I'd never start a fire. I was so happy working here."

She shook his shoulder. "Bennie, I believe you. Now go home and get some dry clothes and something to eat. Hurry, before you get chilled.

We'll sort this out in the morning."

She watched the boy leave. She turned to McGee. He was already scratching figures on a soggy piece of paper. She tried to mentally calculate the damages, and came up with eight thousand at best, including orders lost. How would she ever come up with so much money, she wondered frantically.

"How much, McGee?" she asked.

"I'm guessing between five and six, depending upon what we can save—and if the roof can be repaired and not replaced. Oh, and if we didn't lose any machines."

She shook her head, closed her eyes, and inhaled a long breath to steady herself. Without a word, she cheerlessly heaved herself onto the stallion's cold, slippery back and rode toward the manor. The snow began to fall more rapidly, covering her limp, wet cape in a layer of white. The words of Lone Wolf came back to haunt her, and she felt like someone had kicked her in the chest. The mill had been her fiery ball.

"Oh, Papa," she whispered aloud and looked at the sky, "what do I do now?" A tear slipped down her cheek and landed on the frozen ground. "How will I ever be able to recover such a loss?" She heard the pines rustling in the winter wind. *Wydcliffes just carry on*, they seemed to echo as their lofty tops bowed and swayed.

She thought of Jonathan and was vexed his name entered her thoughts. In part, he was responsible for her misery. He started the finishing mill, he had left her, and he had control of her money. Yet, it was she who was suffering the humiliation of yet another disaster.

In the evening, after a hot bath, Willie penned a letter advising Jonathan of the recent disaster and requesting he release ten thousand dollars from Wydcliffe funds to rebuild the mill as quickly as possible. She forwarded the letter through Bradford Payne.

Two weeks later, as she paced the floor in the study, she received his reply with a crate of oranges:

Dear Willie,
Money request denied. Wait until spring.
Love,
~Jonathan

Astonished and outraged by his reply, she crumbled the paper and flung it into the fire. The mills were rightly hers. He had no right to deny her the money and dismiss her decision like she was a mere child.

Her thoughts flew to Matthew Reed. When she'd met him for dinner, she had talked with him about building a house in town so she could be closer to the mills. He had suggested she sell land to finance it. Now, his suggestion lent even more credibility to the ideas rattling around in her head. Securing a pen, she wrote furiously, without flourish:

Jonathan,
Requesting permission to sell western
one thousand acres to finance the rebuilding
of my half of the mill.
~E. Wilhelmina Wydcliffe

Again, she forwarded the letter through Payne.

Within two weeks, she received his reply accompanied by another crate of oranges:

Dearest Willie,
Permission to sell any lands denied.
Wait until spring.
Love,
~Jonathan

This time, Willie saw black when she read his hastily penned note, and she ripped it to shreds and fed it piece by piece to the dancing flames in the fireplace. Each smoldering piece increased her hatred of his obstinate behavior and challenged her to pursue her original commitment. She would show him she was not a simple-minded female.

Before she went to bed, she scribbled a note to Raven and Thomas in Canada, explaining everything which had happened over the past three months and setting her own plans into action. No one, she decided, would prevent her from reconstructing the mill, including a stupid Limey from the Chesapeake.

She dressed carefully for her appointment with Bradford Payne the next day. A simple gray dress and a bun at the back of her head lent her a matronly appearance, and she had rehearsed every line of persuasion she intended to use the entire way in the carriage.

"I assume, Wilhelmina, you have something on your mind," Payne said as soon as she was seated behind his mahogany desk. He peered at her from behind thick, wire-rimmed glasses.

"I'd like my two-thousand-dollar dowry--**in cash.**"

She stared at him boldly.

Payne smiled. "I wasn't aware you were getting married. Congratulations, Wilhelmina. Who's the lucky man?"

"No one. I just want the cash."

Payne scowled. "This is a bit unusual. I don't quite understand."

She leaned forward and tapped her fingers on the top of his desk. "I know Papa set up a dowry of two thousand dollars for me many years ago—just like he did for Raven before she was married. I want it. Jonathan Wain has no claim to my money whatsoever."

"Yes, but it's supposed to be handed over when you make your choice and *proceed* with the marriage plans," Payne countered.

"Oh for heaven's sake, don't you see my point? I have no intention of ever marrying, and therefore the money, which is rightfully mine, will never be spent." She cast him a placating smile. "Consider this, will you? In the event I do marry after my holdings are released, I'm wealthy enough to afford my own wedding with, or without, the two thousand. We're only talking six months."

Payne shook his head slowly, his green eyes solemn. "I have the feeling this is not what your father intended."

"Mr. Payne, I'm still having trouble understanding what my father's intentions were when he tied my holdings to Jonathan Wain."

Payne sighed. "It was for your protection, my dear."

"A good point," she replied. "Everything else I own is protected, so why the fuss over a pitiful two thousand? The money can be easily returned in half a year."

Payne removed his glasses and mopped his forehead. "I don't like this. I don't like this at all. But I don't see any legal aspects to hamper its release. You win, Wilhelmina. Stop in and sign the papers tomorrow morning."

Without warning, she flew around the desk, nearly upsetting his chair, clenched his hand in hers and jerked it like she was pumping a bucket of water. "You won't regret this," she cried in delight and scurried from the room with her gray skirts flying out the door.

Frowning, the old lawyer shook his head, rubbing his forehead. "I already am. And I'm sure I'll regret it even more when Jonathan Wain gets wind of it."

Later that morning, Sam met Willie at her father's office in the Hornet's Nest. Her face was radiant, with an old familiar sparkle he had not seen since her father's death, and he knew it was not from the bitter cold outside, nor from the glowing red heat of the pot-bellied stove in the corner of the room.

"I know when you're up to no good, Willie," he declared, sinking his old bones into a leather chair beside the stove. He rubbed his hands together to warm them.

"I can do it, Sam." She yanked the pins from the bun at the back of her head and shook her hair free. Droplets of water flew against the iron stove and popped and sizzled. Her shiny hair, unloosened, hung down over her shoulders, giving her the appearance of a innocent child.

"Do what, young lady?"

"Rebuild the finishing mill. But not without your help."

"How much?" The old man muttered an expletive, squinting at her. "How much money do you need, Willie?"

She grinned. "Two thousand. Only two thousand, what with the two thousand I requested from Thomas, two from my dowry, and another source I have yet to approach. I can do it, Sam. I know I can."

The old man scratched his head, his face skeptical. "Maybe you ought to talk to Jonathan about this. He's your partner."

"Absolutely not. Let the bloody pirate sit beside his frozen harbor and ice skate until spring."

If Sam was a man to take life slowly, he realized the girl before him was not. He could see her impatience, in her every movement, every feature, every word. He instantly knew no matter what—including Jonathan's wrath—he would be the last man on earth to deny her a mere two thousand dollars. His love for her was as deep as any father's love.

He rubbed his chin thoughtfully. "I don't have a hankering for a shenanigan like this, my dear, but two thousand it is. Something tells me this is going to cause more trouble and more headaches than the dang two thousand is worth."

"Oh, Sam," she squealed and wrapped her arms around him, knocking his hat to the floor, "you're absolutely charming."

"Still charming, eh?" The old codger laughed gleefully. "A mighty good compliment for an old geezer." He pushed his creaky bones up from the chair, scooped up his hat, and ambled toward the door. He paused. "I'll have your money in the morning, Willie. But Lordy, I sure hope Jonathan never, *ever* hears about this."

With six thousand dollars now promised, Willie had no doubt how to obtain the remainder of the money she desperately needed. She made an appointment with John Pierce for later in the afternoon and wasn't surprised when he agreed to meet her at the Mansion House.

"I've taken the privilege of ordering for you, Miss Wydcliffe," he said, smiling and rising to meet her when she arrived. "Would you like something to drink? Wine, perhaps?"

"Not at the moment, thank you." She raised a glass of water to her lips and anchored her thoughts. "I'm sure you know the finishing mill will take some capital to rebuild. I'd like to start quickly, instead of waiting. I understand you're still interested in the land."

When he nodded, she forced a dazzling smile and continued, "I can't sell the land you want outright until six months has elapsed, and I'm in complete control of all holdings. But I'm willing to offer you first chance if you'll loan me two thousand dollars."

"What's in it for me?" Pierce fixed his snake-like gaze on her, his thick neck bulging under his starched white shirt.

"I'm willing to write an agreement giving you a five percent monthly interest on your two thousand until I can repay it."

A server girl appeared with two glasses of white wine and plates of food. Silence surrounded them as they ate.

Pierce considered the issue before him. He had been hoping for an outright sale with his hands on the property immediately. Inwardly, he had been disturbed by the disclosure of a guardianship. But the proposed railway for the area by the Tyrone and Clearfield Railroad Company wasn't even off its knees yet. It might take another two years. Any type of agreement, which would bind him closer to the land, was a step in the right direction. If he lent her the money now, he would have a bargaining tool to pressure her later. And who was to say she might not need more money before the six months were out? Better yet, now with Matthew Reed wooing her, maybe pressure wouldn't be necessary.

"Miss Wydcliffe, I think you and I may be able to reach an amicable understanding," he finally said.

She smiled. "I have just one more request. Our relationship is strictly business, strictly a private matter, and strictly not to be discussed beyond this room. I would appreciate it, as well, if we could deal with another lawyer besides Bradford Payne."

Pierce stared at her, resisting an itch to reach out and caress her delicate face. He had always liked assertive women. "But of course, my dear. Does Attorney Thompson meet with your approval? I'll make the proper arrangements tomorrow." Aware she might be conscious of his base stirrings, he added, "Surely you can't deny a man admiring beautiful scenery?"

Her retort was quick and short. "Certainly not, Mr. Pierce. But as Sam Bradley always says, *"Beware of beauty. Beneath may lay a dangerous viper."*

He laughed heartily and raised a chunky hand to

toast her. "I'm a man who drinks to beauty when he sees it, Miss Wydcliffe."

She clinked her glass against his.

And I prefer the viper, she thought.

CHAPTER THIRTY

THE ICY WINTER WINDS DIPPED the temperature below zero, much to Willie's amusement and sanity. There was no way she wanted Jonathan to intervene in her present affairs, and she prayed desperately the cruel weather would prevail, hampering any thoughts he might have about seeing the mill disaster firsthand. At least not until spring. By then, she would have everything in order and running smoothly again. To assure herself even further, she forwarded a third letter to Baltimore:

Jonathan:
Mills are now functioning as per your
instructions. Will wait until spring. Stop
the blasted oranges!
~E. Wilhelmina Wydcliffe

When she heard nothing the following two weeks, she breathed a lengthy sigh of relief. He believed her! Already she had proceeded with the repairs, using her dowry money and Sam's. The roof was all but restored, as weather permitted.

Delighted with the progress, she read and reread the note from Thomas LeConte explaining the arrangements he was making to forward the loan safely to her as soon as possible.

Absolutely nothing could go wrong now, she mused gaily as she skimmed the steps to McGee's office with her loan from John Pierce. With the river frozen, all the mill operations were shut down. She missed the singing of the saws and the fragrant scent of sawdust. But soon, come spring, everything would be back to normal. From the reports trickling in from the winter logging camps, Sam and Olaf agreed it was going to be the best year yet.

She dropped the hem of her russet dress, removed her cape, and straightened her ivory pinafore outside McGee's office. Her outfit, youthful in appearance, had been exactly the proper attire to wear to the Attorney Thompson's office earlier in the morning. She had even braided her hair into two loose pigtails and wound them into Swedish knots at the side of each ear. She was sure her youthful, naive appearance had helped get the agreement with Pierce drawn up exactly to the letter. The young lawyer had even insisted she insert a clause releasing her from the agreement if at any time she returned Pierce's money with the accumulated interest.

Later in the day, she promised Matthew Reed she would celebrate her success with him over dinner. He had been pressuring marriage over the last four weeks, and to date, she had been able to hold him at bay, although she wasn't sure for how much longer. Marriage was the farthest thing from her mind. The mills and river were her first love. Her only love. Only the mills and river were constant, never fickle, never betraying her. They were solid. Lasting. They would remain forever.

Entering McGee's office, she tossed her cape over a nearby chair, swung her reticule in the air, twirled, and did a jaunty gig. McGee, seated at his desk, watched her antics with guarded amusement.

"We've done it." She opened her reticule and handed him the bank draft. "The remainder is on its way from Canada."

McGee frowned. "I don't know, Miss Willie," he said, his voice filled with anxiety. "We still have to account for this money. It has to show on the books."

"Ah, McGee, you worry too much. The fiend in Baltimore doesn't have to know where this money came from." She watched the paymaster cringe. "Run it through on a separate account in a separate ledger. After all, it doesn't matter how I secured it. Just think of it as a personal loan to the mills. Criminy, we'll repay the money in the spring before the big-footed devil thaws out or finds out." She watched anxiety transform McGee's face. His body stiffened in alarm.

"Your compliments warm my heart, Willie, my dear," a deep voice drawled from the shadows in the corner of the room, "and your loyalty is extraordinary, but your honesty seems to be in sore need of repair."

Jonathan stepped out and crossed the room to tower over her. He wore a heavy, fur-lined, suede coat that only added to the largeness of his well-built frame.

She froze to the spot, speechless. His hand went directly to her reticule, which he yanked from her grip and tossed to McGee.

"Hold this," he said sternly to the nervous man, "it's a bit too heavy for my liking." His eyes bore holes through her, and the hostile sparks which passed between them were hot enough to melt the ice on the river.

McGee's voice trembled as he spoke, "Maybe we had better sort this out at a more appropriate time, sir."

"Take it easy, McGee," he assured him, "I'm not going to harm my precious little ward, not yet. And certainly not with a witness."

His eyes swept over Willie. Standing demurely before him now, she was as breath-taking as ever, looking as innocent as a school girl setting out for her first day of lessons. The old burning ache, which he had tried to push aside for the last five months, came back stronger than ever. He tried to mask it with a frown.

"I don't suppose you want to explain the money, Wilhelmina, but we'd better start somewhere."

Willie found her voice. "The money, as you refer to it, is my personal loan to the company. This isn't any of your business. It's money I had, and loans from Thomas and other sources. I did nothing wrong. You have no right to interfere."

"Ah, but you're wrong, my dear. We're partners in the finishing mill, and I would have thought you'd have the courtesy to inform this big-footed devil of any decision you had undertaken."

"Partners?" she snapped. "If those ludicrous letters were any indication how you honor your half of our partnership, you can go straight to...."

"Uh, uh, Willie. McGee is here," he warned.

She glanced briefly at the red-faced, flustered paymaster and started over. "Since my knot head of a partner hadn't the courtesy to allow me to quickly rebuild the mill as I requested, I proceeded with the plans myself. We were losing money, orders needed to be filled, and workers were sitting idle. You can't run a mill from Baltimore. One of us had to get off his..." She paused and glanced at Henry McGee. "...mule's backside and start moving."

Jonathan realized she was getting more furious as the discussion ensued. She was more than ready to poke his eyes out. He would have to keep a cool head.

"You'll have to excuse me, Jonathan," she said with a saucy mock tone, "but there are things needing my attention far worse than you." She collected her reticule from McGee and turned to leave.

If her impertinence rankled him, he was determined not let it show. He reached to help her with her cape, but she shrugged off his assistance and threw it over her arm instead.

She reached the door and paused, her hand still on the knob. "If you plan to stay at the manor, I should inform you we have no cook. Hannah is off for a break. Therefore, you must forage for yourself, eat in town...or starve to death."

She slammed the mill door behind her.

Later in the afternoon, as Willie dressed to dine

with Matthew Reed, she chose the most beguiling black velvet dress in her wardrobe. The high neckline was sewn with tiny seed pearls, fashioned in a Greek-like pattern which was replicated on the sides of the tapering sleeves ending with a circle of French lace at the wrist. The dress was simple enough to pass for mourning, drab enough not to be flirtatious, but stylish enough to satisfy the latest tastes in fashion. In fact, it was exactly what she wanted.

With Jonathan underfoot somewhere in the manor, she hurried as fast as she could, abandoning the thought of struggling with her hair and instead letting it tumble haphazardly down her back. She knew she'd have to intercept Matthew and warn him as soon as his carriage arrived.

She grabbed her cape and reached the door in time to see him strolling up the walk, shaking the snow from his sandy hair. His boyish features and lithe body covered with sprinkles of delicate, white flakes reminded her of a child emerging from a snow battle. Maybe, she decided, it was one of the reasons she was drawn to him. He was so opposite Jonathan and presented no threat to her. Maybe he might make a good mate after all.

Almost instantly, before he had time to even speak, she flew into his embrace, encircled his neck, and kissed him boldly on the lips.

"My, this is unorthodox," he said, taken off-guard.

"Let's go, Matthew," she ordered. She grabbed his arm, dragging him toward the carriage, her voice desperate sounding. "Jonathan Wain is back."

"Why is Wain here?" He frowned, stumbling after her.

Willie nudged him onward again. "For the mills, why else? Obviously, not for my health."

Within seconds, sure deliberate footsteps crunched on the walk behind them, and Jonathan's large and panther-like form loomed over them. He had bathed, changed, and removed his day's growth of beard accenting his chiseled profile.

"Dining out as well, Jonathan?" she asked in an icy voice.

"Hardly," he replied in his usual mellow tone, "and neither are you. It seems, Willie, we have a few things to discuss that can't wait."

Matthew rose to her defense. "Seriously, Wain, we have dinner reservations. Please allow the lady to honor her commitment and our plans."

"The lady, if that's what you wish to call her, has never honored her commitments, nor anyone's plans," Jonathan recapitulated. "We have unfinished business to settle first."

Matthew's temper shot up. "Now see here. Surely it can wait."

Jonathan glanced down at Willie and drawled, "I suggest you express your apologies to Reed. We don't want to create a scene." His gray eyes blurred to cold granite, and his implication struck her full-face. The man was hell bent on a fight, and he needed no excuse to start with Matthew Reed. She had no choice but to succumb to his wishes.

She half-pulled, half-pushed Matthew toward the carriage, "He's right, Matthew. It's best if we just postpone our dinner plans temporarily. We need to clear the air of this mill business gnawing at him so we can proceed with our private lives in peace."

She frowned. "I'm sorry."

Reluctantly, Matthew kissed her on the cheek and stepped into the carriage. "Good night, my dear. I'll get word to you soon."

As the carriage rolled away, Willie pulled her cape shut, hugging her body for warmth. She was glad for the bitter cold which stung her face, cooling her embarrassed flushed cheeks.

A carriage, pulled by two matching grays, rounded the corner of the manor and stopped, waiting at the edge of the road.

"I'm not going anyplace with you, Jonathan Wain." A look of defiance crossed her face.

"And I'm not about to discuss this in the freezing cold."

She bristled. "Where are we going?"

"It doesn't matter. Get in the carriage." He reached for her elbow.

She yanked away from his grasp, turned abruptly, and dashed up the muddy lane leading from the manor. She heard him curse as he spun out after her.

Her slippers, she quickly realized, were far from adequate for winter streets. The icy water seeped into her stockings as she raced along. Behind her, she heard the snow crunch with heavy footsteps closing the gap between them.

Everything happened in a horrible blur seconds later. She missed seeing a rut and stumbled into it, her body crashing downward. Instantly, his strong arm grabbed her, pulling her upward, but she fought against his hold and broke free, only long enough to slip on the snow, lose her balance again, and fall into the half-frozen puddle for the second time.

"You swine," she shrieked.

He hauled her to her feet at the same moment she raised her hand to strike him. He deflected it with his upper arm and propelled her soggy body toward the manor.

"You've ruined my gown." She stumbled along beside him. "I hate you."

CHAPTER THIRTY-ONE

JONATHAN FLINCHED INWARDLY. THE WORDS, *I hate you*, were worse than a physical blow, stinging down to the pit of his stomach as he urged Willie through the front door, dragging her past the surprised caretaker. Mud covered her from her eyelids down to her soaked shoes. Her hair hung in dirty strands, caked and matted and sopping wet.

"The lady needs a bath, Conrad," he said, nudging her up the staircase to her room before finally releasing her. She scurried across her bedroom floor, her hair and soiled clothes dripping icy water and mud onto the Oriental rug. She stopped at the window and stared morosely out.

He leaned against the doorjamb while the caretaker shuttled pails of hot water to fill the brass tub behind her dressing screen. He was glad Conrad had earlier fixed the fire in her room to help ward off the cold.

"That'll be all. Thank you, Conrad," he said when the last bucket finally arrived.

"I haven't eaten," she whispered dolefully, her back still turned.

"A plate of food as well." He refused to let down his guard at the door.

Conrad nodded, left quickly, and returned minutes later with an assorted tray of food. This time the poor caretaker scuttled from the room as if his pants were on fire.

Jonathan shut the door, locked it, and dropped the key in his pocket. "My dear, both your bath and the food are getting cold."

Unbuttoning her cape, Willie let it fall to the floor. "I can take a bath without any assistance," she snapped and slid behind the screen.

"No doubt, my dear, but I don't trust you to remain here. Your virtuous nature will have to suffer."

On the other side of the room, he found a seat in a wingback chair and crossed his right leg atop the other knee. From behind the screen, he heard her clothes hit the floor, and just when he thought she had returned to some state of sanity, a sodden heap of clothes flew over the top of the screen to land next to his feet. She moaned in satisfaction at she stepped into the steamy water and began to splash about.

Time slipped away.

Finally, when he could bear it no longer, he barked, "Elizabeth Wilhelmina, no one, not even the devil himself, would accuse me of being a patient person."

Like a quail sprung from a thicket, she jumped up, sending bath water flying onto the floor. Desperately, she searched the bath area for something to dry herself. Not only was there nothing to be found, but also there wasn't a stitch of clothing within reach. She bit her lower lip to keep from shivering.

"Jonathan, I need a towel."

She heard him chuckle, and shortly thereafter, one came sailing over the screen.

"I need clothes as well."

Her peacock dressing gown followed the route of the towel.

Drying herself, she wound the robe tightly around herself before appearing.

"I need a hairbrush, too," she muttered and searched the room.

"Willie, your food is getting cold and my patience is exhausted." He stood to help, recovering it from beneath the pile of clothes on the floor and handed it to her. Spying the heap of filthy, wet garments, he unceremoniously gathered them up, walked to the fire, and heaved them into the flames. They rose up sputtering and crackling as the fire devoured them. "They remind me of widow's weeds," he said in a deadly low voice, "and you are most definitely *not* a widow."

When she gasped in shock, he added, apologetically, "I'll replace them, I promise."

Frowning, she gathered the hairbrush and her tray of food and sat on the bed as she proceeded to eat, too hungry to care what he thought, said, or did.

Jonathan slouched back down into the chair and watched her. She seemed to be as delicate as the china doll in the window at Irwin's General Store. How on earth could anyone so small, so perfect, so exquisite, create such havoc in such a short time?

Moments later, he spoke, "I understand Thomas

LeConte is one of your benefactors as well as Sam Bradley. I should have known you'd rope both into your little scheme, especially since they are far more than just gullible where you're concerned. How much are you bleeding them for?"

Willie chewed on a biscuit, which must have suddenly begun to taste like sawdust, Jonathan conjectured, because she set it aside when he mentioned the loans.

"Four thousand total. Two from Sam and two from Thomas," she said.

"This personal fund," he continued, "How much is involved?"

"That's none of your business."

He leaned forward and said through a hiss, "You may waltz Bradford Payne around, but I don't dance to the same tune. I traveled through snows belly deep and temperatures which would freeze your tongue to the roof of your mouth. I all but broke my neck and that of my horse just to get here. Answer me."

"It's my dowry money," she said quietly and pushed the plate aside, obviously having lost her appetite.

"How did you get it released?"

"I told Attorney Payne I had no intention of ever marrying," she admitted. "Therefore, it was rightfully mine to take now."

"Why, Willie? Why would you do it?"

Her eyes flared, and when she spoke, her tone was almost hysterical. "I needed the money. I don't care if I have to be married in rags, I needed the money to get the finishing mill back on its feet."

Her admission tore at his heart, and he softened.

She was willing to forsake a wedding gown and reception to rebuild a blasted mill. He ran his fingers through his hair in exasperation. Sometimes the fool woman didn't make a wit of sense. He sighed. "How much?"

She stared at him.

"How much did you use of your dowry?" he repeated.

"All of it. Two thousand dollars." She picked up her hairbrush and started to work the tangles from her hair.

"That's six thousand dollars. Where did you get the remainder?"

She grew silent and bent her head, fingering the handle on the brush, certain the fireworks about to explode would shame a Fourth of July celebration. She mustered every ounce of stamina she had. She watched Jonathan stand and step toward the foot of her four-poster bed. His knuckles were white as he clenched a corner spindle.

"For God's sake, tell me."

"John Pierce."

"John Pierce!" he thundered. "How much?"

"Only two thousand."

His stare drilled into her. "How on earth did you squeeze two thousand dollars from that no-account?"

She backed farther on the bed and sent her plate of food crashing to the floor. "I agreed to sell him the thousand acres when it legally becomes mine. He gets first rights to the sale in return for the loan of the money." She reached for her reticule on the night stand, but he intercepted it before her hands could touch it.

"Careful, sweetheart. I know you handle concealed hardware."

"The agreement is inside," she replied weakly.

He extracted the piece of paper, tossing the reticule onto a chair across the room, and scanned the contents. Shortly thereafter, he breathed a sigh of relief, and folded the paper carefully on its already made creases.

"Is it in order?" When he didn't answer her immediately, she asked again. "What's wrong? I know you're not pleased it was John Pierce, but I had no choice." She continued, her voice almost pleading, "Believe me, I never envisioned this would cause a disturbance. I intended to have the money repaid before you found out."

Rubbing his chin thoughtfully, he spoke. "There's no attachment to Pierce other than this agreement?"

"No, none whatsoever."

"Good, I know how much you dislike him, and I wouldn't want him to coerce you into something unwillingly."

He sat down on the edge of the bed and inspected her, his earlier ire melting away. "I would never want him to touch or harm you in any way," he admitted truthfully. "We'll have to get this agreement paid back immediately."

She nodded, relieved, and picked up her brush again, pulling it through her drying tangles. He watched her calmly, saying nothing.

When she finally tossed it aside, she spoke. "Jonathan, I need your consent to marry Matthew Reed. It makes perfect sense since we both share the same interests and love for lumbering. He's been pressuring me for a commitment."

Caught off guard, he raised his head, his eyes widening, his jaw dropping in astonishment. They stared at each other for several seconds before he stood and began pacing the room from the bed to the fireplace. For a time, he rested his hand on the mantle and stared into the flames licking at the logs. Minutes elapsed slowly.

"No," he finally said in a dull voice. "I don't want you to marry him."

Willie riveted her eyes with a lethal glare at his form, black against the red and yellow flames. "Why not? You would be released from playing nurse maid to me and the mills. It would be a perfect solution for everyone."

He turned. "I don't need a reason, but you need my consent. It's my decision. At least for the next six months."

"That's thoughtless and unfair!"

"Is it fair for you to marry a weak, unscrupulous man? Think, Willie, what would your father have said? He hated Matthew Reed." His words poured out in a clipped tone.

"I don't know, but I do know Matthew loves me."

"Oh, you're wrong there, Wilhelmina. He's infatuated with your money and your lumber mills."

"No, that's just not true. He truly cares."

"In a pig's eye!"

"If you allow me to wed Matthew, all your problems will be solved," she pleaded. "You can go back to bloody Baltimore and leave this god-forsaken place for good."

"If you marry Matthew Reed, my problems will

just be compounded," he snarled and threw up his hands. "He'll clean you out of every single penny you own and then start on my half of the investments here."

"Criminy, Jonathan, you can't control my life forever. I can wait six months. After that, you'll have no say in my life, thank the Almighty." She was so overcome with rage she choked the words out and flung her hairbrush violently at him. He ducked. The hairbrush clattered to the floor and skidded toward the fireplace. She lay down on the bed, curling herself into a tight ball, weeping.

He looked at her miserable form atop the rose coverlet and every fiber in his body ached. He moved to the bed, sat down, and scooped her up in his arms, letting her sob against his chest. A strong surge of desire racked through him. His lips found the soft spot by her neck, and he began kissing her tenderly.

"This is why you can't marry Matthew Reed," he whispered huskily, continuing to rain kisses on her, "because I *love* you, Willie. I want you...totally...all of you without restraint...for myself. For the rest of my life."

She stopped crying, the words registering in her brain. She looked up at him through tear-filled eyes, confused. He held her chin firmly as he ground out, "I love you. I've always loved only you. Can't you tell?"

He pulled her closer, his lips finding hers as he kissed her, wanting her with a hunger eating at his very soul. He lost control of all his emotions as his lips and tongue eagerly explored the warm honey interior of her mouth. He demanded of her, and unsure, she returned his kiss with hesitancy.

Forcing himself away, Jonathan lifted his head. "I've wanted you since the first day in the forest. For every cat I saw you stealthily slip food to. The morning I watched you ride Blackjack despite my permission. And I wanted you today when you danced into McGee's office so full of energy. No man on earth is going to take you away from me. No one! When Matthew Reed kissed you by the carriage today, I wanted to destroy him."

He wiped the tears still lingering on her cheek with his thumb and tangled his hand in her honey-brown hair. His lips sought out hers once more. He crushed her pliant form to him.

He could feel her warm, slim body react, and despite her earlier desire to hate him, he knew she was helplessly bound to him by an emotion far greater than hate. She responded to his advances timidly at first, then more eagerly, like a moth unable to resist the light.

Never before had he wanted to please any woman as much as he wanted to please her. But he was not satisfied with that alone, he wanted to possess her, keep her next to him always. He wanted to be bound both mentally and physically. He proceeded to show her just how much he cared as they made love. And after delicious relief flooded through them and made them sleepy, they peacefully dozed in each other's arms.

Willie awakened sometime later to an almost pitch-black room. The fire had burned down, and night was upon them. She moved under the weight of Jonathan's arm wrapped tightly around her, pinning her to him as they lay under her coverlet.

Trying to wiggle free, she heard a low sensuous chuckle, and he snuggled her even tighter to him.

"Jonathan, it's late," she whispered nervously, "and the fire is almost out."

"Hmmm," he whispered, "not this fire." He kissed her on the back of the neck, groaned, and slipped out from beneath the covers into the chilly air. He pulled on his breeches and moved directly to the fire to tend the flames. Within minutes, he had a rosy glow in the room.

She pulled the quilt over her naked body to her chin and watched him.

He lit an oil lantern and hung it on the hook near her bookshelves. "Since we're awake at this ridiculously early hour, what do you propose we do?" He smiled mischievously at her.

"We could get something to eat and drink," she said.

He picked up the dishes from the floor and headed with the tray for the door.

"No, wait. I'll go." She pushed back the covers and pulled on her dressing gown. "You'll never find your way in the dark as easily as I can. Rum?"

He grinned, fished in his pocket for the key, and opened the door.

Shivering, she padded down the hall, returning much too quickly with another tray filled with glasses, water, rum, wine and an assortment of breads and cheese. "Conrad must have anticipated a sweeter ending than the beginning. This was left on the landing."

Willie poured him a drink, glancing up to see him scan the cluttered array of trinkets littering her bookshelves. He fingered the tiny porcelain horse before replacing it and picking up the black rock beside it.

"Where did you get this?" he asked. He held it near the lantern and watched streaks of satin black gleam under the light.

She wrinkled her nose. "Raven and I picked it up when I was a child after we had taken a ride together. It was out by the old stone quarry inside the edge of our western piece of property."

"Can you show me exactly where you found it?"

"I'm not sure. It was so long ago. Raven may know the exact location." She watched him extinguish the lantern and walk to the bed. He sat down, drawing her toward him as he propped himself against the pillow.

"Jonathan, what now?" she asked.

He kissed her tenderly on the forehead. "We repair the mill, get it operating, pay off Pierce immediately, and get married." He paused. "But first, I have to leave for Pittsburgh for a few days. There's a man I meant to contact about a geologist report of the piece of western property we never surveyed since we had no desire to use it. The first thaw, I want someone on the job."

"You don't have to go all the way to Pittsburgh. Kramer can take the samples and do the survey." She didn't want him to leave again.

He shook his head. "No, I've been thinking. Kramer is somehow involved. Maybe some sort of a deal. Maybe he's misrepresented information on reports or mineral surveys, boundaries, whatever. He was much too anxious to see me leave his office the last time I paid him a visit to look over his personal maps of our other holdings. Maybe

Rachael's death wasn't an accident."

"That's ludicrous," she gasped. "It had to be."

"Attempts on people's lives, snakes, broken ropes at the dam, a torched mill are also ludicrous."

Recoiling, she sat up straighter. "But it *was* an accident."

"Why? There were no witnesses. Rachael was a bright, sensitive girl. I can't believe she'd take her life, or one of an unborn child."

"She wouldn't, Jonathan. I talked to Daniel Barrett, and he insisted she wasn't carrying his child. It was an accident. It had to be. She was supposed to meet him at Garret's splash dam, but never showed. They had planned to tell her parents they wanted to marry." She looked helplessly at him as if she was praying he'd understand.

"But we still don't know how she managed to end up dead in the water. All we know is she couldn't swim."

"She could swim," she said. "Not as well as you or me, but she could swim. I taught her two summers ago. Something must have happened. She tired or swam out too far for her own good."

He squinted at her skeptically. "Willie, you and I were raised around water. It's perfectly natural for us to take a dip after a tiring day. But what girl would go swimming just before she was to meet her beau and tell her parents about their marriage plans?" He held up a hand, refusing to let her interrupt as he went on. "Even if she did swim at the splash dam that day, the water was only four feet deep at its best. The spring rains last year had broken the old dam to pieces. If she was in trouble, she could have stood up and walked out."

Stunned, he watched Willie shrink away from him. He knew she had only begun to recover from Rachael's death, and she didn't want to think about the possibility of murder.

"You're doing the same thing I did. Your imagination has gotten the upper hand." She looked at his face, eyes wide, and she shook her head.

He saw a picture of pain and fright cross her face. The last thing he wanted to do was to upset her needlessly. "Maybe you're right," he conceded.

What bothered him most and what he was afraid to disclose was the threat to her safety. He had the feeling disaster was imminent, and he hated the idea of being away from her for any amount of time. Worse yet, he was worried her carefree, trusting nature would put her in a dangerous situation unknowingly. Even if she could competently protect herself, she couldn't do it if the enemy was someone she thought was a friend.

He downed the last of the rum, set his glass aside, and extinguished the candle. Shedding his trousers, he slipped beneath the covers. "Enough talk. Come here," he urged her lovingly.

Willie slid in next to him, his arms already open, eager to hold her close. She felt his breath in her hair, and she kissed him on the neck. "I love you, Jonathan Caleb Wain," she said simply. "Truly, I do."

Emitting a husky growl, he pulled her against his chest, his thick matted hair prickling her skin. He kissed her several times before she asked, "Must you leave, again?"

He sighed. "Yes, the trip to Pittsburgh will kill two birds with one stone. Besides the geologist, there's a man who claims he grew up with John

Pierce. I need to talk to him." He raised himself on an elbow. "While I'm gone, be sure to stay close to Sam and away from Pierce. I'll deal with him when I return."

She nodded, snuggling closer.

"I'm serious, Willie."

"Yes," she mumbled, happy to just be held close while his naked flesh warmed her body. All at once she sat upright and pulled away from his embrace.

"Oh, drat," she hissed, shaking him lightly. "What about Matthew Reed?"

A grin pulled at the corner of his lips. "Well, well, my little lumber princess, you have a slight problem, don't you? You can't marry both of us."

"Get serious," she scolded. She thumped him playfully on the chest. "I need time to tell him properly. Despite your misgivings, he has been exceptionally kind these past months. I mean him no harm, and I do feel sorry for him, being an orphan and all."

The last remark got Jonathan's attention, and he looked at her oddly.

"Jonathan, I have to tell him," she persisted. "I have to explain my feelings."

"Agreed," he murmured thickly. "But finish it quickly. I don't approve of Reed hovering about and drooling over my future wife."

Relieved, and no longer afraid of his wrath, she laughed. "A bit possessive, aren't you?"

He locked his arms around her neck, hungrily kissing her lips as she sank slowly against him. Then he showed her just how possessive he really could be.

CHAPTER THIRTY-TWO

WILLIE TURNED RESTLESSLY IN THE bed, reaching for Jonathan's warm body to ward off the chill that had awakened her. Through half-opened eyes, she realized the bed was empty, and she sat up. Surely what happened last night was not a dream. Her eyes caught the rumpled pillow and traveled down to the foot of the bed where his white shirt lay crumpled as well. She smiled and pushed back the covers, sensing an added weight on her finger. The diamond twinkled brilliantly as she raised her hand before her face. Jonathan must have slipped it on her finger while she slept.

Light seeped into the room from behind the drapes indicating it was later in the morning. She slithered out of bed, shivering, and glanced at the fire which had burned low. If Jonathan had left at daylight and tended the fire, it had to be mid-morning. Donning her robe, she crossed to the door and flung it open, almost colliding with the caretaker who was about to knock. She backed into the room.

Conrad nervously cleared his throat. "Mr. Wain had to leave early this morning." Willie watched his eyes circle the room and land on Jonathan's shirt. "Yes, well, of course. You know that." Red-faced, he tried to get a grip on his thoughts. He stammered. "Mr. Wain doesn't want you to tell Matthew Reed that you have plans to marry him. Marry Mr. Wain, I mean, and he also wants you to stop at Attorney Bradford Payne's office this morning."

She nodded and watched him back out the door before she asked, "I assume you were responsible for the tray on the landing last night?"

He flashed a sheepish smile, his face flushed. "Yes."

"Thank you. That was thoughtful and kind," she said and watched him hustle down the hallway.

Pulling on a pair of riding breeches, she chose a warm flannel shirt and her heavy leather coat to wear for her ride into town. Even though she knew she could wear something more suitable to visit the finicky old lawyer, a dress was impractical. She planned to visit the Henderson's cabin later, located outside of town on a trail so steep it could never be traversed by carriage. Lydia Henderson was ill.

Nimble and frisky from the crisp morning air, Warrior eagerly delivered Willie to the door of Bradford Payne's office where she selected a chair in front of his massive desk. She hoped Jonathan didn't tell the old lawyer about her legal agreement with Pierce. And if he did, she secretly hoped Payne wouldn't hold it against her for choosing a different legal counsel. The man had been her father's lawyer since the lands and mills were purchased and built.

Attorney Payne peered up from over his glasses and reached for a pile of papers at the corner of his desk. "I suppose I should scold you," he said with a little huff. "Telling an old man like me you weren't ever getting married."

His wizened eyes locked on hers as he continued. "Hood-winked that two thousand right out from under my nose, didn't you? Shame on you, Elizabeth Wilhelmina."

Flinching, she muttered, "I'm sorry, Mr. Payne. Truly, I am."

"Yes, well, I suppose even an old codger like me deserves to have someone to keep me on my toes," he admitted in a more cheerful tone. "Before I begin, I want to congratulate you. I know you and Jonathan are planning to be married soon, although he wants no one else to know for the present time. You are one lucky young lady."

Unsure of what to say, she nodded.

"He stopped in my office early this morning and wanted these papers drafted for you to sign. Shall I read them, or shall I just explain their contents?"

"Just give me the pertinent details, Mr. Payne. I trust your judgement."

"Most of the time, that is," he said, clearing his throat and squinting at her.

They looked at each other for a few seconds before they both laughed.

He tapped his pen on some papers in front of him. "First, Jonathan is returning your dowry money, replacing the two thousand with his personal funds accrued from the mills. Jonathan was quite adamant the money be returned to the account as quickly as possible to comply with your father's original wishes."

The old man removed his glasses and wiped his eyes.

She twisted the ring on her finger nervously.

"Second, I need your signature on this agreement I drew up this morning. It simply states upon the immediate occurrence of your marriage to Jonathan, all Wydcliffe holdings will become solely your property with no control by him, including those rights of a legally married spouse. He relinquishes all rights as an heir as well. Naturally, since no children are involved yet, you will have to designate another heir in case of your death." He held the papers out to her. "All I need is your signature."

Shocked, she drew back. "Why?" she uttered.

Attorney Payne leaned back in his chair, crossing his hands over his portly stomach. He scrutinized her in a fatherly fashion. "Quite frankly, Elizabeth Wilhelmina," he said, "at first I thought the big brute wasn't playing with a full deck, but I think your young man is trying to assure you he wants to marry you for love, and not your land or your money. God knows, as wealthy as he is, he doesn't need anymore." He paused. "He wants you to realize his intentions are strictly honorable."

Speechless, she shook her head and stared into space. She had never expected such unselfish generosity and devotion. If she was supposed to be happy, why did she feel like she wanted to cry?

Payne cleared his throat again, handed her the paper, and dipped a pen in ink. "Just sign here, and you can be on your way."

Coming to her senses, she stood and waved him away. "No, give me the papers to read over again. I'll get them back to you." She hardly acknowledged his words of departure as she left with thoughts tumbling inside her head.

Once outside, she tucked the papers into her saddlebags and proceeded to Irwin's General Store to purchase some supplies before riding to the Henderson's cabin.

The ride was long and the day frosty cold, but her heart was as warm as a breeze that caresses a summer afternoon. The significance of what Jonathan did hit her full force. He really did love her. He loved her! It wasn't the money, power, or the mills. How could she have been so blind? She silently promised to make it all up to him the first chance she found.

Sure-footed, Warrior easily maneuvered the steep snowy trail to the Henderson's cabin. The woods were a fairy's domain of white beauty. Even sharp jagged brush piles had been turned into soft shimmering mounds. The snow, starting to fall in feathery flakes, landed on her hat and coat and sparkled in the sunlight. Many times, Willie had to duck pine and hemlock limbs bowing under the weight of fresh snow.

At the cabin, she rode Warrior to a lean-to shack, stacked with wood, dry enough to temporarily ward off the winter wind and snow. She secured the reins on a loose board, dug in her saddlebags, and pulled out a package. "I won't be long, boy," she whispered, patting the animal briskly on his shoulders.

She managed the icy steps leading to the front of the cabin, rapped on the door, and waited until she heard a feeble response.

On a bed in the corner of the room, Lydia Henderson lay, her face pale and drawn. She smiled weakly when she recognized Willie. "Well, hello, Miss Wydcliffe. This is a nice surprise." She coughed hoarsely. "Seems like this cold weather has got me down. You needn't have put yourself out to come all the way up here."

Willie smiled and dropped her hat and coat on a peg by the door. "No trouble, Mrs. Henderson. I thought perhaps a little herbal tea might be welcome." She looked about the room. The dimly lit cabin was sparsely furnished with a table, two chairs, a chest, and a trunk. Along the wall, she noticed a wash counter and an old cook stove. Homemade curtains fashioned from blue flour sacks hung in the two windows. A fireplace, located on another wall, was burning low. The cabin was immaculately kept, even its rough lumber floor swept clean from mud.

She moved to tend the fire, taking logs from a wooden crate beside it. As she fed the dying embers, she felt a wave of guilt wash over her. The furnishings were meager, the surroundings sparse and pathetic. Yet, she knew Henderson's salary could afford far better than this.

As if reading her thoughts, Lydia Henderson spoke, "Our home is not much to look at, compared to others, but Martin has had a bit of a problem for years."

Willie turned, still squatting by the fire, and stared her way, saying nothing.

"I'm sure you know he likes to imbibe in spirits, and on occasion, play a few hands of cards. Right now, he's in debt from the last game. He keeps promising me he'll gamble no more, but I've yet to see it."

Willie stood and crossed the room to the bed. "How about I fix you some tea?" she offered.

"I'd be obliged," the older woman replied. "It's not often we get company up here. I can tell you where to get everything." She brightened. "My mother's china teapot is packed in that trunk by the door. I'd be delighted if you'd use it."

Willie moved to the well-worn trunk and knelt, lifting the high lid. Inside, among the packed linens and wedding quilt, the teapot sat in the corner. She reached to remove it, parting back the linens, when her eye caught the edge of a shiny object. Flipping the corner of a wool blanket aside, she froze. On the bottom of the trunk lay her pearl-handled stiletto gleaming against the dark cherry wood. Her heart thumped wildly, and she stared at it for several moments. It had been Martin Henderson who was involved in the payroll robbery two falls ago.

"Can't you find it?" she heard Lydia faintly calling from the bed. "It should be in the corner on the left-hand side."

With shaking hands, she replaced the blanket, removed the teapot, and fought to gain control of herself. "Yes, it's right here."

Painfully conscious of her heart thudding in her chest, she checked the cook stove which had burned low and threw a few pieces of wood on the fire. Hoisting the water bucket from the counter, she filled a pan to boil. Her hands were still trembling when she untied the package on the table and removed a little sack of tea leaves, dropping them in the bottom of the china pot.

"You might rightly be coming down with the same thing I have," Mrs. Henderson said. "It starts with the chills, you know."

Willie willed her hands to be still. "I've been out in the cold quite a bit this morning. I'm just not used to the warm cabin," she lied. She removed the steamy water from the stove and poured it into the pot to steep. Lydia Henderson, glad to have a woman to talk to, rambled on, but Willie barely heard a word she spoke.

"I brought that teapot from England when I came here as a girl. It was my mother's," the woman said proudly. She looked oddly at Willie's pale face. "Something wrong, Miss Wydcliffe?"

"No, no," Willie stammered. She forced out a tight smile. "It's just since Papa passed away, I've had a lot of things on my mind. Do excuse me, Mrs. Henderson."

"I reckon it couldn't be easy for a young girl like you to have to take over those nasty old mills by yourself," the older woman admitted. "I give you credit—you have spirit."

"Thank you." Still distracted, Willie poured each of them a cup and walked to the bed. "I'm lucky I have Sam Bradley and a fine crew to help me. Without them, I could never have carried on like Papa wanted."

"Suppose so." The woman coughed before taking a sip. "This is really kind of you."

"Pleased to help." Relieved her heart was now beating a steadier rhythm and, with the initial shock worn off, she grew brave. "Thank goodness your husband has been healthy. I'd hate to lose a good man like him. He's our best man for sorting the millpond logs before they're sent up to the saws. I remember he had some problems a while back, and he was ill for a few weeks. I hope everything has gone well since?"

Lydia Henderson grew crimson. "Old Martin is as healthy as a horse. Reckon I shouldn't tell you, but I know you're an understanding sort. Martin wasn't ill those weeks."

"He wasn't?"

"No, he'd been involved in a brawl over some cards and got himself knifed when someone called him a cheat. Took it pretty bad in the shoulder and just needed time to land on his feet again. And I'm really sorry about the whiskey I stole from your father's office, but Martin needed something to ease the pain."

The pulse in Willie's temple began to drum loudly. Her palms began to sweat, and the cup she held almost slipped from them, but she recaptured it without spilling a single drop. She had no doubt now that she had stabbed Martin Henderson.

"You really don't look well, my dear," Lydia remarked.

"I...I'm fine," she replied in a reassuring tone and silently berated herself. Henderson didn't know it was her. Even Jonathan had assumed she was a young boy. "Could I get you some more tea?" she asked.

"Just a little."

The woman held out her cup, and she poured her some. "Who does your husband play cards with?"

Lydia's voice had a sharp edge to it as she spoke. "A bunch of ruffians at Granny Gordon's Tavern, or in that indecent bawdyhouse in town. They're all a bunch of good-for-nothing thieves. Especially that card shark John Pierce."

The conversation ended abruptly when the cabin door flew open and Martin Henderson stepped inside, brushing the snow from his grimy coat. Startled, Willie jumped, and her stomach dived at the sight of the large figure looming in the doorway.

"Martin, shut the door before the warmth leaves," Lydia scolded. "Miss Wydcliffe was kind enough to visit and bring some tea. She just finished tending the fire."

Henderson eyed Willie and ambled to the fireplace, discarding his coat and rubbing his hands in front of the flames.

With as much courage as she could muster, Willie carried her cup to the washboard. The hair at the back of her neck prickled. "I'd better be leaving," she said, reaching for her own hat and coat. She turned toward the bed and forced a weak smile. "I hope you're feeling better soon, ma'am."

Lydia Henderson returned her smile. "No need to hurry off."

"I really must. The snow doesn't look like it's going to end soon."

The woman coughed. "Next time you visit, I hope I can be more hospitable." She eased herself up in the bed. "I do hope this old cold will be gone." She looked over to her husband still hunched by the fire. "Martin, why don't you see that Miss Wydcliffe gets down the mountain without any mishap?"

Willie raised her arms in the air, palms forward. "No, no, that's fine. Don't bother yourself. I'm used to riding in bad weather." She tugged her hat down over her head and reached for the latch on the door.

"No trouble," she heard Henderson say. He pulled on his coat and started after her.

"Honestly, Mr. Henderson," she said, "there's no need to saddle your horse again in this cold, I'll be fine." Her heart began pounding again, so loud she was sure he could hear it.

"I said it's no trouble." He followed her down the steps and headed for the barn.

Unnerved, Willie untied Warrior's reins from the shed and mounted, dreading the man's return. She shuddered, from fear, rather than the cold. The minutes seemed to drag by in misery while a myriad of thoughts swirled about in her mind like the snowflakes in the air around her. How did Henderson fit into the payroll robberies? Was he hired by someone, or did he need money so badly to pay his gambling debts he was forced to steal it with the help of his friends? And who were his companions that day?

Henderson turned his horse toward her, stopped, and signaled for her to take the trail first. She kneed her mount, urging the big horse to move faster, but the animal snorted in annoyance.

"Slow down," Henderson muttered gruffly. "You'll break your horse's neck and your own."

She pulled the reins too sharply, and the gelding snickered in disgust this time. Then, as if sensing another's presence, he picked up his ears listening and meekly settled himself.

Willie's steely gaze searched the long, steep trail. Under a stand of tall pines, a muddy-colored horse waited with its rider. Almost immediately, she recognized the beaver coat before she saw his misshapen face. A sense of relief washed over her as she rode toward Old Joe.

"Sam was worried you wouldn't be home in time for dinner," Old Joe said. "He sent me to get you."

She smiled. It was the most she had ever heard the man say in one breath, and it sounded better than a choir of angels.

"I can take it from here," Old Joe said to Henderson.

Willie turned in her saddle. "Thank you, Mr. Henderson. I hope your wife is up and about soon." She watched the man nod to her and turn his mount around to begin the steep climb toward the cabin.

In silence, she urged her mount forward, waiting barely a second for Old Joe to swing his horse in line behind her. Farther on, she stopped under a stand of pine and waited until he drew up beside her.

"You are a handsome sight for sore eyes."

"I figured as much," he said, grinning.

Willie looked at him suspiciously. "Have you been following me?"

He shrugged. "You might say I've been close by." He stared at her, but refused to say more.

"I know someone told you to follow me, Joe. Who was it?"

"Sam Bradley."

"Sam?"

He nodded and pulled the collar up on his coat.

"Please, Joe, talk to me," she said. "Why did Sam

have me followed?"

"He doesn't trust Henderson. He thinks he's involved with the trouble at the mills."

She took off her hat, showered with snow, and shook it before she resettled it on her head. "Henderson was involved in the payroll robbery two years ago."

"Doesn't surprise me," Joe rejoined. "He's too sneaky for my liking. Even Jonathan suspects he's a lookout man at the Hornet's Nest. When his wife cleaned the offices at night, he had easy access to the mill. We believe he supplies information to whoever is behind all the hassle we're having. Trouble is, we can't catch him in the act."

"But he helped to fight the fire at the finishing mill," she pointed out.

"He had to, so he wouldn't be suspected of any wrongdoings." Old Joe glanced sideways at her. "Didn't it cross your mind that it was odd he was in town the Sunday the mill burned? He's not a god-fearing soul, the saloon was closed, and there are no card games allowed at Granny Gordon's Tavern on the Sabbath."

"Do you think he destroyed McGee's office?"

"Naw. He's not smart enough to decipher all those land contracts. I saw a mill hand reading him a letter sometime back. It has to be Pierce. That footprint Jonathan found on the back of the map matched his size, right down to the cleat mark."

"Why didn't anyone tell me?" she asked, annoyed.

He chuckled. "Didn't see any reason to get you upset when the only evidence we had was one dirty footprint."

At the sound of the man's deep voice and rich

laughter, Warrior snorted and pranced, edging closer to his horse. Puzzled, Willie patted him on the neck, and spoke, "Warrior seems to take a shine to you, Joe." She glanced up in time to see his smile widen.

"I'll be darned." He had been her mysterious savior during the thunderstorm. She shook her head. "Have you rounded up any other spooked horses lately?"

This time he laughed loudly, throwing back his head like it was a funny joke. "You can blame Olaf for that one. He sent me out in that surly downpour when he suspected you weren't heading home. I arrived shortly after you left him and headed for Reed's mill. I needed to go over some timber figures with him and ended up drenched to the skin tailing you instead."

Taken by surprise, she asked, "Did Jonathan ever find out?"

Old Joe shrugged.

Her voice was low, almost pleading. "Dang, Joe, please, don't tell him. He would be furious if he knew I rode to Matthew Reeds mill alone. He doesn't like Matthew, not by a jug full."

The hideous man grinned again. "That makes four of us—Jonathan, Sam, Olaf, and me." Two streams of vapor blew out from his noseless face as his warm breath vaporized in the cold air.

They moved on, and in minutes arrived at the end of the snowy trail. Old Joe halted his mount. "Don't worry, your secret is safe, Miss Willie. I wouldn't want to cause any trouble between you and Mr. Wain. You've done right by me these past two years, and I'm beholding to you. No one takes kindly to this face."

"So tell me, Joe. What really happened to your nose?" She peered up at him. "I certainly don't believe the rumor that it was bitten off in a river fight."

He laughed again and it rippled into the chilly air around them. "I was mauled by a bear when I was a kid. But don't you dare tell a soul. That river fight rumor gives me much more clout with the crew who think I'm one mean cuss."

She nodded, grinning. "You got the jobs, Joe, because you were the best man for them. I didn't do you any favors. You earned them. It looks like I'm the one who owes you. This is twice you've come to my aid."

Old Joe blushed crimson and was at a loss for words.

"Joe," she said, reaching out to pat him on the arm, "You're the most beautiful person I've ever met." She waved a hand to where the paths parted. "Now go home. I can make it back to the manor without a shadow."

CHAPTER THIRTY-THREE

WILLIE SAT JABBING THE INTRICATE rose design on the pillowcase she was attempting to embroider when Matthew Reed arrived the following morning. She couldn't decide whether she was frustrated with her tedious handiwork as she eyed the rows of uneven stitches or with his arrival. She really didn't want to face him, and she remembered Jonathan's pointed warning.

She set the needlework aside, exasperated it didn't look more like Raven's neat delicate stitches she had sewn on many of the bed linens for the manor. In fact, it looked more like she had harpooned the design into the fabric. She silently hoped Jonathan didn't have plans to domesticate her.

Suddenly, she remembered she was wearing Jonathan's engagement ring. She pulled the gleaming display off her finger and dropped it into the pocket of her dress just as Matthew sauntered into the sitting room.

"I thought you'd like to take a carriage ride with me," he said, crossing the room and lightly planting a kiss on her cheek. He seated himself in a wingback chair opposite her. "It's the first warm thaw of the season, perfect for an outing."

Willie glanced up. She hoped he wouldn't see through her false facade. "It's kind of you to offer, Matthew, but I really don't feel like going out."

Actually, she decided, she would have loved to take a ride in the sparkling sunshine, but with Jonathan, who had not yet returned. It had been over a week since he left for Pittsburgh, and she was simply missing him.

Unaware of her inner turmoil, he spoke. "I hear your winter logging operations are doing splendidly. You'll be ahead of every operator come spring. Looks like your one-horse idea of tossing coins to the paupers has succeeded. My men tell me you have rollaways stacked on every river bank in the area."

Willie felt a ripple of mirth. "My crews are incredible. They're ahead of season and have managed not to clear cut any area, leaving enough timber behind to keep Wydcliffe forests intact for years to come."

"Now, Wilhelmina, don't start." His voice grew impatient and irritated. "We've enough timber to build a ladder to heaven."

"Or hell," she shot back. Her crew had told her Matthew had ravaged every bit of timber near his mill to avoid excessive hours of transportation, additional crews, and labor costs.

He sighed. "I didn't come here to fight with you."

"I know," she replied, frowning. "I'm sorry."

He leaned back in the chair with superior coolness. "Have you and Wain settled your business differences yet?"

She picked up the needlework and turned

it slowly in her hands. "Oh, yes, and I should apologize for his brash behavior. We had a trifle misunderstanding about how I was funding the reconstruction of the finishing mill." She beamed inwardly. "It all worked out well in the end. We came to a mutually satisfying agreement."

"Good," he replied, "but I'd be more careful around him. I don't think he has your best interests in mind. I'm just pleased he's gone again. At least we have the grace of his absence for a while."

From his breast pocket, he extracted a slim case. "I brought you a present. Just a small token of my esteem. You don't know how much I've missed you."

At first, she was too stunned to say anything. She stared at him. She couldn't let him profess his love for her. Yet she couldn't disclose her relationship with Jonathan either. She should have sent him away the moment he arrived. Now she'd have to continue the silly farce.

"How kind of you, Matthew." She took the case, flipped the lid open, and stared aghast at the contents. On a bed of blue satin lay the mother-of-pearl necklace and earrings she had lent Rachael Kramer. Her stomach twisted itself in knots, and she felt a queer constriction tighten her chest. Oh, sweet heaven above, did Matthew Reed kill Rachael Kramer?

She took a deep breath, swallowed nervously, and forced her eyes to look at him.

He peered back at her oddly. "Don't you like them?" he asked. "I thought the mother-of-pearl would be perfect for your wardrobe."

Willie felt her heart bang like a drum. She bit her

lower lip. "Yes, I...I like them very...very...much," she stammered.

His next words did little to set her fears to rest. "Wilhelmina, darling, if they're not to your liking, we'll turn them in to the jeweler's tomorrow and choose something more suitable."

"No. No." She swallowed again. "They're beautiful. I'm just overwhelmed." She steadied her nerves. The foolish man had no idea they once belonged to her and were given to Rachael to wear. Yet, how had the jeweler come by them?

"Honestly, my dear, if you don't like them, we can return them."

"No, they're exquisite. Truly they are. I'm just so speechless. You shouldn't have, Matthew."

"Shouldn't have?" His voice cracked. "Why not? We're almost engaged! Surely you know my true feelings by now."

Repressing a sigh, she spoke. "Please, you promised you'd not hurry our relationship. You know I'm fond of you."

"Fond?" He glowered at her. "I should hope you're more than just *fond*." He moved to her and grasped her hands in his. "How many times have I told you that I want to spend the rest of my life with you?"

Her stomach churned madly until she thought she would be sick. She felt dizzy, and her hands felt clammy and cold like icicles. "Please. Must we discuss this now? I don't feel up to it."

He eyed her pale complexion. "I'm sorry, Wilhelmina. Of course, we can discuss this when you're feeling better." He bent forward and touched his thin wet lips to hers, lingering there a moment.

The kiss repulsed her and she pulled away. It was nothing like the firm, fiery ones she had become accustomed to with Jonathan.

He drew back and rose to leave. "I'll call on you tomorrow, my love. I hope you feel better."

She nodded wordlessly, and once he left, she expelled a heavy sigh of relief.

Later in the afternoon, when she entered the jewelry shop, she was greeted by the same Claude Wrigley who had tried to overcharge Jonathan when he first arrived and purchased her new knife.

Without speaking, she dropped the opened mother-of-pearl jewelry box on the counter before him.

"You don't like them?" Wrigley's forehead creased itself in worry lines.

"Oh, no. They're perfectly lovely." She forced a smile. "In fact, they're so beautiful, I'd like to purchase a set exactly like them for Raven."

The jeweler removed his glasses, rubbed the bridge of his nose, and mopped the sweat popping out on his forehead. "I'm afraid it's impossible. I've only the one set."

Feigning alarm, Willie took a step backward. "Tell me it's not possible, Mr. Wrigley. I've fallen in love with these," she lied, "and I was hoping to surprise my sister with a matching set. Could you please order them? I'm willing to pay more than a fair price."

The jeweler's face turned red around his ears. "Actually, these were turned in to me for cash," he admitted, "but I assure you, they're not second hand. I doubt they've ever been worn. They were in perfect condition when I purchased them."

"I see." The jeweler had to be the poorest liar she'd ever met. And certainly, a dishonest businessman who had no qualms about selling used goods.

"Could you possibly tell me who turned them in?" she asked. "I'd approach him with the utmost discretion, I assure you."

Wrigley hesitated.

Willie knew it wasn't good business to divulge a person who pawned goods for cash. "I just want to verify there's not another set. We've always shopped here." She hoped he'd realize the importance of their prior business transactions. There were times when greed over-rode common sense.

And this was one of them.

Wrigley looked at her cautiously. "Ezra Hawkins sold them to me, although I have no idea how he came by them. You understand I don't make it a habit of procuring used jewelry. I have a reputation to uphold, but these were worth every penny."

Willie dropped the jewelry box in her reticule. "I appreciate your help. I'd be delighted if I could find an identical set." Faking a warm smile she hardly felt, she shot through the door and stood trembling on the street, gulping in breaths of fresh cold air.

Ezra Hawkins. What could he possibly have to do with Rachael Kramer? Certainly he didn't kill her. Hawkins was ornery, but surely not a killer. She doubted Hawkins and Rachael had ever been acquainted with each other. The only possibility was if Rachael's parents sold them to Hawkins to secure some cash. But why sell them to Ezra Hawkins and not directly to the jeweler? Now she was more confused than ever.

Sam lumbered up the walk, pulling his ragged

coat around him tighter as he approached. The blustery cold wind whipped at his mop of hair peeking out from the old dilapidated hat he had worn for what seemed like decades.

"Gall darn bones don't take kindly to this spiteful weather," he grumbled. "You look like you've just seen a ghost, Willie."

"No," she lied. "Just feeling a little cold, too." She wasn't about to tell him her latest discovery, not until she had a talk with Rachael's mother. "I'm headed for the Kramers to chat with Rachael's mother and see how she's doing."

Sam squinted at her with an odd look. "Don't be late for dinner, young lady," he warned. "Conrad has prepared something special, and he's not as understanding as Hannah Svenson when it comes to your shenanigans."

Willie never reached Rachael Kramer's house.

Riding to the eastern end of town, she met with an angry John Pierce instead. He sat atop his dark mount as massive and formidable as always. His contemptuous grimace rolled over her when she stopped at the snow-covered lane leading to Kramer's house.

"Well, well, the beautiful Miss Wydcliffe. Or is it the treacherous Miss Busy Body?" he ground out. Hatred laced his voice.

She watched him withdraw a pistol from under his coat.

"I don't understand," she said in a choked voice. Fear slowly crept up the back of her neck.

"Understand, is it? I think you understand too much already. Snoopy **clever** witch, aren't you? You and I are about to take a little ride. It seems I can't wait to collect what's due me. You might be clever enough to convince Matthew Reed that Wain and you are little more than business associates, but I'm no fool. The rock on your hand is not exactly a token of friendship."

She glanced at the ring and up at Pierce's mottled face. "What does my betrothal to Jonathan Wain have to do with you?"

"Plenty, little lady. We had a bargain. The land was supposed to be mine."

"It is," she insisted, trying not to sound frantic.

"Not with Wain as your husband," he snarled. "Surely you don't think I'm a dolt."

"If it's the land you want, I'm sure we can reach an agreement without the use of a gun."

He grinned and pinned his beady eyes on her, like a rattler ready to strike. "Oh, we're about to reach an agreement. Move! And don't try anything crafty, my dear, unless you want to meet the same fate as your little friend did. We're about to see the winter sights downriver."

Too frightened to resist, Willie rode ahead of Pierce, knowing full well the gun was trained on her back. It didn't take her long to realize they were headed for the Black Widow, now deserted because of winter logging. She prayed silently to herself this was one day Old Joe had been instructed to follow her. She prayed Jonathan was back in town as well.

CHAPTER THIRTY-FOUR

WHEN WILLIE DIDN'T RETURN TO the manor for dinner, Jonathan knew something was amiss. After checking further, he found she never arrived at the Kramer home as well.

Now, as he rode up the slippery mountain to Henderson's cabin, he tried to determine all the logical places she could safely be. He could think of none. Not one.

Quietly, he rode in behind the cabin and tethered his horse behind the shed, covering the distance to the barn where the door was ajar. Fear and anger began to well up inside him. Kicking the door open with a booted foot, he almost tore it off its hinges. Light flooded into the stables as it clattered against the barn wall.

Caught off guard, Henderson whirled around to face him and met the cold barrel of Jonathan's gun.

"Where is she?" he demanded.

"Who?"

"Don't play silly games with me—Willie Wydcliffe." He looked at Henderson's meager belongings spread out on the straw at his feet. "I see you're taking a little trip. You really surprise me,

Henderson, leaving your poor sick wife behind to manage for herself."

"You don't understand, it's nothing like that," the surly man stammered.

"What's the problem? Isn't Pierce paying you enough to stick around?"

Startled, Henderson gawked at him and his gruff voice faltered. "You can't pin nothin' on me. Nothin'."

"No?" Jonathan countered. His expression was dangerously amused. "There's the matter of a stolen payroll, a dead girl and horse, an attempt on my life. I think I have enough evidence to keep your belly full of prison food for a long time."

"You can't pin any killings on me." Henderson's voice had taken on a frightened tone. "It was Pierce who cut those ropes to the holding dam, and Leb Luther who poisoned the horse and tried twice to kill you. I'm blameless."

"Is that so?" Jonathan's voice was smooth and icy. "You were the lookout man for the past two years, that's conspiracy. I have no doubt you also helped Luther and Hawkins."

"I had no choice," Henderson admitted. "Pierce had the deed to my land, and I was in debt up to my ears. I never wanted Miss Willie hurt. Pierce promised we'd only scare her old man a little. By the time I realized he was serious about getting that land of hers, I was in too deep to get out."

"You'll never learn, will you, Henderson?" Jonathan's eyes narrowed, and he threw him a look of disgust. "When did it occur to you Pierce was a card shark and a thief?"

"Too late," the man lamented. "I couldn't pull

out. He threatened to kill my wife. What are you going to do?"

"That depends upon you. I want to know where Willie is right now. Tell me, and you're free to go. But if I find out you lied, or any harm has come to her, I'll hunt you down and knock your lying teeth down your throat before I kill you. A sound thrashing would make me feel better, but I don't have time. You leaving the area for good will make me a very pleased man. Understand?"

Henderson nodded. Cowering, he backed himself against a horse stall. "Pierce is taking her to the Black Widow to sign over the land legally to him."

Jonathan spun about and raced wildly for his horse, ignoring the logger slumped against the stall, his body trembling with fright.

If Trade Wind had ever shown his best, Jonathan was sure the beast was outdoing himself that afternoon. They rode like there was no tomorrow, and little of today. He knew Pierce would never be content to release Willie once she signed over the land. She knew too much.

He whipped his mount until he drew near the Black Widow. Two horses, their saddles snow-covered, stood hunched and stiff-legged in the cold. He recognized both Willie's mount and John Pierce's. Alighting noiselessly, knowing there would be company soon, he waited for several minutes until Matthew Reed rode up and slipped in the side door. He skirted the mill and cautiously moved to the back door.

Inside, John Pierce sat contentedly on an old plank bench with his gun aimed at Willie, who was slouched on the floor in a corner of the room.

He laughed menacingly at her. "So, Miss Wydcliffe, it's almost over except for a few last details." He glanced up as a cold draft followed Matthew Reed through the door.

The young man was out of breath and his face was beet red from the fierce cold. He rubbed his hands together and eyed Pierce skeptically. "You said there would be no violence, Pierce." He looked over at Willie, shivering even though she wore a heavy leather jacket. Her reticule lay on the floor next to her. She stared up at him with terror-glazed eyes.

"Did I now?" Pierce emitted a maniac-like peal of laughter, his beady eyes glowing like a hungry wolf. "Maybe one of us should share his warmth with this little beauty here. She looks cold."

"Now wait one minute, we had a deal."

"Shut up, you lily-livered fop," Pierce growled. "I'm making the deals."

Willie cringed at his fierce temper. There was no way she was going to make it out alive. She prayed someone had seen her leaving town. Surely Sam would begin to worry when she didn't arrive for dinner. But she was notorious for not being on time. How long would it take the household to begin to worry, she wondered, as another wave of fear washed over her.

"You filthy scum!" The words slipped from her lips as terror fueled her anger. She bolted to her feet. "The only way you'll ever touch me is if I'm dead."

Pierce howled, licking his protruding lips seductively. "Feisty little logger lass, aren't you?" He started toward her when Jonathan came crashing through the door.

"Drop it, Pierce," he growled. "I'd love to blow every hair clean off your head and soil those fancy clothes you're wearing. Just give me a reason."

Pierce turned and dropped his pistol. Jonathan motioned both men over to the makeshift bench. "You all right, Willie?" he asked, his husky voice sounding like music to her ears.

"Remind me I'm supposed to be in church on Sunday morning. I need to send up some prayers of gratitude." She moved next to him. "How did you know I was here?"

"It seems Pierce's lookout man got a little weak-kneed. Henderson did an entire one act performance just a few hours ago, before agreeing to clear out for good." He eyed Pierce scornfully. "You really spun an intricate web."

Willie's voice interrupted him. "Jonathan, he wants the land. He wanted me to sign it over."

"I know. It seems Mr. Pierce here is involved in quite a lot of deals. Go ahead, you piece of horse dung, tell her why you wanted that land. Why you wanted it *all* to yourself." He glanced at Reed and added sarcastically, "This might prove enlightening to you as well."

Matthew Reed glared at Pierce. "What does he mean *all to yourself?*"

"It seems Pierce is out for revenge," Jonathan said. "The land he wants—and which Willie now owns—once belonged to his brother." He cast a disgusted glance at Pierce. "How appropriate, the tale begins and ends here, doesn't it?"

Jonathan turned to Willie. "Remember the widow who shot her husband's killer? Vanessa

Rowles? She was Matthew Reed's mother. And it was John Pierce's older brother that she killed to avenge her husband's death. It didn't matter though, did it, Pierce? You always hated him, ever since you were young?"

"Damn right," Pierce snarled out. "I hated my brother. He used to beat me when I was a kid. He was a good-for-nothing bully. But I loved her. I loved Vanessa Rowles...before she died." He turned and looked scathingly at Matthew Reed. "She died bearing you. I sent her to New York, knowing she was carrying a child and had to avoid the law. I was hoping that someday we'd be married. She changed her name from Rowles to Reed, and she made me promise if anything ever happened to her, I'd see her child was taken care of. But I hated you, Reed. I hated you from the night she died having you. You killed her. And I loved her!" Pierce's eyes blazed at a bewildered Matthew Reed.

"And the land was mine," Pierce spat at him. "Mine! My brother won it honestly from your spineless father who didn't know how to play cards. Stupid fool."

Jonathan scoffed. "*Honestly won*? Come, come. As honestly as you took the deed to Henderson's plot on the mountain, Pierce? It was your brother who taught you to become a fantastic cheat. But the land was never yours or his. It was incorrectly deeded. **Wain and Wydcliffe** bought it at an honest price after it was put up for sale."

"Liar!" Pierce screamed. "It's mine. It's mine and everything beneath it is mine."

Willie stared at the screeching man for several

moments. It all made sense. Her father's words came flying back to her, haunting her, ringing in her ears. "Papa said...'that's the key to all this. It's cold, it's dark...beneath...it's black.' *Coal,*" she sputtered. "Papa meant *coal,* not cold."

Jonathan smiled, pleased with her discovery. "You had the clue in your room, just sitting on your shelves waiting to be discovered. Sadly, it was too late when your father discovered it."

Leveling a bitter gaze at Pierce, he snorted derisively. "It also seems Mr. Pierce is involved in a deal to bring the railroad into the area. If it came through, and he owned the land, he'd be a very wealthy man in a few short years. Your only mistake was leaving your calling card in McGee's office. Had I never seen your cleat mark on the back of a paper, I would never have sent an investigator to New England where you claimed you once lived. Funny thing, though, all the pieces to the mystery were in New York instead. Changing Vanessa Rowles's name to Reed covered your tracks pretty well. Well almost."

Jonathan turned to Willie. "Had your father not talked to me about Pierce purchasing horses in New York, I might never have pieced it all together." He shook his head, amused. "How could a man who knew nothing about horseflesh, know so much about horses in New York? But you, Willie, put the rest of the puzzle together when you told me Reed was an orphan. Remember that evening, sweetheart?"

Willie blushed crimson.

Abruptly, the door flew open. A medium-framed figure entered and pointed a gun at Jonathan.

"Drop the gun, or you're the most handsome dead man in these woods."

Jonathan regarded the trouser-clad figure. "Well, well. Welcome, Clara," he said in a silky voice without losing stride. The pistol he held hit the floor with a sharp thump, only to be retrieved by Pierce. "Didn't rightly think you'd be around. Yet, you always liked hot situations."

Clara Ferguson removed her hat and her frizzy hair tumbled out over her shoulders. "Amusing, Jonathan, quite amusing. You don't seem surprised? I'm so disappointed." She closed the door, still leveling the gun at him and dropped a leather satchel on the table.

Jonathan watched Willie look up at him with frightened surprise. "Didn't you know, Willie, darling, that Clara was involved as well? Dear Clara threw in with Pierce as soon as she found out her father's land was valuable—and not necessarily as a cozy homestead. Clara was the little snake in the grass who was the hardest to flush out. Seen any good fires lately, my dear?" he taunted her.

"You started the fire at the mill in town?" Willie asked in an incredulous whisper.

Jonathan smiled, a cold calculating smile. "Clara had me stumped, Willie, but not Sam Bradley. He found it unusual Clara was one of only two people who were not present when the finishing mill burned. Her parents were even there. The entire town was there, I hear. Now, didn't it seem odd that the person who hated you the most didn't show her face to bask in your misfortune?"

"Don't be silly, Jonathan," Clara replied hotly. "You can't prove anything."

"No?" he goaded her. "How about snakes, Clara? Have you and Ezra Hawkins seen any large rattlers lately?" Clara's eyes widened as he spoke. She laughed shrilly, hysterically, enjoying his wit.

"You put the snake in the barn?" Reed asked, looking askance at her.

Willie stared at Clara while bits and pieces of information sifted through her mind. "No," she muttered. "Ezra Hawkins put the snake in the barn, and Hawkins was the lookout man when Clara torched the mill. Henderson was there to fight the fire, but Hawkins never showed his face either. Clara was also at the Hornet's Nest the day it was ransacked helping Pierce to steal the deed to the land. I smelled woman's perfume. Fortunately, the deed was still at the manor."

"Well done, Willie," Jonathan said smoothly. "We'll never see poor Hawkins though. He packed up and left town immediately after the blaze, before the ashes were even cold, once he found out the Hornet's Nest crew were riled and looking for blood."

"That only leaves Rachael Kramer's death unanswered," Willie said, her gaze circling the trio.

"Yes," Jonathan admitted and looked askance at Pierce. "But I never suspected you as a killer, Pierce, or Hawkins either, for that matter. You don't like to dirty your immaculate hands, and Hawkins was crazy, but not a killer. I guess that leaves you, Reed, with the blood on your hands."

Willie looked at Matthew Reed's astonished face. She whipped her head around to face Clara. "No," she said, "you killed Rachael Kramer, didn't you, Clara? And you paid Hawkins off with the jewelry you took from her dead body."

She looked scornfully at Reed. "The same jewelry Hawkins hocked to the jeweler and you bought and gave to me. The same jewelry I lent to Rachael to wear to Clara's birthday party, or didn't you know that?"

Furious, her pent-up anger exploding, Willie hissed, "Why Rachael? Why kill Rachael? Was it spite? To scare me? Or were you trying to scare Kramer into not divulging any information?"

Clara's eyes caught fire, and she swore a string of expletives. "Wrong on all three counts, you little trollop. You Wydcliffes wouldn't give up. You had it all and wanted more. Jonathan had to pursue the damn land issue and couldn't be satisfied with the altered maps and charts furnished by Kramer. Unfortunately, Rachael found out about her father's wrongdoings. But Kramer didn't have much choice. He owed a lot of money to Pierce over a stupid game of cards. I had to kill Rachael. I couldn't take the chance she would keep her mouth shut with you as her best friend. Why, Wilhelmina, didn't you just sell the land to Pierce? You had money, you didn't need more."

Pierce interrupted, his tone commanding, "Get on with it, Clara. We don't have all day to waste."

Clara extracted some pieces of paper from the leather satchel along with a bottle of ink and a pen. She smiled maliciously at the group. "This will all work out better than I ever dreamed. After Willie signs the papers giving the land to Pierce, we do away with all three of you. After all, no one will question her signature on the deeds since we have the agreement saying she was indebted to Pierce for a loan."

"Three?" Matthew Reed sucked in a breath of air, looking suspiciously at John Pierce and Clara Ferguson.

"Surely you aren't stupid enough to think we'd let you be part of this whole scheme, Matthew?" Clara hissed. "No, you're part of my plan to dispense with Jonathan and Willie. We shoot each of you with different pistols, planting them near the bodies. Two devoted lovers quarrel over the same woman. Both die. How touching."

Matthew Reed gasped. Sheer black fright swept over his face.

Deceptively calm, Willie raised a questioning brow at Clara. "And me?" she asked.

"You drown like Rachael Kramer." Clara cast out the words without any remorse. "You discover your dead lovers' bodies and are so distraught you commit suicide. No one will ever question it."

"I'm impressed, Clara," Jonathan uttered in a lazy voice. "But what if someone followed us? Surely you don't think I'd come here alone."

"You're lying, Jonathan," she spit back. "No one in town even knows you've returned. No one saw Willie leave. Now, my dear Wilhelmina, sign here if you don't want to be the first to visit the Pearly Gates."

Clara placed the agreement on the table with the bottle of ink and a pen. Willie glanced at her reticule on the floor and up at Jonathan. He leveled a cautious gaze back at her. There would never be enough time to dive for the gun inside it without one of them getting shot. It was too risky. Both were powerless to move for fear of getting the other person hurt.

Willie's heart beat a loud staccato as her left hand, steady and sure, picked up the pen, the other reaching for the bottle of ink. Grasping the jar at the base, she flung it upward and tossed the contents into Clara's eyes and face. At the same moment, Jonathan lunged forward and knocked the gun out of Pierce's hand, grappling him to the floor.

Clara shrieked wildly, trying to wipe the ink from her eyes, but Willie grabbed her and shoved her to the floor. Neither of them noticed Reed heading straight for the door, leaving them to struggle with their captors.

Willie knew Clara Ferguson was no match for her. She exceeded her in height and weight, but certainly not dexterity or strength. She slipped her stiletto from her boot, placed a knee on Clara's chest and grabbed her by the hair. She touched the tip of the blade to her throat. She could hear Jonathan and Pierce scuffling behind her.

The door flew open and Old Joe and Olaf entered, surveying the chaos.

Willie, still clutching Clara by the hair, spit into her face, "Move one inch, Clara, and I will scalp this frizz off your head so fast you'll beg to die. Or maybe I'll just slit your throat. Did you give Rachael a nice clean death? Or did she suffer?" Tears stung her eyes, but her anger was so fueled she started to violently shake the girl by her hair, pounding her head against the rough plank floor boards.

Old Joe laid a restraining hand on her arm. "Enough, Miss Willie," he said calmly, prying the stiletto from her fingers. "The law will try her for murder."

Willie rose to see Jonathan still pummeling hard blows into Pierce, who lay pinned against the wall. "You'd better stop him, too," she said, coming to her senses. "He's angry enough to destroy that river rat as well." She watched him continue to rain angry blows on the limp figure.

"Leave him recognizable for the trial," she heard Old Joe say as he and Olaf forcefully pulled Jonathan away from Pierce.

Jonathan straightened and wiped the blood from his lips, at the same moment Willie flew into his arms, hugging him fiercely. They turned and watched Sam Bradley boot Matthew Reed through the doorway.

"Material witness." Sam snorted. "Cowardly buffoon tried to slip out the back."

"How did you know where to find us?" she asked.

Sam picked up an old wooden bucket filled with water. "Joe, here, lost you in town, but had enough sense to latch onto Jonathan coming from Henderson's cabin. As soon as Joe realized where Jonathan was headed, he came back for help." He held the bucket over Pierce's limp form. "I think I'm going to enjoy this," he rasped. He flung half of it onto him. He turned and looked at Clara. Her face was smeared with ink, and more dripped from her hair into her eyes and onto the floor. "Looks like you could use a bath, too, gal," he added gleefully, heaving the rest over her. She shrieked hysterically as the shock of the cold water hit her in the face.

Sam grinned impishly.

CHAPTER THIRTY-FIVE

Mid April, 1858

IT WAS A BALMY APRIL morning, just perfect for a wedding. Bradford Payne had requested to see both Jonathan and Willie before the ceremony, and they had agreed to meet him at the manor in the early morning. Despite the household staff's superstitious nature, Willie had pressed the idea as well. She had business she wanted to deal with. She was certain after everything that had happened over the last two years, nothing—just nothing—could go wrong.

When she met Payne and Jonathan inside the large oak-paneled doors of the study, both were sipping rum like it was an after-dinner drink, even though it was six o'clock in the morning.

"I thought you weren't nervous," she said, eyeing the drink Jonathan casually held. He was leaning against the bookcase. His hair was tousled, and it was obvious he had already been out for an early morning ride.

"I'm not, sweetheart," he replied in a husky tone, "but Payne seems to have a need to steady his jangled nerves, and I can't let him drink alone."

Bradford Payne laughed with gusto, setting his glass aside. "You young people certainly have a way of peeling a few extra years from my life with all your antics. There's still some legal work to clear up before this marriage takes place today."

Willie interrupted, handing Jonathan the unsigned papers she had received earlier in the lawyer's office. "This will be rather simple, Mr. Payne." She looked into Jonathan's eyes. "It's a partnership to the end."

Jonathan barely glanced at the unsigned agreement Payne had drawn up and folded the papers, handing them to him. "Are you sure, Willie? There's a lot of money involved now with the land and its mineral rights. You once told me you wanted to be the largest lumbering operator this side of the Mississippi. With the monies from the coal rights, you can do it now."

She smiled radiantly, overflowing with love. "We can do it, you mean. Burn the blasted papers, Mr. Payne."

Payne cleared his throat and handed Willie another document. "It's the deed to the Wasp," he explained. His green eyes, gleaming like summer lightening, were full of amusement. "Sam wanted to be sure you and Jonathan received your wedding present early. It's deeded to both of you. I believe his exact words were 'to get the gall darn harness off my neck and get the final laugh on Dalton Wydcliffe.'"

Willie shook her head. "He didn't have to do this. Sam really felt saddled with the responsibility of that mill. Wait until he hears we're going to make him general foreman of all the mills while we're away in Baltimore." She handed it to Jonathan before asking, "I wonder why he just didn't sell and rid himself of it immediately?"

"Why?" Payne asked, perplexed. "Sam would never break up Wydcliffe holdings, especially since it was your father's first mill, and he knew you'd refuse to buy it back, thinking he rightly deserved it. The old codger doesn't need money, he's got more than enough."

"He won't have any if someone ever finds out where he stashes it. Papa said Sam distrusted banks and safes."

Payne's mouth twisted into a soft smile. "That he does. But the old geezer is digging up money, not burying it. He invested in silver mines on the coast a few years ago, and cash has been pouring in since. Wilhelmina, Sam Bradley is one of the wealthiest men in this town."

"Sam?" Willie gawked at Payne, astonished. She thought she knew everything about him. "Why does he persist in wearing a battered felt hat, living like a pauper, and working like a dog?"

Payne smiled. "If Sam Bradley decided to be an honest prominent citizen, he says he wouldn't be able to walk through the front doors of the Sawdust Bin for a snort of medicine without causing a stir among the Bible-thumping town folk. This way, he moves about town at his leisure without any commotion. The old fogey sees no need for money. At present, he has plans to build a large home on Front Street to house orphaned children. He's even badgered Red Ruby into helping decorate it, and my wife into running it."

"I'll be damned," Jonathan muttered. "Why doesn't he just retire?" He remembered the old man working atop a teamster's sleigh in the bitter cold.

"He said he'll die if he doesn't work," Payne returned. "He feels he's lived to be seventy-six because he never sits still. He loves the woods and the lumbering business. More importantly, he stayed with your father because of loyalty and, of course, for Elizabeth Wilhelmina."

"Me?" Her voice raised in surprise.

Payne removed his wire rims, mopped his sweaty brow, and settled the glasses on his nose again. "Sam had one weakness, Miss Willie. He could never live down the death of his little daughter, no matter how hard he tried. From the day you started to stumble around in the sawdust piles at the mills, Sam found peace with himself. In his heart and mind, he just adopted you instead. Your father couldn't ever deny him the love he had for you, and always hoped Sam's extra love might, in some small way, make up for the mother's love you never had. So Dalton was content to share you with Sam, and he couldn't have selected a better man."

"You're spot on," Jonathan said quietly. He watched Willie lower her head and swipe at her eyes with the back of her hands.

"It might be easier to understand if I give you this letter," Attorney Payne said. "I certainly don't want to make this day a melancholy one. This was supposed to be given to you after your marriage, but since it's only five hours away, and since you've spent your dowry money once, my dear, I don't believe I'm too premature in handing it over to you now."

Willie immediately recognized the script on the outside of the envelope as her father's. Her heart thudded wildly. With shaking hands, she accepted it, extracting the letter inside. Her tawny hair flowed down over her shoulder, shading her face, as she read:

Dearest Elizabeth Wilhelmina,

If you are reading this letter, it means you have married Jonathan Wain. I can't tell you how happy I am for you. He's a good man. Rest assured, I never distrusted your ability to run the mills, even though my will might have indicated otherwise. It was not my idea, but rather Sam Bradley's idea to set up the will as I did.

Not only was Sam afraid for your welfare upon my death, but also the romantic old coot believed Jonathan was the only suitable person for you to marry. He felt keeping a link between both of you until you were a year older could do no harm. But don't blame Sam, he never gives up. Did I ever tell you it was Sam who introduced me to your mother?

You know I've always loved you, always trusted you—no father could be more proud of any daughter. Don't pine for me, Willie, just be happy... because Wydcliffes carry on.

Your loving father,
~Dalton Wydcliffe

Willie's eyes watered again as a wave of relief surged though her. So her father had always believed in her abilities to run the operations, and he even knew the will would disturb her. Today was not a day to cry, it was a day to rejoice. She passed the letter to Jonathan who accepted it with a wary frown.

"Are you sure you want me to read this?" he asked. She nodded, and he walked to the fireplace, scanning the pages quickly.

"Criminy!" Her old familiar exclamation slipped from his lips. "What a meddling old-timer."

Jonathan glanced up to see her smiling, and he returned it, crossing the room to embrace her as his lips met hers passionately. They never noticed Bradford Payne slip quietly out of the study, leaving them alone.

After a minute, he disengaged himself from her and peered into the depths of her velvet brown eyes. "You're beautiful, my love, and darn frustrating at this moment. Let's get this wedding started soon."

She giggled. "I do have to go, Jonathan. I need time to get ready properly."

He drew her fast against him again as his mouth came down hard on hers. His lips were hungry for her and demanded her response again. After a while, he released her, raising his head, his fog-colored gaze penetrating hers. "Just one thing, Elizabeth Wilhelmina Wydcliffe, all I ask is one thing before we're wed."

"What is it?"

"Don't be late!"

Willie stood beside Sam Bradley in a simple ivory gown that only seemed to enhance her beauty. Her hair, unbound, spilled down her back and was pulled away from her face by two diamond studded combs, a present from Raven, her matron of honor. She watched Nicole bounce gaily down the aisle scattering wild cherry petals before she and Sam stepped out.

The little country church was overflowing with people. She easily recognized the faces of her logging crews and their families who had jammed in the pews, even standing three people deep at the back of the church. She had never seen the crews look so clean in her entire life. All decked out in their Sunday best, the men had shaved or trimmed their beards, and their hair was cut and tamed. Many grinned sheepishly her way, and she smiled demurely back at them, her eyes glistening. They all cared. They all had come.

For this special occasion, Sam had bought a new gray suit, and even though he looked like his shirt collar was choking the wind out of him, his jovial mood was not to be deterred. His plastered salt and pepper hair looked out of place, but his grin was as wide as the Susquehanna River during the spring flood season as he delivered her to Jonathan.

Earlier, he had met Jonathan in the vestibule and had presented him with his own special wedding present, an old battered cigar box tied up with twine.

"What is it?" Jonathan had asked, warily, looking up to catch the mirth in the old man's eyes.

"It's a wedding present," Sam said, "but you can't take it on your trip to Baltimore. I'll have to hold on to it until you return."

Curious, Jonathan untied the twine and lifted the lid. Inside were Willie's gun and stiletto.

"You stole these?" he asked incredulously.

The old codger let out a peal of laughter. "Not exactly. Just borrowed them without her knowledge. It's a long trip to Maryland, son. Knowing Willie, I thought it best if you'd arrive in one piece when you introduce her to your family. A honeymoon is one time in a man's life he deserves to have the edge."

Now, clad in a dark ebony suit to match his wind-blown black hair, Jonathan's heart raced when Willie's hand touched his, and together they began to recite their vows, their solemn voices never wavering. He smiled lovingly down at her and slipped a gold filigree ring on her finger, holding her hand firmly, but gently, to reassure her that the ceremony was almost at an end.

When at last, it drew to a close, and he swept her into his arms and kissed her soundly, rekindling the fires of previous nights, a wild hoot went up from the back of the church where the Hornet's Nest crew stood jammed together. Their whooping, cheering, and rowdy behavior urged others to join in until the noise rose in intensity and everyone was clapping, shouting, or whistling their approval of the radiant young couple. The clatter finally grew so boisterous it shook the rafters of the tiny church and rattled the windows.

"Looks like you have a lot of free kisses to dispense to this ugly bunch, Mrs. Wain." Jonathan grinned, ushering her up the aisle amid the throngs of onlookers. "Just be sure to save a few for your new husband."

It was Sam Bradley who grabbed her first, just outside the doors of the church, and crushed her to him as swarms of loggers eagerly shouldered their way toward the bride to wish her well.

Jonathan stepped graciously aside and watched the spirited proceedings. He'd let them delight in having a moment with his new wife, knowing she was a part of them, a part of the mills, a part of the river, and a part of the land. She was the little girl they had all helped to raise.

Yes, he'd let them have their moment.

He planned to have a lifetime of them.

**If you have enjoyed this novel,
please consider leaving an honest review.**

ALSO BY JUDY ANN DAVIS

Red Fox Woman
Under Starry Skies
Key to Love
Four White Roses
Up on the Roof and Other Stories
Sweet Kiss
Three Merry Mysteries

Visit Judy Ann on...

HER BLOG:
www.judyanndavis.blogspot.com/

THE WEB:
www.judyanndavis.com

FACEBOOK:
www.facebook.com/JudyAnnDavisAuthor

TWITTER:
www.twitter.com/JudyAnnDavis4

AMAZON AUTHOR PAGE:
www.amazon.com/Judy-Ann-Davis/e/B006GXN502/

PINTEREST:
www.pinterest.com/judyanndavis44/

GOODREADS:
www.goodreads.com/author/show/4353662.Judy_Ann_Davis

A WORD ABOUT THE AUTHOR...

Judy Ann Davis began her career in writing as a copy and continuity writer for radio and television in Scranton, Pennsylvania. She holds a degree in Journalism and Communications and has written for industry and education throughout her career.

Over a dozen of her short stories have appeared in various literary and small magazines and anthologies, and have received numerous awards. Her first novel, *Red Fox Woman*, won a finalist place in the Best Book Awards by USA Book News and International Book Awards by International Book News. Her contemporary romantic suspense and comedy, *Four White Roses*, was a finalist in the Book Excellence Awards and the Georgia Romance Writers' Maggie Awards.

When Judy Ann is not behind a computer, you can find her looking for anything humorous to make her laugh or swinging a golf club where the chuckles are few.

She is a member of Pennwriters, Inc. and Romance Writers of America. She divides her time between Central Pennsylvania and New Smyrna Beach, Florida.

SPECIAL THANKS TO...

Suzanne Webster, my long-time friend and talented editor, and the Killion Group

Made in the USA
Monee, IL
21 November 2020